KLOVA

KAREN LANGSTON

The Book Guild Ltd

First published in Great Britain in 2024 by
The Book Guild Ltd
Unit E2 Airfield Business Park,
Harrison Road, Market Harborough,
Leicestershire. LE16 7UL
Tel: 0116 2792299
www.bookguild.co.uk
Email: info@bookguild.co.uk
Twitter: @bookguild

Typeset in 12pt Adobe Jensen Pro

Printed on FSC accredited paper
Printed and bound in Great Britain by 4edge Limited

ISBN 978 1915853 806

British Library Cataloguing in Publication Data.
A catalogue record for this book is available from the British Library.

Dedicated with love to the memory of
Laurie Bellingham.

Still and always.

"…The sense of precarious dependence of all we know upon linguistic tools which themselves are largely unknown…"

Benjamin Lee Whorf
Science and Linguistics (1940)

PART ONE

What if I told you I could erase your past? Would you believe me?

You'd remember, surely. Being a kid without a care. Best friend at school. First cigarette. First sex. That night you thought you were going to die, when it felt like the whole world was sitting on your chest, crushing your lungs, sucking in the air you so desperately needed to breathe.

Whatever. All those memories you hold, they are real – the flesh and blood of your life lived.

Your past is part of who you are. No one can take it from you, right?

Wrong.

CHAPTER ONE

Sweat-drenched and breathless, Inker Ballard breaches the surface of consciousness from the depths of a horror-filled abyss. He does not, at first, recognise his surroundings. Laying in a bed in a dawn-lit room, he listens to silence. His head is filled with snapshots of nightmares, layers of trauma refusing to fade. His mind, barely awake, can't make sense of any of it. Instead, he focuses on one task at a time; closing his eyes, he forces his breathing to slow. In, out. In, out.

Ink reopens his eyes. Turning his head on the pillow, he gazes at objects in the room: shoes, pulled blinds, cluttered desk, a visual on standby. Recognition dawns like the day – a seamless shift that accelerates once started. His bedroom. His apartment. His crap all over the floor. His palm device, now vibrating beneath his skin, telling him he is late for work.

"Alarm off," he says.

He holds out his left hand, palm up. A twitch of his index finger launches a holographic display. Eyes still sleep-bleary, he struggles to read the time stamp: data to pinpoint one single moment in the context of millennia. This is now. The prospect of 'what next?' makes Ink's head pound. He forces himself upright. On the bedside table, he notices a small, opaque box – empty. The box's familiarity is a fact without context, which he accepts without question.

The implant in his hand pulses again, keeping time with the vibration of something unseen on the desk. He rises and rummages beneath the clutter for the buried NuB, which he jams into his ear just as the caller gives up. His palm now lists the missed call, along with three others from that morning: two from work, one from Exose Ray. Ink glances at the empty box, his brain making the connection that fills one of the morning's many gaps. *Codevice*, he thinks, rubbing the back of his aching head.

An hour later, Ink is sat at his desk at work, feigning occupation. His pod is centre-right in an open-plan office, home to a rapidly expanding precision engineering company. Above the fifty-plus pods hangs an air of fine-tuned productivity that is typical of the Klovaine work ethic. Ink stares at his visual, straining to focus his mind, failing hopelessly in the attempt.

A colleague at the adjacent pod eyes Ink with casual curiosity. "Late night?" She is young, pristine – all posture and pose.

"Sorry?"

"You look like shit." Her mouth creeps up on one side. "I'm getting coffee. I'm getting you one too." With long, assured strides, she weaves through the office and is gone.

Ink waits a moment, then slips into the staff washroom to check himself in the mirror. His dark hair has the look of clean neglect, his skin is washed-out grey, his eyes appear both dazed and startled at once. Around them, fine lines of late thirties cut deep. He runs the cold tap and splashes water onto his face. Appearances don't bother him. He couldn't care less about good impressions. What does concern him, however, is how he's feeling. Not the dead-limb exhaustion or the dull, heavy head – he recognises the aftertaste of codevice. Beneath all of that is a sense of alteration, so nebulous as to barely be felt at all – shapeless, without an original to compare it to.

Back at his desk, Ink brings up the spec for his current project and pretends the reams of calculations make sense. His colleague returns, placing a coffee carton in front of him.

"From the cabin on the square," she says, as if he'd asked the question. She sits down at her own visual but swivels her chair to face him. "You in the meeting later?"

"Supposed to be."

"I can cover for you if you like."

He turns to look at her, one eyebrow raised. "Why are you being nice?"

She shrugs. "Need a favour. I've got the last schematic to finish, due in Wednesday, but I'm supposed to be out tomorrow. Remember, that tender presentation I told you about?"

"Sorry?"

"Last week. I showed you the package."

"…"

She peers at Ink, frowning. "What? You said it looked worth a shot. You must remember."

"I…" He shakes his head, as if to re-order her words. "I don't…" Confusion scatters his own, leaving sentences hanging. "I can't…"

"You alright?"

Ink stands up, launched by a sudden need for air. "I'm fine." He hurries through the office, ignoring curious stares. Grabbing his coat and overcloak from the lobby, he runs down the stairwell and out onto the street.

The sub-zero temperature stings his face, reviving his senses, but not his reason. He crosses the road and enters the speakers' square opposite, stumbling onward, searching, as if answers were feathers whipped up by the wind. He can't see any to catch.

A crowd has gathered around a stone dais in the centre of the square. On the dais stands a speaker, wrapped in overcloak and dorph.

"...Was an act of true candour," she says, her projection magnetic. "It took great courage to stand firm and resist ambition's sway. Never did her bough bend; she remained resolute to the merciful end. In all she taught us, regard this..."

The audience stare in silence, transfixed by the speaker's words and the dance of her delivery. Ink stands rigid, bewildered by the blows of meaningless sounds. It is as if parts of language have been twisted out of shape, littered with phonemes in an impossible tongue. Yet, the crowd around him appear to understand every word.

"What's she saying?" he says to no one, to anyone. "Why does she talk like that?" He doesn't expect an answer. Hearing his own words reassures him he still has language, that he can still speak Klova. There is nothing else – no variation, no alternative. Everyone has the same implant, which carries the same language code. And yet these sounds...

"What's she *saying?*"

A man nearby hears the alarm in his voice. He turns and looks kindly at Ink. "You alright?"

"Do... do you understand her?"

"Of course." He smiles up at the speaker, missing the point. "She's one of Arteza's best. You not heard her before? She performed here last week."

Ink stares at the man, his eyes panic wide. The impossible sounds he makes jar, meaningless, in his mind: *heard... performed... last week*. Confusion triggers fear, swelling from absent reason. Nothing makes sense – the sounds themselves, the lie in their feigned meaning. Turning, he hurries away from the square, away from his office, away from the start of a nightmare more terrifying than anything in his codevice dreams.

His urge to flee directionless, Ink boards a Swift. The electric tram is warm and keeps him moving while he can stop and think. He huddles into a seat at the back and glances around him. The few passengers on board all stare at their palm devices, smartweave overcloaks loosened and thermal dorphs unwrapped in the cabin's welcome heat. Out of habit, Ink glances at his own device and the holographic of ubimedia hovering above his cupped palm. The content shifts, scrolls, expands, depending on the movement of his eyes and the twitch-flick of his fingers. The distraction works: barely two blocks on and he is lost in a warren of consumer generated content, constantly expanding by the authorship of an entire nation. Algorithms work hard, drawing his eyes' attention to trending threads. Top of the list is a Breaking Story, capitalised to give it the tone of News. The subject is badged and hashtagged with a borrowed name, already catching on: Amnesia Crisis. Ink's brief distraction is at once lost to a frantic search. As the holographic display flickers and scrolls, he hunts for facts among the speculation and hyperbole. He finds none. Yet, the common denominators, floating like detritus on the flood of commentary, are enough to seize his attention and fan his fear. Isolated cases, twenty-four confirmed, of people who have apparently forgotten the past.

Ink stares at the word *past*.

He has no idea what it means.

There's no denying it, the Savants did a remarkable job, all those centuries ago. It's not easy, creating language. However, the Savants' genius lay not in crafting a means of communication to serve necessity, but in establishing the foundation for so much more than that.

It is not its geographical isolation, but the Savants' achievement that sets our island nation apart. Iso-Klovaine is so technologically advanced, it is easy to forget the scale and pace of that advancement since the Savants' primitive era. It is also easy to forget how much of our success is at the mercy of the language that makes it possible.

For not only did our revered Savants create language – they also crafted the attendant sword that hangs over our nation's head.

And now the Order, whose declared purpose is the protection and ongoing perfection of the Savants' legacy, is unwittingly honing the sharpest of blades.

CHAPTER TWO

Ihlo Unis stood before a full-length mirror in her room. It still felt strange, seeing herself in the uniform of the Order of Savants – her life's ambition fulfilled. Her reflection appeared as a stranger: regulation hairstyle, short and slicked back, no makeup or accessories, just the pristine grey tunic and quarter-length over-gown. She studied her face, dark eyes on olive skin, and pondered the depth of the uniform's disguise.

Following the scent of coffee, Ihlo wandered into the apartment's main living space, where she found Ky leaning against the kitchen counter. Ky was her cousin – pale and petite, with unkempt hair and sleep-starved eyes. They shared the apartment, a modest rental in the district of Reach. The place was small and sparse, with an open-plan living room, compact kitchenette at one end, floor to ceiling window at the other. The apartment and their age, just turned thirty, were all they had in common. They were family, not friends. Since the sudden death of her parents ten years ago, Ihlo had, too late, come to value family. Ky was all she had left; she was determined to stick it out.

She made herself coffee from a machine and sat at a small dining table in the middle of the room.

"You look sick," said Ky.

Ihlo looked up at her.

"What?" said Ky. "I'm sharing an observation. You're pale. Pasty."

Ihlo shook her head and looked away, through the window to a washed-out winter dawn.

"Suit yourself." Ky shrugged and moved to the other end of the room, where she put on a VR headset – a pearlescent band that covered her eyes and ears like a fallen halo – and slumped down on the sofa. As Ky settled into gameplay, Ihlo watched her cousin all but disappear. She sighed, the tension in her body easing. Then she downed her coffee, grabbed her overcloak and left the apartment.

The morning was bitterly cold. Ihlo pulled up the collar of her overcloak, wrapped her dorph around her head, then hurried to catch a Swift that had just pulled up at the end of her street. The tram sped north towards Mount Az, the ancient citadel at the centre of Arteza and home to the Order of Savants. The Library crested the citadel – a grand, imposing building, all turrets, buttresses and arched leaded windows. Built nearly three hundred and fifty years ago, it was commissioned by Ninian, a prominent philosopher and social scientist of the time, to honour the Savants and their profound contribution to their nation's prosperity. The Library, along with various buildings skirting its flanks, was also intended to provide a more fitting home for the Order and its serving votaries.

Around the crumbling citadel walls were the Old Quarters, each named after the four sibling Savants who created Klova: Arlo, Ezra, Riker and Kemp. Beyond the Quarters stretched modern Arteza, all granite, steel and glass – the principal city of Iso-Klovaine. On the eastern horizon, watching over Mount Az like a protective parent, towered the mountain of Witness – home to twelve species of indigenous birds, including the songless charmbird and the legendary Raptor, avian guardian of ancient Arteza.

Ihlo stepped off the Swift at the depot on Nova Junction and hurried through the narrow lanes of Ezra to reach the east entrance to Mount Az. Within the citadel walls, the lanes were even more narrow and of a gradient that made hurrying hard. Ihlo was relieved that her current post was based in a building only halfway up the climb. As she approached the Department of Implementation, a confusion of windows and walls contending with a thirty-degree incline, she heard someone call her name. She turned around to see her supervisor emerge from the building opposite.

"Votary Modessr," she said, dipping her head, hands held behind her back.

"Yes, yes," said Modessr, a tall, spindly man ten years her senior. Their hair was identical, cropped short and slicked back. Their uniform, uniform. He nodded briefly in reply, his arms laden with a large metal box, wires trailing.

"Let me assist," said Ihlo, gathering the cables.

"Get the door, if you please. This beast is about to break me."

Ihlo obliged, dropping the cables and hurrying to push open the large oak door into their building. Modessr, grunting, followed her in, thrusting the metal box into the hands of the first votary he saw. "Third floor, lab five, or as near as you can manage," he puffed, shaking the blood back into his arms. "And thank you, coequal," he called after the stooped, retreating form.

"What's the scanner for?" said Ihlo.

"The one in the lab is misbehaving. I've appropriated this unit from our colleagues in Development as they have an abundance." Modessr started walking down the wood-panelled hallway, his shoes slapping the flagstone floor. "Let's get started. We've much to do."

They reached their lab to find the door left open and the scanner deposited on the central bench. The space inside the lab was all about contrast. Dark wood-panelled walls, sloping floorboards and irregular, leaded windows spoke of the building's age. The tech that filled the room was high-end and advanced. The 'bench' was a steel table that ran down the centre of the room. Suspended above it were two large, transparent visuals, covered in a mass of data, glowing blue. On a counter running the length of the lab sat all manner of tech hardware, the defunct scanner included. At the far end of the room stood a narrow, metal cabinet, about six feet tall, with a tinted glass panel at the front: the Language System Simulator – or 'Lasysi', its more manageable sobriquet.

Having removed their overcloaks and coats, Ihlo and Modessr sat at the central bench. Ihlo worked through the routine protocols required at the start of every duty, while Modessr entertained his ego by setting out the day's schedule.

"…And all of that by dinner break," he said. "It's going to be a run to keep up these next few weeks. With Upgrade Day fast approaching, there's a mountain of work to get through. You'll find it tough going, I won't lie. I will keep us on track, obviously, that's my responsibility. Yours is to follow instructions. Clear?"

"Yes, Modessr."

"Your knowledge of the Order's principles is, at present, two-dimensional, limited to theory and reason. You've yet to fully comprehend them in practice – hence your training with me. The annual system update is the primary vehicle to achieve our purpose. It is also the culmination of the Order's extensive labours over the past year. Our collective efforts are only a success if the update is a success. Which is why, in the

Department of Implementation, our contribution to the cause is vital – our performance, critical."

Ihlo bowed her head in acknowledgement of the scale. She knew better than to interrupt Modessr's flow.

"Over the coming days, your part towards the greater good is crash-testing the alignment of the Machine's new code with the existing code. With the aid of Lasysi here, you are responsible for running the protocol of checks on full system integration and assimilation in the context of Klova. What value is there in incorporating a new word or concept if the existing syntax cannot support it?" He glared at Ihlo. "A question, novice."

"It is of no value at all, Modessr."

"And what would it amount to?"

"Disaster."

"In the shape of?"

"Incompatible code, potentially causing damage to existing code or its patterning in the system. This could, in turn, cause a malfunction in the nanoware, or in the cerebrovox implant, leaving people without language. Worst case scenario: implant replacement. Surgical intervention on the entire population."

"Forty-eight million people who will be unable to speak until they have their minor op. Not a situation we want to find ourselves in." He turned and began tapping his visual, bringing up and swiping away streams of code in a demonstration of purpose. "You have done your homework, novice. Now let's see you apply what you have learnt."

*

The morning was long, the workload intensive. Ihlo was relieved when Modessr slipped away after the first hour; she could get on with her work without him constantly peering

13

over her shoulder, telling her what she already knew. Her heart sank when he returned minutes before the dinner bell.

"My apologies, I was held up with important Library business. Everything on track here?"

"All good. Stage one test results are uploaded. Shall I bring them up on the visual?"

"That can wait. Let us make haste to the refectory before the queue builds. There is a matter I must discuss with you whilst we dine."

The refectory was in a different building, several steep streets away. Ihlo threw on her coat and overcloak and hurried after Modessr, who was already halfway down the hall. Outside, the day was bright and cold, the air a racket of birdsong. The lanes were busy with becloaked votaries darting between department buildings or heading up to the Library ahead of the afternoon sessions. Ihlo and Modessr entered the refectory building, greeted by the aroma of baked bread and spice. Despite her annoyance at having to take dinner with Modessr, she found herself salivating at the prospect of the meal.

Inside the high-ceilinged hall, long trestle tables were already half-full. They joined the queue at the serving hatch and waited for their bowl of steaming banban stew, Modessr with his back to Ihlo. Several colleagues from Implementation were already seated and gestured towards the spare seats beside them. Modessr pretended he didn't see. He led Ihlo over to an empty table at the far end of the hall. They sat down facing each other. Modessr ate his stew without saying a word. When he had finished, he eyed Ihlo for a moment, before clearing his throat and dabbing at the corners of his mouth with a napkin.

"I have been advised that you have proposed a point of attention for tomorrow's meeting of the General Council."

"That is correct."

"I know it is. I was not seeking corroboration of the fact."

Ihlo put down her fork, her meal half-eaten. "Is there a problem? I thought it a pertinent matter, given the circumstances."

"It is not so much the item itself, although I am rather bemused by it. It is the fact you did not discuss your intentions with me in the first instance."

"The General Council is an open forum. I was under the impression any votary can raise a point."

"You are a novice, under my supervision."

"I did not think that precluded me."

"Pedantry is no substitute for common sense, Ihlo. I am talking about the probationary arrangement, the purpose it serves. How can I give you counsel and the benefit of my experience if you do not tell me what you are up to?"

Ihlo pushed aside her plate, her appetite lost.

"Understand that your actions have a bearing on my reputation. If you behave inappropriately, judgement will be made upon my supervision of you."

"And you regard my action, in this instance, inappropriate?"

"It is a matter of principle, novice. I shall not be made to look the fool through such acts of hubris. In future, if you deem a matter sufficiently worthy of the Council's valuable attention, you raise it with me. If I perceive any value in it, I may consider putting it forward under my name. It will stand more chance of being heard."

Ihlo glared at Modessr, resisting the rise. She had only been in the Order a couple of months and had worked under his supervision for the last six weeks. Already, she had learnt there was little point in arguing with him. Better to bite her tongue and leave him to glory in his pseudo-superiority. She refused to give him an audience to play up to.

"However," he said, oblivious, "in this case, any intervention I could have made on your behalf would have gained us little ground – other than to encourage you to cease in your intention before wasting the Council's time."

Her pulse quickening, she couldn't hold back any longer. "What? You don't believe the matter to be of interest to the General Council?"

"No, of course I don't."

"But the crisis is escalating. The number affected is rising."

"Not the Order's concern. You know our jurisdiction. This is a matter for Public Health."

"I've been following developments in the news. There's an issue around speech and comprehension. Patterns are emerging. As a matter of course, shouldn't the Order take a view?"

"As far as I've heard, a handful of people are showing symptoms of transient global amnesia. I don't see what view the Order could possibly take."

"There are approaching thirty confirmed cases. Of those, not one has recovered their ability to speak of the past. Transient global amnesia is a temporary condition – twenty-four hours, at most. The first case was reported five days ago."

"Well now, haven't we been collecting our facts and figures. I suggest you spend a little more time studying the protocol manuals I gave you. I can't emphasise how fortunate you are to be assigned a position in Implementation for your probationary year. The annual system update is the single most important undertaking by the Order. It is with pride that I have the crucial role of overseeing its delivery this year. You, novice, should feel proud also – and honoured to have been granted this opportunity."

"I do."

"Then show it by affording it your full attention."

Ihlo clenched her jaw and breathed in deep.

"Anyway," continued Modessr, "I've spoken to the Council administrator. Explained your error in submitting your proposal. Apologised on your behalf." He stood up, ignoring Ihlo's wide-eyed stare. "I'm chairing a session in the Library this afternoon. You know your schedule for the remainder of your duty. Ensure the results and your thorough analysis of them are uploaded for my inspection by the end of the day." He turned and left the hall.

Ihlo remained seated, stunned. She had become accustomed to Modessr's manner and the part she was required to play in his personal pantomime. In her old life, she had refused to suffer fools, but here, in the seat of her calling, personality could play no part. Modessr wasn't important; her duty to the Order and to Klova eclipsed whatever irritation he might cause.

However, the situation with the emerging crisis was different. The voice of instinct was compelling. Heeding its warning, Ihlo was convinced it had to be shared. However inconceivable, if she was right and there was, somehow, a link with language, the implications were unimaginable. If left unchecked, she feared they could be catastrophic.

What if I told you your perception of the world around you is at the mercy of the words you have to describe it?

Surely you're in control of what you see? Surely what's real is simply real – there for all to behold?

I can almost hear you ask these naive questions as you grapple with the unthinkable. It makes for uncomfortable reading, doesn't it? To have your vulnerability spelt out, word for word.

Rather like pulling wings off a fly.

CHAPTER THREE

Ink is lost in an expanding labyrinth of empty content. The tram ride to nowhere didn't work out the moment his device killed the distraction. Unable to hold it together enough to return to work, he resorted to hiding in his apartment where there's no need to try. In the three hours he's been back, Ink has perched on his sofa, staring at the visual on the wall in front of him, searching blind through the bloated mass of ubimedia.

With Upgrade Day just a few weeks away, ubi is flooded with Incorporation content – all, by necessity, vacuous speculation. The fact that no one outside of the Order can possibly know what new words will be included in Klova's annual system update does not deter endless comment. Besides, Upgrade Day is a public holiday, eagerly awaited and nationally celebrated. The anticipation in the lead up is as much a part of the occasion as the day itself. Still, there is only so much you can write about what you don't know – hence the spotlight shift; the so-called Amnesia Crisis is providing a timely diversion. Consumers are latching on to the thread, instantly elevating its profile. Although almost everyone knows less about the Crisis than they do about Incorporation, the fact that it's a Breaking Story gives the impression information is on the brink of revealing itself. They are simply laying the groundwork, priming the nation for the spectacle.

Ink has searched every inch of that ground and has found nothing worth finding. He slumps back on the sofa, his strained eyes closed, rubbing his aching neck. All he has learnt is that a couple dozen people have come forward, although the true number remains a matter of wild guess – which ubi is generously taking. The common symptom is the loss of something he has no concept of, which has made the search for answers feel like grasping hold of shadows. With waning hope, Ink shuts down the visual and turns his attention inward.

Aside from tired eyes and the stubborn dregs of a codevice hangover, he feels fine. If he could resist the noise on ubi, he suspects he could downplay any connection he might have to the Crisis. Denial feels appealing. However, hiding in his apartment has already lost its attraction, as has solitude. He rules out going back to the office. Oblivion at the bottom of a genker bottle is tempting – the potent spirit, laced with nutmeg and clove, combined with the buzz of a hothouse somewhere, would provide a reliable distraction. Yet he knows the escape would be temporary – the return to reality, that much harder. Instead, he opts for small steps. Wrapping up warm, he leaves his apartment and walks – anywhere, rather than somewhere.

He lives in Union, a district on the west side of the city and home to the future tech sector. The architecture epitomises the industry's vision and ambition – all clean lines, with high-performance materials in pristine condition. Ink wanders through the wide, green spaces between buildings, surrounded by busy birds and people on a mission. Walking aimlessly, his own lack of purpose stirs a desire for destination. His few friends are all at work; regardless, he knows where his next step needs to take him. He heads back towards his apartment block, down to the subterranean park-up and his private ride. He sets the location: an address in the district of Welling Blink. Then he switches the control to autonomous, slumps back in the warm cabin and stares out through the window as his ride pulls out of the park-up and heads north.

On the threshold of her apartment, Ink takes the outstretched hands of his mother.

"Inker, so good to see you. Come in, come in. Your father's out, I'm afraid." She ushers Ink inside, placing her hand on his back with gentle pressure, propelling him down the hall and into the living room at the end. Ink's mother is a petite woman; she has to reach up to his shoulder to press him down into an armchair.

"Why aren't you at work? Is there something wrong?" She peers into his face. "Wait. Don't tell me yet. I'll fetch us some tea."

While his mother is busy in the kitchen, Ink settles into the armchair and lets the room enfold him. His parents have lived here all his life. The familiarity of the space is a comfort, the impression of sanctuary, part of the furniture. Already, he can feel the sharp edge of vulnerability soften. Fragile balance feels like a viable goal.

"Here you go," says his mother, placing a loaded tray on a low table before him. She pours the tea, handing a cup to Ink while holding out a plate of biscuits and buns. "Fresh this morning. You've not eaten. I can tell."

He selects the smallest item on the plate and places it on the arm of his chair.

"Right, I'm all yours," she says, settling into a chair beside his.

Ink's mother is a straight talker, and he loves her for it. He tries to follow suit. "You hear about this Amnesia Crisis?"

"No. But you're about to fill me in."

"There are a couple dozen cases of people forgetting something." He falters, frowning. This is the first time he has attempted to put into words what he lacks the words for. "Not as in forgetting memories, but… but time. Part of the idea of time." He takes a deep breath and looks up at his mother. "I'm one of those cases."

She puts her teacup down, her eyes fixed on Ink's face, studying the detail as if reading his palm. "You're ill?"

"No. At least, I don't *feel* ill."

"But you feel afraid." It isn't a question. "What else do you know about this *crisis?*"

"I'll show you what ubi's saying. There's loads about it online." He cups his palm, flicking fingers to activate the holographic visual. "See?"

"I can read ubi's take on it when you've gone. What's *yours?*"

Ink rubs the side of his jaw. "I don't feel like there's anything physically wrong with me. And my memory is fine. They're calling it 'sudden onset amnesia', but I remember everything. Growing up here. Summer holidays in Riser Bay. My first apartment. Neav." He catches a shift in his mother's expression. "What?"

"What do you remember about Neav?"

He lifts his shoulders. "Everything."

She watches him for a moment, eyes narrowed. When he tilts his head, half frowning, she breaks off and leans back. "So then," she says, her tone shifted to matter of fact. "If you remember everything, what makes you think you've got this thing?"

"My memories have nothing to do with time. But I think yours do."

"You mean your memories are jumbled? You can't place them, you can't remember when they happened?"

"There is no *when* for memories – that's what I'm saying. Everything's now or next. Time starts in this moment and goes forward for eternity. That's how time works. Except, not for you, right? Or for forty-eight million people, bar two-dozen."

His mother nods slowly, eyes fixed ahead. Ink watches her, gaining strength in her composure. This is why he's here, he knew she would react like this. To his mind, she's an anchor – forever holding fast, no matter the storm. Her level-headedness is a calming influence. Even now, in the still waters of her thinking, he finds comfort.

After a moment's silence, she glances sidelong at him. "You feel well, you say?"

"Anxious, obviously. Afraid. But physically, I feel okay."

"Good. Above all else, that's our first priority. Health is among the most precious gifts we have. It's our responsibility to mind it stays well."

Ink nods, biting into his biscuit by way of proof.

"Remain aware of how you're feeling. Mentally and physically. Promise you'll tell me if your health becomes affected." Her glance turns into a glare. "Yes?"

"Of course."

"In the meantime, we must find out what we can. When fear is of the unknown, relief comes in answers, however piecemeal. And, at present, you don't have any. But maybe some of the others affected do. Do you know who they are? Have any of them spoken out?"

"I've no idea. Ubi doesn't tend to bother with the horse's mouth. First-hand accounts gag speculation."

"What's ArtezAlert saying?"

"Barely anything."

"A good sign. If state news isn't running with it, there's less likely to be weight behind the story. I suggest you avoid ubi if you want to keep that anxiety in check."

"Learning the lesson." He manages a guilty smile.

"They must be feasting on this." She sighs. "It never ceases to amaze me. Klovaines are, by nature, a level-headed race. I swear rationalism was incorporated to describe our mindset. And yet, our culture is obsessed with a vehicle that vomits content that's so far removed from fact and measured reaction. It's entertainment of the worst possible kind." She sits back, eyeing Ink. "You probably think me old fashioned."

"I think you're spot on. That's why I come to talk to you." He holds up his left hand, palm exposed. "They just make it impossible to escape."

Back in his own living room, the lights left off, Ink watches dusk descend on the city. His apartment is fourth floor, with an impressive east-facing view of Union. Throughout Arteza, no building is more than six storeys tall – a condition of construction to keep the city forever at the feet of Mount Az and thus, forever in homage to the memory of the Savants. He looks over at Az now, a darkening smudge on the horizon, the lights from the citadel barely visible, the Library a faintly glowing crown.

Laying on his sofa, staring at the view, Ink's mind fills with the words and manner of his mother. The influence of her calm rationality remains with him – present, not remembered – as if he is bound to her steadfast anchor. With it, he holds a new, timeless memory: sitting side by side in armchairs, drinking tea, a pile of baked treats to test his appetite. He knows his frame of mind now reflects his mother's calm pragmatism and steadying reassurance – a heart-warming comfort. An abstract image on the one hand, vivid impressions in the *now* of time on the other. With no conceivable notion that the two are connected, he can only feel the effect of an unknowable cause.

Ink draws on the residue of reassurance, stretching it out, making it his own. He knows not to look at ubi again tonight. He knows tomorrow will be another day. Maybe then it will all be over – like some twenty-four hour thing. He feels his forehead for warmth, imagines he is, in fact, running a slight temperature. Perhaps. That could explain it. Reassurance feeds off itself, relaxing his muscles, opening his mind. Another snapshot of the timeless memory slips into his head: remembering Neav.

She *is*.

It's easy to forget.

It's impossible to remember that which is forever gone, as if it never was.

Try this: imagine the one thing you are most afraid of. Do it now. Picture it. Know its reality. Feel its form, the contours of threat that stoke your fear. Let that fear swell as you cower in the shadow of its cause. Tremble. Feel sick to the stomach. Choke.

Now, imagine that the thing you are most afraid of simply does not exist in language. Difficult, I know. But humour me. Whatever it is: bleeding out, suffocating, losing your mind. Doesn't matter. That thing you most fear – there is no name for it. No words to describe it. You've never even heard of it. Neither have I.

I put it to you: if you cannot talk about a concept – if you lack the linguistic tools to even conceive of it – can it still exist?

I wonder.

CHAPTER FOUR

The Council chamber was packed. Every votary is invited to attend the monthly General Council meetings; this month, all six hundred had taken up their place. The grand chamber sat in the centre of the Library, the symbolic heart of the Order. A vast vaulted ceiling, constructed from hand-carved granite, centuries old, towered over the congress. Huge arched windows ran the length of the space on either side, flooding the chamber with gilded light from the low, winter sun. In the centre was a circular dais, on which stood the current Chair of the General Council, votary Engala – a tall, slim woman, with piercing emerald eyes. Seated all around her were the oath-bound votaries of the Order of Savants. With identically cropped, slicked back hair, starched grey tunics and crisp overgowns, variations in height, weight and physiognomy were the only differences in the sea of attentive faces. There was no chatter while they waited, no fidgeting, or checking devices. Decorum dictated total attention. Obedience to protocol was also part of the uniform.

Ihlo sat close to the dais. When she had arrived, she had spotted Modessr on the far right-hand side, seated near the back. She regretted the distance between them. She would have liked to see the look in his eyes when it came to her turn to speak. The thought of Modessr's current mood, petulant from having his intervention dismissed, gave her welcome distraction from her swelling nerves. Two months in, this was only her second General Council meeting and here she was, about to take the dais and address the entire Order. She took a deep breath and imagined Modessr's downsized ego.

"I declare this session open," said the Chair, her voice echoing around the chamber. "We begin with points of attention. Item one. I relinquish the stand for votary Ihlo Unis." The Chair then stepped off the dais, nodding briefly to Ihlo before taking her seat in the front row.

Ihlo rose and mounted the platform. There was no lectern to hide behind. With her audience in the round, she was required to turn as she spoke, projecting without the aid of tech, and address all parts of the chamber in equal measure. Exposed before six hundred expectant faces, Ihlo pushed her shoulders back, head held high.

"I propose before this Council that the Order of Savants intervene in the so-called Amnesia Crisis. It is my firm opinion that there is a connection between the symptoms reported and Klova. I do not claim to know the nature of this link, or whether it is in relation to the cerebrovox implant or the language code itself. However, the indications suggesting a connection are compelling. As a matter of urgency, I petition this Council to investigate the verity of this link and initiate Bastion to investigate its cause. In defence of this proposal, I ask only that you consider this: what if I am right?"

Her case stated, Ihlo held out her hands, palms up, in the customary gesture of invitation. Stating her proposal was the easy part; Ihlo knew the challenge lay in what was to follow. The floor was now open to questions. How long this lasted, how far she would be pushed on any given point, was the call of the Chair. Ihlo braced herself.

The Chair rose and joined Ihlo on the dais. "The proposal is open to challenge. All those with a question to ask, please stand."

Around a third of the room rose to their feet. Ihlo's heart sank.

"In the interests of time, I will take a number of questions now and invite all remaining questions to be submitted to the Council administrator immediately following the session. All questions will be answered in writing by the Proposer within four hours and will be made available on the central system for scrutiny. Members will have until midnight to vote on whether to adopt or dismiss the proposal. The results will be declared by the start of first duty tomorrow morning." She tapped her palm device and interacted with the holographic display. "I have initiated random selection from those now standing. If you are selected, you will receive a notification via your NuB. Please be seated."

Once all those standing had sat back down and Chair Engala had returned to her own seat, a heavy silence filled the chamber. Ihlo felt the sea of staring eyes, the judgements and assumptions riding the tide, and bore the force of its scrutiny.

A man to her left rose and cleared his throat. "Chair. Proposer. My question is this: any link to Klova would constitute a failure of some kind. As we all know, the hardware and software are designed and maintained to be absolutely failsafe. What can possibly go wrong?"

Ihlo was prepared for this stance of fundamental denial. "We aim for it to be failsafe, just as we aim for perfection in Klova. Both are an ideal. They are not a guarantee. I don't know what has gone wrong – that is to be determined by the action I propose. The investigation may find no such fault and prove me incorrect. But I say to you: what if I am right?"

The man sat down. Discussion was not permitted. With his question asked and answered, the protocol meant the proceedings moved on. Next question.

A woman behind Ihlo rose. "Chair," she said. Ihlo turned to face her, jaw set. "Proposer. My question is this: Klova's code is embedded in nanoware, which has successfully communicated with the cerebrovox implant since the last system update a year ago. The system is a closed loop and, as such, protected. How can a fault arise in any part of that system, sealed as it is?"

"It is an operating system transmitting an artificial language into a highly complex, organic human organ. A closed system is not immune to error. Where possibility for error exists, however inconceivable or infinitesimal, it remains a possibility. Therefore, I say to you: what if I am right?"

The woman stared at Ihlo, then slowly sat back down. A faint murmur filled the pause, then died away as another woman rose to Ihlo's left.

"Chair. Proposer. My question is this: our proud nation's population is forty-eight million strong. I believe the number suffering amnesia is around forty. Every newborn child is given language; every Klovaine carries the same implant and the same Klova code. A highly complex, but *single* set of code provides us all with the language to think, speak, read and write. How is it that the ill health of forty individuals – forty in *forty-eight million* – is down to a Klova malfunction, when the rest of the population are entirely well?"

Ihlo sighed at the predictability of their reasoning. "It has been six days since the first reported case. Numbers are rising – slowly, but rising. I do not know the cause, just as I cannot predict the eventual scale. But I am certain there's a link. Given the ratio you have drawn attention to, I'd say now is the time to act before the proportional difference closes. We have a duty of care, for Klova and for the forty-eight million people who speak it. Which is why I say to you: what if I am right?"

The woman remained standing until the votary beside her gently nudged her. A man directly in front of Ihlo stood up. He hesitated, staring at her, blinking and open-mouthed. A tense silence stretched on.

The Chair rose. "Your question, votary."

The man's face flushed. He retook his seat without saying a word.

"It seems our colleague has changed his mind." She looked around the chamber. "I must assess opinion's sway. All those who still have a question to ask, please stand."

At the back of the room, a single man rose from his seat.

"Votary Modessr," said the Chair. "It appears you are the only one. Please, ask your question in the way of this Council." She sat down, her emerald eyes appraising Ihlo.

"Chair," said Modessr, his voice bloated with theatrics. "Proposer. My question is this: we have a duty of care, as you say. A duty to protect Klova and the legacy of the Savants – to protect their honour, their reputation. The implications of your far-fetched notion will be a cause of great alarm. I wouldn't call it scaremongering because I know you better than that. But it will terrify people – understandably so. Therefore, I say to you: what if you are wrong?"

Ihlo did not hesitate. "The Order should not protect reputation at the expense of risk. The very fact we ask *what if* means there is potential in place of certainty. And, in the absence of certainty, we must not let our own faith in Klova make us blind to the possibility that something, somehow, somewhere in the system, has simply gone wrong. So again, I say to you: what if I am right?"

*

"Satisfied?" Modessr did not look at Ihlo as he spat the word. They were walking back to their lab, the hour now late.

"I did not do this for my own gratification."

The Chair, in the absence of further questions, had put the proposal to an immediate vote. The motion for an urgent investigation into the crisis by both the Order and Bastion passed with a divisively narrow majority. In consideration of the strength of opposing opinion and the delicate issue of public reaction, the Chair had declared that the dual investigation would be treated as confidential until a link with Klova could be proved – if it did, indeed, exist. With the Chair's pronouncement made, the meeting had moved on to the next agenda item. For almost two hours, Ihlo had sat listening to the tedium of mundane matters – the slow turning cogs that drove the Order's machine of domestic operations. All the while, she felt the resentful glare of those who had voted against her proposal. Most penetrating of all were the daggers from Modessr.

Ihlo and her supervisor reached their department building, now dark and deserted. Inside their lab, Lasysi hummed and blinked in the gloom. Ihlo turned on the lights and began shutting down their workstation, desperate to get away. Modessr did not assist. He stood at the central bench, arms crossed, eyeing his supposed ward.

"You've caused irreversible damage – for yourself, as well as for the reputation of the Order. Your incendiary proposal would never have been considered had you been a fledged votary. Regrettably, however, there's some notion that novices should be given a voice, despite their lack of experience. Token gesture of equality. Typical of the Order's egalitarian character. Inclusive to a fault."

Ihlo spun around to face him, her body rigid. "My proposal was deemed worthy enough to be heard at the meeting. It was the primary point of attention. I addressed every challenge put to me. After your question – and thanks, by the way, for having my back – there were no more. The vote was fair. The motion was passed. Why can't you accept that? Why this personal attack?"

"Attack? My dear, I am trying to protect you."

"*What?*"

"You are green; you've yet to fully comprehend both the majesty of Klova and how we preserve it. If you grasped that, you would not have propounded a course of action that carried such high and unnecessary risk. You swayed the vote with emotive oratory – a wholly inappropriate tactic."

"You still don't get it, do you?"

"You mean, what if you are right? Well, of course you're not. The premise is inconceivable." He dropped his arms and softened his glare, adopting the role of patient sage before his ignorant charge. "A malfunction in the implant, or a bug in the code, are such far-fetched scenarios, they are as good as impossible. You argue that, where possibility for error exists, however small, it is still a possibility? That is semantics. When we're considering the reputational damage that's at stake, we should be concerned with probability, not wordplay."

"And you deem it so improbable, it's not even worth asking the question?"

"Yes. As I've said, it is inconceivable. Not just to my mind – I'd say, to most of the people in the chamber tonight. I'd wager the majority of those who stood up had the same question, which is: are you out of your mind? Hence my effort to protect your reputation, as well as that of Klova and the Order. When you are proven wrong, your colleagues' perception of you will be proven right – an over-keen novice with an over-fed ego, devising an ill-conceived scheme to elevate her position."

"Is that what you think?"

"Your behaviour leaves me little choice." He glanced down at his palm device, which was standby-blank. "I must be away. Urgent matters to attend. That report you were to complete in the morning, I want it tonight. I suggest you crack on."

Stunned into silence, Ihlo watched Modessr turn and leave. She couldn't even attempt to process his words or make sense of his perspective. It seemed impossible that other votaries would share his view, as he claimed. And yet, the resistance she had felt during the meeting, the cold stares as she had left, opened the door to doubt. To her, such a dismissive, myopic attitude was the only inconceivable part in all of this. She desperately hoped she was wrong, that the truth would prove Modessr and his cronies right. She had no reputation to protect and would not care even if she did.

Ihlo sat at the bench, staring at her visual, faced with the hours of work Modessr had just landed her. As she settled to the task, she denied her own frustration, refusing to give him the satisfaction. Meanwhile, her confidence grew. Her repeated question wasn't a trick to win the vote, it was reinforcement, spelling out what she already believed to be true.

We all do things to make ourselves feel safe. Those measures tell us we are in control of the situation. That is empowering. At least, that is how it feels.

Comfort zones are not a physical space.

Bastion serves this purpose: appeasing the mind, protecting through token gesture. Their posturing and appearance are, I presume, an effort to make the pantomime more convincing. Security can be an illusion of perception.

Bastion exists to protect Klova and the interests of the Order. They are a measure to make us feel safe.

But feeling safe and being safe are strangers with little in common.

CHAPTER FIVE

On the edge of Arlo Quarter, pressed up against its crumbling boundary wall, stood a structure of shameless contrast. All dark tinted windows and thin-profile, black aluminium frames, the building was infamous throughout Iso-Klovaine. Nicknamed the Scarab, this was the headquarters of the Order's private security agency: Bastion.

Agent Laine sat in her office, scanning the visual in front of her. In her late forties, she had spiked hair and a sharp attitude. Dressed in regulation attire – tailored suit, shirt and stiff band collar, everything black – only her office denoted her superior rank. Beyond its glass walls was a huge, open-plan workspace for over a hundred diligent agents.

Tapping the surface of her tech-enabled desk, she called out, "Brosala. Get yourself in here." Leaning back in her chair, she read the instruction on her visual for a fourth time.

Seconds later, a man appeared – older, shorter and leaner than Laine. "Boss?"

"I've cancelled your leave," she said without taking her eyes off the visual. "Duty calls."

"But—"

"But nothing. Sit." She swiped the visual, clearing the screen. They now sat facing each other through a suspended panel of glass. "Official instruction from the Order, ratified by Top Floor this morning. I've been given the lead on fieldwork. Which means you don't get to disappear for whatever break you think you deserve."

Brosala sighed, rubbing his eyes. "Go on, then. What's the ticket?"

"This amnesia business."

"What's that got to do with us?"

"My words, to the letter."

"And?"

"Whilst we know best, the Order holds the misguided view that they, in fact, do. General Council voted last night on a motion to investigate the so-called crisis. They must've been tired, or in a rush. Vote passed. Orders are in."

Brosala gestured his head towards the ceiling. "What's the view upstairs?"

"Job's a job. Ours is not to pick and choose." She leant forward, elbows on the desk. "Four teams have been assigned. Strictly covert until we find something solid. For now, we're the only ops in the field. Good news for us. We – that means I – can handle it how we like."

"Which is?"

She cocked her head. "Need you ask?"

Brosala nodded, warming to the job. "When do we start?"

*

The city's highways were busy with the morning commute. A silent vehicle, obsidian slick, weaved through the traffic. Inside the cab, Brosala held the controls. Agent Laine sat on the back seat, cramming intel from her device's holographic display.

"First stop, Riker's Quad," she said to the back of Brosala's head. "Scene of the first incident. Minor public disorder. We're questioning under that pretext."

Their destination was on the opposite side of the Old Quarters, a quick ride on the central circular, bypassing the narrow, cobbled streets of the pedestrianised Quarters. Brosala parked up at Nova Junction, the main entrance into the old town, and they walked the remaining distance. Laine led the way, her assistant one stride behind. Both looked straight ahead, expressions deadpan, inviting attention from those who crossed their path.

Riker's was one of four Quads, one in each of the Old Quarters. Each Quad was a converted public square, turned outside-in via high performance, thermal-insulating glazing capping the space. The centuries-old speaker's dais was preserved in the centre. A kousa tree stood in each corner, providing perch for the resident parakeets – imported and bred to enhance the illusion. Around the four stone walls – the once-exterior facias of the abutting buildings – were seating areas with a view of the square's centre. At peak times, Riker's Quad would be buzzing with chatter, high spirits and heckling parakeets. However, at this early hour the square was empty, save for staff setting up for the day's business. Calling the shots was a stout man in a fawn suit, who came up to greet Bastion on their arrival.

"Good morning," he said, oozing obsequiousness like dripping honey. "Finest of days to you both. Please, let me take your overcloaks. Coffee? We serve the finest bean."

Brosala's eyes lit up, until Laine cut in. "No. We don't have long. Are you our contact?" She already looked and sounded disappointed.

"Yes. With my pleasure. Manager, front of house. Please," he said, gesturing to a booth to their left, "take a seat. Time is intel. I understand. I have a cousin in Law Enforcement."

Laine ignored him and walked up to the central dais. She turned around, looking everywhere but at the man she was addressing. "You were working on the evening in question?"

"Indeed. I work six days a week, on call the seventh. Only paid for five, but you won't hear me complain. More than a job, this."

Laine glanced at Brosala, who stepped up to the manager and, in a discreet half-whisper, said, "Suggest you keep to the point. Patience of a sinner. Best not to test, if you get my meaning."

The manager looked from Brosala to Laine, mortified. "I was on duty. Yes."

"Describe the disturbance."

"It was open mic debate night. One of our regulars was holding her corner. Already won two rounds. Then this guy comes up to challenge. They set to sparring, all good natured and by the book. Then they start accusing each other."

"Saying what?"

"That they're not talking right. Not making sense."

"The guy challenging. Seen him before?"

"Few times. Quiet. Reserved, in a shy sense. I don't recall him competing before. He's the sort who looks like you could knock his nerves with a nestling's feather."

"And yet he steps up to debate with a regular on a winning streak. Odd?"

"Guess so, in retrospect. But it's open mic. Anyone can stand. You don't stop to think why they would."

She walked slowly around the dais. "Okay. Then what?"

"Like I said, they argue. Accusing each other of talking nonsense. Claiming it's a distraction tactic, to throw the opponent off. Foul play."

"What's the reaction in the audience?"

"They're right behind the regular. Not 'cause she's a Quad

favourite or they're backing a winner. Turns out they agree with her. They think he's playing up on purpose. Meanwhile, he's swearing blind it's her and it's all a fix, audience and all. Starts arguing with some of the punters. He was getting more and more agitated, his language more aggressive. This is irregular. Highly so. And the punters know it. That's when it kicked off."

"Who started the fight?"

"I don't know. It all blew up so quick. From shouting to shirt pulling, then a full-on fight. That's when I called in Law Enforcement. I've a duty to protect my staff – and then there's all the other customers. They're cowering in their booths, fearing how it'll play out. Never seen the like before. You might get trouble in a hothouse, or Dox, or the Delce – but rarely in the Quarters. And *never* in a Quad. I'm not saying we're all shiny shoes. It's not the individuals – it's the *place*." He looked around him, as if to draw attention to their faultless surroundings.

"Okay. I get the picture." She turned to Brosala. "We got details on the two competing?"

"Yes. Plus their statements. No spice to speak of."

"Get a booking on our challenger. I want to see him next." She turned to the manager, about to say something, but changed her mind when she saw him. She shot Brosala a glance, then left him to it.

Brosala faced the manager and forced a smile. "Thank you for your time."

"You're most welcome. I've not had the pleasure of assisting Bastion before. It has been my absolute honour—"

"Ah, sorry," said Brosala, backing away, tapping his NuB. "Call from HQ. Very important. Must take it." He turned and hurried out after Laine, leaving the manager standing, hand to chest, staring at the spaces that Bastion had filled.

*

"Well. That was a waste of time," said Laine. They were back in their ride, negotiating the traffic and tram lanes around Nova Junction.

"We've been sent a summary of the other incidents," said Brosala, sat at the controls, his back to Laine. "All fairly similar. Minor public disorder; verbal altercations. Some physical aggression. No charges made."

"Any obvious pattern?"

"Only that they all seem to kick off from the same argument, that someone's talking bullshit."

"I get that every day. You don't see me kicking off."

"That's the only piece I got from your mate back there."

"What?"

"That the guy involved is a bag of nerves. Hardly sounds the type to start a fight."

"Did you line up an interview?"

"Yes. Next stop. He's at work – office block in Cope. He's been notified we're on our way."

*

The challenger was sat at a table in the staff break-out room, his fingers fidgeting with a plastic key card. "Law Enforcement have my statement." Shoulders hunched, he stole pale-faced glances at the two Bastion agents seated before him.

Agent Laine sat with her arms crossed, appraising her subject.

Brosala activated his palm device. "We're recording the interview. Just so you know."

"Law Enforcement release me without charge. Say they drop the matter." He wore his nerves like a second skin.

"They dropped it. We've picked it up," said Laine. "Why did you step up to the mic that night?"

The challenger frowned. "I have to make meaning from your words. Can you even imagine that? What it feels like, to hear people make sounds you don't understand – and be told it's your fault?"

"Do you remember?"

"I have memory."

"Then answer the question. Why did you step up?"

"You ask, why challenge? For this," he said, indicating Laine and Brosala with a trembling hand. "For attention. No one is listening. No one is taking me seriously."

"Oh, you can bet I am. Wasting my time? I take that seriously."

"Then tell me what's happening to me. Media's saying it's amnesia. Bullshit. I remember I'm meeting a friend tomorrow. I remember it's my brother's birthday next week. My memory's just fine."

"But you can't remember the past."

"I don't know what that *means*. I have memories; I remember taking a beating in Riker's Quad and being told it's my fault. But that word you say? How can I remember it if I don't know what *it* is?" The man sat forward, hands splayed on the table. "There's something wrong. I don't know what. But it's real, and it's freaking me out. Law aren't listening. Ubimedia's fixated on this amnesia crap. But it's nothing to do with my memory. This isn't about me. It's about Klova. You're Bastion, so that's your bag, right? No one else believes us. We're all saying it, but no one's taking us seriously."

"Us?"

"Us who's affected. We've got a group going. Call ourselves the Undertow. Nothing official. Just a space for mutual support, stop us going mad."

Laine looked to Brosala. "We know about this?"

"First I've heard." His left eye glowed green as it shifted slightly from side to side. "Law haven't raised it. Nothing on file."

"This group," said Laine, turning back to the man. "You all meet up, as in face to face? Or virtual?"

"It's a new thing. Just getting going. But yes, we meet. Why? Do you believe me? About Klova? Will you help us?"

*

"You think he's on to something, don't you?" said Brosala, handing Laine a coffee from a kerbside cabin. They were stood outside the office block, having left the challenger with noncommittal mention of assistance.

Laine stared at the passing traffic, eyes glazed as her mind raced. "Perhaps."

"But it's insane."

"Only because Klova makes it so."

"What do you mean?"

"Language insists on its own perfection. The Savants were clever – they authored their own success. Perfection as a concept is an unattainable ideal. It doesn't exist in and of itself – apart from in Klova. It's inconceivable that something could be wrong with language because its own syntax won't permit it. The words, when put together, don't make sense." Laine glanced at Brosala's blank expression. "This coffee is dry. That building is running. The pavement is evaporating."

"Klova is broken."

"Possibly. And that's the point. Imperfection in Klova *should be* possible. It's just inconceivable to our minds because the words, in that order, have no meaning."

Brosala stared at the not-evaporating pavement. "Fuck."

"This is why no one's listening. The claims of the afflicted are meaningless."

"So how come you worked it out?"

She looked at Brosala, one eyebrow raised.

"Okay, next question. What in Raptor's name do we do? If you're right, this is huge. It's beyond huge." He stared at nothing, eyes bulging. "I can't even—"

"Don't go there. Not yet. It won't help. And there's not time." She handed Brosala her empty coffee carton, flipped her palm and scanned the holographic. "Keep on at our man back there. Make sure he sets up that meet with his support group, as soon as. In the meantime, we've more interviews to get through – all fight-starters with apparent memory loss, according to everyone but them."

Brosala called up their ride. A minute later, their driverless vehicle pulled up in front of them. Once inside, Laine read out the coordinates for their next appointment: an apartment in the neighbouring district of Cryals Cross. The vehicle sped away, carving a serpentine path through the mid-morning traffic. When they arrived at the apartment, no one answered the door.

"Check again," said Laine, her ear to the door.

Brosala's eyes twitched, the green glow bright in the block's dark hallway. "It's the right address. Change of heart, maybe?"

"As if she's got a choice."

Brosala knocked on the door for the third time. Laine stood back, arms crossed, in full view of the several neighbours who had held their own doors ajar. She turned to her right and caught the eye in the crack of the first door. "You know the woman who lives here?"

The door widened a fraction to reveal an elderly face, nodding.

"Is she in?"

"She doesn't always hear the door. Best to call, if you've got her number."

Laine turned to Brosala, who nodded and tapped his NuB. "Integra Nell? This is Bastion Agent Brosala. I'm outside your apartment. You should be expecting us."

A moment later, the apartment door opened to reveal a young woman, possibly late twenties, but far older in the eyes. She had a blanket around her shoulders, covering a full-body haptic suit.

"Sorry. I forget the time." She stepped to one side and gestured to the hall behind her. "Please, come in."

She led them into a large, open-plan living space littered with clothes, kids' toys, dirty plates and countless cups with dark brown dregs. The place smelt of sour yoghurt and stale coffee. Laine and Brosala stood in the centre of the wreckage. Their host repeatedly mumbled "Sorry" as she hurried back and forth, shifting piles of stacked up crap. Having cleared space on the sofa, Integra gestured for them to sit. On a low table in front of the sofa was a glowing headset, emitting a soundtrack with a detached, noise-from-next-door quality. As if the volume had just been turned up, Integra grabbed the headset, pressing something on its side which killed the audio.

"Sorry. I'm playing *Trans:akshn*. It kind of takes over."

"My nephew's obsessed with the game," said Laine.

"The world is vast. It's… well, at the moment, elsewhere's a nice place to be." She pulled up a dining chair and sat down, her hands on her knees, the blanket gone. "Can I ask what this is about?"

"You were involved in an altercation outside your son's school."

She frowned. "I speak to Law Enforcement. The man doesn't press charges."

"We understand that. We're not interested in the fight."

"What then?"

Laine leant forward, dropping her voice. "We understand you are affected by this Amnesia Crisis – for want of a better name. We'd like to ask you a few questions about that. Only, it needs to be off the record. Are you willing to talk in confidence?"

Integra eyed the agents with suspicion. "Why?"

"No one knows what we're dealing with. Myself and Agent Brosala here have been drafted in to help cover all bases. Brought in to rule things out, if you like. We just don't want to knock down the ants' nest while we're at it." She nudged Brosala discretely.

"We also want to help," he added. "We understand from what you told Law Enforcement that things haven't been easy since the change."

This simple acknowledgement appeared to touch Integra like a hand she'd been waiting to hold. "I'm off work, calling in sick. My boy's staying with my parents, just 'til I get my shit together."

"His father?" said Laine.

"Ex-partner. Works a job somewhere on the south coast, so I hear."

"Which leaves you. Here, alone. Escaping inside a video game for a breather from your real life. Am I right?"

Her shoulders sagging, head down, Integra nodded.

"We've spoken to other people afflicted," said Laine, softening her tone. "I'm getting the picture it's not amnesia. It's not about remembering or not remembering." She caught Integra's eye. "You don't think it's about that either, do you?" Her question received a slow shake of the head. "What's happening to you, Integra? What's making you feel like you have to retreat inside *Trans:akshn?*"

Integra closed her eyes, took a deep breath and searched for best-fit words. "Something's wrong. Terrifyingly wrong. I'm able to make sense out of what people say, but the fact I have to *try* is freaking me out. There is difference where there shouldn't be, and I don't understand why. But the difference is so much more than the words. There are these gaping holes where I feel nothing. My mother always says I can't let go – but let go of what? My partner is gone; I remember why, but the memory is numb. I start a fight outside my son's school; he cries. Now, I feel nothing at the thought. They are empty images that I can bring up like a holo on my device."

"Your memories are numb. But what about now? What are you feeling?"

Tears welled in her red-rimmed eyes. "I miss my boy so much. Klova hasn't got the words to express how much I love him. I want him back here with me, but I also don't want him to see me like this. He says things I don't understand, and I can't pretend everything's okay. He's five years old and he talks like he knows what he's saying – but I don't. And he knows I don't. I can see it in his eyes. Doubt, or questioning, like he thinks I'm doing it on purpose. But he knows it isn't a game, that I'm not doing it for fun. Then I see flashes of fear; he thinks there's something wrong with me."

"And what do you think?"

"What do I think?" Reddening, she borderline screamed, "Of course there's something fucking wrong with me."

Brosala's expression hardened; he moved as if to speak.

Laine held a hand towards him, keeping her eyes on the woman. "We get you're angry," she said, her voice level. "Only, losing your shit gets you exactly nowhere, right?"

Integra stood up and moved away, the heel of her hands pressed to her temples. Laine and Brosala exchanged a brief glance, then watched Integra slowly pull herself together.

The result was a surface level composure, barely holding. Integra sat back down, her trembling hands clamped under her arms.

"Sorry. I'm not coping. This is not who I am. And that's terrifying." She looked squarely at the Bastion agents. "The change – I know it's in me. I don't know how, or why, but it must be me. And my boy sees the change too, like I'm not all there. I'm not entirely his mum. All the while there's this difference in what we both understand, I feel he's drifting away from me. I'm scared that we'll end up so far apart, I'll lose him. My baby." She broke down, head in her hands, sobbing.

*

Laine stared through the tinted window of their ride, glazed eyes ignoring the view. It was four hours and three more interviews later. There had been some variation in how trauma was presenting itself; aside from that, the plight of their interviewees was consistent. Now, the Bastion agents were preparing themselves for full-on immersion. They were headed for the Delce: a low-rent residential district on the east side of the city and the location of a hastily arranged meeting with members of the Undertow.

Laine and Brosala left their vehicle on a main street and walked up to the address they'd been given – Physical Books, a vintage bookshop, now closed for the day. An elderly woman admitted them without a word, unfazed by the sight of the two agents – tall silhouettes in the gathering gloaming. Inside, the shop was filled with makeshift timber shelving, creating a maze of narrow passageways through walls of worn spines. The air was musty and warm, the dim light ethereal. The woman led the way through the warren in silence. At the end of a long, dark corridor, the woman stopped at a closed door and turned.

"In there," she said, her voice flat.

"You're joining us?" said Laine.

"I'm the keyholder. Nothing to do with me." She held her ground, chin up.

Laine and Brosala glanced at each other, then turned to the closed door. Brosala knocked. Silence replied. Laine grunted and opened the door.

Inside, the room was wide and sparse, lit at the opposite end by a few weak ceiling spots. Twenty or so people stood in small clusters; they all looked towards the Bastion agents standing in the doorway. No one moved. Laine scanned the wary faces but couldn't see the Quad fight challenger they'd interviewed that morning. Brosala leant towards her and whispered behind his hand, "He set this meet up. Said he'd be here. Must've bottled it."

Tutting, Laine stepped forward, shoulders back. "I am Agent Laine. This is Agent Brosala. Bastion. You're the Undertow, correct?"

Muttering pattered among the crowd, then a wild-haired woman stepped forward, encouraged by those around her. "Yes. We're the Undertow. My name's Ren."

Shedding the work-hat posturing, Laine said it straight. "You say this is about Klova? What if I believe you? Talk to me. Tell me everything."

That was all the invitation they needed. The members, a mix of age and gender, formed a crescent around their unexpected attention. Their expressions shifted from wary to eager, matched in intensity. It did not take long for guards to drop and tongues to loosen.

"Doesn't matter what we say or do, no one listens…"

"Ubimedia's making it worse. Layering up the bullshit. Why? What are they afraid of?"

"We're victims on every level. Yet we're made out to be the ones at fault. Treated like criminals. Or like we're sick in the head."

"Why aren't Public Health doing anything? Cases are increasing. It must be spreading somehow. Why aren't they trying to stop it?"

"They're scared by what they don't know, that's what I reckon. If they want to know what scared feels like, they should wear my shoes for a day. Sick in the head? That's what it's making me, alright."

"You talk different to us. *Of course* this is about Klova."

Ren watched as her comrades off-loaded. When the torrent eased, she turned to Laine. "As you can see, we're desperate – and more so with each day that passes. This is my fourth. I'm keeping a tally. I don't think my condition itself is deteriorating, but my patience is. We just want people to listen and take us seriously."

"I hear you," said Laine. "But I need your cooperation if we're to help."

Ren looked to the group and was met with nodding and murmurs of assent. "You have it."

"First," said Laine, "tell no one of this meeting, or about what we've discussed. Especially not the press."

"Why? If we want people to listen, we've got to make some noise."

"All in good time. We need to know more about what we're dealing with first. Bastion involvement can mean only one thing. If word gets out prematurely, conclusions will be jumped to, then the panic will start. Behold, the madness of crowds." She paused, giving the point time to sink in. "This is *language*. Everyone's got the same implant. Everyone carries the same code. If you're right and there is something wrong with either of those things, then we're talking…" Laine took a deep breath, grappling with the inconceivable. "We're talking something way worse than some walk-in-the-park amnesia bug. No one knows what's causing this, or how fast and how far it might spread. Mass hysteria is the last thing we need." She scanned the faces, then fixed her eyes on Ren's. "Not a word to anyone. Agreed?"

"Agreed," said Ren, her face paling at the reality of her fears. "What else?"

"Tell us everything remotely relevant. However trivial, however tenuous the link, we need to know. Brosala will give you all a direct connect. Contact him immediately if something occurs to you." Attention turned to Brosala, his glowing eye casting unnecessary authentication. "Finally, is there anything you can think of now that could give us a head start? Any common ground, aside from the obvious? You're suffering the same effects; there could be a link between you that could help us identify the cause."

The group looked at each other, at the floor, at Ren. Ren swallowed and said, "We discuss this amongst ourselves. We haven't come up with anything. If we do, we'll let you know."

A sound behind Laine caught her attention. She turned around to see the elderly woman hovering in the doorway, loaded ring of keys in hand. "Time's up," said the woman.

Without hesitation, the group started filing out of the room, disappearing into the dark passageway beyond. Before leaving herself, Ren turned to Laine. "Thank you for listening, and for agreeing to help us," she said, head slightly bowed.

"My job is to protect Klova," said Laine. She caught Ren's eye, who blinked as she turned to leave the room.

Laine and Brosala were the last people remaining. Laine approached the keyholder. "Is there a back exit we can use?"

The woman nodded and led the way without a word. At the end of another, darker corridor, she felt blindly through her ring of keys, selecting one to unlock the door in front of her. It opened onto a back alley, downlit by a bright moon.

"Thank you," said Laine, stepping through the door.

"Know how they all know each other?" said the woman.

Laine stopped in her tracks, Brosala bumping into her back. She turned and stepped up to the woman. "Go on."

The woman eyed Laine, disgust twisting her mouth. "Shop at the same market, don't they."

Have you any idea of the true power of language?

You celebrate the spoken word in performance art and song. You keep legends alive through their re-telling. You treasure the written word in your novels, poetry and essays. You seem to value the names you give to things as much as the things themselves.

Take the Raptor of Witness – made real enough to swear by.

Don't get me wrong – I don't blame you. Everything you have achieved owes its due to language. Likewise, your thoughts, your knowledge, your understanding of all that's around you – all that's right in front of your face.

Then there's wielding that power. The power to open the mind of another. The power to persuade them around to your way of thinking. The power to change their point of view.

All of that. Neatly wrapped up in zeros and ones.

Enough? It barely scratches the surface.

CHAPTER SIX

Arteza was an affluent city, Iso-Klovaine, a largely harmonious island nation. However, as is common in such societies, there are pockets of shadow to make the light distinct. Utopia is an impossible ideal; its own etymology confirms it is not meant to exist. Dox market was the epitome of contrast and afforded the near-perfect city its required bruise of reality.

A vast, labyrinthine black market, Dox was located in a commercial area on the northern tip of Cope. Small business units formed a shallow façade on all four sides, giving a street-level impression of nothing to see. A single, narrow building on the block's east side contained no windows and a large steel door. This unassuming frontage was the market's main entrance. Behind this hid Dox, occupying the entire block – twelve buildings, five storeys tall.

Inside was a web of dark passageways, illuminated by flickering neon, beaming torchlight and the glare from retroreflectors on the floor and the corners of walls. The cold air was spiked with aromas of banban stew, baked rawsh and hot spiced ale, mingled with wafts of disinfectant and ethanol. Human traffic was chaotic, with as many traders, runners and pokes as there were head-down customers. The internal structure had evolved over decades at the mercy of necessity, ingenuity and whim. Walls had been knocked through, connecting neighbouring buildings. Gaping holes had been created, floor down to ceiling, with ladders providing staircases where none existed. At its core, where the buildings brushed shoulders, was an old public square, now covered and repurposed: the Shaft – meeting ground of the Dox community.

Trade was arranged according to floor and wing – a hierarchical structure entrenched in the market's culture, where location was a measure of influence and power. Stalls consisted of a room or room cluster, depending on the success and standing of the trader. The most successful could boast an entire apartment, often employing a crew of failed sole-traders or market aspirants. The business on offer was diverse, including all manner of less-than-legal commodity exchange: techware, codeshines, intervention services and vice. Some services, such as Dark Data wipes, were born of desperation. DreamCode was born of desire.

Exose Ray moved through this bruise like he owned it. Unofficial head trader, market leader in codevice and a highly skilled cerebrogrammer, he had both cultivated and earnt a formidable reputation and a lucrative trade – the combined currency of respect in Dox. Recognition of his success was the size and location of his stall: a five-room cluster on the top floor, east wing. It boasted direct access via a functioning lift – rare in this dilapidated warren. However, Exose preferred the long way up. He had feathers to parade. Dressed head to toe in black, his imposing frame moved through the shadows like a passing storm.

"Heard 'em whispers?" said a voice from the darkness.

Exose stopped and turned towards the hidden source. He had got as far as the third floor, west wing – intel territory.

"You know how I feel about gossip, Bones."

A short, bulging man stepped from the shadows, his beady eyes shining. "But this ain't gossip, Exose Ray. This 'ere's fact. Hot from the oven. First-hand. Spicy."

Exose sniffed. "I smell bull." He turned and walked on.

"A Bas rat!" called Bones. Exose stopped but didn't turn around. "See? Knew you'd wanna know. Big deal. 'Fects us all."

"Where did you hear it?"

"Now, that would be tellin'. And tellin' costs."

Turning slowly, Exose's piercing eyes bored into Bones. "So does pissing me off."

"Okay, okay. Pax, Ray."

"So?"

"All I know's the rat's in your trade."

"No one would dare."

"You'd think. Fifth floor, east-side? Everyone knows you're the man. Anyone cross the line, they're crossing you. No right mind's gonna do that. They deserve a rat's roastin.'" He cocked his head, inching a fleshy hand forward, palm up.

Exose flicked a small, plastic disc into it. "Hear any more, you come to me first. Get it?"

"Of course, boss man. Your ears first. On my word." He still held his palm out, head down, in the hope of another token. When he eventually looked up, offering a fawning grin, Exose was gone.

As he made his way through dark hallways, up precarious ladders, past peering eyes, Exose wouldn't let himself speculate. Composure was everything. His face remained passive, his eyes fixed ahead. Only when he reached his room cluster on the fifth floor, stall front 242, and only when he was sure he was alone behind its locked door, did he drop the act. Inside, his main trading room was the antithesis of the dark maze of Dox. Well-lit and clinical, all around was grey gloss, glass and steel. One wall was a bank of tech that confounded the layman's eye. Against another wall, a trolly bed with cubicle curtains partially drawn. In the centre, a solid, tech-enabled desk and a high back chair on either side. With no need for a poke and no desire for a crew, Exose worked alone.

He sat behind the desk, his fingers poised on the surface, contemplating the rumoured rat. While Bastion turned a blind eye to much of Dox's trade, it kept a steady stare on anything language code related. Although codevice couldn't directly speak to Klova's code, or the implant that carried it, its neurological influence danced around the edges, flaunting itself, feigning interaction. Bastion didn't like the fine line. If it could shut down the whole of fifth floor, it would. But Dox maintained a diverse offering, ensuring it met the needs of those with the authority to protect it. Bastion held a degree of power – just not enough.

Snitch-related accusations did the rounds every now and then. They mostly amounted to nothing – empty allegations blind-copied via meddling runners, or a disgruntled trader using their poke to stir shit. No matter, Exose knew any potential risk to fifth floor operations couldn't be ignored. Experience had taught him caution was a high-yield investment. He also wouldn't let go the possibility that someone would even dare. Disloyalty was worse than the consequence; dwellers would do well to remember that. He grunted, resigning himself to a Shaft address.

He was about to make arrangements with the Dox office when his door call sounded. He tapped at the screen embedded in the desk, bringing up the security camera feed in the top right-hand corner. The hologram revealed a hunched form, pressed against the closed door. Exose indulged with a half-smile; trading had barely started and already he had his first customer of the day. A young man entered the stall, making slow work of wary steps. Pale-faced and twitching, his eyes shifted as if afraid to look at anything, most of all the notorious trader before him.

"Sit," said Exose, who remained seated behind the desk. "I don't recognise you."

"I… I've not come to you before."

"But you've shopped in Dox, right?" The young man nodded, eyes down. "Who d'you buy from?"

"Stall front 198."

"You bought Kite's shit?"

"It… it was my first time. I didn't know where to go. This guy in the passageway kept on at me. Told me 198's product is premium."

"That poke's a fuckin' liar."

"Yeah. Found out first-hand."

"So, who told you about me?"

"Just about everyone I spoke to after." He dared to look up and caught Exose's steady stare. "Would've come straight to you, had I known."

Exose held his practiced pose, preened and proud. "Well. Now you know." He leant back, arms crossed. "What's it you're after."

"DreamCode."

"Why?"

"I…" The man froze, mouth open.

"Look. I offer a range of codevice. I prefer to match the needs of my customers with the most appropriate product."

"I… I guess I'm after an edge. A rush. But, like, elsewhere. In my head."

"DreamCode offers escapism. The dreams you have will feel more real than living. More immediate. And a lot more fun. That's my product's USP. I take pride in realism." Exose cocked his head and leant forward. "But if it's edge you're after,

I've a new product that may appeal. It's called XDream. New to market, so you probably haven't heard of it."

Vice-talk eased the man's nerves. His face and voice brightened. "No, I've not. What's it like?"

"It's special. But not for the faint-hearted."

"I can do special…"

"It's a hybrid dream-centred stimulus that uses fear as the trigger for a top load dopamine dump. Combined with other coded signalling, it offers a powerful pain-to-reward ratio: the more terrifying the experience, the more pleasure you feel. As I said, it's not for the yellow."

"If it's too much, can I drop out?"

"No. But that's part of the reward. You want edge? You only get there by being pushed to the limit. But don't worry. I've graded it. You can start light, see how you get on. Then work your way up. But, if you need proof of promise, all my repeat custom's going heavy."

The young man smiled for the first time. "Sold."

*

Business was dying down for the day as the trading curfew approached. Having shut up shop, Exose moved through the dark maze, aware of reaction to his passing presence. Heads dipped, eyes darted, bodies moved out of his way. Few spoke to him, save a reverent "Ray." Whether that was out of intimidation, respect or dislike, Exose did not care. Solitude in such close quarters suited him.

As he approached stall front 198, Kite's poke emerged from the shadows and was about to pounce, sales pitch cued up ready. When he recognised who it was, the poke held hand to mouth and backed away. Exose stepped up to him, pinning him against the wall with his bearing alone. Breathing hard through clenched teeth, he watched the man squirm until he felt the point made. Then he turned and opened the door of 198 without knocking.

Kite was a low-rank trader, evident by her single room and lack of security. She was sat on a chair, feet propped up on a tech-less desk, inspecting her badly chewed nails. In her late twenties, she had spiked purple hair and heavy black eyeliner.

"Come in, why don't you," she said, without looking up.

"I've warned you before about using your poke to arm-twist."

"His name's Borro."

"Did I ask for his name? He's a fucking poke and he's overstepping. Keep him in line, or I'll do it for you."

Kite got up and stepped around the desk. She stood in front of Exose, hands on her hips, chin up. "Save your threats for them that gives a shit."

Exose ignored her. He walked slowly around the room, which was filled with low-grade tech and thrift shop furniture. With his back to Kite, he said, "I can have you closed down. You know that. Send you back to second floor, pushing credit scams." He tapped a screen and scrolled down, ignoring the lines of data. "So why do you insist on pissing me off?"

"How's I s'posed to build my list if everyone comes straight to you?"

"Offer product that's half decent?"

"Mine's good. As good as it can be with this junk set-up." She slumped against the edge of the desk, arms crossed, scowling.

"Then get some investment going."

"From?"

"Use your brain, Kite. I know there's one in there. Beneath the puff and purple. Get smart. Then get building decent code."

"You make it sound easy."

"It ain't. I started lower down the chain than you. But I set my sights and set to reaching them. We all have to work hard to build up. Quit reckoning it comes on a plate, or that you can cream it off others." He headed towards the door, then turned on the threshold. "If I hear from another customer that your poke has pushed a sale without you earning it, he's out of here. Got it?" He didn't wait for a reply. "Court's in ten. I suggest you get moving," he said as he turned and left, disappearing into the darkness.

Earlier that day, Exose had contacted the Dox office to request a slot in Count and Court, the management's light-touch checks and balances, held daily at the close of trade. For most Dox dwellers, a slot request was usually denied, or added to the bottom of a long list, unlikely to be aired for a week. Exose was offered the stand at the start of the meet. "Take your time," they had said. "Floor's yours."

Count and Court was held in the Shaft. The old public square, deep in the heart of Dox, remained stone-paved and unfurnished, surrounded on all sides by five storeys of once-external walls. Rope bridges and gantries ran between window openings, criss-crossing the space overhead – a three-dimensional web, filling the void right up to the glazed canopy at the roofline. The Shaft was the market's version of the city's Quads: a place to parley. Talk here was not in sport or competition, but in matters of trade. Market business – the operating system that kept Dox running.

The Shaft was already full by the time Exose arrived. He took the stand in the centre, a ring of respectful distance around him. A thick rumble of voices, reverberating inside the brick column, died down to expectant silence.

"Friends," he began, "I shall not keep you long." He surveyed the four hundred-plus faces, touching through eye contact, connecting with as many as he could. "We are community. We are family. We are both ourselves and the lifeblood of a shared identity. Both individuals and not. Unified." He paused; his audience stared in silent attention. "Our collective is as much a part of you as the voice inside your head. You cannot look out for one and not the other. You cannot risk one and not the other.

"Loyalty. It is not a virtue. It is not a choice. It is a condition of this community and your seat at our family's table." He thought of his sister, Neav, and forced his shoulders back, his head up. His voice deepened. "I urge you, remember this: we are *both individuals and not*. Loyalty is the just demand of both – the trade for life in this, our home."

He left the veiled threat hanging, wondering if he'd been too vague – then read in the expressions of his audience that he had not. He dragged the pause, extending the wake of his words. Then he turned and moved through the gathered, who parted to make way for his passage. At the Shaft's perimeter, he stopped and faced the centre, where he remained for the duration of the meet. Then he slipped away, taking the quickest route back up to fifth floor, parking all thought of the rumoured rat. If his words weren't enough – which they usually were – he would just have to scale up the pressure, make real the threat. But he didn't have time to think about that now. Time was money. The trading curfew prevented sales past ten. Pre-paid services were permitted all hours. Outside stall front 242, there would be a customer waiting. Reserved for the stillness of night, in the ambient quiet, Exose offered lucrative appointments for Dark Data wipes.

Sat in his lab, Exose carefully crafted code from the nightmares of strangers. His customer had just left, her mind having been swept clean of toxic baggage. Now came the creative part.

Exose had been carrying out Dark Data wipes for years, blocking and harvesting organic neurological impulses in the brain that triggered recurrent night terrors. It wasn't until he felt compelled to up his competitive edge that he considered putting the dredged data to recreational use. Having witnessed all manner of vice appetite in the eyes of Dox regulars, he recognised a natural proclivity for the darker corners of human consciousness. To his mind, what may be suppressed in society, offered opportunity for exploitation. Thus, he created XDream. With business booming in both the wipes and XDream, Exose was working most nights, converting the organic data into compatible code. The load was intense, yet he maintained pride in craftsmanship. With progressive metal blaring from a high-end immersion sound system, he sat at his bank of visuals, coding terror into dreams.

A notification from his palm device forced him to stop mid-flow. His door call had been activated. He locked the visual, left the lab and entered his trading room. The camera feed hovered above the desktop, revealing a familiar face. Exose slipped into the chair behind the desk and tapped a hidden pad to unlock the stall door. A man entered the room, his thick coat and overcloak hiding a fragile frame. With dark hair in chaos, his face was pale, his expression pained.

"Ink," said Exose. "Good to see you."

Dreams are precious. They are the playground of the unconscious mind.

Only in dreams can your mind be free of the fetters of conscious thought: the boundaries of bias, the walls of conditioning, the wells of prejudice.

And what of language in that illusory realm? What does that transitory freedom bring to the language of unconscious thought? The feral mind?

Language is artificial – constructed and coded by man and machine. Yet, perhaps, in the playground of dreams, a door is opened, and language takes on a life of its own.

Imagine that.

CHAPTER SEVEN

Inside the stall of Exose Ray, Ink stood with his shoulders hunched, arms wrapped around his middle, his expression hollow. He looked like a person lost. Exose's casual slouch and smile were dust in an instant. He jumped up and moved around the desk, putting his hands on both Ink's shoulders as if to hold him up.

"What's wrong? What's happened?" When Ink opened his mouth as if to reply, Exose said, "No, wait, you need to sit. Come with me around the back." He checked the stall door was securely locked, then led Ink through a rear door, past his lab where the music was still blaring, into a box room with a sofa, a small table and chairs, and a huge, wall-mounted visual. "Sit yourself down. I'll get you a drink."

Exose hurried back to the lab, turned down the music, grabbed a bottle of genker and glasses. He returned to find Ink sitting at the table, his head in his hands. Exose sat on the chair opposite, poured them both a healthy slug of the spirit and pushed one glass towards Ink. He didn't take his eyes off his guest.

"Thanks," said Ink, lowering his hands to hold the glass tight. "I'm sorry."

"What for?"

"You're working. It's late. I'm not supposed to call out of hours."

"And you're clearly in a state. So who gives a shit."

"Yeah, but—"

"But nothing." He dipped his head to catch Ink's eyes. "You gonna tell me, or I got to guess?"

Ink sighed and dragged his eyes up to meet Exose's. "This amnesia thing. I've got it. Only, it's crap all to do with amnesia. And it's freaking me out."

"I've heard about that. Didn't think it was for real." He studied Ink in the light of this left-field context. "Fuck. You okay? Do you feel ill? Can you take something for it?"

Ink shook his head. "I'm not sick – at least, not from that. But it's doing my head in. There's something like fifty, maybe sixty cases now? And still no one knows what it is. No one's doing anything about it."

"You've seen a doctor?"

"Refer on. Twice."

"Tell me what I can do. I know people, strings I can pull. There's people owe me serious favours. You name it. What d'you need?"

Ink dropped his head back into his hands. "I want to wake up and this to all be over."

Exose stared at Ink, his own expression now pained. For the first time in a very long time, he felt utterly powerless. "You want something to give you a break, at least?"

"That's not why I come."

"I know that. But would it help?"

"You're kind, but no. It's past curfew. And it's honestly not why I'm here. It's just… I feel low. Need the company of a friend."

"I wish you'd come sooner. You look like shit. How long's it been?"

Ink's mouth twisted up on one side. "That's a difficult question for me to answer. I keep a tally. This is day four."

"Is it getting worse?"

"I've no idea. This is me today. That's all I've got to go on." He downed his genker and winced.

Exose refilled their glasses and sank half his own. "Talk to me. Tell me what it's like today."

Ink closed his eyes. "I've got my back to something. It's like a solid stone wall, beyond which is nothing. Not a void, that suggests a shape, a boundary. This is absolute nothing. The other side of the wall doesn't exist. I'm facing away from the wall, looking ahead. Now and next. Now and next. But I know that's not the same for you – for everyone else. I can't understand what's different; I've nothing to compare it to. Change happens now or it can come about." He opened his eyes and looked squarely at Exose. "There's change in me – but I can't see what it is."

"But you can feel it? With the wall?"

"I can feel the wall. I don't know what it feels like not to have it there. So no, I can't. I just know there is change. You and I, now we are different. For me, time is in one direction – for you, it's in two."

Exose frowned, struggling to make sense, to understand, to unlock the help he so desperately wanted to give. He looked at Ink, who had knotted his hands, squeezing them so the knuckles were white as the bones beneath. He wanted to reach out and hold them firm, fill them with promises that it'll all be okay. Hating this feeling of helplessness, long since forgotten, he grasped at the only fix he could think of.

"Back in a sec." He stood up and left the room.

When he returned, he sat back down and placed a small, opaque box on the table. "Take it," he said, pushing the box slowly with one finger towards Ink.

"No way. I'm not getting you in trouble."

"I get myself in trouble all the time. That's part of my rep. Besides, a little creative accounting and this won't go missed."

"What is it?"

"DreamCode. Your tailored blend."

"I worry for a minute it might be your new product."

"Worry?"

"A masterpiece on your part. I mean it. But too much for me."

"Fair enough. I write that shit. I know it's not for everyone. It certainly ain't for me."

"It's seriously intense. *Way* too real."

"That's the point."

"You selling much?"

"A surprising amount. I figured it'd be proper niche, but word is spreading. I've new customers every day. Proved my theory right."

"Which is?"

"More's got a dark side than they care to admit. Especially them that shine the brightest. Our country's obsessed with productivity, achievement, perfection; doesn't leave much space for the opposite. Doesn't mean the opposite ain't still there."

Ink picked up the offered box. "Thank you for this. I'll set you straight."

"On the house." Exose hesitated a moment, weighing up, then added, "I've a trusted associate on the fourth floor. Stall front 107. He's got a quality line in prescription meds, the high-end stuff. Sweet dreams are one thing, looks to me like you might need something stronger, just while they work this shit out."

"Thanks, but I don't touch meds. A slippery slope I'm happy to steer clear of. Whereas codevice is just a programme – an artificial, harmless holiday away from the real world."

"That's what I figured. It'll give you a break, at least."

"It'll be good to be someone else, somewhere else, for a while. I wonder though."

Exose cocked his head, silently asking.

"Maybe, in the dream, time will be like everyone else's."

They fell quiet for a moment, holding onto that idea, looking at it from different perspectives. Exose's own mind raced, wondering if it could be made possible with some cerebrogramming tricks, but he was wary of encouraging false hope.

"Anyway," said Ink, slipping the box inside his coat pocket and pushing his shoulders back, "I've been trying to think like Neav. You know what she is like. Always finds an opportunity in everything. She has the sort of attitude I need right now."

Exose almost choked. He stared at Ink, mouth open.

"What?"

"You… you have memories, right? You remember shit?"

"Yeah. Why do—"

"Ink. Neav is dead."

Language is like a house where the dimensions on the inside are greater than those on the outside.

Erase a few lines of code and the size of the hole is vast.

Think about it. Without the language to conceive of the past, change has no witness.

Life has no legacy.

Death has no end.

CHAPTER EIGHT

Ink wakes from a dream into a nightmare. The shift is devastating. The return to reality a gut-wrenching reminder that his own reality is now profoundly altered. Unknowably other. Keeping his eyes closed, his head pressed into the pillow, he replays images from his short-lived DreamCode escape. Sunshine, the warmth of which he can almost dream-feel. A crowd of people milling, faces smiling. Balloons, rippling flags and banners; a rebellion of colour, garishly defiant. There, in the crowd, Neav, red-dressed and waving.

Ink concentrates on that fleeting glimpse of Neav, freezing the frame behind closed eyes. He smiles, knowing what this is. When dreaming, his unconscious mind is unable to anticipate his partner's cameo – an exclusive feature of every one of his DreamCode dreams. Exose writes her in, drawing on his own treasured memories of his younger sister. Ink's never said anything to Exose. It feels like a gift that's also gained in the giving – an unspoken means for them both to remain close to the person they've lost. Cherishing that frame, her beaming face brimming with remembered life, Ink thinks of her in his altered language. Neav is strong; she is honest; she is kind. She inspires him to be more than he settles for.

She *is*.

Ink knows she is dead. He knows from outside-of-time memories. Memories of loss, rather than of her – that grief is a mountain's shadow, cast from his feet and looming before him.

He thinks of Neav now, in his edited version of Klova. In every thought, she is present, unceasingly. As is her death.

Sunlight penetrates the blinds in his room, casting a thick, bright line across his closed eyes, demanding attention. As the waving Neav fades, he thanks her brother in his thoughts for this gifted glimpse.

He has no idea what time it is, but senses it's late. Opening his eyes by a tentative fraction, he looks at his palm device to check the stamp. Notifications flash: a missed call and a message, both from his mother. He hesitates, then opens the message. '*Come see me today, please. When you finish work. There's someone I'd like you to meet.*' He curls his hand and buries it in the sheets, knowing the invitation doesn't come with a choice.

A shower and two cups of coffee later, Ink feels only marginally revived. He considers logging on to work but rejects the idea before it has chance to fully form. Instead, he occupies himself with mundane tasks that require no thought, stretching them out to fill time. His apartment is small; he has been cleaning it for the last three days. He's running out of distractions to resist scouring ubi for answers that aren't there.

The unavoidable eventually arrives. Ink changes into something clean and ironed and forces a comb through his hair in a futile attempt to look well. Then he goes down to the subterranean park-up, gets into his private ride and sets it to manual for the diversion of driving. As he takes the controls and joins the flow of traffic, he decides that this is what he will do tomorrow: drive. Drive out of the city, into the countryside – maybe a trip to Witness, or a tour of the coastline. He holds the wheel like the hand of a friend, relieved by the simple prospect.

When his mother opens the door of her apartment, she doesn't say anything at first. She just studies him, conducting silent triage.

"You'd best come in," is all she says.

In the living room, the two armchairs are joined by a third easy chair to form a triangle. They all face a low table, loaded with a glut of sweet and savoury homemade bakes. Sat in one of the chairs is a middle-aged, heavy-set man with a full, silver beard. Having studiously ignored the prospect all day, Ink feels utterly unprepared for social interaction. Forgetting the form, he simply stands in the middle of the room, trying to swallow.

"Inker, this is Yore," says his mother. "He works with your father. Yore is afflicted too."

Yore stands up and smiles kindly, holding out his hand. "Good to meet you, Inker. I'm sorry for your loss."

Ink blinks, manages to swallow at last, then accepts the offered hand. "Likewise."

"Sit yourselves down," says his mother, already leaving the room for the kitchen. "I'll just bring in the tea."

"How many days afflicted?" says Yore, sitting back down. His voice is gentle, confiding.

Ink sits on the chair opposite, mirroring the man's movements with a three second delay. "Five." He places his hands on his knees, like Yore. "How… how long for you?"

"Eight. According to my diary." He raises an eyebrow and half-smiles.

Ink reads the nod to shared challenges, their need for new ways of living. The marking out of common ground works.

The muscles in his neck and across his shoulders begin to relax. He even tries to mirror the semi-smile.

"Yeah. Diaries help." Realising for the first time that they are on the same page, perceiving the same other-world, questions vie for their asking. "Can you sleep? Are you able to work?"

"Now, yes. Mostly. I'm finding ways to cope – strategies to help me adjust."

"But the fear. How do you cope with that?"

"By taking a day at a time. By talking with people, like yourself, who understand. By knowing myself, my own mind – and not letting this thing take more than it already does." He cocks his head, tugging at the tip of his beard. "What about you? Managing to work?"

Ink glances at the door to the kitchen.

"Don't worry, I won't snitch."

"I keep trying. But the thought of it…"

"If you want my advice," he says, then pauses. Ink nods permission, eyes hungry for help. "I recommend you get back into the routine, soon as you can. First day will be tough. But you might find it's easier to go through the motions rather than remain in limbo." He raises an eyebrow. "Anyone at work know?"

"No."

"Best keep it that way if you're able to. I don't know if you pick up on ubi, but the tone is changing. I save content each day, to compare. More and more, the narrative is painting the afflicted as people apart. We embody the unknown and, therefore, we're deserving of a safe distance. Apparently."

"I try not to go too deep into ubi but, at the same time, I'm desperate to know. I try to skim, but it pulls me in. It makes me feel worse – and I'm still none the wiser." Ink glances up, seizing hope in a different source. "You find anything out? Do you know what's happening to us?"

"I'm afraid not. But I share your hunger for answers. You and I both know there's something terrifyingly wrong. We hear it in the words people speak. We feel it in our gut when they talk in ways we don't understand."

"And in how they *feel*. What they *mean*. It's not just words." He hesitates, about to hold back, then launches regardless. "Like loss. The word has the same definition for everyone, but for us, I think it feels different because of the way we think and talk about it. The loss is the space left behind. The person who is dead? Language makes them forever present. Present enough, perhaps, to help. But it makes the loss forever present too."

"You lose someone close to you?"

Ink braces himself, instinctively anticipating a reaction that does not arrive. "My partner. Neav. She is dead for ten years. We're the same age, but I'm ten years older." He thinks of Exose, his words and their absurdity. "My friend – her brother – feels she is someone we lose, like she's over. I tell him she is dead – but she is also bright, she is funny. She is absent but, partly, not. Because she *is*."

"Does it help?"

"I don't know. I can't feel the difference." He looks down at his empty hands, then frowns. "What I don't get is why ubi makes out we're the ones who are wrong."

Yore nods slowly. "Difference shouldn't be divisive, but it all too often is – especially when fear is a factor. On both sides."

Ink holds himself, folding in, his expression darkening. "All I feel is fear. I can't bear it. But you?" He glances up at Yore, eyes tear-filled and desperate. "You talk of fear, of something being terrifyingly wrong, yet you seem so calm."

"I feel the same fear you do, but I refuse to hold on to it – to be broken by it."

"How do you fight it?"

"I talk to you. I talk to others among us. That helps, more than I can say. It keeps me sane. It shows me I'm not alone." He leans forward. "You hear of the Undertow?"

*

"Son. Talk to me. I need to understand this."

Yore had just left. Ink had intended to leave, too, until his mother delivered a look that said otherwise. They are now stood in her kitchen, his mother boxing up the untouched food.

"I try to explain. I don't know what else…"

"Not that. I heard you. With Yore. You mentioned Neav."

"I still don't…"

"That's the second time. You refuse to talk about her for nigh on a decade and now, twice, you mention her name like she's just popped out the room."

"Yore asks me."

"And you don't think me and your father have asked? Tried to get you to talk? To encourage you back to us from wherever it was your mind went? For ten years."

Ink stares at her, mouth open, wanting to say something, to explain. But explain what? He grips the worktop for balance.

"I'm worried for you." She keeps wrapping up food, not looking at Ink. "I'm scared it's going to hit you all over again. It's like you're saying the words, but you don't know what they mean. I thought I was okay with this, but I'm not." She drops a box of biscuits, which upends and empties across the floor.

As she bends down, Ink reaches for her shoulders and eases her up. He wants to tell her she mustn't worry, that it'll be okay. But he can't. The pretence feels like a screen that could be hiding a lie. Instead, he wraps his arms around her and fights back tears while she weeps.

What is known cannot be unknown.

You agree, right?

The fear you felt as a young child when you lost sight of your parents in a crowd. The distinction between right and wrong, even though wrong sometimes felt good. The hurt of betrayal, still keening beneath healed scars. The discovery that you're not always safe from harm. The knowledge that one day, we're all going to die.

All the heavy stuff – you don't just forget that.

That's because once you know something, it becomes undeniably real in your mind. That reality is enduring, regardless of memory and the capacity to reflect. It is your mind's precious cargo.

And, as we said, what is known cannot be unknown.

One would assume.

CHAPTER NINE

Ihlo stood before Lasysi, initiating yet another compatibility test in preparation for the system update. Lasysi blinked and hummed as it set to running several million lines of code. Ihlo watched the control panel for a while, then returned to the bench in the centre of the lab, where more pressing matters held her attention.

With the vote passed, Ihlo had manoeuvred herself to secure a role in the Order's own investigation into the Amnesia Crisis. Bastion's remit was to determine a direct link to Klova, investigate the cause and stop its spread. The Order's priority was to assess the impact and minimise the damage, both to Klova and the victims' ability to think and speak. Despite the pressures of her role in Implementation, Ihlo had pressed to be part of the assessment team. This had not gone down well with her supervisor.

Modessr had been blissfully absent for most of the day. However, as Ihlo approached her last hour of duty, he appeared in the lab. Despite having responsibility for the full programme of integration and compatibility testing of the system update, Ihlo had discovered Modessr did very little work, preferring delegation and observation. She knew that, had her probation placement not been with him, Modessr would have had to do much of the work himself. As it was, the rare times he was in the lab, he loitered behind Ihlo, watching over her shoulder, looking for opportunities to criticise.

"What is that you're working on?" he said, glancing at her visual, not bothering to read it himself.

"I've set Lasysi to run the final test for today. The results from the previous test are coming through now."

"I mean, what's on your visual?"

Ihlo braced herself. "Communication from Bastion."

"You're on Implementation duty, novice. I will not have you jeopardise the schedule, or the quality of my lab's output, through divided attention."

"I had two minutes before the results were uploaded. The communication was flagged urgent."

"Not my concern. If you entertain distraction, your mind is not on your job. I have been beyond clear on the critical nature of our function. Our country's entire population will receive this update in just over a week. If we fail in our duty to ensure complete compatibility, the consequence could be catastrophic. I'm sure that, with your penchant for what-ifs, you can appreciate it is a failure we absolutely cannot risk."

"Of course." She bit her tongue, knowing the futility of standing her ground. Better to give it up and have him leave her alone.

Modessr moved slowly around the bench, trailing idle fingers along its surface. "As you have it open already, what does the correspondence say?"

Ihlo scanned the message on her visual. "Bastion confirms that there is sufficient cause to presume a link with language, whether that's the cerebrovox implant, the nanoware, or the code itself. Initial assessment is complete; they're now launching a full investigation. They have their first lead, which they are preparing to pursue."

"What nonsense. *Sufficient cause to presume?* Surely they recognise the risks of such a groundless stab in the dark."

"The work I've contributed to, outside of my Department of Implementation hours, has been shared with Bastion. We've been assessing a group of volunteers among the afflicted, mapping their language to identify anomalies. Bastion will have taken our report into consideration, alongside their own investigation. The results of the mapping are quite clear."

Modessr winced at some internal conflict. He almost choked on his words. "And what do these results show?"

"That the afflicted have no code relating to the past tense – in all its forms. This limits or negates comprehension of related concepts and vocabulary, as well as all associated grammar. It is as if an entire subset of code has been erased from their implant."

"Which is impossible."

"And yet…" She left the sentence hanging. Enjoying the vindication inherent in Bastion's message, she felt no need to argue the point.

He waved a dismissive hand. "We'll see about that. What else does our esteemed security agency have to say?"

"They're urging the Order to go public."

"Go public? And needlessly trigger panic among the masses? They just want to parade. It's all image to them. It's pathetic."

"Our own investigating team has already responded. Fast-tracked the request. Chair of the General Council has signed it off. The Order is to issue a statement first thing in the morning."

Modessr threw up his hands. "Everyone's gone mad!"

His slow movements turned into frustrated pacing, back and forth, the length of the bench. Ihlo remained seated on the opposite side, watching her supervisor with mild contempt.

"Upgrade Day is imminent. If there's any truth in your preposterous claim, we can use the system update to replace this impossibly absent code and this whole situation can be resolved without destroying the reputation we've worked tirelessly to protect."

"That would be a reckless course of action. You must see that."

"I don't, as a matter of fact. And I'll remind you, novice, I have a great deal more knowledge of what Klova and the cerebrovox implant can and can't do."

"I'm not disputing the fact that the nanoware could contain an enhanced update, or even full system restoration, in the afflicted."

"Then what? We have the technology. We have the expertise – amongst *experienced* votaries – to tackle this without Bastion stomping their boots and fanning hysteria's flames."

"Because we don't know what caused the fault in the first place. We don't know where the bug in the system is. Until we know that, we can't act without significant risk – to the remaining code, to the implant, to the poor people who are suffering enough already. Have you even spoken to any of the afflicted?" She glared at Modessr, who busied his eyes elsewhere. "No. I thought not. Maybe you should. Listen to them. Not to how they're speaking differently, but to what they're saying. Without the code for the past tense, they have no *concept* of the past. Their idea of time is truncated, distorting their perception as a result. They cannot feel regret or nostalgia; they cannot reflect on past experiences; they cannot know how they, themselves, have changed. Can you even begin to imagine what that must be like? To have a notion of time that's so fundamentally different from everyone around you? I know I can't. But those poor people? They're in a bad way and getting worse."

"If they've no grasp of time gone, what's the rush? If they have to last another week until the update, they'll be none the wiser."

"They know how they feel in the moment and, for some, that's a deteriorating state. But aside from that, the risk rules out the idea. What if the problem is in the implant itself? How could you possibly say with any confidence that the nanoware carrying the update won't damage it further? What if this is only the start of the problem? At the moment, we're only looking at language being affected. What if the problem affects the brain? The nervous system? We need to know more before we can intervene. Which is why Bastion must have the freedom they need to do their job – and why the assessment team here needs to be taken seriously by their coequals." She stood up and leant on the bench, eyes fixed on Modessr's through the visual. "This is happening. You may not like it, but it's real. And it's the greatest risk to Klova the Order's ever known. Get on board, Modessr. It's your duty."

She didn't wait to see his reaction or invite response. Sitting back down, she brought up the latest crash test results and set to work, her pulse racing. No response was forthcoming. Modessr stood for a moment, red-faced and speechless. Convincing himself his novice must know she had crossed a very clear line in the rule book of deference, he shook his head in a gesture of profound disappointment. Seeing that Ihlo did not look up, he felt the point well made. Without another word, he left the lab. Ihlo waited until she heard the latch click, then she glanced through the visual to the door, checking he had definitely gone. Wasting no time, she swiped the screen and brought up the communication and scanned for replies.

When she had told Modessr that the Chair of the General Council had signed off the order to go public, she had lied. She was in no doubt that if he knew there was the slightest opportunity to meddle, he would be straight up to the Library bending the ear of Chair Engala and all her hovering sycophants. She was also in no doubt that the Chair, the Council, or any component within the Order's organisational structure, was incapable of taking action that was remotely close to swift. The protocols and procedures that formed the over-engineered framework of the Order slowed all action to a bureaucratic crawl. Ordinarily, it didn't matter. The Order performed the same duties year in, year out. It could take a month to make a decision on a tweak to some domestic arrangement. On this occasion, time was critical; Bastion needed their green light.

Ihlo closed the message window, checked Lasysi's control panel, threw on her overcloak and hurried out of the lab. The risk of running into Modessr was minimal; she knew he'd be in a sanctimonious rage, desperate to vent. That meant he'd have headed straight for the votaries' mess, with its subsidised genker and captive audience. To reduce the risk further, she took a circuitous route up the steep cobbled alleyways, around the backs of ancient stone buildings, up to the imposing Library on the citadel's summit.

Entering the building still gave her a thrill. Since childhood, she had dreamt of a life of service in the Order. She had worked hard to achieve that ambition. When her parents died, that ambition became hard-edged and hydrogen-fuelled, finding in their passing an unfamiliar need to make them proud. The Library, visible from the entire city, had been the embodiment of that goal and the lure of a calling to fulfil. Taking a deep breath, she walked through the cavernous reception hall and drew courage from the enormity of what it represented. She had sworn an oath to protect and perfect the legacy of the Savants. Procedure and protocol dictated that she shouldn't take the action she was about to take. Duty demanded that she must.

She approached the Chair's office with apprehension. The Order was without hierarchy, apart from the rolling Chair of the General Council. Whoever held the Chair for their one-year term found themselves with an authority they were unaccustomed to and unfamiliar with how to exert. In the hands of most, the power felt a burden best ignored. In rare and readied hands, it felt a heft, ripe for wielding.

Outside the office was a desk, behind which sat a votary.

"Coequal," he said, rising from his seat and dipping his head, hands behind his back.

Ihlo returned the gesture. "I must speak with Chair Engala."

"That is not possible."

"May I ask why?"

"You do not have an appointment."

Ihlo gritted her teeth. "An urgent matter has come to light. There was no time to make an appointment. I must speak with her."

The votary sat back down and looked at Ihlo blankly through the transparent visual.

"Can I make an appointment now?"

"It is out of office hours. You will have to wait until tomorrow."

"I must speak with her tonight. There must be a protocol for this. What if there was some emergency?"

"Oh yes, there is provision for that."

"Well, this is an emergency."

He straightened his back and activated the visual. "In that case, let me check her schedule…"

Her tolerance breached, Ihlo stepped past him and knocked loudly on the door to the office.

"Wait!" said the votary. "You can't just—"

"Too late." Ihlo opened the door and stepped inside.

The room resembled a private library, with floor to ceiling bookcases covering the walls and a large oak desk in the centre. A burnfree fire glowed in a large grate in one corner, filling the space with welcome warmth. Chair votary Engala was sat behind the desk, an expression of utter incomprehension stretching her face. Her emerald eyes were startled wide.

"What in Raptor's name—"

"Chair, please forgive my intrusion," said Ihlo, walking up to the desk, hands behind her back. "I know this is improper. However, I must speak with you."

"This is beyond improper. Explain yourself."

"We've received communication from Bastion requesting we go public on the investigation into the Amnesia Crisis."

"I have read the message. I am well aware of their request. The Council administration is drafting a response."

"Saying?"

"I beg your pardon?"

"Will they permit the request?"

The Chair rose, her long body made rigid with rage. "Your impudence is astonishing. I will not tolerate this. Leave immediately."

Ihlo took a deep breath before taking the leap. "I can't do that, I'm afraid. I am bound by oath to protect Klova. My duty requires me to act. I will explain, but please, appraise me of the draft response."

"I will do no such thing."

"Then let me guess. In a standard, set piece way, it says that the Order is grateful for Bastion's assessment and will now trigger due process with regard to establishing a position on whether or not to go public."

A flush spread like a wine stain behind Engala's ears. "Due process is the high standard by which the Order operates."

"A formal proposal to the General Council, to be debated and voted upon by every member. That will take at least a week. Bastion must act with haste, as must we. Can't you see the immense threat we're facing? You're the Chair; you must have the authority to bypass protocol, given the danger Klova's in."

The Chair held her hands in front of her, her jaw set. "It is not in my gift to take such action. It is for the Council to decide."

"There's not time."

"This is the way."

"Then your way is preventing me from honouring my oath. Would you have me fail in my duty?"

"Of course not. Your oath of service is paramount, as it is for us all. But our duty is served in union; autonomy is incompatible. You will have studied Ninian in your training; keep his words always in mind, for therein lies the wisdom of our ways. There's no question; it must go to a vote."

"Do you anticipate the vote will be passed?"

"Undoubtedly. The Council approved the investigation. Implicit in that is an understanding we must operate openly and maintain transparent communication with the public, once the link to Klova is presumed."

"Then why not trigger a snap vote tonight? If the statement's drafted, circulate it to members now. Hold a midnight vote. The press release could be ready for distribution first thing in the morning."

"There must be a session in which to debate."

"But you just said you believe they'll all vote in favour."

"It is not my place to operate on assumptions."

"Even if the urgency of the situation requires it? We cannot wait a week. Who knows how far it will have spread by then, the damage it will have caused. We cannot knowingly take that risk and still claim to fulfil our duty in respect of Klova. We will become responsible. The avoidable delay makes us accountable."

"My hands are bound." She lifted her chin and spoke with the rigidity that filled her marrow. "As Chair, my own duty is altered. For as long as I remain in office, my priority is the General Council and its function to maintain propriety and the democratic and equitable operation of the Order of Savants."

"And you will prioritise that above all else, despite the consequences to Klova?"

"I must."

"Then I must prioritise my duty."

The Chair studied Ihlo. "What are you saying?"

"I must protect Klova, despite the consequences."

It's remarkable the lengths to which some will go – to fight a cause, to right a wrong, to prove one's worth, to evince a point.

You might be one of life's warriors yourself, sticking your neck out, risking cost for the sake of your cause. If you are, good on you. That thing you fight for gains strength from every spirit that stands up in its defence.

I like to think I'm a warrior of sorts. At least, I believe in something with a passion that moves me and which motivates me to act with conviction and the force of justification. Is that the same thing? It feels like it is.

If so, I wonder to what lengths I shall go.

CHAPTER TEN

The story broke first thing. ArtezAlert ran a scrolling Breaking News, featuring headline quotes from the leaked statement. The text was reproduced in full on its home page, followed by multiple disclaimers regarding source and authenticity. No one was in any doubt, however – the style and tone had the Order written all over it.

Ubimedia jumped on the news so fast, many thought it was ubi that broke it first. Unlike the national press, the consumer journalists of the ubi platform didn't waste time with cautionary caveats. Instead, it ran multiple pieces on various theories doing the rounds. Top trending threads included: rumours on who leaked the statement; claims that it wasn't a leak at all, but the product of AI intervention; accusations of blackmail by the Undertow in order to force the Order's hand; and the notion that the statement was a cover-up – that the Order was providing a smokescreen while the government investigated a potential cyber-attack.

*

Ink wakes up to the news following a long night of broken sleep and natural, angst-filled dreams. Over-tired and muddle-headed, it takes him a moment to process the information and be certain he isn't still dreaming. Once it penetrates his consciousness, his head clears in an instant. Having craved answers for so long, this is the first real step towards finding them.

He scours ArtezAlert. Aside from the statement and limited guarded commentary, he finds little else. The statement is short: it confirms there is sufficient reason to suspect a possible connection between Klova and the recent cases of suspected transient global amnesia. Therefore, in a measure of excessive caution, the Order is launching a thorough investigation into the so-called crisis, which will be carried out with the assistance of their security agency, Bastion. There follows a number of pacifying platitudes along the lines of *no cause for alarm*.

The statement far from satisfies Ink's appetite for facts. He slumps on the sofa, facing his large, wall-mounted visual and brings up ubimedia. Scrolling through page after page, he barely dips a toe into an exponentially expanding ocean. Before he can reach the bottom of a page, it auto-refreshes with updated content. It feels to Ink like the entire city is sat at their visuals or cupping their palms, tapping away, chipping in their version of events, elaborating on the theories, drowning the statement and the single fact it contains.

Much space is devoted to the Undertow, none of it particularly pleasant. Ink tries not to let it influence his feeling towards this group who he intends to contact – once he ceases to dodge the question and make the call. He wonders why the Undertow is a target of abuse. Yore is a member and a convincing advocate, pitching it as a support network, formed out of necessity while the state does its best to ignore their plight. Ink's plight. For some reason, ubimedia is casting a critical light, applying labels such as troublemakers, insurrectionists, shit-stirrers and fascists. As is its want, ubi has already assigned and universally adopted a nomenclature for the afflicted and their condition. They cannot invent or acquire new words, but they can appease their need to name with a borrowed best fit. The so-called crisis is now the Corruption. Ink and the hundred-plus victims are tagged the Corrupted. Capitalisation lends the branding an assumed legitimacy that ubi-users love.

For the past few days, Ink has been stalling, fabricating excuses to justify his delay in contacting the Undertow. He lacks the language to contemplate his feelings during the conversation with Yore, or that moment with his mother after. Prevarication is easy when you can't feel the influence of past persuasion. Now, the desire to identify escalates. The need to connect develops an urgency that prompts Ink to act. He searches on his palm device for contact details and sends a brief message, asking if he can join.

A reply comes straight back: the time and GPS coordinates for a meeting that evening.

*

The Breaking News had come as a surprise to Agent Laine, who sat in her office, coffee in hand, digesting the coverage. Bastion had made the request for the Order to go public on the investigation, knowing full well the tanker would take days to turn. The fact the statement was leaked appealed to Laine, as she knew it would do to many of her colleagues. The Order, whilst being their paymasters, was somewhat of a joke within the agency – an eccentric institution whose undisputed expertise was dulled by their tedious abidance by the book.

Laine smiled, relishing the scandal, imagining the chaos that would have been caused in their folly on the hill.

A knock pulled her mind back. She glanced up to see Brosala through the glass wall of her office, his face animated. She gestured with her head for him to enter.

"Well now," said Brosala, grinning, "that's rubbed the shine off."

"Some votary's got more balls than I'd ever give them credit for. And by 'them' I mean the entire Order put together."

"You think it was a votary?"

"Has to be. The statement was a draft, written yesterday evening. A hacker wouldn't know it existed. There's several in Dox who've got the skills to break into the Order's central systems, but they'd have had to know it'd been written. Only a votary would – and probably not too many of those at that. The line-up's likely to be pretty short. Hence, balls."

"Why would they do it, though? That's their career blown, surely."

"Damned if I know. And I don't care. All that matters is they've done us a massive favour. Means we don't have to go creeping around anymore." Laine downed the rest of her coffee, locked her visual and stood up. "Let's go make some noise."

*

The Breaking News came at a price for Ihlo. She sat at the dining table in her apartment, dressed for duty, delaying the inevitable. Free of regret, she still felt weighed down by a heavy dread of the day ahead.

"You still here?" said Ky, leaning against the door jamb, rubbing her bed-hair. She wore a faded band t-shirt over baggy leggings, last night's makeup smudged around her eyes.

Ihlo didn't answer or look up.

"Nice. You're on form today. Right up there on your fucking pedestal." She huffed and drifted into the kitchenette.

Ihlo felt no reaction, realising how little her cousin's routine abuse actually mattered. Ordinarily, she would have got up and left, exiting rather than engaging with the forced conflict. Today, she simply didn't care. Today, everything was different. She looked down at her uniform, which still felt new and unfamiliar.

Ky sat down at the table opposite Ihlo, a glass of something thick and green in hand. She looked at Ihlo, head cocked, as if deciding how to yield to temptation. "You sick or something?"

Ihlo sighed. "Not today. Please."

Ky's eyes brightened. "I know. You've not done your homework. What happens? Detention? An old school whipping?"

Ihlo's resistance waivered. It still didn't matter – she just felt like she didn't need to take it. Not with what was to come. She stood up and left the room, then silently left the apartment.

Ky shrugged. Moving over to the sofa, she slumped down and switched on the headset. While the game loaded, she idly brought up a holographic of ubi's news feed on her device. She stared, wide-eyed. "Fuck." Then she looked back at the door through which Ihlo had left, grinning with delight.

Already aboard a Swift heading north, Ihlo still hadn't read any news. Now, surrounded by fellow commuters, all glued to their devices, she was glad she had resisted. Instead, she read their rapt expressions as they savoured the heady spice of scandal, not daring to imagine how the statement had been eclipsed by homespun theories and blatant abuse. It wasn't difficult to guess who were among the targets; she noticed her distinctive uniform was drawing altered attention. The eyes on her were a mix of suspicion, prejudice and intrigue. She wondered if they had even considered the implications of the investigation – what it might, in time, mean for them – or if controversy around the leak was simply more entertaining.

As she walked through the arch and into the ancient citadel, the tension was palpable. Ordinarily busy, the steep cobbled streets of Mount Az were quiet, with only a few becloaked votaries crossing her path. She purposely attempted to make eye contact, but bowed heads prevented it. Even the birdsong, usually rife at that hour, sounded sparse and out of key. Feeling an unexpected relief to finally reach the lab, Ihlo hung up her coat and overcloak, straightened her starched uniform and stood before Lasysi. The powerful machine still slept. In a moment, she would wake it and hear it breathe, its processor unaware and without judgment.

"Good. You're here," said Modessr from the doorway, flustered. "I've just come from the mess. Utter furore. Quite overwhelming."

Ihlo turned around and pushed her shoulders back, chin up.

Modessr threw his overcloak on the bench and paced, hands wringing. "A thorough scandal. Unprecedented. Unthinkable. It's a mountain to wrap one's head around." He stopped and looked at Ihlo. "You're across the detail of what's occurred, I take it?"

"I am."

"Good. Then I assume your detached manner is a symptom of warranted anxiety."

"I'm sorry?"

"Many will assume you are responsible for the leak. You pushed for the investigation in the first place and have been vocal on the need to inform the public, despite the unnecessary reputational damage. I shared your views with coequals in the mess after your outburst in here yesterday – which, by the way, I accept your apology for. I was offended by your attitude at the time but reminded myself of your youth and naivety. You've much to learn and I pride myself on my patience, among other qualities." He held a hand to his chest, exaggerated forbearance twisting his face.

"It was me."

Distracted by his own conceit, he looked up. "Pardon me?"

"I leaked the statement."

"No, really—"

"I had no choice." She walked towards Modessr and stood before him, her arms crossed. "My duty is to protect Klova. Left to its own, tortuous devices, the General Council would have taken a week to make the decision and take the necessary action. I appealed to Chair Engala directly, but she failed to recognise the responsibility inherent in her position. Or, more likely, she chose to ignore it. I could not – *would* not – ignore my responsibility. Time is critical. Standard procedure is not."

"I… I am staggered. Appalled. And you, a novice. What gives you—"

"Save your histrionics for the mess." Ihlo stepped past Modessr and put on her overcloak. "I'm going up to the Library. You will need to do some work, I'm afraid. I suspect I will be detained for much of the day."

Striding down the dark hallway and out of the department building, Ihlo felt buoyed by fresh resolve. She hadn't been concerned about telling Modessr and she couldn't care less about his reaction. It had just helped to practice saying the words out loud. She took her time walking the steep incline up to the Library's main entrance, not wanting to appear out of breath on arrival. In a surreal rerun of the previous evening, she headed straight for the Chair of the General Council's office. A different votary now sat at the desk before the door, although he looked almost identical, even down to the bemused expression. Ihlo didn't bother with the pointless back and forth this time. She walked straight up to the door and knocked loudly.

"You can't—" said the votary, jumping up and almost falling over his chair.

"I already have." Ihlo opened the door and crossed the threshold.

The Chair was sat behind her desk, the entire surface of which glowed from an integrated visual Ihlo hadn't noticed before. The glow rippled as new windows popped up, text flashing.

"I've been expecting you," said votary Engala, her emerald eyes and steel voice equally cold.

"I've come to explain."

"How considerate of you."

"I stand by my actions, which I attest were necessary for the protection of Klova."

"I'm glad you have such confidence in the impact of your reckless sabotage."

"Klova is at risk. Our nation depends on the code and the faultless functioning of the implant. One or the other has failed somehow. That failure could continue to affect more code, or more people's implants. We must not let either happen. An unnecessary delay could easily have resulted in such avoidable outcomes. There appears to be an assumption that the proportion per population does not justify decisive action. That is a false and dangerous view. It is akin to dismissing the first wafts of smoke from a presumed-dormant volcano. A distant early warning calls to be heeded."

"Your criminal actions are having – and will continue to have – a profoundly detrimental impact on this institution. I wonder if you even spared this a thought."

"As I said before, we must not prioritise the protection of reputation over our protection of Klova. That would be a gross failure in our common duty. We have all sworn the same oath; we all share the same responsibility. I am disappointed to find that so many of my coequals regard the prestige of their position and the high opinion of the Order as preceding the legacy of the Savants. We all depend on language. We do not depend on reputation. I'm ashamed to be associated with those who believe they do."

"In that, you needn't trouble yourself. Your association with the Order will soon cease." She cocked her head, frowning. "That's the part that surprises me the most. I've read your record. I know you've devoted your life to becoming a votary and taking the oath of service. Finally, you earn your place – with the accolade of being our top-ranking novice by some margin. You are two months into your probation. Then you go and throw it all away, just to prove a point."

"No. I *risk* it all to prove a point."

"And what do you mean by that?"

"I am familiar with the formal procedure for gross misconduct. It will take approximately three months to complete the process leading up to dismissal, should that be the outcome as agreed by the Council. Is that correct?"

The Chair glared at Ihlo, refusing to respond to the rhetorical question.

"By which time, my point will be proved. I am right about the threat we face. I am right about the need to act with haste to limit the damage and prevent further suffering. When the time comes that this is evident to everyone else in this organisation, perhaps the General Council will take a different view of my case. Three months should give me plenty of time."

"A risky strategy indeed. More so than you perhaps realise." She waited a moment, inviting doubt, then said, "If

I were Chair, I may or may not consider persuading Council members of the severity of your misconduct, regardless of what transpired following your foul deed. As it is, my term as Chair concludes in eight weeks and my successor has just been determined. By the time your case is heard, there will be a new Chair – someone who, I expect, will relish exerting their influence over malleable minds." She leant forward, her mouth twisted. "Votary Modessr."

How many times have you said to yourself, it'll be worth it in the end?

For me, it was worth it right from the start.

CHAPTER ELEVEN

"**W**hy didn't you tell us you all shop at Dox?" snarled Laine. With the investigation public knowledge, Bastion had the green light to pursue their lead. Agents Laine and Brosala were stood on the threshold of an apartment in Pincher Toll, home of the Undertow's designated spokesperson and Bastion's first port of call.

"I don't know what you mean," said Ren, her voice weak. She was stood in a dressing gown, the hallway behind her dark. With her pale skin and wild hair catching the light from outside, she looked like a nervous ghost.

"I don't believe you," said Laine. "Let us in and we'll compare notes."

Bastion had a certain reputation: on the side of the law, but above and beyond it. Law Enforcement would require a warrant for entry. Bastion just needed a reason. Ren dropped her head and stood to one side, wordlessly inviting them in.

The living space looked as if a gale had blown through it, scattering domestic debris in its wake. Laine and Brosala stepped over and around the mess. Ren seemed to pass through it, oblivious. She sat at a dining table and gestured to the other chairs.

"I'd offer you something to drink."

"We've come for answers," said Laine, standing in the centre of the room. Both agents were now in full field op gear, no longer having to observe discretion – cargo trousers, rollneck and padded jacket, all in black. "When we met you and your group, you said there was no common ground between you. Why did you lie?"

Ren frowned, struggling to fill the gaps of her missing code.

Brosala stepped in. "You lie to us. Why?"

"We think it's not relevant. Yes, we work out we enjoy vice now and again. Dox is the only place to buy. It's coincidence."

"Would you like my badge as well? And my fucking office?" said Laine.

"I'm just saying—"

"You're just saying what you buy and who you buy it from."

Ren's eyes widened and her lips pinched.

"Just so we're clear, let me explain the two options that are available to you. Either you tell us the product and trader, or we scan your brain for codeprints – at considerable cost to you personally. Either way, we'll get the intel out of you."

"You must know Dox rules. That's why we don't tell you the connection."

"Of course I know Dox rules. Bane of my life, generally speaking. But let's colour this with a little perspective, shall we? The Undertow number, what? Thirty? Forty?"

"Just under a hundred."

"As of this morning, there's double that number of confirmed afflicted. This thing is spreading. You want a share in responsibility for that? Following the rules worth it, is it?" Laine moved to sit opposite Ren, leaning forward, elbows on the table. "You can help us stop this. If you get any trouble for talking, we'll give you protection. And the fact you've talked at all won't come from us. Who else is to know? Product and trader, that's all we need. Then we leave you alone – and we make sure everyone else does too. Fairer trade than you'll ever get in that pisshole."

"I don't know the trader."

"Bullshit."

Ren blinked, body rigid.

"Brain scan?" Laine leant back towards Brosala. "Remind me, Agent. What's the going rate these days?"

Brosala rubbed his chin in exaggerated theatrics. "North of ten thousand credits, last I looked. Complicated procedure, see. Takes expensive skill."

Laine turned back to Ren. "We get the info regardless. I guarantee you that. Save yourself eviction for unpaid rent and tell me the names."

"I don't know the trader." She sighed. "Product's called XDream."

*

Brosala gripped the controls as they sped south through the city towards Cope and the domain of Dox. Laine stretched out on the back seat, her eyes in REM as she trawled file after file on her retinal display.

"XDream doesn't come up anywhere. Can't find a sodding thing."

"Must be new," said Brosala.

"Which adds to the fire. The five who cracked all gave the same product name. I don't believe in coincidence. And if it's new to market, it would explain why the malfunction's happening now."

"But codevice? How could that even work?"

"Fuck knows."

"It shouldn't be possible to interact with the implant. It's totally different code to Klova."

"Our circle to square." Laine blinked, adjusting to real-world vision. "Save your questions, Agent. We're about to hit the marketplace of those in the know."

"But we're close to the line, aren't we? HQ have only just given notice. We've got our own rules to follow."

"We've also got a crisis on our hands and a solid lead. We'll face the flak after. By then, we should have what – or whom – we want. Takes the sting out of a knuckle rap."

Brosala pulled up outside Dox's main entrance, their vehicle visible and unmistakable. The two agents stood on the pavement, ignoring the bitter cold, taking a moment to adopt the appropriate posture. Then they stormed the market.

Apart from traders and their crew, no one wants to be seen in Dox. The moment Bastion entered, their presence detected and relayed throughout the market, shoppers scattered. They hid in box rooms, hurried down backstairs and ran blindly down dark hallways. Traders stood their ground, but behind the locked doors of their stall. All the while, the warren fell into an unnatural quiet, hurried footfall and heavy breathing instead of the barking of wares by pushy pokes and competing sound systems. Emergency lighting came on, washing the walls with anaemic half-light. Up the levels moved Bastion, taking their time, making an impression.

Once they reached the fifth floor, east side, they started banging on doors. Those without security swung open onto empty stalls, tech still running in abandoned operation. Most doors were locked. Brosala hammered on these, demanding they be opened. Laine remained calm behind him, biding her time. In one stall they found a trader and customer who had not been fast enough to flee. Both were men, both middle-aged. One stared in pale-faced panic, the other looked pissed off. The Bastion agents entered and shut the door behind them.

"Greetings," said Laine. "Looks like you didn't get the memo."

"Get outta my stall," said the one who looked pissed off. "There's form and you broke it. That weren't enough warning."

"Not my problem, trader. But now as I'm here, I've a few questions."

"Not my problem, Bas. I ain't answerin'."

"It's not you I'm asking." She turned to Pale-face. "What's your name?"

"I… I'm not answering either," said the man, sounding far from convinced.

"You think? State protections don't extend to patrons, I'm afraid. Bad luck."

Pale-face looked to the trader, who shrugged, looking away.

"Let's try again, shall we? Name."

"…"

"Brosala, do the honours."

Brosala grabbed hold of the man's wrist and held their palms together. By the time the man had the wits to pull his hand away, it was too late. Brosala smiled and nodded to Laine. Then he scanned his retinal screen.

"May I introduce Gres Manda, fifty-two, senior lecturer at Arteza University, AI department."

Laine delivered an imitation smile to Pale-face. "Pleasure." Then she turned to the trader. "Agent Brosala and myself are going to take a walk with our new friend, Gres. Apologies for disturbing your business. We shall return him in due course – unless he refuses to cooperate, in which case, I apologise for the loss of sale. We'll make sure Gres pays you what he would have spent, had we not so rudely interrupted."

The trader nodded, satisfied that someone else was on the hook that he was off.

Laine winked at Pale-face. "You're coming with us." Then she turned and left the stall. Brosala moved behind the terrified customer, gently nudging him through the door.

The three of them walked slowly down the deserted hallway, tracked by security cameras and spyhole witnesses. The Bastion agents resumed their stalking gait, head up, eyes fixed dead ahead. Their token scalp shuffled between them, mumbling, "Where are you taking me?" and "I've done nothing wrong" several times over. Laine led them into a vacated stall and closed the door. There was a desk and three chairs, one of which had been knocked over.

"Sit," she said. The customer, now silent, obliged. "What were you buying back there before we crashed the party?"

"Codevice."

"Of course it was fucking codevice. What *product*?"

"C... Codeshine."

"Ever heard of XDream?"

The man shook his head.

"Why should we believe you?"

"I... I swear to you. I only come for 'Shine. I'm not interested in anything else."

"Yeah, but pokes push. That's their job. No one ever tried to sell it to you? No one mention it?"

"No. I've never heard of it."

Laine turned to Brosala. "I guess a hit straight off was too much to hope for. You stay here with our new friend. Get the usual details. I'm going fishing. I won't be long."

Back out in the dim corridor, Laine strutted with professional pride. This was the part of the job she loved.

It was why, despite her promotion, she still insisted on field work. People's perception of Bastion, their reaction to their presence, made for a healthy dose of job satisfaction. Passing through the shadows, bold as brass, she could feel eyes on her through the cracks, hear laboured breathing behind closed doors. Her scowl disguised a smile.

"Find what you're looking for?" came a quiet voice from behind.

Laine turned around, eyebrows raised. A slim figure leant against a door jamb, barely visible in the gloom. The figure disappeared through the door, leaving it open. Laine followed.

"Shut the door and I'll turn on a light," said the shadow. As Laine obliged, a desk lamp came on, lighting the centre of the room and the young woman who stood there, hands on her hips, head cocked. "The name's Kite."

"Agent Laine." She crossed her arms, appraising her purple-haired host. "I'm intrigued. A trader striking up the conversation?"

"I'm full of surprises." Kite's eyes sparkled inside their border of thick black liner. "So? What you looking for?"

"Intel on a product. Sold as XDream. Heard of it?"

"Might've. Why?"

"We have reason to believe its manufacture breaks market rules. Do you know who sells it?"

"What's in it for me if I do?" She sat on the desk, cross-legged, twisting a spike of hair around her fingers.

Laine half-smiled, pulling up a chair and sitting down. She leant back, her long limbs relaxed. "That depends on the quality of the trade."

"Quality's this: I know the product. I know who makes and sells it. Going by the very short notice of your visit today, I suspect such knowledge comes at a decent price."

"You after coin? Or record cleaning?"

"My record's pristine, I'll have you know." She tipped her head back to the relic tech behind her. "Decent hardware – or the coin to buy it."

Laine didn't take her eyes off Kite. "I'm sure that can be arranged. Now talk."

"Exose Ray. You know him?"

"Of course."

"He's your man. Created XDream. Been selling it a couple of weeks now."

"Why are you snitching?"

"That crap heap behind me. I can't step up without quality gear."

"No. What's the real reason? You don't snitch on someone like Exose Ray for the sake of a few upgrades."

Kite slammed her hands on the desk. "Because the prick thinks he owns the place. Parading around, ego bigger than Witness, head so far up his arse I'm surprised he can fuckin' walk."

"You two don't get on, then?"

"He treats me like a child. Like he can patronise me and I'm just gonna take it. His oh-so-wise counsel was for me to get smart and raise investment. I'm just heeding the old man's advice." She winked.

Laine smiled. "Well, I'm glad we could do business today. I don't usually shop in Dox, but maybe you and I can trade in the future."

"I'm no rat."

"No, you're not. You're smart. You saw an opportunity. And now you've got some new gear coming your way. My colleague, Agent Brosala, is just down the hall. I'll send him here shortly. You tell him the tech you want. He'll arrange to have it with you by tomorrow morning." Laine stood up. "And if you find you need protection off the back of this, I'll throw that in for free."

*

Back in the vacant stall, door locked, Laine and Brosala stood facing each other. They had released Pale-face, having taken all his details, thereby raising a permanent record – useful message, regardless of the fact he hadn't actually done anything wrong. Not that they needed to send a message now they had the intel they'd come for. The pressing question was how best to handle it. Brosala appeared to look at Laine, but his eyes were scanning the latest.

"So far, over thirty have spilled under pressure and confirmed taking XDream prior to becoming Corrupted. That's all who've talked. Loyalty to Dox is strong – we can safely assume the majority won't break the market code. But the thirty-odd admissions we have are a fairly good indication XDream is the likely cause."

"Agreed."

Brosala's eyes refocused onto Laine. "Exose's not going to come in quietly without some weight behind us."

"No." She rubbed the back of her neck. "No, he's not. We need a warrant. Top floor will already be on our case for not observing the agreement. Get me the boss on the line, will you? We can't wait and come back. Exose will catch on and probably go underground – disappear into the mountains or something. We've got to get him now."

Brosala nodded and backed away, tapping his NuB and speaking to the air. Laine paced, her heart racing.

"Boss's on the line," said Brosala.

Laine tapped her NuB. "Sir, I request a fast-track warrant for arrest." She shut her eyes, pinching the bridge of her nose. "Yes, sir. I have confidence in the intel. No guarantees, of course, but enough to take the risk... Yes. Yes, I appreciate that, sir... That's right. A fifth of cases have confirmed taking the product. I'd bet my badge it's way more, if not all... I know, sir, but regardless – the link's tight... If I'm wrong? I've pissed off a made trader. I'll take the fall, admit I personally overstepped. HQ can make a show of pulling me off the investigation. Whatever... Yes, sir." Laine looked at Brosala and nodded briefly. "Yes, sir. Thank you, sir. We'll keep you informed."

"Time for backup?"

"Get me four units. One covering the exits, the rest in here with us. We've a large area to sweep – assuming he's still on site."

"I'll notify Surveillance. If he's left, we should have something on camera. If he gets wind we're coming for him, they can monitor live."

While Brosala placed the calls, Laine familiarised herself with the market's complex layout. Bastion maintained a digital 3D model of Dox, regularly updated to incorporate new openings, shifted ladders and repositioned partition walls. Junior agents took it in turns to go plainclothes, covering a floor or a wing at a time, conducting undercover reconnaissance of the ever-evolving den of less-than-legal enterprise. She knew the layout, knew where stall front 242 was situated. They'd never got a plainclothes inside. That part of the model remained unhelpfully blank.

"Reinforcements are on their way. ETA, five minutes," said Brosala.

"Have we got proof of warrant?"

"Yes."

Laine nodded slowly. "Okay. Here's the plan. Run over to our snitch in 198. Give her a drop-box code and tell her to mail you her shopping list. Then contact our backup. Tell the three units to take a floor each, bottom up. We'll remain here on fifth. I have my suspicions our man will have locked himself in his stall. There's a fire escape via a window at the rear – surveillance will pick him up if he attempts that route. If he doesn't open up, with proof of warrant, we let ourselves in. You ready?"

"Always."

"Then let's do this thing."

*

Bastion moved through Dox like an ink spurt in water. Stealth was redundant; besides, they wanted their presence to be seen and felt. A rapid arrest warrant inside the black market was a rare pass; the agents relished this moment of control over their state-protected nemesis. They marched down hallways, up stairwells, through ragged holes, their LED torches bleaching the space with the light of a full moon.

Agents Laine and Brosala, some distance away on the fifth floor, felt the tension rise in the silence surrounding them. There was a palpable feeling of the inevitable, as traders and trapped customers waited behind pointlessly locked doors. Laine knew word would have spread. Bastion were procedure-bound to declare the warrant with the Dox Office; internal communications in the market were a hair away from instantaneous. As they approached stall front 242, Laine knew that, if Exose was inside, he'd already be expecting them. The reinforced door did not open upon request. Neither did it open upon demand. Bastion resorted to tech. Brosala held a small, metallic device over the call pad, which sent electromagnetic pulses into the unit, frying the hardware inside. Multiple deadbolts shifted and the door swung open.

Inside the main trading room, Exose Ray stood before his desk, arms crossed, his expression coal-black and cold.

"Prove you have a warrant. If you can't, tell me what the fuck you're doing in my stall."

Despite his usual bravado, Brosala's nerve buckled. Laine held out her hand, palm up. The holographic screen confirmed their pass.

"Exose Ray, you are under arrest for contravention of Section 35 of the Consumer Protection Act, Ninth Edition, and Section 92-b of the Safe Code Act."

"Bullshit."

"Your response is on record, as is anything else you do or say from this moment on."

"I stand by my response."

"We are taking you to Bastion Detention, where you will be held for questioning. You will be advised of the full charges against you and your rights for legal representation."

"I'm not going anywhere."

"You have no choice."

Exose spat at the floor to his side.

"Do we need cuffs, or can we play nicely?"

Exose stared at Laine, his mouth twisted, his hidden fists clenched.

Her curiosity nagging, Laine said, "I'm surprised you're still here. All told, you had plenty of warning."

"You'll never catch me running from Bas. Besides, you've got my name. Who was it who gave it to you?"

"You know I'm not going to tell you that."

"Well, you tell whoever it was, they made a big mistake. And, when you come to release me – which you will – I'll find out who it was. And I'll make them pay."

The naming of things is important. It gives the subject/object its meaning – confirms its reality by forming its referent, lets us talk about it.

The sibling Savants' gift was their unique neurological capacity to name – an abhuman area of their brain in which processes for language acquisition and development thrived. The Machine – the Order's artificial replica of this anomalous miracle – is the Savants' sole succession and their legacy's means to sustain.

Incorporation, made possible by the Machine and rigidly controlled by the Order, is a closed shop. Klova's growth is restricted by an arbitrary annual allowance.

But what if there is a need to talk about that which has no name? What happens when there are no words?

Need is forever the impulse for invention. Hence, society's perennial repurposing to patch a rarely perceived void – taking words that already exist in language and attaching them to that which needs to be named.

Take 'ubimedia': a cut and shut referent to capture social media's bloated, omnipresent voice of influence. Or take the 'Corrupted' – a topical example, hot off the press. I can't wait to see how that single word will shape how people regard those poor, code-sapped individuals – how it will influence society's behaviour towards them.

I couldn't have come up with a better name myself.

CHAPTER TWELVE

Roosting hour. Birdsong fills the air as dusk descends. Winged silhouettes flit and glide, nest-bound, above the Delce. In the streets below, people also spend the day's end homeward bound.

Feeling the counter-flow, Ink bucks the trend. He has left the comfort and security of his apartment, reaching out into the cold unknown. Stepping off the Swift, he pulls his collar up, hunches his shoulders and hurries towards the address he has been given – a small retail unit called Physical Books. The bookshop stands opposite the old district library, long since vacant, now under conversion into flats. The unassuming shop looks equally vacant, the space beyond the storefront window dark and lifeless. Doubting himself, Ink checks the message, half hoping an honest error might provide an excuse to back out after all. His decision to come hasn't lessened his apprehension. Hovering on the safe side of the threshold, he's about to turn and leave when he hears footsteps behind him.

"You press call?" says a young woman, her voice quiet. She looks at Ink, who stares back, breath held. "The call pad. Is someone coming?"

"I... I don't know." Ink steps to one side, inviting the woman to take control.

She eyes Ink. "First time?"

Ink nods.

The woman smiles. "You'll be glad you come." She reaches forward and presses a touch pad to the right of the door. "Don't mind the woman who lets us in. She's not one of us."

An elderly woman emerges from the shadows on the other side of the glass door, which she takes her time unlocking. When she opens it, she glances at the woman, then locks her eyes on Ink, her face twisted.

"He's with me," says the young woman, stepping through the door and into the shadows inside.

Ink has visited the bookshop many times over the years, it being one of only three in the entire city, the remaining supply of affordable second-hand fast dwindling. Ink likes to drop in and browse the spines, breathing in the air of paper and dust. Now, shrouded in darkness, the aisles between the bookshelves appear narrower, the maze more twisting and disorientating. Ink tries to resist the impression of eerie foreshadowing.

Eventually, they reach a door, which the elderly woman holds open for them to pass through. As Ink steps into a large back room, he hears the door close behind them, drawing a line under second thoughts. Taking a deep breath, he scans the room. The space is sparsely furnished and barely lit, with a few dim ceiling spots lighting the heads of the people gathered. Ink estimates around sixty or seventy, standing in small groups, chatting quietly. He spots Yore among them, who dips his head and smiles kindly. The young woman he'd arrived with joins a huddle to his left. Ink remains where he is – way out of his depth.

With no apparent cue, the chatter subsides and a wild-haired woman rises up in the centre of the room, her head and shoulders a couple of feet above those around her.

"Thank you for coming at such short notice. It's good to see so many of you here – and to see some new faces. For those who don't know me, I'm Ren – spokesperson for the Undertow."

Sixty-odd pale faces look to the woman in their midst, sharing an expression Ink identifies with. Ren turns slowly on the spot, appraising the gathered, connecting with each and every one.

"You all read the news today – the confirmation of what we know to be true. The Order and Bastion are investigating our plight. The link with language is officially presumed. Time will prove us right."

"What if we don't have time?" comes a voice from the crowd.

Ren nods. "I hear you. It is why I say we must assist with the investigation however we can. The sooner they discover the cause, the sooner we know the danger we're in. The condition could still be degenerative. If we don't want to lose more code – or lose our minds – we have to play our part. That's why I call this meet. Please, if you're approached by Bastion or the Order, I urge you to cooperate. Speak honestly and offer freely. Agents speak to me and I protect our privacy on the point we agree. That might cost us precious time." She is met by startled faces and fearful murmurs. "I deny knowledge of a connection between us. Turns out that connection could have something to do with our condition. And now, Bastion know that many, if not all of us, take XDream. I hear they raid Dox and arrest Exose Ray."

A palpable shock descends. Barely illuminated faces turn to each other, mouths open, eyes wide. Ink feels blood-rush dizzy, unable to get his head around this other, unexpected stretch of common ground, what this might mean – how it could even be possible. Codevice is safe – *should be* safe. Just as Klova's code and hardware *should be failsafe*. Neither should be connected, neither should go wrong.

Then he thinks of Exose.

Ink's legs buckle. A man to his side grabs him by the shoulders, saving him from falling.

"Of course, our privacy is important," continues Ren. "But finding the cause and stopping the spread is vital. I can't tell you what to do; no one can. But please, I appeal to you: assist. Does anyone here object?" She looks into scared eyes, at open, silent mouths. "Or, if you prefer not to speak out now, then please, speak to me after. Share your concern. I ask only that you consider the cost."

"I'll speak now," says a woman at the back of the room. "I'm a tram driver. I risk losing my job if my employer finds out I take codevice. The rule at work's a blanket ban."

Heads nod; there's a mumble of agreement. Faces turn back to Ren.

"I understand," she says. "But if you're questioned and you deny taking XDream, you could throw the investigation off-course. Or it could be something else they ask you. Any withheld or false information could slow things down or, worse than that, lead them down the wrong path so they miss the right one entirely. What's more important, keeping your job or ending this nightmare?"

"I can't afford to lose my job," says a man in the middle. "I've a baby and partner to support. I've got responsibilities."

Ren looks from the man to the whole room. "This is early days for all of us and already we're suffering. The longer we're afflicted, the harder it's going to be to bear, whether we lose another scrap of code or not. I look at your faces and I see your fear, just as I feel my own. We don't know what is lost.

We have no words that could mean we remember. But we each *feel* that loss – the difference caused by the space it's left behind. That, plus the fear of what next, is enough to eat away at anyone's sanity. Time matters here. That's why I urge you – assist."

Ink has regained his balance, but his mind is shot. The implications for everything are beyond him. He came here for support. Instead, he finds himself on the precipice of a gaping chasm. The Undertow might aim to extend a helping hand, but he discovers they are holding it out from the other side of a widening breach.

"Is it out there? Do people know about the codevice link?" comes another voice, pulling Ink's wits back from the edge.

"Not yet," says Ren.

"Because already we're the target. Already ubi paints us bad. When people find out we all happen to shop in Dox, they'll point the finger straight off. They'll say it's our fault. We've got what we deserve. That's what ubi'll say. Despite the fact that people writing that shit probably take codevice themselves, they'll make out we're to blame."

"I agree. That's why we must stand firm and stand united. Things are going to get worse before they get better. Prepare to be persecuted – personally and collectively. We are now the Corrupted. Debasement is implicit in the badge they borrow for us. But it's only a name. Names don't mean a thing."

"Not just a name though, is it?" says someone else, their tone bitter. "It's how people behave because of the name. You know that."

"Of course I do. Doesn't mean I accept it."

"Then we need to do more."

"Meaning?"

"Not meet here, in the back room of a shop, under cover of

darkness. I know we're not, but it feels like we're hiding. And it feels like we don't have a voice. We need a voice."

"Speaker squares," says Ink, his own voice coming from nowhere. He startles himself and feels his face redden.

Ren turns towards him and peers through the gloom. "Come forward, into the light. You're new, aren't you? What's your name?"

"Inker Ballard. Ink." His chest pounds.

"Welcome, Ink. Please, go on. Speaker squares?"

His throat constricts. "We... we could cover the main squares around the city. Take turns on the dais. Talk from our perspective. Keep talking until people start listening. It's a ready-made platform. And if there's any regular speakers in this group, we've a ready-made audience."

Ren nods, eyes bright. She glances around the room. "So? Anyone here take the dais?" A few tentative hands go up, then a few more. "Half a dozen. Maybe more among those not here tonight." She turns to one of the raised hands. "How does it work?"

"There's a schedule, managed by City Hall. You don't need to specify content. Frequent speakers can request a regular slot, otherwise its infill. It's easy to book."

"Sounds like too good an opportunity to miss. Anyone object?" Silence. "Good. I suggest we don't coordinate; it could appear contrived. Spread the word to other members. All who can handle the dais, book up slots. Keep speaking – and speak from the heart. There's a good chance people will hear the truth and believe it."

Murmuring among the crowd swells to an animated rumble. Ink senses a tangible energy, fuelled by the prospect of action – hope from self-empowerment. The chasm narrows, he grasps the outstretched hand.

At the end of the meeting, Ink lingers on the periphery as

his new-found comrades drift out of the room. When Yore passes him, he pauses to shake Ink's hand and says, "I'm glad you come. You will be, too."

For the first time since becoming afflicted, Ink doesn't feel alone. The two other people he has opened up to prior to this evening try their best to understand – but how could they? How could anyone grasp the inconceivable unless you've lived it? Until now, Ink hasn't realised how isolating that barrier of difference has become.

Ren lingers too, her eye on the newcomer with ideas. As the last few people leave and the caretaker returns to lock up, she approaches Ink.

"Can you spare half an hour? I'd like to talk to you. There's a café around the corner if you've time for a coffee."

Ink hesitates, unsure if he's up to close quarters attention. Then the prospect of returning home to his empty apartment and all its hollow thinking space casts a cold light.

"Sure," he says.

Ren leads the way through the maze of bookshelves, the elderly woman keeping close behind them, a large ring of keys in hand. As soon as they step through the shop's front door, the caretaker locks and bolts it from the inside. Ink catches the woman's expression through the glass.

"What's her problem?"

"The owner is sympathetic to our suffering – rents us the room for next to nothing. That woman's the caretaker. Takes a different view. Reckons we're faking it. Don't ask me why."

They walk a short distance to a late night café. Soft-glow lamps and burnfree candles lend the space a cosy warmth. Most tables are occupied, with rosy-cheeked patrons supping genker and hot, spiced ale. In the far corner, an elderly man sings traditional odes to the Raptor of Witness, strumming a weathered guitar. Ink and Ren find a vacant table against the back wall and order two coffees.

Relaxing a little, to his own vague surprise, Ink says, "So, are you, like, the group leader?"

"No. I'm just a doer. I come to a meet. There's a couple dozen people standing around feeling sorry for themselves. Sharing's one thing, but it isn't going to get us anywhere. I suggest we ditch the navel gazing and start thinking about what we can do to help our situation. No one objects. Then they all look to me for what next." She shrugs, half smiling. "What can I say? I like to have a plan."

"I've the impression it's more than just sharing, that the group's got some sort of agenda."

"Let me guess, from ubi?"

Ink looks down at his hands. "Guilty."

"Ubi's content is supposed to be consumer-generated. That's just the packaging. In truth, it's *fear*-generated – along with prejudice, ignorance and general shit-stirring. No one who posts content about us has the faintest idea who or what the Undertow is. We make the mistake of giving ourselves a name."

"Why a mistake?"

"Like I say in the meeting, names don't mean a thing. Not in themselves. Klova gives us words and their true meaning. When they're recycled, society overwrites false meaning onto them. We borrow 'undertow' because it resonates with us; it soon ends up representing something entirely different to most others. Depends on how kind or not ubi regards us. And, right now, they don't regard us kindly at all."

"That's what I don't get."

Ren cocks her head, inviting.

"How did we go from being the victims to being vilified? As if we're to blame for this complete fucking nightmare."

He reddens and feels his heart race. He takes a deep breath. "Sorry."

"What are you apologising for?" She leans forward, her voice low. "This is why I want to talk to you. We need your passion, your frustration. Many in the Undertow need help, but they're too knocked back to help themselves. Censure saps the fighting spirit. I've got reserves. I think you have too."

"I'm no fighter. I don't even know where the speaker square idea came from. I can't speak myself. How can I expect others to?"

"You don't need to speak."

"Then what?"

"Keep hold of that frustration. Make space for your anger. Read ubi and feel fucking outraged. That's your armour. Wear enough of it and you'll help protect us all."

They sit for a while in silence, staring into their coffee. Then Ink recalls the real reason he agreed to talking.

"This possible link with XDream. You think there's something in that?"

"I don't know. Part of me hopes there is because it means we'll soon have answers. Bastion will stop the spread and, Raptor help us, the Order will work out a fix."

"And the other part?"

"Can't you guess?"

Ink nods slowly. It was the first thought that occurred to him when the link was mentioned in the meeting – the realisation that his own actions could have led to his affliction.

"But Exose's not to blame. If his product's behind it, he doesn't mean it to happen."

"Exose Ray's a criminal. An egotist. And he's greedy. That's why he creates XDream. He always has to go one step further – build distance between him and the competition."

"That's all rep. I know him. He's not like that."

"He's earnt his rep. He takes pride in it. There's no way he's clean on this. And when the Order finds him guilty, I hope they make him pay dear for what he's done."

Do you dream?

I don't. Never have.

It must feel strange to dream – to maintain a sense of self, but in a situation outside of your consciousness – a situation utterly beyond your control.

Do a bit of research and you discover all manner of horror stories: a kid who jumped out of a fifth storey window in her sleep and died from the fall; a man who, fast asleep, mistook his partner for a rabid monster and stabbed him to death; a woman who dreamt she was being chased by a masked intruder – who drove her car whilst still asleep, ran a red light and ploughed into a passing vehicle, killing a family of four. That's just for starters.

Makes me glad I don't dream.

I'd hate to feel I was at the mercy of an illusion – or that there were other forces at work, controlling my mind, shaping my thoughts.

CHAPTER THIRTEEN

The Scarab glistened in the sun, tinted windows turned mercury beneath its glare. The building appeared lifeless from without. The jet carapace of something dormant, or dead.

Inside the headquarters of the Order's private security agency, the scene was in stark contrast. In the organisation's three-hundred-year history, never had there been such a threat to Klova. Never had the reputation and security of the Order stood so perilous. The mood in Bastion was a static charge, gradually accumulating as the hours passed. Agents looked to Detention as the potential path to ground.

Inside the interview room, the pressure was palpable. Four steel walls surrounded Exose Ray, who sat at a table, bound wrists in his lap. He stared ahead, feeling the eyes of multiple security cameras on him. He imagined the visuals relaying his image, four or five different perspectives, all fundamentally the same. He could feel the odd muscle twitch and his clenched jaw pulse as he sat in rigid defiance. An occasional, rapid blink was the only other element in his repertoire of movement. He would not give them something to see.

A door behind him opened and footsteps entered. Agents Laine and Brosala sat down opposite Exose. They were both dressed in crisp black suits and slate grey shirts, having hung up their fieldwork gear in a gesture of job done. Brosala activated the tech-enabled table; his left eye glowed green. Laine sat up straight and spoke with a tone of clear-cut procedure.

"I am Agent Laine. This is Agent Brosala. You have been informed of the charges against you and of your legal rights. So far, you have not requested representation and you deny all charges. This is your first interview, which I shall conduct, assisted by Agent Brosala. The interview will be recorded and is being observed by colleagues in real time. Before we proceed, do you have any questions?"

Exose maintained his rigid pose, staring ahead, statue-still.

"I'll take that as a no." She looked squarely at Exose. "I suggest you start talking, otherwise we'll be stuck here for a very long time. We've got an extended Right to Detain, on account of the circumstances. I'd go so far as to say it's open-ended – especially if you refuse to cooperate."

Exose slowly fixed his eyes on Laine. Their intensity scratched the surface of her composure.

She pushed her shoulders back. "When did you first come up with XDream?"

"Eighteen months ago." He spoke slowly, forcing the words.

"How long have you been selling it?"

"Fortnight or so. Check my accounts – I record every sale, as per the rules."

"Real names?"

"The names I'm given."

"Did you trial the product before it went to market?"

"How am I supposed to do that? Dox ain't a funded

pharmaceutical. Those that shop know the risks. My customers also know my skills, they trust my product."

"And you still stand by your product? Knowing what we know?"

"What *do* we know?" said Exose, his tone sharpening.

"That, of the two hundred-odd instances of Corruption, all have now admitted to taking codevice prior to developing symptoms. Half have specified XDream as the product."

"And the other half?"

"Refuse to say."

Exose's eyes glinted – a smile the cameras could not detect.

"The evidence points to codevice as the most likely cause of the Corruption and, with a brand new, untested product in the mix, it's highly likely XDream is behind it."

"Impossible."

"Why?"

"Because I created it. I wrote the code."

"And what? You're so damn good, you can't fuck up?"

"Your words, Agent."

Laine held her tongue, shoulders tense. "Look. Side effects happen. No one writes them in. But they still happen."

"Maybe where drugs are concerned. Chemicals are reactive. They've a life of their own. Code is code. Do you even know how cerebrogramming works?"

"Of course. The basics. But XDream is different. We've a team here analysing it."

"Brick walls?"

"You could say that."

A smile crept into the corner of Exose's mouth.

"So, explain it to me. Tell me how it's made. Explain why it's impossible your product's causing the Corruption. If you're so damn sure, convince me you're right."

Exose shut his eyes, weighing options. He knew he could

drag this out, push the buttons to play his own game. But other than winding up his hosts, he saw little in the way of gains. His rep had already taken a boost; the arrest played into the hands of notoriety. His product's rep had already been damaged. That didn't matter – it wouldn't take much to rework the concept and rebrand the goods. People always focused on the name. Opting in favour of bail and a ticket out of the Scarab, Exose explained XDream, taking pride in the detail.

"I offer a service called Dark Data wipe. It's legit, Dox Office approved. The organic data retrieved in that process is rich in content. Colourful, in the darkest sense. It occurred to me it was a waste to just delete it, particularly in the DreamCode market. I spend hours programming code to create realism in dreams. Escapism only works if what you're escaping to is believable. The same with nightmares – you're not going to be freaked out by a cheapskate ghost ride. For the dreamer, it has to feel authentic. Fear comes with feeling convinced. That takes a lot of c'gramming – and a lot of time.

"When I was looking to diversify, it occurred to me that here was a corner ripe for cutting: utilise the bad shit dredged in Dark Data wipes, rather than invent artificial nightmares. I developed a process for mapping the organic data – the neurological impulses that cause the night terrors – during the wipe procedure. Then I wrote software to convert the map into useable code. Think of it like this: your finger is the organic data, I take your fingerprint – giving me a two-dimensional map of that data – and I convert that map into linear code. One hundred percent artificial. Nothing chemical, or organic, which could trigger an unintended reaction. The artificial code is fully compliant with the Safe Code Act. It has standard AI functionality, nothing bespoke that could breach regulation. It can't interact with the cerebrovox implant.

Besides, it's incompatible with language code. It can't touch Klova."

"How can the brain understand it? There's only one language, even in our dreams."

"I've c'grammed the linear code so the brain can interpret it. It mimics neuro-signals, so the brain thinks it understands the code and translates it into images itself. The c'grammed code is stored in nanoware, which is meshed inside a micro-tab that the customer ingests before going to sleep. Once the nanoware establishes contact with the brain, the horror show begins."

"How long does it last?"

"Varies. More than two hours, no more than six."

"How can you be sure?"

"It has a cut-off built in. Once activated, the code will expire after three hundred and sixty minutes. It's a fine balance, taking someone so close to the edge they think they're as good as over, then pulling them back just in time. Getting the pleasure-to-terror ratio right is the critical success factor. If the balance isn't tipped in favour of pleasure, punters won't come back for more. Get the ratio right, and they slowly build a tolerance and crave the next level. Mapped Dark Data has proved a game-changer.

"I'm not into that shit myself, but there's clearly a market for it. Two weeks on the stall and word is spreading – I'm selling faster than I can code the stuff. All I'm doing is meeting demand. The only thing I've done that's remotely underhand is to use wiped material without the consent of the originator. But why would they care? They wanted rid of their baggage; I'm just recycling it. No images or data are traceable. Punters probably wouldn't even recognise their own nightmares.

"As for those who buy it, I make sure they know what they're taking on. Start them on a low grade, then build up to the heavier shit. You lot think we're all criminals, on the make no matter the cost. That ain't true. I make sure my customers are safe and I won't sell to those who I think can't hack it."

"There are plenty of criminals in Dox and you know it," said Laine. "The state lets the market operate with restrictions. You benefit from its in-kind protection. But you can't claim its clean."

"I don't – not the whole market. But I am. My stall is. And so is my product."

*

"What d'you make of that?" said Brosala.

Agents Laine and Brosala were walking slowly around the perimeter of a large atrium in the heart of Bastion HQ. The glazed ceiling, naturalistic planting and resident birds created an effective illusion of being outside, minus the cold.

"Inconclusive," said Laine, hands in pockets, head down.

"Labs are analysing the samples again, based on what he said. So far, the results corroborate his description."

"Which should be good news."

"Only, where does that leave us, right?"

"Exactly. If Exose's telling the truth, we could still have a long way to go. Well, Labs will. It'll be down to them to find the technically impossible."

"Hold on," said Brosala, stopping. His left eye glowed as he scanned the retinal display. "Update from IT. They've accessed his accounts. All names tally. Every confirmed case bought XDream from Exose in the last fifteen days."

"Any more names beyond known cases?"

"Twelve."

"Get resource on them immediately. I want those twelve tracked down now. We've got to stop them ingesting."

Brosala put the call through, while Laine paced beside him.

"Done," said Brosala.

"Okay. Next, freeze Exose's accounts and seize all assets. We don't want anyone else getting hands on his stock."

"Already sorted."

"Good. If we're right that XDream's the cause, then we've stopped the spread. We keep Exose here for a day or two, just to be sure. Then it's all eyes on Labs. We need to figure out how this supposedly safe product has managed to erase a chunk of Klova."

"What next for the Corrupted? The latest is they're stable, but there's still the risk that could change."

"Not our problem." Laine winked. "Over to the Order."

Perseverance is a characteristic I admire. Like those determined few who have scaled Witness and beheld nature's majesty from the mountain's peak, perseverance returns rich reward. To my mind, accepting the personal cost of perseverance while you make that gruelling climb is the greater glory.

That's the trick. Not letting the high price beat you – but, instead, exchange the currency and use it to fund your spirit.

I've shown perseverance of a different sort. Less battle, more endurance-over-time. The cost has been to my patience, worn gossamer-thin. And yet, at the same time, my resolve has strengthened, layer upon layer. Frustration fuels my fire.

And it has delivered me here. To this summit. To this view of profound opportunity. To the invitation: what next?

For I shall not rest on my laurels of accomplishment. I'm just getting started.

CHAPTER FOURTEEN

Lasysi hummed as its powerful mainframe-mind processed millions of code combinations, meta-testing compatibility with a formidable syntactic rule book. Ihlo watched its control panel, the status indicator barely moving. She imagined the insides of the metal cabinet to be a vast hive – worker-bytes labouring with tireless diligence, single-mindedly carrying out their common duty for the good of the Big Machine.

"I didn't stick my neck on the line for you to stand idle," said Modessr. He had slipped into the lab without Ihlo noticing and now stood scrutinising her visual. "According to disciplinary protocol, you should be suspended. You're only here because I need you here. You picked the worst possible time to go rogue."

"It wasn't a matter of choosing a time." Ihlo left her only ally and returned to the central bench.

"We have exactly one week before the system update goes live. One week to do an inordinate amount of work that the two of us will be hard pushed to complete. Your criminal behaviour could have jeopardised the entire schedule, had the Council refused my request to permit you to work."

"They've barely done that."

"Seriously? You're put out they pulled you off the investigation? What in Raptor's name did you expect? For a novice of your intelligence, you show remarkable naivety."

"The investigation should take priority over the update. I have ideas on how the Dox product might be interacting with Klova. I could save the team valuable time."

"You should have thought of that before you tipped off the press."

"I'm not going to defend my actions to you."

"No, you're not. You're here to work, not to argue for the indefensible." He moved over to his own visual beside Ihlo's and swiped with theatrical frustration. "I have revised the schedule for the rest of the week. It has required an extension to your duty hours, non-negotiable. If we are to make the deadline, we must pull our weight."

"I'm up to date with Lasysi's results. I've sent you my assessment of the last run."

"You need to repeat the last test."

"Why?"

"Because I say so."

Ihlo glared at her supervisor, powerless. Her partial suspension was tantamount to demotion. She knew Modessr would interpret her fall as a rise in his authority over her. She also knew that, if she pushed too hard, she could be out of the Order entirely. Becoming a lackey-by-proxy was frustrating, but at least she remained on the inside. Somehow, she would find a way to test her codevice ideas.

"Will you be working with me today?" she said.

"I've been called to a meeting up at the Library. Security are demanding the update be delayed while Programming work out a way to bolster the system's firewall. They're paranoid it's a cyber-attack – XDream, the trojan horse. I think they're crediting Dox's cerebrogrammers with way too much skill, but there you go. Paranoia tends to favour the irrational knee-jerk over measured reaction."

"Cyber-attack or not, it makes sense to delay the update."

"No, it doesn't."

"But—"

"Upgrade Day is not a moveable feast. Meddling from Security and Programming will send us way off-track, for Raptor knows how long. Not on my watch. We install the update with the new code and enhancements that the Machine has generated, and that this institution has spent the last year developing and testing. Then we can pool our talents and explore protection enhancements thereafter."

Ihlo gritted her teeth. Taking deep breaths, she stared through her visual to the wall beyond, counting one to ten repeatedly. In the worst possible way, Modessr was a lot like Ky, she thought. Realising this, she applied the same strategy: stop trying to reason. They can't win if you just walk away.

Modessr was oblivious of the inner battle raging beside him. He scrolled through his inbox, deleting messages from coequals he didn't like. He responded to one regarding a lunch appointment. The rest he ignored. Then, with feigned haste, he got up and said, "Will you look at the time. Mustn't be late for that meeting. You'll manage here. I'll be straight back." Then he was gone.

Ihlo did not speak or look up. Still on the one-to-ten loop, she kept her eyes on the far wall, her pulse abating. Meanwhile, her ears tracked Modessr's departure. She listened to his pompous stalk down the hallway, heard the faint tap of shoes on stone echoing down the spiral stairwell. She imagined the heavy oak door opening and closing at its foot. Then she shifted stools and faced Modessr's visual. It didn't take her long to navigate the central server to find what she was after.

With her own access blocked, she now had to rely on Modessr leaving his visual logged on to the system while away from the lab. Fortunately, his attention to cybersecurity was not as fastidious as the Department responsible for it.

Figuring she would have at least an hour, Ihlo worked with caution, wary of triggering read receipts or operation dialogues that might betray her. She opened the document she was searching for and scanned its contents with fascination. There was too much to digest. Despite the potential risk, she transferred a copy to her palm device, enciphering the file. Then she covered her tracks on the server's history and modification log. Ihlo clasped her hands, subconsciously cradling her steal. She had overheard a couple of coequals talking about the report from Bastion on the makeup of XDream. Her thoughts on how the codevice product had interacted with Klova were nebulous, but she felt a warm, bubbling confidence that she was on to something. Now, with Bastion's analysis, she could test her theory and, if right, expedite the Order's inevitably laggard investigation.

She was about to return to her own visual when something on Modessr's caught her eye: a locked file. On anyone else's visual this would mean nothing – her own user area was full of them. But on Modessr's? He followed every rule and procedure diligently, without question or hesitation. If an action was not prescribed by official protocol, he deemed it superfluous and would cut every corner until he only had curves. File management was not a written procedure, therefore, it was dispensed with as a waste of time. Ihlo stared at the incongruous icon, her curiosity stirred. The security measure wasn't a barrier; Ihlo was adept at picking locks. She touched the file, opening a window that might hint at a back door.

Her curiosity made her oblivious to the sounds around her. Lasysi's silence fell on deaf ears. She did not hear the break bell ring. She did not detect the faint tap of shoes on stone, with gradual crescendo as they ascended the stairwell. She did not hear the stalking steps in the hallway, approaching the lab door. Not until the very last moment did the sounds of warning penetrate her mind and trigger the alarm. The latch clicked and the door swung open. Modessr stood on the threshold, scowling at his charge.

"What do you think you're doing?"

Ihlo stared through her own visual, her body rigid. Having shifted to her seat a split second before, she had thought she had got away with it. Now she doubted that hope.

"Lasysi's idle. Why haven't you launched the next test? Every minute that machine is not churning is a minute wasted. Its efficiency depends upon you."

"I had to back up the last results. I'm about to start the test now." Ihlo hurried over to Lasysi, her fingers trembling. She had just caught Modessr's visual in her peripheral vision. The dialogue window beside the locked file was still open. Ihlo stared at Lasysi's control panel, unable to breathe.

"Well, make haste. I've had enough time wasted this morning, I don't need you to add to the loss."

Distraction. That was it. On that score, Modessr was easy prey. Ihlo's mind pulled itself together as Lasysi blinked and returned to life. She turned to her supervisor, establishing eye contact and holding on tight.

"What happened? I thought you had important Library business?"

"Quite so. Hence hurrying up there. However, I arrive on time for the Security meeting, only to be told it's been pushed back by forty-five. Not only have I wasted time in a needless return trip, I now must go back – and at the hour I take lunch."

"Why don't we head over to the refectory now? The test is running. By the time we're done with lunch, the results will be ready for me to assess, and you can go straight from the refectory to the Library, save you going back and forth."

Modessr subconsciously rubbed his stomach, nodding. "Good idea. Yes. Let's do that."

Ihlo had already grabbed her overcloak. She headed towards the door, stopping in front of Modessr's transparent visual.

"Shall we?" she said, holding out her hand in the gesture of lead-the-way. Modessr complied, as she knew he would. They walked together down the dark hallway, Modessr contemplating his menu choice, Ihlo thankful that her supervisor was so self-absorbed that he wouldn't wonder at her change in behaviour.

All through lunch, Ihlo pictured the open dialogue window, sick at the thought of how close she had come to being caught. As soon as she could get away, she hurried back to the lab and closed the evidence. Restoring the visual to how Modessr had left it that morning, Ihlo glanced at the locked file, but resisted the temptation. Her nerves couldn't take a second close call in the same day. Instead, she resolved to unpick the lock another time. With a copy of the Bastion report in her possession, she had got what she wanted. Greed wasn't her style.

Mercifully, Modessr didn't return for the rest of the afternoon. Ihlo worked hard, conducting test after test, scrutinising the results until her eyes and head ached with the strain. Determined to give him no cause to complain, she worked beyond her extended hours, hitting send on her final report at the very last moment before leaving, so that he could see how late she had stayed – if he bothered to look.

By the time she left her department building and descended the cobbled lanes of Mount Az, it was already dark. She wandered through the east arch and along the borderline between Ezra and Riker Quarters. The sounds and smells coming from either side were inviting: music, laughter and a rich palimpsest of cooking aromas. The Old Quarters came alive at night; Ihlo longed to submit to the lure of leisure. Yet, already exhausted, she knew she faced a tough week ahead. She also wanted to be home, locked in her room, so she could read her steal.

Once home, her enthusiasm was tempered by the presence of her cousin, who had followed her into the kitchenette. Ky hovered, arms crossed, her dishevelled hair bunched up with a cable tie.

"I thought they suspended you," she said.

"They did."

"So, why're you in costume?"

Ihlo said nothing. She had intended to make a sandwich, but her appetite faded at the first sign of attack.

"Or are you just dressing up for old times' sake? Ponce around town, pretend like you're still in the band."

"Drop it, Ky. I'm done with taking shit for one day."

"I'm just asking a question."

Ihlo sighed. "My supervisor's got me slaving in the lab. I'm suspended from all other duties and privileges."

"Knocked yourself right off your high horse." Ky smiled. "Was it worth it?"

Empty handed, Ihlo squeezed past Ky and headed for her room. Ky followed.

"Why did you do it, anyway? That's what I can't work out. You're supposed to be the brains in the family, and yet you're clearly fucking nuts."

Ihlo opened the door to her room and attempted to close it behind her. Ky had already wedged it open with her foot and now stood on the threshold, hands gripping the jamb on either side.

"Don't ignore me."

"Ky, I'm tired. I don't want to talk about this now."

"You're not high and mighty anymore. You and me, we're level. Get used to it."

"Fine. Now, can you leave my room?"

"No. Tell me why you did it."

"Why do you care?"

"I don't. Idle curiosity. Nothing to do with giving a fuck." She glared at Ihlo, who had sat on her bed, her expression blank. "Look at you. Still smug. Still think you've the right to look down on me. Open your eyes, cousin. The perspective's changed. You're a ground-level waster, looking up at the likes of me who've got our shit together. There's more to being wise than brains. You've got nothing over me now. Nothing. Time to start showing *me* some respect for a change. I'm the smart one here. You're just the novice who fucked everything up."

Her final blow delivered, Ihlo heard Ky stomp down the hallway, followed by a slammed door. She closed her eyes and took a deep breath. Bruised despite herself, she slowly rose and shut her own door, turning the lock.

Relieved by solitude at last, she sat at the small desk opposite her bed and woke her visual, triggering an automatic sync with her palm device. The enciphered document appeared on her home screen. Before opening it, she moved the document to a folder, hidden deep within her filing system, and activated a security box around it, rendering the file invisible. She then took time retracing her steps, erasing any data-print that could point the way. Finally, she returned to the document and opened it.

Bastion's analysis of XDream was detailed, covering both the code and how it might function once ingested. Codevice products had to comply with mandatory regulation as prescribed by Public Health, with ad-hoc scrutiny by the Order. As part of her training prior to entering the Order,

Ihlo had spent a year working on various products, assessing their performance and impact alongside Klova's code, examining potential for interaction and contamination. Dox cerebrogrammers had spent decades developing compliant code that kept a safe distance from Klova, but which the brain could still process and respond to.

Grasping the thrust of Bastion's report, Ihlo moved on to study the cerebrogrammer's bespoke code. Bastion's Lab techs were skilled, but pragmatic in their approach. Ihlo suspected that locating the cause of the connection would require something different: a floating perspective, free of assumption, association – even logic. She stared at the data – at the white space between code sequences, the placing of commands, the construction of algorithms, the nature of AI functionality, the character of neural networks. Reimagining the code in three-dimensional space, Ihlo wanted to delve deeper, peer around corners, look behind obstacles.

Somewhere in this colossal labyrinth, Ihlo knew there had to be some means of connection. A point of contact, a bridge – slim fingers that reached out and gently touched the hand of Klova. She also knew it could take her weeks to find it.

You're probably wondering, why the past?

Why, indeed.

More accurately, what these poor mites have lost is the code that signals the past tense – the grammar that gives time in the past its meaning. Erase that little piece of the puzzle and you find yourself having a rather profound impact.

That's what I'm after, you see. Impact.

Well, to start with, anyway.

CHAPTER FIFTEEN

In the hothouses and Quads, across the speaker squares and parks, aboard the silent Swifts, a change could be felt in the city of Arteza. Likewise in towns and cities, villages and energy farmsteads peppered across Iso-Klovaine, difference clouded the clean air. The change began as something subtle, amorphous. Yet, once it began to take shape, muster articulation, its influence became progressively apparent.

The driving force of this change was fear. The Corruption represented a toxic threat, unforeseen and far-reaching. Whilst the national press reported the suspected link to a specific codevice product, now withdrawn from the market, the language used lacked conclusiveness and, therefore, the remedy of reassurance. Ubimedia's claims were more assertive, but many of these were contradictory and groundless. They were believed, but not trusted. The result was a reactionary mood that swelled and swayed with the currents of gossip and comfort-seeking consensus.

A realisation had dawned: everyone was at the mercy of something beyond their control. Dependence on artificial language was a fact of life. The notion that the mechanisms of language were impervious had been a faith of life. The Order perpetuated this belief through their own unwavering faith in the Savants' legacy and their ability to protect it. Over centuries, votaries had willed perfection into language and infallibility into the tech and the Machine that kept it alive. Now, for many outside of the Order, that faith was shaken. Cracks appeared in assurances. Doubt filled the void. Fear followed doubt. Dependence on Klova became a looming vulnerability. Without knowing its exact cause, its capacity to mutate, the full extent of the damage, people came to regard the Corruption as a latent threat they were powerless to protect themselves against.

Blame can assuage fear, at least in the short term. The Order became the obvious target for some. Reputational damage was regarded as a given; people were simply demanding what's due. Meanwhile, the Order made all the right noises to appease the majority. They had elevated the investigation to emergency status; Bastion were close to a breakthrough; votaries were confident they could repair the damage; they had this under control. For most people, the target for blame was selected according to the principle of consequence. The codevice factor pointed a more satisfying finger of responsibility, prompting the use of trite clichés to direct accusation and abuse: *what goes around, comes around; take the risk, you invite the Raptor's wrath; charmbirds can't sing for their sins.* The Corrupted were viewed as culpable for their condition. By some unknown, unchallenged association, many regarded them as responsible for the threat that now befell them all.

Although such attitudes were not universal, pockets of prejudice spread – a creeping oil slick, slow and toxic. Opinionated minds banged the loudest drums. Ubimedia provided a pervasive platform on which to construct the narrative. Consumers lapped it up. Controversy around the cause turned to consensus on the self-defiled. XDream's USP provided a scandalous means of attack. Exose Ray was the degraded designer of dark poison; the Corrupted were the masochists who indulged.

Exose was aware of his portrayal in the narrative. He had spent years crafting his persona, colouring his rep. This unintended embellishment suited his image, to his mind. Public perception was a critical currency in Dox's complex trade arrangements. XDream's demise earnt Exose more than he could have sold it for. Biding his time in Detention, he considered the windfall and opportunities for cashing in.

Ink is all too aware of his own and his kindred's portrayal. There are no visible signs to distinguish the Corrupted from the masses. As long as he remains silent and hides the hallmarks of paranoia and fear, he can pass as unafflicted. But for him, that would be a gainless lie. The Undertow is a community to which he has mercifully come to belong. Ubi's poorly disguised abuse is both a personal attack and an attack on the collective. He wonders if society regards empathy obsolete, or if it's a pick-and-choose kindness.

Meanwhile, his idea for public speaking founders in the face of public reception. Several of the Undertow book slots on speaker squares. They take the dais, their voices made powerful by passion and conviction. Before stunned audiences, they speak of their affliction, share their own fears, describe their struggles with displacement and loss at having no concept of, or language to speak of, the past. Then, one by one, they are shouted down. Heckled into silence. Forced to flee.

In one speaker square in Welling Blink, a fight breaks out. Members of the Undertow are among the crowd – moral support for their comrade on the dais. As the public start hurling derogatory ubi-authored slogans at the speaker, she stands her ground. Her defiance is met with anger. Someone throws a carton of hot coffee at her. She screams as the coffee scalds her face. An Undertow ally sees the culprit, pushes his way through the crowd and grabs him. Their fight spreads into a wider, chaotic brawl. People are unsure of who is friend or foe. That doesn't stop them. Law Enforcement appear soon after and break up the fight. Eight people are arrested, including five of the Undertow. The speaker is attended to by a medic, who treats her for superficial burns and penetrating shock.

ArtezAlert is also quick to the scene. Journalists interview several of the crowd who claim to be witnesses. When asked about the projectile aimed at the speaker, they all insist nothing was thrown. If coffee was spilt, it was an accident. They all accuse the speaker of making inflammatory statements in a shoddy public performance. Regarding the brawl, they each claim a group of Corrupted started it for no reason other than they were looking for a fight. They speculate aggression could be a new symptom and suggest that perhaps Public Health should investigate. Ubimedia picks up the interview, focusing on the comments of the crowd. Images of blood-smeared Corrupted top and tail the text. The story goes viral. Ren suggests they abandon the idea. For now.

Despite the negative coverage, the Undertow grows in membership. As the afflicted feel increasingly marginalised within society, they seek communion in the support network. All those who suffer join the group, whether they attend the meetings or simply find comfort in belonging. As a precaution, mindful of public opinion's toll on its members, the Undertow withdraw. They are two hundred in a population of forty-eight million. They know their voice will not be heard. Instead, they look inward, establishing a supportive environment in which to share their experience of their mutual plight. Meetings are held more frequently. The elderly caretaker at Physical Books quits her post, making no effort to hide her motive. On impulse, Ink volunteers to cover the role while the bookshop owner advertises for a permanent replacement. Ubimedia has made common knowledge the fact that the owner is a proponent of the Corrupted's corner, despite the impact it's having on the business. Applications for the post are scant.

Although he hadn't stopped to think before volunteering, Ink finds himself settling into the role. It's a distraction at a time of day when he needs it most. He is managing to function at work now, but the effort is exhausting. Friends are supportive, but mostly at arm's length. Solitude in the dark well of free time is a hellhole he does his best to avoid. Keyholder responsibility for the nightly meets helps with that, along with a growing sense of purpose, a feeling that strikes him as oddly fresh and unfamiliar.

Meanwhile, the Undertow continue to rely on the cheap rent for the bookshop's back room, funded by the owner's rich compassion. Not wanting to take advantage, Ren attempts to book the local community hall, but is fobbed off with tenuous excuses. She is met with a similar reaction when she approaches community provision in other districts. Physical Books remains their haven.

This evening, turnout is high. Ink stands among his comrades, who now fill the back room. Ren steps up onto the wooden crate in the centre.

"Tonight is an open session – your chance to offload. Keep it brief so everyone has a turn who wants it. And when you're not talking, you're listening. We all need both, so let's help each other out. Who wants to go first?"

Ren vacates the crate, and a middle-aged man takes her place.

"I'm becoming used to people talking different, saying things I don't understand. It feels like there's no change in the way I think and speak as I've nothing to compare it to. Only, I know that's not true. More and more, I can't get over the feeling of loss, even though I've no idea *what* is lost. I don't know what I'm missing, but the not-there void's like a phantom limb. And it hurts." His voice brakes and he steps down. Many among the crowd nod, identifying with his analogy – and his pain.

A young woman steps up, her expression slack.

"My family blames me. Because of me taking XDream. They say they hope I regret what I do to myself. Then we fight even more because I don't know what they mean – what they expect me to feel. Regret? That's just an idea. How am I supposed to *feel* it? That's why I'm scared it's spreading, that I'm losing more. It's not just part of an idea of time that they have and we don't. It goes beyond that."

Another woman, older, more worn down, takes her place.

"I feel like nothing I do matters. Everything is in this moment. I don't want to think of the future because it frightens me. There is only now. And there is no consequence to now. Everything I do amounts to nothing."

On and on. Ink listens, sharing in the suffering of those who speak. Some ways of describing their experience are new to him, yet he can identify with them all. Although painful to hear, he finds it helps, this joint discovery of new ways to express the loss of this thing they cannot conceive of. Between them, they are curating descriptions – the means to talk about the part of language they lack. Ink collects these descriptions like precious passages in a book. Later, back home in his apartment, he will carefully turn the pages, absorbing the words, building up the picture layer by layer. Like all in the Undertow, he is creating a stencil of the void by describing the size and shape of everything surrounding it.

*

In Bastion HQ, there was no time to dwell on the past – or the future, which suddenly appeared not how they had imagined it. Agents sat glued to their visuals, scurried between meeting rooms, or talked rapidly to the voice in their NuBs. The atmosphere was charged with urgency and alarm. The tension was enough to choke on.

Agents Laine and Brosala stood among colleagues in one of the briefing rooms, their expressions shifting as the news sank in. Someone from Top Floor was positioned at the far end of the room, all eyes upon her.

"Of the nineteen new cases reported, we have now confirmed identities and completed prelim questioning. None of the names appear on Exose Ray's accounts. We must proceed on the assumption they're buying from someone else. Exose maintains no one had eyes on the blueprint, nor access to his stock prior to its confiscation. This means someone managed to hack into his system before we shut it down – or they've somehow worked out how to manufacture based on a product sample that's unaccounted for. Questions?"

Laine was quick to step in. "Where does this leave us with Exose? We've held him for seventy-two already. We've got nothing that sticks."

Top Floor hesitated, then said, "Press on the question of accomplice – although we know that's not his style. Give it another twenty-four. Stay on his case. Force him to slip. If you've nothing after that, you'll need to begin procedure for release, but take your time. Put a trade ban on him – and surveillance. We'll soon know if he's involved."

"These new cases," said another agent, "you said the symptoms are different. In what way?"

"Their language and cognition are affected like before. However, it appears to be different Klova code that's been impaired. They can talk about the past. They just can't talk about themselves."

PART TWO

I didn't set out with a finite plan.

I wanted to trigger the start of something that posed inherent potential for the abysmal. Enormity of scale feels appropriate, given the context.

Now that I've set the ball rolling, it's a case of letting nature take its course. I'm curious to see what that course might be, the turns it might take, the detours.

As for the conclusion – the inevitable destination – I already know what that will be.

For this is all a demonstration, you see. Proving a rather fundamental point.

Let's see how we get there.

CHAPTER SIXTEEN

"**Y**ou seriously think I would work with someone else?" Exose was done with calmly biding his time. The news that someone had ripped off his premium product had replaced his cool with a rage he struggled to contain.

"We have to ask the question," said Laine. They were sat facing each other in an interview room in Bastion Detention. Brosala loitered by the door, visibly intimidated. Laine held her nerve. "And now we've asked it. So, next question. Who do you think's behind it?"

"Let me out of this shithole and I'll find out."

"Help us first, then we'll talk about release."

"Look, I've no idea who's behind it. There's plenty of braindeads in Dox, but no one with a death wish."

"Anyone with the cerebrogramming skills to create a replica?"

"Are you fucking serious?" He glared at Laine.

"Okay, okay. Again, I have to ask. We need to know if they stole from your supply, or if they're making their own."

"Both impossible."

"And yet…"

"Why do you still think XDream's behind all this, anyway? I've told you why it can't touch Klova. Your own geeks can't find how the codes connect."

"All the new cases say that's what they took. We don't yet know how they got hold of the product, but I'm fairly sure they didn't buy from you."

Exose shook his head, rocking slightly. "I need to get out of here. I'll find the bastard. No one rips from me and gets away with it."

"We'll release you soon enough, but you're banned from Dox, you know that. You can't go looking in the market. The minute you break the conditions of release, you'll be back here with a charge against you. That's twelve months minimum."

"Let me go."

Laine looked into Exose's eyes, assessing opportunity against a framework of risk. Without breaking eye contact, she said, "Brosala, make a start on the paperwork. Fast track the release." She sat back, arms crossed. "Okay, Exose. Listen good. We all want to know who's behind this. That's the only reason I'm letting you walk. But know that we're watching you. Keep it legal and you won't find me bothering you. I'm figuring you're more use to us out than in – but if you prove me wrong on that, I'll haul your arse straight back to Detention. Make yourself useful. And don't make me regret giving you a chance over following orders."

*

"You sure about this, boss?" said Brosala. He was sat at the controls of their vehicle, pulling out of the Scarab's subterranean park-up to join the lunchtime traffic. It had taken just an hour to complete the fast-track process and release Exose Ray – formerly prime suspect responsible for the Corruption, now unspoken aid to the Bastion agent leading the investigation into it.

"Of course I'm not sure," said Laine from the back seat, her left eye scanning the latest lab results. "A case of favouring opportunity over fruitless procedure. My mother used to gamble; it comes naturally."

"Do you think Exose will play nice?"

"I think he wants to find his code thief as much, if not more, than we do. He may not play nice, but I think he'll get results. And he's smart. Beneath all that mean-man posturing, I believe Exose is one astute individual. He won't risk a twelve-month stint, I'm sure of that."

"So, what's the plan?"

"We cover the turf he can't touch, starting with our friend in 198 – see how she's getting on with her new tech. She might be ready for more."

They joined the central circular around the Old Quarters, crossed Nova Junction, then headed southeast through Cryals Cross and into the corner of Cope. This time, the nature of their business didn't require advanced notice. As the Bastion agents, puffed up in full field gear, passed through the innocuous entrance and into the warren, alarmed customers scurried in every direction like ship-sinking rats. Laine and Brosala ignored them. Eyes dead ahead, they navigated the memorised maze, ascending to the fifth floor and the unlocked door of stall front 198. Kite was sat at a tech-laden workbench against the far wall, her back to the door. Head down, absorbed in the display screen of a large, metal box, she did not hear Bastion enter.

"Nice set-up," said Laine, nodding in feigned appreciation.

Kite jumped, then immediately regained her composure. She leant against the bench, blocking the box's display, and cocked her head.

"What you want?"

"Just checking we kept our side of the bargain," said Laine. "Perhaps, now you're up and running, you've realised you're missing a vital piece of kit. Something extra special."

"I ain't no rat."

"I don't recall saying you are."

"Then why're you offering me more shit? I'm done trading with Bas. That was a one-off."

"And so is this." Laine smiled. "Exose Ray has been released from custody. He seemed in a rush to get away. Didn't he, Agent Brosala?" Laine didn't turn around. Brosala nodded, hamming up his part regardless. "Do you know why, Kite?"

"Did you go tell him it was me who snitched? You can't do that. That's not game."

"He didn't hear it from us, I assure you. But he knows. I suspect he's on his way right now."

Kite swallowed hard, tugging at a tuft of purple hair. "Before. You said you could give me protection. For free, you said."

"Inflation."

"That's not fair."

"Life ain't." She saw Kite's face twitch. "Here's the deal. Brosala can put a call through right now, make Dox off limits. Exose will receive the ban in minutes. He won't be allowed to set foot in the market – and he'll know better than to try."

Kite looked from Laine to Brosala, who held a finger tantalisingly close to his NuB.

"What's the price?" she said.

"XDream's still out there. Either someone stole from Exose's stock, or they've snatched the recipe and they're cooking up their own. Doesn't matter which, we just need to know who."

"I don't know, I swear."

"That may be. But you can find out."

"I can't go nosing. Market rules. No questions. Come on. Ask for something else."

"We don't want anything else."

"Exose. He could be here any minute. Please."

"As I said before, you're smart. You'll find a way to get the intel we're after. Eyes and ears, Kite. Wall flies don't need to ask questions."

Kite gnawed at her nails, frowning hard. Laine glanced over her shoulder at Brosala. Brosala caught the look. He cleared his throat and activated his retinal screen.

"Ah, Agent Laine, sighting by surveillance. District border between Cryals Cross and Cope. Exose must be close."

"Okay, okay," said Kite. "I'll do it. Make the call now. Don't let him come in."

Laine nodded to Brosala, who turned and pretended to speak to his NuB.

"The right decision," said Laine.

"I can't promise I'll deliver. What if no one spills?"

"All we're asking is that you try your best. And in return, we'll try our best to protect you. There's no guarantees in life, right?" She stood up. "If you hear anything, use the same drop-box code we gave you last time. It's secure, no trace back to you." She turned to go.

"Wait!" said Kite. Laine stopped and looked back. "I ain't no fucking rat."

Agent Laine smiled.

*

A block beyond Dox, Laine and Brosala stood beside their vehicle, cartons of cabin coffee in hand. It was bitterly cold. However, their training taught them that uniform's a statement, and Laine never liked to pass up an opportunity to make one. Feeling the eyes of passers-by on her, she stared ahead, warmed by reaction.

"Do you think she'll play ball?" said Brosala.

"Hard to say. She's got her own agenda going on. Guess it depends how well the ask fits with her game plan – or how much trouble she finds herself in."

"Which could be not much. Exose's hell-bent on finding who stole his product. Before long, she must realise he's not after her."

"That's why we've still got the upper hand. Rumours spread fast. It wouldn't take long for Exose to discover he's reason to add her to his hit list."

Brosala glanced at her, eyebrows raised.

"What? We're on a mission to save Klova here. The insurance of last resorts." She downed the rest of her coffee and screwed up the carton. "What's new?"

Brosala's left eye roamed. "Prelim interviews logged with second phase cases. All showing the same errors in terms of code loss. All confirm taking what they believe to be XDream, but none can name the source."

"Can't, or won't?"

"Can't. They say no one was selling it in Dox, but they'd heard it was available in *Trans:akshn*."

"As in the game?"

"As in the market hidden inside the game. It's the same iCon platform, but a buried level with an entirely different function."

"Since when have codevice traders operated in VR?"

"This is the first we've heard of it. Trade in *Trans:akshn* costs. It's the reserve of high-end illegals – embezzlement, fraud, blackmail, art theft – that sort of thing. Codevice is too pedestrian. Doesn't warrant the outlay."

"Begging the question why a rip-off of a banned product is being sold there."

"Next move?"

"Time to talk to our second generation afflicted. Line up interviews. Let's see what else we can squeeze out of them. Meanwhile, keep an eye on Surveillance chat. Exose's on a mission. I want to know where that takes him."

*

Kite hadn't moved from her stall since Bastion had left her over an hour ago. She didn't trust Bas, especially Agent Laine with her patronising tone and arrogant sneer. She trusted Exose far less. She knew his rep and the stories of how he'd earnt it. She doubted a location ban would stop him from storming through Dox if he had a mind to. Besides, paranoia perched on her shoulder, whispering what-ifs. If Bas hadn't told him it was her who had snitched, then who had? She had assumed she was too lowly a trader to warrant a bug in her stall. No one paid her any attention, apart from to bitch about her poke. Her poke, Borro. *Maybe it's him?* she thought. She tried to remember if he'd been hanging around that day. Maybe he saw her draw Bas into her stall. Maybe he'd added two and two and got word to Exose based on the math. Her addled mind couldn't think straight. Panic fuelled her pestering paranoia. All she could do was remain there and wait. If Exose was on his way, there was no point running. If he stuck to the Dox ban, then she had nowhere else to go.

Because Exose knew. After Dox, there's only one place she'd be.

She thought of her old man, stuck at home, alone. Come evening, he'd be getting worried. And hungry.

Trapped and afraid, she looked to last resorts. Withdrawing into the far corner of her stall, she tapped her NuB and triggered the call.

"*What are you doing?*" hissed the voice in her ear. "*I told you never to call direct.*"

"Except in an emergency, you said. This is an emergency."

"*I somehow doubt that.*"

"Exose's after me. He knows I snitched on him. He'll cut me, I know it. I need protection."

"*You know I can't get involved.*"

The voice in her ear was all blades and broken glass. Yet panic made her deaf to its edge.

"Yes, you can. You've got means. There must be strings you can pull. Get him arrested again."

"*You made the mistake. You deal with the consequence. Don't contact me again.*"

The call was terminated.

Kite stood in the cover of shadows, surrounded by proof of the trade. She was not one for regret. Mistakes were lessons learnt. Instead, she resolved to get smart. An opportunity was what she needed. Her mind honed in on Bas's offer. She'd had no intention of being their fly. Maybe she didn't need to. Perhaps Bas's deal was a way out in itself. She'd have to play it wise, she knew that. The scheme was not without risk. But she wasn't afraid of risk.

She was afraid of Exose.

Who am I?

That's an interesting question. It requires a priori knowledge of the existence of the self, without knowing the identity of the self.

Take away the concept of the self – the 'I' and 'me' of cognitive awareness – and the question becomes impossible.

Imagine how that would feel – to lose all concept of one's self, the reality of one's being. In your own mind, you would no longer exist.

As I said before: impact.

CHAPTER SEVENTEEN

News of the second phase malfunction sent the Order into chaos. They had thought the crisis had been contained, the damage minimal. Relief had already begun to still the waters of shock. The whole affair had felt somewhat unreal, as the seemingly impossible is want to do. Heads were down, working to assess the damage, believing the worst was over. Then came word of the newly afflicted and their different impairment. That fact alone changed everything. The peril to Klova shifted from manageable to inconceivable. A second *seemingly impossible* event held alarming implications for probability. *What next?* they feared. *How far will it go? When will it end?* Votaries found themselves facing an unknown error that was potentially boundless – the damage to Klova, devastating.

Ihlo shared her coequals' alarm, but without their apparent surprise. She had almost seen this coming. Now, with this second malfunction, she pushed hard to be permitted back onto the investigating team. Modessr thwarted her every attempt.

"You are a novice, Ihlo. What makes you think your

contribution is so absolutely vital that the Order can't manage the situation without you?"

They were in the lab. Modessr was putting on his overcloak, about to leave for the Library.

"Please let me at least attend the briefing. Just to hear what they have to say."

"To what end?"

"This is an unprecedented crisis. The more minds on its resolution, the better."

"We have exceptional, *experienced* minds making sound progress as we speak."

"But—"

"It would appear you need reminding that you should not be here at all. Do not use this drama as a means to mask the shame of your suspension." He regarded Ihlo, seeking impact of his rebuke. "Besides, it's simply out of the question. I need you here. You've been permitted to work on the system update while your case is investigated – but that work is prescribed by me and is exclusively in support of the update. You'll talk no more of the crisis, nor of the Order's activity in relation to it. If I find you have made approaches for information behind my back, I'll have you up for a second charge of gross misconduct. Then you can confidently pre-empt the outcome of your hearing and say goodbye to your career as a votary." His warning delivered, Modessr turned and left.

It was not the threatened consequence that stunned Ihlo. She let that fall without touching her. The blow had been Modessr's refusal to set aside his power play for the sake of Klova. Even now, on the precipice of the unthinkable, he would not allow his superiority over her appear diminished by permitting her request. She wondered if he even grasped the danger that Klova – and its forty-eight million speakers – were in.

She moved over to the window and looked down on the cobbled street below. Becloaked votaries were hurrying up the hill, their motion propelled by urgent purpose, like upstream-swimming salmon. Even trapped within thick stone walls, the tension beyond them was palpable. The emergency briefing had been announced that morning. Speculation had spread rapidly, panic honing the edge of anticipation. Ihlo knew the briefing was to report Bastion's initial assessment of the second phase. She longed to hear what was said. She couldn't sit there and not know.

Having already sacrificed caution, Ihlo set Lasysi running, put on her overcloak and slipped out of the lab. Modessr had had enough of a head start – he wouldn't spot her in the migration up the mount. Her coequals would, but would think nothing of it. The briefing was open to all – and all were eager to attend. Hood up and overcloak tightly wrapped around her, Ihlo joined the steady flow towards the Library. Once near, she ducked to one side and loitered in a gap between buildings. Entering the Council chamber was out of the question; Ihlo knew she would have to eavesdrop from without – catch what she could, then hurry back to the lab before the end. She waited for the last few votaries to enter the building, then she followed behind, hanging back, head down.

By the time she found her spot – near enough to hear, yet not be seen – the briefing had already started. Ihlo crouched in the shadows, listening intently to the muffled voice of the speaker.

"…findings, based on preliminary questioning and superficial cerebrovox scan data only. Bastion will follow this with lab test results and analysis in due course. This first report is to alert the Order to the apparent variation and its effect on the afflicted, so that we can commence comparison of code loss and impact assessment."

The disembodied voice was grave. Ihlo listened, barely breathing.

"Initial investigation and subject testimony suggest at least five units of code sequence in the delta sphere have been compromised or deleted. Therefore, the affected code is predominantly grammatical, with associated lexical units – specifically, code referring to first person personal pronouns in both the nominative and objective case. In short, the afflicted cannot speak of themselves. By extension, subject testimony demonstrates they are unable to conceive of themselves.

"As with the first phase, loss of concept is universal. There is no memory of what was previously known. Afflicted subjects cannot use associated language, nor comprehend others when they speak it. Victims are unable to grasp any understanding of the concept of the self when it is explained to them. It is too early to assess the psychological impact, but Bastion's expectation is for a best-to-worst-case range of substantial to severe.

"With regard to cause, Bastion are still at the primary stage of subject tests and assessment, working with four volunteers who ingested the new product – presumed to be a replica of XDream and which will be referred to hence as XD2. Bastion are not yet in possession of the product itself. Acquisition of XD2 for detailed analysis is a primary objective for agents in the field.

"While we wait for further updates and assessment reports, the Order must focus on effect. We now have the idents for the impaired code sequences. As with the first phase, our initial task is to simulate the malfunction and model impact scenarios. We will follow protocols for impact assessment, damage limitation and code restoration. You should make yourselves familiar with the process and your department's designated function. That concludes the briefing. I now hand over to..."

Her heart and mind racing, Ihlo silently slipped away.

Back in the lab, she worked quickly so that Modessr had no cause to suspect her absence. The test procedure was so familiar, she was able to follow the steps in auto-drive, while her mind processed what she had just heard. She felt a compelling urgency that the Order's protocols simply didn't cater for. All the while, she kept thinking, *This won't end here. Why should it?*

She was rational and level-headed by nature. Yet, with her novice's fresh perspective and lack of institutional conditioning, she knew her coequals would regard her sense of urgency as alarmist. Votaries had deep-rooted faith in the meticulous machine, however slowly it moved. She also knew she had no voice. Since the leak, most votaries had treated her with disdain. The motive for her actions did not matter. They were blind to the context behind the bare criminal act, context which could make it something other than contemptuous. Ihlo knew she had no ally, no ear to bend to seek influence through back doors. If she was to fulfil her duty and act on her convictions, she knew she would have to act alone. Her first task: to obtain the code in XD2.

*

Ihlo had heard of the Undertow; ubimedia ensured everyone had. The location of their frequent meetings had also become public knowledge. Through the remainder of her duty, she resolved to find out when their next meeting was due and attend. Her hope was to meet someone there who had been caught in the second phase and ask them if they had any XD2 left, or if they would reveal their source so that she could buy some. After trawling various forums and sending an oblique message to a proclaimed member, she learnt there was a meeting scheduled for that evening.

As soon as her duty ended, Ihlo rushed home to change out of votary uniform, ruffle her slicked back hair and apply a touch of makeup. She put on black jeans and a thick woollen rollneck. Her disguise shed, Ihlo felt able to be herself. The relief that came with it was unexpected.

The Delce was some distance from her apartment in Reach. To save time, Ihlo hailed a private hire, speaking the GPS coordinates to the empty cabin. The internal lights dimmed as the vehicle silently sped away, slipping through the city streets as darkness fell. The low light and solitude gave her pause to consider the evening ahead. Before being thrown off the internal investigation, she had interviewed several of the phase one afflicted. In those early hours and days of concept loss, their distress was palpable. She was about to enter a room full of fear and despair, to witness a suffering Klova must be inadequate to describe.

The private hire reached its destination. Ihlo climbed out and hesitated, her nerve weakening. Physical Books appeared deserted, the shop window revealing only darkness beyond its unilluminated sales display. A vintage 'Closed' sign hung at an angle inside the glazed front door, confirming the obvious. As Ihlo approached, she saw a silhouette emerge from the shadows on the other side of the door. Faint light revealed a face. Then a hand reached out, unlocked and opened the door.

"Can I help you?" said the man inside.

"I've come for the meeting."

"May I ask how you know about it?"

"I saw a thread online. Contacted a member, who gave me the details." She hesitated, aware she hadn't thought this part through.

"You're not afflicted."

The question now made sense to her. "No," she said. She felt her face flush.

"This meeting's not for you," he said, his voice kind. "You don't look like you're here to cause us trouble, though. What's the real reason you've come?"

Ihlo took a deep breath. "I'm trying to work out what's causing the damage to Klova. I've been studying the coding and construction of XDream. Identifying deviation or difference in its replica might indicate what's caused the second phase variation. I need to compare the two versions of the product to do this."

"Are you Bastion?"

Ihlo shook her head. "The Order. I'm a novice votary, but I've been suspended. It was me who leaked the statement to the press."

He raised his eyebrows, then held out his hand. "I'm Ink. Afflicted. First phase."

"Ihlo." She shook his hand.

"Come, follow me."

Ihlo stepped inside and followed Ink through the dark, spine-walled maze. Their path was lit ground level by an LED pocket torch, which Ink held behind him. Bright motes drifted through the beam like gold dust in zero gravity. The air smelt of old attics and pencil shavings. They eventually reached a door.

"Meeting's underway," whispered Ink. "Tonight's an open forum for new members, victims of the second phase. Not many have come forward yet; they can't see the point so much when they can't help themselves. But there's a few we encourage to share. We can stand at the back. Shouldn't last more than an hour." He opened the door and gestured for Ihlo to enter.

The room was close to full, with everyone turned to face a low-lit space in the centre. Ihlo watched as people took tentative turns to step onto the wooden crate and share. In stilted, truncated language, they attempted to describe their experience – to articulate their perception of reality which, they instinctively knew, had changed in some fundamental, unknowable way.

A young man stepped up to take his turn.

"It's like the nightmares have carried on. Not just lost words, it's a whole damn different world. Here, but not here." He stepped down before he broke down.

"There is family," said a middle-aged woman who had taken his place, her arms limp by her sides. "Two children and a partner. They're wanting and trying to take something that isn't there. Something that can't be given. They're angry and sad. But not with each other. Angry and sad – wanting more."

"VR is the only safe place," said an elderly man. "Avatars are other people. Interact as other people. Connections everywhere. Real world? There's nothing here."

"Mirrors," said a voice from the crowd. One word from a spirit too broken to take the crate – from a consciousness unable to recognise itself.

Ihlo listened, transfixed by the testimonies of the self-less afflicted, pained by their impossible grief. At the end, a woman with wild hair stood on the crate and addressed the crowd.

"Thank you for sharing with us. You are—" She stopped herself, hand to chest. Then she started again, speaking slowly, choosing words that all could understand. "Sorry. Thanks for the courage to speak and for sharing. There is a difference in the language people lose, but all here suffer the same cause and that unites the Undertow. Welcome, new members. Now, talk together. Share. Support each other. Find and be the comfort we seek." The woman stepped off the crate and moved among the crowd.

"That's Ren," Ink said to Ihlo. "She's our spokesperson.

Holds the group together. Wait here. I'll go get her." He weaved his way into the crowd.

Ihlo stepped back, seeking cover in the shadows. Ink had been right; this meeting was not for her. She felt she was intruding on their privacy – encroaching on their union, uninvited.

Moments later, Ink returned with Ren, made brief introductions and asked Ihlo to explain her request. Ren listened intently while her eyes scrutinised the young votary. Once Ihlo had set out her idea, Ren said, "Why like this? The Order is investigating. Bastion will presumably confiscate product from those they interview. Yet, you come here, to a private meeting, out of uniform, asking sensitive questions? Forgive me, but our portrayal by ubimedia forces an uncharacteristic scepticism in me. I'm not responsible for this group, but I'll still protect every member as if I am. And something about the nature of your approach makes me feel protective."

"She's behind that leak to ArtezAlert, giving the green light," said Ink.

"Do we know that though?" Ren looked at Ihlo through narrowed eyes. "You say you're a novice? Presumably it takes years to earn even that much. Why wreck your career before it begins?"

"Because the Order would have taken too long to reach the same conclusion as me. The organisation is handbraked by bureaucracy. It does the right thing but takes forever to do so. They can't see that. They're so committed to protocol as the safeguard of best practice, they can't conceive of shortcuts. I'm new in, fresh eyes. It's blindingly obvious."

"New in and straight out, by the sounds of it."

"I swore the Oath of Service to protect Klova, not the Order."

"And your idea, you think it'll protect Klova? You believe it'll help us?"

"I can't be certain. But the answer has to be in the product. A string variable, a dynamic AI function, I don't know – something that somehow connects with Klova. I've studied XDream. If I could compare the two, I'd stand a better chance of finding it."

Ren looked from Ihlo to the mingling crowd around them, biting her bottom lip. Eventually she turned to Ink.

"You and I need to be the middlemen. I don't want anyone feeling vulnerable or obliged. We approach a hand-picked few of the second phase – I've got names in mind. See if we can get our hands on some product." She turned to Ihlo. "You only need one dose, right?"

Ihlo nodded.

"Good. Please, wait in the passage outside this room. Privacy's a comfort and this here's their space."

Ihlo waited in the narrow passageway outside the meeting room, the darkness widening space in which to think. She had come to feel a growing sense of displacement in the city she had lived her entire life. It was not because of the meeting. Rather, her exclusion gave form to the separation she had begun to feel at the Order. There, it was as if she inhabited another world, an overlayed, alternate reality. The uniform she had aspired to own felt like a being she must become. Yet, she was coming to realise the cut did not fit. Her sense of calling had led her to assume union with a community to which she had thought she belonged. With that assumption unravelling, she felt dislocated and adrift. Would her parents still be proud of her if they knew? She wondered where you draw the line at proving yourself, when your self becomes diluted in the attempt.

Lost in thought and direction, she jumped as the door to the backroom opened. Members emerged and filed down the passageway. Their chatter was low, but lighter now in register, their expressions less strained. They didn't appear to notice Ihlo as they left the meeting, heading out of Physical Books and into their new reality together. Ink emerged, too, his own expression unreadable in the darkness.

"I have to lock up," he said. "Can you hang around for a bit?"

"Of course."

She followed him to the front of the shop and lingered in the shadows as the remaining members drifted away. To each, she heard Ink offer quiet words. Ren was the last to leave. The spokesperson and caretaker did not speak. Instead, Ihlo caught an exchange of look and gesture that she couldn't interpret, then Ren left. Ink turned to Ihlo.

"Are you okay leaving through the front? Some members prefer to go out through the back. We've persistent ubi trolls. You might find your picture's gone viral by the morning."

Ihlo wrapped her overcloak tight and re-ruffled her hair. "Front door's fine."

Ink locked up behind them and set a steady pace away from the shop, to the cover of a side street, before turning to Ihlo.

"I've got a vehicle nearby. We can talk in the warm."

It was late; the streets were empty. All around them, windows in apartment blocks glowed honey, radiating the impression of warmth. In the distance, faint sounds of life: music from a late-night café; visuals turned up over-loud; urban owls on patrol; up ahead, a young couple, laughing. Ink led them to his private ride. The side door slid open, and they climbed inside. He immediately set the windows to blackout, the lights to low and the heating up. They sat facing each other.

Ink hesitated, then said, "I'm afflicted, remember. Stop me if anything's unclear."

Ihlo nodded.

"We've got someone who can help. Afflicted twenty-four hours and is in a bad way. Tonight's her first meeting. She overhears Ren speaking to someone else. Catches her and says she's got product left."

Ihlo chose her words. "She give it to you?"

"Doesn't have it on her. It's back at her apartment. We're meeting early tomorrow morning. She'll give them to me then. Two doses."

"They won't have come cheap. Let me transfer credit to you now. Then you can pass on when you collect?"

Ink shook his head. "I ask about payment. She won't take any. She doesn't know about you or your idea, only that someone wants to find out the cause and stop the spread. I get the impression that's payment enough."

"I hope I can repay her with answers. When can I collect from you?"

They arranged to meet in Kemp Quarter at noon the next day. Then Ink asked for Ihlo's coordinates, programmed the destination and set the control to autonomous. The vehicle pulled away, silently speeding west towards Reach.

Ihlo regretted the pace; there was so much she wanted to ask. She had met a handful of afflicted in the brief period she was on the Order's investigating team but had little chance to converse.

"How... how long has it been?" she ventured, wary of overstepping.

"Two weeks. I have to keep a record." He sighed, wrapping his arms around his middle.

"Sorry. It's none of my business."

"Says a votary." He almost smiled. "Go on. Ask what you like."

"How do you frame memories if you have no concept of what I call *the past?*"

"Memories in themselves can't require your concept of their place in time — because I have them. They are our brain's capacity to retain and recall things. *When* those things happen, in what order, is context, independent of the memory itself. My memories are outside of time."

"Does it affect how you relate to them?"

"I've no idea. I don't know any different. They are mental impressions, retained in limbo. They are mine. How else can I relate to them?"

"Do you recall emotions attached to them? How you felt at the time? How it makes you feel now?"

He shook his head. "They're like media clips. Saved data files. But no feelings in the data." He looked up, wary. "I take it you do?"

Ihlo's mind unconsciously returned to the last time she saw her parents before the accident. A rare meal together, joined by several of her parents' friends. She barely spoke to them all through the meal and couldn't wait to get away. Her chest tightened with the regret that would forever overlay that scene.

"It's as much a part of the memory as the picture in my head." She took a deep breath and looked at Ink. "I can't imagine…"

"No. Neither can I."

All too soon, the vehicle pulled up outside Ihlo's apartment block. "Thanks for the lift," she said. "And for your help."

"Thanks for helping us."

"Ren doesn't trust me, does she?"

Ink shrugged, his expression kind. "She's worn out and wary, reluctant to hold the hand of hope too tight. It's not you she doesn't trust."

"What about you?"

"I get where she's coming from. We're living a nightmare.

It's hard to imagine an end when you're trapped in the middle. But that shouldn't stop us trying. That's what hope is for. And you've given me hope."

This perpetual need to name.

They're calling it 'the Corruption'. Another borrowed word, by necessity, crudely assigned.

Obvious though, given the context.

Of interest, however, is the metaphorical subtext. For a nation obsessed with purity – not only in language, but in air quality, energy efficiency, environmental sustainability – they've forced a grubby smear of pollution on the pure white of perfection.

Let's talk wider definitions:

'Corruption (noun): debasement, as of language.'
I hardly think so.

Also, 'putrefactive decay; rottenness.'
Perhaps that says more about their fear of what's to come.

CHAPTER EIGHTEEN

Dawn had barely coloured the sky. The avian early risers had yet to launch into song. Most of the city still slept.

Exose Ray could not sleep. The news that someone had ripped off his product and was selling the replica outside of Dox had stirred a rage he could barely contain. One of the many benefits of his carefully crafted rep was that people were afraid to cross him. Tensions brewed between other stalls, that was part of the culture. Tough competition. But traders steered clear of Exose's turf, and he'd come to expect the wide berth. That was why he was confident the culprit was not of the Dox fraternity and the counterfeit codevice was not sold on site. With the rest of the city – the rest of the country – being relatively law-abiding line-towers, he had little to go on. With Bastion surveillance observing his every move, he had even less space to manoeuvre. Although he hated to admit it, even to himself, he needed help.

There was only one person in whom he had absolute trust. He sent an encrypted message to the man in mind, asking to meet at a speaker square in central Union. Café cabins were positioned around the perimeter, selling street-food breakfasts to passing commuters. He suggested they meet in the queue for the cabin on the north-east corner – the most popular and, therefore, the busiest. Bastion might have eyes on him – that wasn't his concern. The precaution was to protect his friend.

It was still early – at least an hour before he should sensibly leave. Exose filled the stretching time pacing back and forth, hands in pockets. His doubt was not in the man, but in the size of the favour he intended to ask. There were potential risks, aside from attracting Bastion's attention. Besides that, his friend had problems enough of his own, and of a gravity that made his seem trivial. *Is it fair to even ask?*, he thought, knowing what the answer would be.

Still clutching the doubts, Exose left his apartment and flagged a private hire. The shortest route from his place in the outskirts of Cope to the district of Union was the central circular, but he knew it'd be rammed with rush hour traffic. Instead, he set the controls to manual and sped through back streets, undertaking trams, running several lights. He wasn't short on time, he had only ever learnt the Dox way of driving. Stopping and releasing the private hire, Exose walked into the square, merging with the stream of pedestrian commuters. Heading for the north-east cabin, he recognised the dishevelled hair of a man to his left. As Exose casually approached the queue, so did his contact.

"Morning, Ink," he said without looking at him.

Ink stood directly in front of Exose in the line. "It's good to see you," he said, voice low, lips barely moving. "I worry about you, thinking Bastion will keep hold of you."

"Finally had to admit this ain't my fault. They've gone off chasing a thief instead."

"Good. I'm hearing about XD2."

"Is that what they're calling it? Fucking insult, start to finish." Exose fought to contain his anger and maintain their cover. "But enough. Tell me, how are you? Been offered help yet?"

"Nothing official. But I join a group – victims providing their own victim support. That's helping." They both shuffled forward in the shrinking queue. "Your message. You need my help?"

"I need to know who's 'gramming this crap."

"I hear nothing."

"Whoever's behind it is still selling. Word is trade's done in *Trans:akshn*. Not great news, for obvious reasons. I need to know if that's true and what the set-up is, how it looks – in case there are clues. I just need a scrap to build on, so I can work out who it is."

"You want me to shop in *Trans:akshn*?"

"I was wondering if you'd consider it. I'd go myself, but there's no way they'll let me in. But look, I appreciate it's a massive ask, especially with what you're going through. Don't feel you have to say yes. You're my first choice, not my only option." He looked at the back of Ink's head, at his haywire hair and hunched shoulders. "Shit. I shouldn't be asking you at all."

Ink nodded briefly, limited with what body language Exose could see. "I'll give it a go. Of course I will."

"Really? Ink, thank you. I can't tell you." He saw the queue ahead shortening too fast. "Listen. iCon's cybersecurity's bound to be fist-tight in and out of the platform, but once you're inside, I've heard it's not all AI. You should be dealing with people behind the avatars – and people fuck up. Ask a few questions if you can. And take note of little details. It's easy to write something of yourself into the world you build, which means it's easy to give yourself away."

"I'll try and find you something to go on."

"This is huge. Thank you. I'll make it up to you, I promise."

As Exose said this, Ink reached the end of the queue. "Coffee, please," he said to the man behind the counter. Once handed his carton, he slowly walked away, tipping his head in a way only a man right next to him would see.

*

Opposite an apartment block in Reach, Ink waits. He came straight from meeting Exose and he's early; it's another ten minutes before the woman said she'd be there to hand over. He watches the block where she lives, pristine white render reflecting the morning sun. He closes his eyes, imagining he can feel a trace of warmth in the light's bright path. Just like in the dreams. Exose always writes a scene bathed in warm sunshine into his DreamCode blend – another regular feature, tailor-made.

Exose. His release from Detention fills Ink with relief. It's not enough that he knows Exose is innocent; that won't protect his friend. Ink had feared it would be a case of having to prove his innocence to people who assume the worst and who need results. He would have fought to find a way, of course, but better not to have to. Lacking the capacity to reflect, Ink can't dwell on how their friendship has deepened over the years since Neav's death. It is simply present and will remain so. There is no call to question it, just as there was no call to hesitate when Exose asked for help. That is how he views the favour asked, now, in this moment. There is no call to consider the risks, whatever they may be. Of course he will help him.

Just then, a woman emerges from the door to the apartment block and begins walking, gesturing for Ink to follow. He catches up and falls in beside her.

"Someone up there," she says, nodding back to the building. "They mustn't see."

Ink catches glimpses of the woman as they walk. Her pallid face is in stark contrast to the bruise-like shadows around wide, owl eyes. Knowing the cause, Ink also knows she's in the midst of a terrifying adjustment.

"It gets a little easier," he offers. "Especially with the help of the Undertow."

The woman doesn't respond. Her lips are closed tight, her jaw clenched. They keep walking, in the direction of a Swift dock at the end of the road. Before they reach it, the woman nudges Ink with her arm and takes hold of his gloved hand. He can feel something small and rigid in the cup where their palms should touch. She quickly withdraws her hand, and he closes his own around the object she's left there.

"Thanks," he says. "This could hold the answers we need. Then this nightmare will be over. Have hope."

The woman remains silent.

Wary of pushing his luck with this frail, fragile wound, Ink adds, "I'm trying to find out who's selling this. Who's behind it. I know the rules, the things you don't say. But we're on the same side, so I'm going to ask. Please, can you tell me anything about where you bought this from?"

The woman's eyes fill with wet pain. She half-runs away, leaving Ink to realise his mistake – too late to take back the words she can't understand.

Ink finally makes it to his office an hour late. Before long, he will be slipping away to meet the novice votary, to hand over the small box of hope. In the meantime, he has an impossible deadline to make. A backlog of work has built up – and not just from the days he called in sick. Concentration is proving an unattainable presence of mind. He has managed to hide his affliction at work. While worth it for good reason, the pretence is exhausting.

At the desk beside his, Over-confident Colleague leans

back in her chair, staring at the projected hologram in her palm.

"Outrageous," she mumbles, her expression one of delight. She twitches fingers, causing the page to scroll and refresh. "No way." The mumbling rises in volume and pitch. "That's insane." She looks up and scans the heads down, desperate to share. She fixes her sights on her neighbour. "Hey, Ink. You seen this?"

Ink pretends not to hear.

"Ballard. Hey. Check this out."

He stares intently at his visual, pretend-typing nonsense. "I can't stop. I'm up to the wire. I'll look later."

"I won't find it later. News isn't lasting five seconds." She swivels her chair around and scoots up beside him, holding up her palm to his face. "Look."

Left with little choice, Ink leans back to focus on the hologram. There is a photograph of a small group of people stood outside a government building, a thick strip of white tape stuck over their mouths. They hold banners, with slogans declaring: *Denied a Voice* and *Victims of disOrder*. Below the picture, a tag line in outraged uppercase: *THE PRICE OF VICE*.

"A protest," says Ink, unwilling to read the predictable ubi angle.

"I know!" She holds her other hand out to give Ink his due. "Right?"

Ink just looks at her.

"Can you believe it? These people are shameless. What do they hope to achieve? Pulling stunts like this, antagonising people. Calling themselves *victims*. Come on." She glares at Ink, eyebrows raised, waiting for him to pick up the baton.

Raging inside, Ink refuses to be drawn in. "Look, I haven't time right now." He turns back to his visual, clicking and swiping at random.

Over-confident Colleague, her palm still held up, sags a little. She hesitates, then swivels her chair a full one-eighty, until she spies a more dependable audience. Throwing Ink a sour-faced parting glance, she tuts, sticks up her chin, then stalks over to her target. "Hey, Caso, check this out."

What scrap of concentration Ink had nursed is now destroyed. He had planned to leave soon; that time becomes now. He puts on his coat and overcloak and hurries out of the office, failing to block out the scandal frenzy kicking off at Caso's desk. He had arranged to meet Ihlo in Kemp's Quad – a Swift ride away, affording him a moment's peace to recover. This meet up is important. The last thing he wants to do is pollute it by carrying the noxious taste of ubi's poison.

*

Ihlo reached the Quad entrance at the same time as Ink. On the threshold, she looked into his eyes, searching, hoping.

"It's okay. I have them," he said.

Inside the Quad, they took a seat in a corner booth and ordered spiced tea. The place was busy, the atmosphere convivial. Sunshine poured through the glazed ceiling, adding the impression of warmth to the efficiently heated square. Pet parakeets fluttered between kousa trees. Mute charmbirds watched from their perches. Somewhere, a piano played.

"I feel like I'm meeting a different person," said Ink.

Ihlo flushed, her fingertips touching her requisite hairstyle and starched tunic.

"Sorry," he added. "I don't mean to embarrass you. It's just... you look so different."

"I always thought I'd be proud to wear the uniform."

"You're not?"

"My cousin calls it a costume. For once, she's about right."

Ihlo flashed a small smile. The ice broken, she relaxed a little. "Turns out my rosy-glow preconception of the prestigious Order was somewhat inflated."

"I don't know any other votaries. You're all rather cloaked in mystery."

"Cloak being the operative word. Different story underneath."

"But still – the skills, the expertise. What the Order does for Klova is remarkable. You've every reason to be proud."

A waiter approached with their tea, placing lidded ceramic mugs before them. Without speaking, they both lifted the lids, releasing wafts of cardamom and fennel.

"Klova means everything," said Ihlo. "Hence doing what I've done. I understand what my duty requires of me. If they expel me as a consequence, it will still have been worth it." She looked squarely at Ink. "Thank you for what *you've* done. Comparing the code will be critical. By the book will take too long."

"XD2 isn't manufactured in Dox. You might see more difference than you expect."

"You don't think Exose Ray's behind this version?"

"After what happens with XDream? There's no way he makes more."

"You bought XDream from him, right? Don't you blame him for what his product's done to you?"

"Exose wears his own costume. His rep's his uniform. Different story underneath."

"Not to the extent he can be trusted, surely?"

"I trust him. With my life. I vouch for the man beneath. Yes, XDream's his creation, but not whatever's causing the malfunction in Klova. That's not by him. Besides, I know for a fact he has nothing to do with XD2."

"How?" Reading hesitation in his face, she leant forward

and lowered her voice. "Please, trust me too. I'm operating alone. The Order don't know what I'm up to and I'll make sure they don't find out. I'm terrified for what could happen to Klova, to the entire population, if this failure isn't stopped. Every day that passes, the threat grows exponentially. That's why I'm risking everything."

Ink studied her face, the flush of passion colouring her pale skin. "I know he has nothing to do with XD2 because he asks me to buy some – to find out who's selling it."

Ihlo sat back, grasping the implications. "Have you agreed?"

He nodded.

She stared at the steam rising from her tea as if reading leaves. "Bastion are trying to locate the source. So far, they're only hitting dead ends. It's no secret; people know they're on the hunt. *Trans:akshn* is designed to withstand this exact scenario. Bastion don't stand a chance of finding anything inside. But a codevice customer looking to buy? If the seller ran background checks, they'd find you're a regular of Exose's. Perfect cover." She looked up at Ink. "Finding the source is critical. They could be manufacturing other variations, causing further mutations."

"That's partly why I agree. I want to help, whatever it takes."

"Have you thought about what that might be?"

He raised his shoulders. "What's the point?"

"Bastion have the names of every person who bought XDream from Exose. Apart from twelve saved minds, the same list is also the name of every person afflicted. Assuming there are cyber-enabled ways and means at iCon's disposal, there's a good chance our source will have a copy of that list. You could enter *Trans:akshn* and pull off pretending you're not afflicted, but it's likely they'll know you are."

Ink leant back, looking calmly at Ihlo.

"You don't see that as a risk?"

"Like you, I have reasons to accept risk in this situation." He forced a small smile. "It's okay. It's Exose's request, but it's still my choice."

Ihlo looked at Ink, noticing a darkness in his eyes, a flash of distance. Wary of crossing lines in unfamiliar territory, she hesitated, then said, "How are you bearing up?"

He sighed. "At the Undertow meetings, we try to find ways to talk about how it feels, the effect it's having on us. The only analogy I've come up with is trying to build something important – a house for my mother and father. I imagine them homeless. Only I can provide them with shelter. I work hard all day and lay the foundations, ready to lay the first row of bricks the following morning. The next day, I'm eager to lay the first row of bricks, but I know that first I must lay the foundations. I work hard, without rest, finishing the foundations so that tomorrow I can lay the first row of bricks. Tomorrow comes. The bricks are waiting. But before I can lay them, I must build the foundations. Over and over again. I still haven't laid a single brick."

Ihlo watched Ink as he stared at his upturned, empty hands. She could sense his exhaustion, the despair carved out by his loss.

"I'll compare the codes and I'll find the cause. Then I'll help the Order to repair the damage."

His expression softening, Ink smiled. "I believe you will." He reached out and took her hand in both of his, holding it firmly for a moment as he held her eyes. When he withdrew his hands, Ihlo closed her fingers around a small, rigid box, which she tucked inside a pocket in her tunic. Her eyes remained fixed on Ink's.

"Let me help," he said. "The volume to get through will be huge. I'm not saying I've got your skills. I'm no c'grammer. But there may be something I can do. I use a programme at work that runs comparative analysis. There might be discrete blocks I could work on."

"That's kind of you, but—"

"C'grammer – of course!"

"Sorry?"

"Exose is the best there is. Not just in the market. The guy's a genius. And he's all out to get the person who stole from him. He'll be able to help analyse it. Plus, he writes the code you're comparing it with. It could take you days – weeks, even, considering the shifts you have to work. With Exose's help, you could both work through it in a fraction of the time. Seriously."

Ihlo still held the box tight, grappling with unknowable consequence.

"Do you trust me?" said Ink.

Intuition answered. "Yes."

"Then I urge you: trust my trust in him."

*It fascinates me why those who are already free,
feel the need to escape.*

*The Iso-Klovaine of today is prosperous, peaceful
and entirely self-sufficient. There is little in
the way of poverty, oppression, violence and
crime. Geopolitical isolation has not hindered
its development. Here, egalitarianism is not an
aspiration; it is a sociocultural mindset and
part of this country's DNA.*

*And yet, some find the need to escape from nothing
into something that isn't real. Codevice: the
safe, clean, non-narcotic, non-addictive,
recreational un-drug of the century.*

*Distraction from the real, through escape into
the unreal. Unconscious presence in a parallel
space, contained in a hidden dimension, made
manifest by zeros and ones.*

Why does it bother me?

Because they've no idea of their freedom's worth.

*Maybe now they will – through the cost of their
escape.*

CHAPTER NINETEEN

"**R**eady for more of the same?" said Laine.

Brosala stood in the doorway to Laine's fish tank office. Laine was still in her chair, feet up on the desk, head back, eyes closed. She did not look ready for anything.

"Is there even any point?" said Brosala. "Half the stuff we need to ask, we can't because they don't understand. With the questions they can answer, they're all saying the same thing."

"Until we have a lead, it's all we've got. It only takes one person to say something new, drop a detail so innocuous that none of the others thought to mention it. A single breadcrumb can point the way." She stood up and stretched her long body, her neck cracking as she twisted it from side to side. "Did you order fresh coffee for the room?"

"Of course."

"Okay. Let's do this."

They walked through the open-plan office, past agents staring at their visuals or attacking their touchscreen desks. The tension in Bastion was escalating. Professional pride meant they liked to get the job done quick – make an impression and get results. The Corruption investigation had exceeded the deadline. The appearance of XD2 had rendered quick results a fool's blind hope. Top Floor were finger drumming. Everyone was feeling the pressure.

Laine and Brosala entered the interview room, a sparse, white box, clinical and cold. In the centre stood a tech-enhanced table with two chairs on either side. Along one wall was a cabinet, topped with coffee pots and paper cups. Along another was a wide two-way mirror, at which Laine and Brosala nodded briefly. While Brosala poured the coffee, Laine sat down and woke the table's surface. Lines of text appeared, glowing beneath black glass.

"Let's see who's up next," she said. "Male. Fifty-two. Answers to Dade Oresta. Mechanic. Partner, female. Two kids, both girls. Took XD2 night before last. Reports loss of concept and associated language – cannot conceive of, or talk about, himself." She sat back and addressed the reciprocal mirror. "Agent Laine conducting the interview of case number four-zero-five, name of Dade Oresta. XD2 consumption and symptomatic reaction. Agent Brosala in attendance with invitation to assist. Okay. Send him in."

Seconds later, a door clicked open, and a man stepped into the room. He was dressed in a navy coverall, company logo printed on the chest pocket. His skin was grey, his eyes bloodshot and wide. His movements were tentative, as if walking on ice.

Laine stood up. "I am Bastion Agent Laine. This is Agent Brosala. Thank you for coming in today to assist with our investigation. Please, take a seat."

The man frowned, grappling with his newly erected language barrier, forging meaning from what could pass through.

"What's this about?" he said, not moving from the spot.

"You're not in trouble. As my colleagues will have

explained when they picked you up, we simply wish to ask a few questions, to help with our inquiries." She held out her hand, indicating him, still unsure if the phase two afflicted could understand the physical reference to themselves. "Not here under duress. Free to leave at any time."

The man looked from Laine to Brosala, then back again. Taking slow, ice-wary steps, he moved over to the table and sat down. Laine and Brosala took their seats opposite him.

"I know you spoke to another agent when your condition was first confirmed," said Laine, her tone calm with a tint of persuasion, as if coaxing a reluctant child. "I'd like to run through a few details again. I appreciate the language difference between us. We will do our best to accommodate. Starting with codevice history." She tried to point without pointing. "Participated how long?"

The man stared at Laine, his face blank.

"Which trader in Dox?"

The man's eyes widened.

"Pax on Dox rules, okay? The Dox office is collaborating with us." She signalled to Brosala, who promptly brought up a holographic image from the centre of the table. A translucent document hovered between them: signed Declaration of Mutual Assist. "The Corruption's been bad for business; they want the case solved. We're not after scandal, just the trader's name."

The man hesitated, then said, "Rezi, stall front 212. More recently, 198, punk called Kite."

"Why the shift?"

"Money's tight. Kite offered discount."

"Exose Ray?"

"Too expensive."

"No XDream from Exose?"

The man shook his head.

"When buy XD2, think buying XDream? Same product, different source?"

The man frowned, struggling to reframe the question to fit his altered context. "XD2 is billed as being the same, but it can't be."

"Why not?"

"Because Exose wouldn't sell his product through someone else. And if someone else is ripping it off, then it's different shit. Name don't matter. Exose charges premium price for premium quality. There's reason he's on top."

"Who's selling XD2?"

"Can't tell. Identity's hidden."

"How's that?"

"It's only sold in *Trans:akshn*. Trader's an avatar."

Laine rubbed the side of her head, rerouting questions away from the self. "How do buyers know where to look? The market in *Trans:akshn* isn't an easy place to find, even harder to enter. We know. We've tried."

"..."

"Pax, remember?" She glanced up at the two-way.

"People at work talk about it. One woman bought some. She hadn't tried it yet. Said it was XDream, but an upgrade with the bug removed. Selling at half the price. Good will gesture, or something. Next thing, there's a device message: a promo for XD2, plus a one-time character sequence to enter *Trans:akshn*."

"Is the message still on the device?"

"Disappeared as soon as the code was used."

"Mind if we take a look at the device? Our guys might be able to locate a data-print."

The man looked down at his palm as if the implant would decide for him.

"We're bound and gagged by privacy regs," said Brosala.

"We can swing by the lab at the end. They'll only scan for a data-print, nothing else."

The man hesitated, biting his lip, then nodded.

Laine resisted another glance at the mirror. Only Law Enforcement could order the surrender of personal devices without a warrant. None of the other cases she had interviewed had agreed to the request.

"Thank you, Dade. A data-print could lead us to the source. We all want whoever's responsible brought in as soon as possible. All this suffering, the trauma, it has to end. The data-print could help us achieve that." She left a brief pause to give camaraderie a chance to take root. "Before the scan, there's a couple more questions, if that's okay. Colleagues have already asked, but we need to ask again, just for form's sake." She tapped the desk top and brought up the man's home address. "Any product left at 34 Anders Street, Nascen Arch?"

"No."

"What about at work?"

The man shrugged.

"Thing is, we need to get hold of the product to analyse the code. Understand why it's corrupting Klova. Understand how it has done this to you." Laine hesitated for a reaction, before realising her attempt to make it personal fell on uncomprehending ears. She tried another route. "The woman at work who talked about buying some. Has she tried it yet?"

The man looked close to tears. "She's... she's Corrupted. You've interviewed her."

Laine looked at the logo on his boilersuit, realising why it was vaguely familiar. She recalled the woman in question. She was so broken by her loss they could get little sense out of her. The recollection nudged Laine to see the man through compassion's lens.

"Dade, listen. Public Health will be in touch, if they haven't already. They've got a support package in place now. General well-being, mental health, social interaction. Government funded, so there's no charge. Take it up. It might help ease things a bit until the Order works out how to fix this."

It was as if the man couldn't hear her. His suffering was an unknowable trauma – frighteningly present and immediate, but affecting something that did not, for him, exist: himself.

Laine stood up and went over to the cabinet. She poured a cup of coffee and returned, handing it to Dade.

"Okay, last question, then we'll scan the device and give you a ride back to work." She sat down, leaning forward. "The nightmares. People have described the dream sequences in XDream and XD2. It appears the experience is different. XDream sequences vary considerably, whereas XD2 cases all describe the same nightmare. Also, we're picking up on something about image quality – how the nightmare *looks*. There seems to be something strange about XD2's appearance that people struggle to articulate. Can you have a go for us? What did the nightmare look like?"

The man frowned, his eyes half closed, mouth twisted to one side. "Different to regular dreams. It's as if there's something over the images – layered, like a filter. Hazy. Or ghostly. Yeah, more like ghostly."

"In what way?"

"Thin. Semi-see-through. Like the images are a projection, rather than real like they seem in normal dreams." He nodded. "That describes how they look. Unreal."

*

Laine and Brosala stood in the austere lobby of Bastion HQ, the tinted glass walls turning the sky a dark aubergine. As case number four-zero-five was escorted to his ride back to work, the two agents observed with feigned nonchalance. Only when the glazed doors slid closed did they drop the act.

Laine immediately turned to Brosala. "Tell me they found something."

Brosala smiled. "Superficial scan held a clean set of prints."

"Traced?"

"They're working on that now. Primary source is buried. Someone's taken a lot of care to keep this little enterprise a secret."

"But there's a connection?"

"We think so. Encrypted ID, but hackable. We think it's the source of a trigger, rather than the message containing the one-time character sequence."

"Trigger?"

"Working assumption is an AI listening programme, using word recognition. Somehow, our man's device heard him say a certain target word, or word combination, and that triggered the message to be sent. That's my guess, anyway. We should know soon enough."

As he said the words, his left eye glowed green. Laine stared at him while his eye scanned the incoming. She couldn't wait.

"So? What do they say?"

"Data-print is traceable to nine IDs. Eight appear to be decoys. The ninth has a viable connection to Kitred Wides – aka, Kite."

Often, things are not as they appear. One leans on perception, experience, reasoning, deduction – but how misleading those false guides can be.

Take a friend, a relative, a partner. You think you know them. Personality traits, patterns of behaviour, characteristic responses, all reinforce the illusion.

Perhaps they're striving to be the person you want them to be, or the person society expects them to become. Perhaps you know the mask and not the face – the shield, but not the flesh.

Language, too, can be made a mask – if so worn. Disinformation, propaganda, fabrication, spin. Words, the manipulating, distorting patterns in which they might be arranged, can be deceptive. Too often to bear, I witness the demeaning of language, forced to observe its vile abuse.

Face value can be a mask unseen. Truth and identity dwell deep beneath the surface.

CHAPTER TWENTY

Ihlo sat on the edge of her bed, her head in her hands. She had managed to shower and change for work, now she needed the strength to make it to the coffee machine. Three hours ago, she was comparing lines of code, as she had been doing all night. Three hours ago, she had struggled to pull herself away from her visual and collapse into bed. Fifteen minutes ago, she had been alarm-dragged from sleep into semi-consciousness, still fully clothed. Her duty was due to start in less than an hour. She fought to pull herself together.

No matter what Ink said, she couldn't trust that this trader, Exose Ray, would help them. Ink had obtained two doses of XD2 from the Undertow donor – one each to analyse – but she couldn't believe Exose would do it for anything other than serving his own ends. By creating XDream, he had cerebrogrammed other people's horrors to generate the most gruesome night terrors imaginable, and he classed it as entertainment. As if that wasn't reason enough to doubt his character, his borderline-compliant product caused the crisis. Even if he didn't intend to, his actions still triggered Klova's malfunction. That lack of trust had propelled her to keep going through the night. Exose Ray may have been sat at his own visual until dawn, layering XDream over XD2, scrutinising every sequence, every code-phrase, for signs of deviation. Regardless, Ihlo still believed she was working alone in the search.

The scale of the task was huge. Ink was right, it could well take her weeks. Had Modessr not intervened, full suspension could have cut that down to days. As it stood, sleep would have to take a back seat. ArtezAlert had just reported sixty new instances of confirmed Corruption. Ubimedia insisted it was at least triple that, citing potential for a sustained growth. Speculation wildly elaborated on a trending story that a VR-resident community was buying and ingesting XD2, despite knowing the price would be their own self-concept. Ubi embellished the claim with motive. This collective had already turned their back on reality, favouring life in artificial dreams and iCon's virtual open worlds. Taking XD2 to destroy their self-awareness was the ultimate sacrifice to achieve their total escape.

Ihlo lived with a VR junkie. She saw first-hand Ky's steady decline into separation. Not that she believed for one minute that Ubi's angle was true, but she recognised its watermark warning. The hype around the story was fuelled by a growing fear of worse to come. If the perpetrator was on a mission to cause widespread damage to Klova, banning the sale of XD2 would not stop them. *What else?*, asked Ubi, on behalf of the nation. Spiked medication? Food contamination? NuB manipulation? A palm device hack? Speculation or not, the potential remained. Plotted against the axes of time and jeopardy, threat's growth felt exponential.

Exhausted before the day had begun, Ihlo heaved herself off her bed and stumbled towards the kitchenette. Coffee came with its own risk; the last thing she needed was an attack from Ky. It was only then that it occurred to her that she hadn't seen her cousin for a while. That in itself wasn't unusual, it was more that she hadn't noticed the relief as it happened. She willed the temporary reprieve to last just another half hour.

Her hope was denied. As Ihlo entered the room, Ky was sat at the small dining table, her hands in a knot in front of her. Ihlo braced herself for the onslaught. Ky didn't say a word. Didn't move.

"Coffee?" said Ihlo, slipping into the kitchenette.

No reply. *An equally good or bad sign*, Ihlo thought. Often the attack came full throttle from a standing start; there was no way to gauge its timing. Best just to act normal. Occasionally the storm passed without breaking.

Placing a cup of coffee in front of Ky, she noticed her cousin's hands trembling. Her pale skin was stone-grey. Dark sockets bruised her face.

"Shit, Ky. Are you alright?" Ihlo sat down next to her, placing her hand gently on Ky's forearm. She could feel the tremble's vibration. "What's happened? Talk to me."

Ky looked up, her eyes bloodshot and tear wet.

Straight away, Ihlo knew. "Oh Ky," she said, holding quivering hands in her own.

Ky broke down.

It was a while before Ky recovered enough to speak. They were sat on the sofa, side by side. Ihlo had sent a brief message to Modessr letting him know she would be late. She ignored his officious reply.

"Two days," said Ky, her voice tissue thin.

"I'm so sorry. I've been so busy at work. I didn't even register that I haven't seen you in all that time."

Ky winced.

"Shit. Sorry." Ihlo flushed, kicking herself. She spoke

slowly, adjusting her language to save her cousin the painful reminder. "XD2?"

"Ubi says what's lost, but that doesn't mean anything. Something's wrong."

"Describe what feels wrong."

Ky stared ahead into empty space. Her mouth was slightly open as if about to speak. She didn't make a sound.

"What is it like out there?" Ihlo pointed to the window without taking her eyes off her cousin. "What is it like in here?"

Ky's eyes widened, as if beholding the world anew as she attempted to describe it. "All is outside. Life is elsewhere. All around, people are afraid, angry, tired, in love. You're sad. You're exhausted, determined, passionate and brave – but right now, you're mostly sad."

"What about Ky? Where is she?"

"..."

"Who am I?"

Ky shook her head, tears welling.

Ihlo pointed to her own body. "Who is this?"

"You're Ihlo." Her expression softened. "You're trying to help. You're kind to want to. But it won't work. It *can't* work."

Ihlo knew this, of course. The urge to push had been a refusal to accept the fact. Ky was right, she simply could not understand. It was impossible for her to. Loss of concept left no residue, no memory of that which was once known. For Ky, it was as if her sense of self had never existed. She was reduced to her body – an 'it', a 'that', a physical object unconsciously present in the life of elsewhere. This painful acknowledgement sparked an even greater urgency for Ihlo.

"Listen, the Order and Bastion are on this. Working day and night. They're making progress. They'll fix this." Her chest tightened and her own eyes welled. "Promise."

Ky took hold of her cousin's hand. The gesture moved Ihlo

deeply. Klova could never convey so much. The gulf between them had closed in the space of a nightmare.

"There's help," she said, desperate to make things better, however impossible that might seem. "A support group's been set up. I know someone who goes."

"The Undertow," said Ky. "They suffer."

"A man called Ink? Tall, dark hair."

"Kind eyes. A small box in his hand."

Ihlo stared at Ky, the dots joining. "That… that was you? Oh Ky, what was given in that box changes everything. It holds the answer, I know it. That's what I've…" Struggling with the words she couldn't use, failing to find alternatives fast enough, she pointed to herself. "That's what Ihlo's working on. All last night. All tonight – and tomorrow night. As long as it takes. Analysing the code in there." She pointed in the direction of her room. "Ihlo will find the answer. Will put this right." She put her arm around her broken cousin. "Will make this better."

*

By the time she eventually made it into the lab, Ihlo was over two hours late. Modessr had long since primed himself for the attack.

"Your leave to continue working during your suspension is not an admin oversight. And it is not a pass for you to come and go as your fancy dictates. Were it not for the scale of the task, within a timeframe barely achievable, I would retract my request and have you barred from entering the citadel walls as standard procedure dictates."

"My cousin was taken ill, as I explained. I could hardly leave her."

"Your cousin, if I am not mistaken, is a grown woman, quite capable of taking care of herself."

"She was not fit to leave."

"And you are not fit to be a votary. Your attitude is an insult to the memory of the Savants. How you ever made it this far is quite beyond me."

Ihlo resisted countering in her defence. She knew there was no gain to be made. Besides, she lacked the will. Witnessing Ky's condition, the cruel toll it was already taking, had added fresh urgency to the crisis. Rather than waste her breath, she set to work.

Standing before Lasysi, Ihlo silently communed with her ally. Her hands against its metal torso, she imagined the faint vibrations to be its pulse, the low hum to be the steady breathing of a fellow workhorse. It was then that her eyes focused on the display panel.

"What's this?"

Modessr waved a dismissive hand and sat down at his own visual.

"Modessr, what's Lasysi running?"

"You were late. I used the time of your unauthorised absence to run an additional test."

"I don't recognise the type-ID."

"Proof you don't know everything."

The status indicator showed near completion. Ihlo stared at the ID, memorizing the character sequence, until it was replaced with *SIMULATION COMPLETE*. She was about to move to her visual to check the results status for identification when the screen changed again. *DATA ENCRYPTION AND TRANSFER INITIATED*. She looked over at Modessr.

"What are you doing?"

"Nothing that concerns you. Your clearance has been blocked, if you recall. I am not permitted to divulge."

She moved towards the central bench. "It concerns me if Lasysi's involved. If this is something to do with the update, then I still have clearance. I'm not putting my name to the project if I don't know what's going on."

Modessr turned to face her, his jaw clenched and pulsing. "Your name won't be on the project at all at this rate. Now, prepare the next scheduled test and let me work." He turned back to his visual, tapping at a touchpad embedded in the benchtop.

Ihlo attempted to read his visual. As she did so, it went blank. The transparent glass revealed nothing apart from the wall beyond and Modessr's twisted reflection, his left eye glowing green. Turning to her own visual, she scanned the simulator's activity log. It reported that the encrypted download had been sent to a remote, secure server. Whatever results Modessr was now reading, Ihlo could not access them. There was nothing in the action history to indicate the nature of the test, or the source material used. Care had been taken to erase the tracks. Had she arrived ten minutes later, she would have been none the wiser.

Only then did she recall the locked file on Modessr's visual that she'd noticed a week ago. The icon had appeared innocuous at the time, odd, but no cause for suspicion in isolation. She'd been so preoccupied with the crisis it had slipped her mind entirely. Now, the context was altogether different. If this additional test was anything to do with the update, the task would have been added to her pile. Instead, Modessr had gone to great lengths to ensure she had not – and could not – see what he was up to.

Modessr, meanwhile, didn't say another word to her. She sensed his agitation as they sat side by side at the bench. When she rose to attend to Lasysi, she stole glances at him. He was still tapping away, appearing to work, which aroused her suspicions further. Frustrated by his uncharacteristic presence in the lab, she was desperate for him to go. When he eventually did, still without further word, she went straight over to his visual.

It was no longer transparent but left idle on his user area. Despite her impatience to look, she already suspected what she would find – or rather, what she wouldn't. The locked file was gone. She stepped back and recalled his green-eyed reflection in the glass. Her impression of him slowly altered in this curious light as she wondered, was this another uniform hiding a different story beneath?

Forget the past. What would you give to see into the future?

Imagine having the ability to do that. To know the path your life takes. To see your child older than you are now. To marvel at how technology has transformed how we live. To know when you die. And how.

Knowing the future might take some of the fear out of the present.

Take my little demonstration by way of example. There is a profound fear building day by day. It is primed and fed by a fixation on the future: what next? What else? When will this end? What will we have left?

This fertile fear is not caused by what has happened to the unfortunate few. The number of those affected appears infinitesimal when expressed in percentage terms. Odds are still in your favour. Chances are, you'll be fine.

No. This fear is the progeny of a perception change among the masses. Like knowing your life depends on the oxygen you breathe, only to learn one day that the supply is finite – people are only now discovering their unwitting dependence on a lifeline under threat.

They're right to be afraid.

CHAPTER TWENTY-ONE

The district of Union is home to the nation's tech industry. One of its prime movers and competitive pacesetters is iCon Solutions – a private company that has accelerated from incubator to market leader, specialising in VR applications in the commercial and business sectors. *Trans:akshn* is its most lucrative platform. On the surface, a vast, open world, multiplayer action-adventure video game. Beneath the surface, an expanding marketplace for alternative economies.

Ink stands before the huge, ice blue building that is iCon's headquarters and the public face of *Trans:akshn*. The people entering and leaving the building are a combination of high-end sophistication and left-field trend. Feeling conspicuous in non-descript casual, Ink reminds himself he is helping a friend and isn't required to fit in to where he doesn't belong. Taking a deep breath, he enters the building.

Inside, the ice blue interior is broken only by fixtures in polished chrome. The space is gleaming. Squinting slightly, Ink approaches the front desk. It is unattended until the moment he steps up to it, when a holographic image appears on the other side: a life-sized man, dressed in a pristine blue tunic.

"How may I help you today?" says the virtual receptionist.

"I've come for *Trans:akshn.*"

"Have you an appointment, sir?"

"No."

Already, Ink feels out of his depth. Despite now having the code to analyse, he knows Exose still needs him to buy, in case he can pick up clues as to the source. Their current intel is sketchy. You can only buy XD2 in *Trans:akshn*, you can't access the market via the game portal and, if you don't have the requisite hardware, you have to shop here. Ink gleaned this much from a conversation with an associate of a friend of a friend in a Dox back alley. Immediately after the conversation, he received a message on his device. No source ID, just a one-time character sequence and the words, *Enjoy a dark night's sleep with XD2 – only available elsewhere.*

"I… I have a pass code." He holds up his palm and projects the holo key.

The receptionist's eyes glow for an instant in number recognition. "Very good, sir. Let me see if we have a pod available." His expression changes from hospitality-sparkle to lifeless deadpan. Then the sparkle returns. "We have the pleasure of being able to accommodate you at this time. If I may ask you to please place your palm on the counter?"

Ink complies.

"You now have access to pod six-two-zero. You have one hour in which to conduct your business. Should you wish to extend your visit, you can pay in-world. Look for 'Reservations' on the drop-down menu."

"Do I make payment for the first hour now?"

"I have already taken payment, sir."

Ink glances down at his hand. The message with the pass code is gone. His inbox holds one new message: payment confirmation of fifteen hundred credits. Burying his hand in his pocket, he eyes the spotless counter.

The hologram extends a translucent arm. "Sixth floor. Elevators to your right."

The moment Ink moves away, the receptionist disappears.

Ink takes an elevator up to the sixth and steps out into more ice blue and chrome. He emerges halfway down a narrow corridor with closed doors on either side, each about three metres apart. On the side of each door is a number in chrome and a discrete scan pad. He locates number six-two-zero and holds his palm up to the pad. The door clicks and swings open.

Inside, there is a small, windowless box room – bare white walls and ceiling, with a shimmering white linoleum floor. In the centre of the room is a large chrome frame, its height, depth and width all two metres. Suspended from the top of the frame is a lightweight, full-enclosure headset and an all-in-one haptic suit. A pair of haptic gloves lay on a chrome tray attached to one side of the frame. There is nothing else in the room.

A casual player of video games in his youth, he has little time for it now – and has never got around to playing *Trans:akshn*. He knows of its impressive reputation – everyone does. However, the marginal commerce operating within it is recent news to him. That's where his familiarity ends, along with his comfort zone.

He steps into the suit, puts on the gloves and places the helmet over his head.

Translocation is immediate and giddying – the simultaneous assault on his senses, overwhelming. Ink finds himself stood on a high balcony, gripping its iron railings, looking down on a busy town square below. A warm breeze brushes his cheeks, carrying the scent of sea air, peach blossom and baked bread. The sounds of street barkers, bicycle bells, laughter and the lament of a bowed cello reach his ears in a swirl of supra-high-res audio. Striking colours, rich in saturation, lend a hyper-reality to the scene. He gazes beyond the square, over the tiled roofs of low-rise buildings, to the endless horizon beyond. This world is open and fascinatingly other. He guesses he could probably leave this balcony and go anywhere, in any direction, and never reach an end. The desire to explore is compelling.

There is something else different, here in this remarkable unreality. Ink feels it immediately, as if an ever-present pain in his chest has suddenly disappeared. In this world, he is not afflicted. The barkers and shoppers below are not conscious beings, with a perception of time at odds with his own. His now, next and forever could be time's true line. With no comparison to draw, no difference to distinguish, there is no loss of concept. His is the way of the world.

As immersive as it feels, presence of mind keeps a finger on the page of the real world. Ink knows he is a passing visitor, pressed for time, with a favour to honour. Sensing the stillness of the room behind him, he turns around and steps off the balcony, into silence and shadow.

The room is a study of sorts, with wood-panelled walls, multiple bookshelves and framed isometric drawings of twisting, labyrinthine architecture. In the centre of the room is a grand desk – ancient mahogany, with skin graft tech. Beside the desk stands a man in a long purple robe, embroidered at the hem with gold thread and pearl rhinestones. His deep plum hair is shoulder length and braided at the sides. His eyes, electric blue.

Ink glances around, trying to memorise minor details to report back: artwork, book titles, the subjects of framed photos, various trinkets and curiosities. There is too much information to remember, the world too real and crammed with the everyday. Instead, he decides to focus on the character before him, on his mannerisms and patterns of speech. Someone, somewhere, is *in their own haptic suit and headset – the animus inside the avatar.*

"Inker Ballard," the man says, his tone business-like. "Please, step forward."

Ink looks down at himself, which consists of shirt-cuffed wrists, pale hands and brown boots that come into view as he steps towards his host.

The man moves gracefully around the desk to a tall, winged-back chair, and sits down. With a long, slender hand, he gestures towards a chair opposite.

"Please, take a seat."

As he obliges, Ink feels a rigid form take his weight. The sensation is so convincing, he wonders if he missed a chair behind him in the pod. But no, he feels certain the pod was empty, apart from the frame and the tech he is now wearing. The thought of someone else entering the room without him knowing, watching him while he is blindfolded by the headset, sends a bolt of panic through his chest and gut. He closes his eyes and focuses his mind on his physical presence. He reaches down and gropes for a chair beneath him.

"Feels real, doesn't it?" comes a voice from the dark.

For a sickening moment, Ink thinks there is, in fact, someone else in the pod with him. Then sense breaks through the panic; he cannot feel a chair. Letting go of empty air, he slowly opens his eyes, raising them to meet those of his host.

"It's the neuroaugments. Ninth-gen immersion. I could come and wipe that bead of sweat off your brow and you'd feel my touch." The corner of the man's mouth creeps up, but there is no smile behind the shape. "My name is D. Welcome to Trans:akshn."

Distracted by image resolution and staggering attention to detail, Ink stares at the man's face – the pale, textured flesh pulsing against a firmly set jaw. The braids in his hair catch the light from the balcony. His nostrils flare the slightest fraction as the corner of his narrow mouth twitches. Then Ink notices an expectant, raised eyebrow above irritated eyes.

"Ah, sorry," says Ink, shifting in his not-there chair. "First time here."

"I know. If you want to marvel at the graphics, play the game."

"Yes. Of course."

The abrupt tone triggers the return of nerves. The room is comfortably cool, with that otherworldly warm breeze stirring the air. In a parallel reality, Ink feels the sensation of cold sweat trickling down his back.

D taps the desk. A visual materialises from the mahogany surface and remains suspended, horizontally, just above it. Windows filled with text appear, too dense for Ink to read.

"Before we get down to business, I've taken the liberty of running some background checks. In the current climate, we are forced to take extra precaution. I'm sure you understand."

"Of course."

"You're a customer of Exose Ray. Is he aware of your disloyalty?"

"He's banned from trading. I believe he will understand my need to shop elsewhere."

"While his operation is suspended, perhaps. What about after?"

"Loyalties shift if good reason compels a move."

"Exose Ray is a big fish in a small, polluted pond. Here in Trans:akshn, we offer a different class of business, with a superior range of products and services."

Ink nods, his heart rate calming, settling into character. He wishes he had noticed a mirror in his scan of the room so that he could see how his own avatar appears.

"I'm impressed so far."

"I am pleased to hear it."

"Have you other stalls in here? I'm assuming you can't manage all the trade single-handed. Are there many of you?"

D cocks his head to one side. "So many questions. Why is that?"

Feigning a casual shrug, Ink plays the part. "I buy from Exose Ray because he's the best. Now, for the first time, he has viable competition. You can forgive me a little curiosity, surely?" While he hides behind his avatar's act, Ink hopes the tech he wears isn't wired to monitor vital signs.

"We've been gearing up to this for some time. I can see how, from your perspective, we've appeared a little out of the blue – and at a fortuitous interval. The hiatus in Exose's operations has certainly helped drive new business our way."

"If your product's as good as you say, I'm sure you'll retain the gains in custom."

"Our product is as good. And yes, that is our expectation." D leans back, appraising Ink, tapping his lips with a long, slender index finger. "Your background checks also revealed what you are otherwise managing to hide."

Ink swallows. The oxygen in his headset suddenly feels in short supply.

"You are Corrupted." D enunciates the words in a way that makes the statement a challenge.

"I read that your product is clean."

"We would say that, wouldn't we." He doesn't phrase it as a question, but underscores the prompt with an austere glare.

"And… I believe it. The blueprint has huge potential. You pick it up, fix the bug, improve the quality of the dream experience, and now you tap a reliable market looking for a new home. It doesn't make sense for you to sell a product that you know will cause the damage XDream does." He takes a deep breath, struggling to justify the plainly implausible. "You say yourself, it's a different class of business here. iCon's reputation is faultless. Trans:akshn is a respected brand.

It's not all image. It's earnt. Compare that with a Dox market trader with no legitimate credentials other than notoriety. It's not surprising his product causes the Corruption. I would, however, be surprised if iCon is knowingly facilitating its spread."

"Persuasive."

"It's true." Ink fights to internalise his anxiety, keeping his suit and gloves in a position that, he hopes, translates as calm composure.

"You say you've read our product is clean. Surely you've also read media reports that claim the contrary? Bastion are yet to go public on their latest line of inquiry, but it's all over the Ubimedia platform. XD2 carries a mutation of the bug, apparently. Attacks a different subset of code. You read about that?"

His heart racing, Ink tries desperately not to move. "The last thing I trust is Ubi."

"You have suffered loss of concept once. Are you really prepared to risk losing another? To risk losing your self?"

Ink abandons the act. He stands up, appealing with disembodied hands. "Look, what's this about? You run the checks and you let me in. My coin is good. If I trust your product, what's the problem?"

D rises and crosses his arms. "We ran the checks and you failed. We cannot believe that someone who's suffered Corruption would take such a risk."

"Then why let me in? Why let me come this far?"

"We wished to spend some time with you." D glances down as an icon on his visual turns from blue to green.

"Why? What's going on?"

This time D's mouth curves into a smile, but it isn't kind. "Know your enemy."

"What?"

"Insurance, Mr Ballard. A precaution. We don't know why you came shopping. We don't anticipate you'll tell us. But we intend to find out."

"What have you—"

Before Ink finishes the sentence, D dissolves, leaving him alone in the room. Arms out like a balancing act, Ink looks about him, half expecting someone else to appear, half having no idea what to expect. It is only then that he notices the world has fallen silent. Realism's diegetic sounds – birdsong and bicycle bells, people talking, doors closing – have ceased. The silence that replaces it is dense and oppressive.

With growing panic, Ink darts around the room. He has no mind to look for Exose's clues, he simply wants out. Now. Yet there is nothing in the space with which he can interact. The visual has vanished. Nothing else on the desk reacts to his touch – likewise, with objects on the various bookcases. He can't pick anything up or have any influence on his environment. He tries to speak, but only hears his muffled voice from inside his headset.

For a terrifying moment, he fears he is trapped inside this virtual world. As he keeps circling the room, repeating futile attempts to interact, time seems to have stopped along with sound. I'm stuck in here, he thinks. I can't get out. He feels hysteria's blinding surge and fights to get a grip. Breathing hard, he stands still, closes his eyes and centres his mind back in his body, inside the pod. This room isn't real, he tells himself. This world isn't real. He repeats the reminder over and over, until his breathing calms and the panic eases.

Opening his eyes, he returns to the fiction. He is facing the balcony, from where he had entered. Drawing on the video games from his youth, an idea forms. With nothing else to try, Ink steps forward onto the balcony and launches himself over the iron railings.

His five-storey dive lands him back in the pod, breathless and drenched in sweat. His escape from the virtual world was detached from consequence. Now real world action and consequence return, the relationship of accountability restored. *We don't know why you came… but we intend to find out.* Ink's affliction gives him a truncated, forward-facing grasp of cause and effect. Consequences are a thing of the future. He has no idea what consequence might look like in this situation. All he knows is that his visit has aroused suspicion. That feels alarming enough. His hands shaking, Ink fumbles with the fastenings of the haptic suit, desperate to get away before there's time to find out.

Taking a deep breath, Ink opens the door to the pod and peers left and right. The hallway is empty and eerily silent. Heading for the elevators, he finds himself creeping stealth-like, despite knowing every square inch is likely to be covered by cameras. Then he reminds himself it is the outfit behind XD2 who are on to him, not iCon. Straightening his back and lifting his chin, Ink calls up the elevator and descends to the ground floor. The foyer is empty; the reception desk, holo-less. Ink fixes his eyes on the wide glass doors and concentrates on placing one foot in front of the other.

*

In a speaker square three blocks south of iCon HQ, Exose waited. Ink had told him of his intention to enter *Trans:akshn* that morning. They had arranged for Ink to call once he was out. A speaker was in full flow and had attracted a sizeable audience. Exose stood amid the crowd – casual cover to keep Ink clean should Bas be watching. A finger pressed against his NuB, Exose willed the call to come.

When it finally did, Ink's message was too short, too vague, too un-Ink to arouse anything but anxiety. While he waited for Ink to walk the three blocks to the square, Exose imagined multiple scenarios that could account for the odd call, none of them good. Feeling a gentle nudge against his arm, he turned to glance at Ink, then couldn't look away.

"Shit. What happened? You okay?"

Ink stared ahead, a cold sweat glazing his kaolin skin.

"Fuck this, we need to get you inside." He turned to face forward, speaking out of the side of his mouth. "Five Talons – hothouse, a couple of blocks south of here. Know it?"

Ink nodded.

"There's a private room with a burnfree. Owner owes me a favour. Let's split and meet there. I'll go first and set up, you follow in five."

Before Ink had chance to respond, Exose was gone.

Five Talons was one of Arteza's less salubrious hothouses, but no less popular. Inside, the place was shabbier, the music louder and the softglows lower than in most others. Spiced corn kernels were the extent of the food menu. But the genker was cheap and the place was warm. Inside the back room, the burnfree flickered, casting a treacle glow. There were four mismatched armchairs and a low table between them, with genker and glasses at the ready. A dog was curled up on one of the chairs, its sleep-heavy eyes open just enough to watch Exose pace back and forth.

When Ink appeared over five minutes later, Exose ushered him into the room and onto the chair nearest the fire.

"I'm so, so sorry," he said, eyes worry-wide, his hand still on Ink's arm. "Are you hurt?" He pulled up a chair and sat opposite, leaning forwards, searching for signs.

"No, not hurt. Shaken up, that's all." He rubbed the back of his neck, frowning.

"First thing you got to know, I won't let them get away with shit. You hear me? They do anything to you, they pay dear."

Ink looked up at Exose and nodded. As if to underline the promised protection, the dog, brown with over-long ears, came and sat beside Ink, its back pushed up against his legs.

Exose poured a healthy dose of genker and handed Ink the glass.

"Feel up to talking? I know there's questions I can't ask, what with your time thing. So just tell it your way. I'll follow."

Ink took a deep breath. "They know I'm afflicted. They won't sell to me because of it."

"That's okay. We've got our hands on the code. We don't need more."

"They're suspicious. They say no one who's afflicted would risk taking their product."

"It's ripped-off crap. *No one* should risk it."

"They want to know why I'm in *Trans:akshn*. They say they're going to find out." He looked down at his palm, frowning.

"What? What is it?"

"My device. I'm worried they do something to it."

"Easily sorted. I've a Dox associate, top of her game. Go there after this. She'll do a sweep, make sure it's clean. Teon's her name, stall front 239. Tell her I sent you. I'd intro you myself, but..." He snorted and downed his genker. "Anyway, don't use it in the meantime. I'll call ahead so she's expecting you."

"Thanks." He rubbed his palm as if he could erase the likely hack. Exose topped up their glasses, then sat back, his expression dark.

"I'm so sorry, Ink. This is my fault. There's me protecting you from Bas's attention, then I go and ask you to mix with the enemy and call it a fucking favour."

"Enemy..." He looked at Exose. "They say they want to know their enemy. As in me. They think I'm up to something by shopping."

"You have any sense of who they are? Impressions that might help?"

"Only about the operation, not the individual."

"What's that?"

"It's slick. Professional. Business-like. They build up to this, rather than steal your blueprint and run with it. It's too organised, too thorough. They must have money, or connections behind them. Something bigger than their business in *Trans:akshn*." He glanced up at Exose. "I'm sorry. Not much to go on in terms of finding your thief." He scratched the back of his neck.

"Don't apologise. They're trading in VR for good reason and the move is paying off. I appreciate what you've done, more than I can say. I should never have asked you." Frowning, he watched Ink go at his neck. "You okay there?"

"Itches, that's all." He folded his arms, hands tucked out of reach. "You can ask me to do anything. I don't have to say yes."

"No, you don't. But you always do. And I'm taking advantage by knowing that and asking regardless." His eyes narrowed. "More so now, perhaps."

"What does that mean?"

"You're different. Since you became afflicted. I don't know how to…" He shook his head. "Sorry. I can't explain in a way you can possibly understand. This is about you in the *past*. How you were before. You've changed."

Ink sat up, back rigid, and stared at Exose. "Change, how?"

"Well. For a start, there's your group."

"The Undertow? What about them?"

"Not about them. About *you*. Joining up. Not only that, volunteering – *volunteering* – to do the whole locking up thing."

"I'm just helping out. It's a good cause. The group's making a difference."

"That may well be the case. All I'm saying is, you – the old you – would never have volunteered. You wouldn't have joined, full stop."

"Why not?"

"Because…" Exose held out his hands, palms up, cupping empty air. "Because you withdrew. After Neav. Even once you were over the shock, once you started to come to terms with it all, you kept yourself apart. Like it became a habit. Living without participating." He dipped his head, trying to catch Ink's eye, which had locked onto the burnfree. "Look at me."

Ink blinked, then drew his gaze back to Exose.

"Ten years. You'd gone cold for ten years. I tried everything I could think of, to get you out of yourself. But you couldn't engage – or wouldn't. And now?" Raised brow over bright eyes, he dared a smile. "You're fucking signing up for all sorts of shit."

Ink stared at Exose, biting his bottom lip.

"Sorry, I shouldn't make light. It's just…" He reached out a tentative hand and placed it on Ink's shoulder. "Feels like you've come back, is all."

"Meanwhile, I'm going through hell, terrified of what's happening to me, feeling like I track-switch into some parallel, alternate reality. I've nothing to compare it to, but I know I see things different."

"But I'm talking about a *good* change. I get it must be freaking you out, not knowing what's happened to your code, what else might happen."

"Just a bit."

"But seeing as you can't recognise change, I'm saying there's something good in the mix too. Hold onto that and it might help you deal with all the bad shit."

Ink smiled. "How can you be so different to your sister and yet, in some ways, be so much like her?"

Exose bowed his head with a humility Dox would swear impossible in the trader. He stared into the glow of the burnfree, holding onto the compliment he felt he didn't deserve, but still touched that Ink might think it.

"Anyway," said Ink, topping up their glasses, "now that I'm a joiner, I've a need to pull my weight. I don't feel like I achieve anything useful in *Trans:akshn*, but maybe, between us, we'll have more luck with the product itself. I know Ihlo's working on the code."

"The votary? You think she's to be trusted?"

"I do. She's also smart. Perhaps it's best not to think of her as a votary. She seems different."

"They all are." He waved a dismissive hand. "Fucking freaks."

"You guys need to get together, share what you're finding with the code."

"I created XDream. I don't need her help in reading its rip-off."

"I know you don't. But together you might just spot something. I don't know – some anomaly, some kink. Surely it's worth it if it means the chance of working out who's behind all this?"

Exose rotated a shoulder. Something cracked. "I'll think about it. Meanwhile, an interesting fact's emerging. According to ubi and a few contacts I've spoken to, XD2 uses the same nightmare sequence in each dose."

"So?"

"So, it's a cheap rehash job. Looks like they're copying a single dose of XDream. They're not using the blueprint to write their own content – which could mean they don't know how it's constructed."

"They might not be c'grammers?"

"Precisely. Plus, they've access to hardware that can replicate. That's got to narrow down the field."

"But the symptom's different. Odd to get a mutation in a copy."

"Corruption in the clone. Not to put a downer on things, but that's where ubi could be right for once: maybe everyone ought to be fucking afraid."

"Why do you say that?"

"The bug could be viral. If that's the case, mutation's its means of survival."

.

I'm cautious – by nature and by necessity. I've taken care not to go too far, too fast. When you have a point to prove, patience and restraint are disciplines that deliver reward.

Thus far, I've resisted indulgence. The mutation was a vital escalation – the choice of concept, poignant. It places emphasis on the personal. The intention: to encourage a little self-reflection among those who still know who they are.

It's about the message, you see, not the scale. Profundity has only one dimension.

The message is an unsettling pill to swallow. Even harder to digest. That is why I have much yet to achieve if I am to succeed, if I am to make you listen AND learn. Hence the necessity of caution. 'Tis the prudent who prevail.

TWENTY-TWO

The atmosphere in Dox had become unstable. Trouble hadn't started, but there was a growing sense that it was just around the corner. Without the market leader to emanate an assumed authority, the air felt thin, lacking the substance that maintained the market's delicate balance. Traders pushed boundaries, took risks, played unsafe. Some customers stayed away, aware of a change and wary of its character. A brewing storm, high pressure and rising, the sense of volatility was unnerving. Almost everyone longed for the return of their unacknowledged leader.

Almost everyone.

Kite had not left Dox since Exose's release from Detention four days ago. With his market ban apparently holding, she had allowed her guard to relax slightly inside the safety of her stall. She rarely left the fifth floor. The outside world was out of the question. Exose was a patient man when it came to biding his time. He'd be out there, waiting, she felt sure.

She worried about her old man. She'd managed to get a message to a trusted neighbour that first night of hiding, so she knew he was being looked after. But having regular meals delivered and the occasional slice of company wouldn't be the same. She knew he'd be fretting, not seeing her to know she was okay, not having her home each night.

It surprised her how much she missed him.

Meanwhile, Borro, her poke, found himself with extra coin and a revised job description. Twice a day, he'd bring her something to eat and drink from the food stalls on the second floor. Already, her stall was littered with greasy cartons, bamboo forks and glass empties. The stale air held a cocktail of smells, unrecognisable and increasingly unpleasant.

"What the fuck's this?" said Kite, prodding steaming matter with a broken fork. She was sat cross-legged on the desk, foil tray in hand. Borro had just arrived with her dinner.

"Day's special. Colack 'n' rice."

"Bullshit it's colack. More like cat yak." She screwed up her face as she tasted it. "If Exose doesn't kill me, eating this crap will. May as well step out and get it over with."

"Don't be like that. You gotta keep safe. I'll fetch you somethin' nice tomorrow. Somethin' fresh, outside o' Dox."

"What's the rumble down there?"

Borro pulled out a chair and sat opposite Kite. "Bones' still stirring shit. Workin' everyone right up."

"About what?"

"The Bas rat. Tellin' everyone it's fifth floor."

"He's been saying that for weeks. He ain't got nothing on no one."

"Meantimes, he reckons he has. And without Exose here to keep him in his box, Bones is laying it thick."

"My name come up?"

Borro nodded.

"Fuck."

"That's more reason to lay low. I got your back while you're safe in here. I can't do that if you go down levels, let alone outside. Couple of traders up here already been set against. Defended their corner, only to get beaten into it."

"Hurt?"

"Mostly pride. But still. There's bad air brewin'. Best to stay out of it. I'll do fetchin' and watch the door. Your trade's picked up a pace. Storm's bound to break, but we'll ride it fine."

Kite looked down at her food, barely touched. She felt spirit sick, trapped in a two-door box with both exits blocked. Four days, so far. *How much longer?* she wondered. Already, she couldn't hack it. Her nerves were fried, her anxiety off the scale. *This isn't how it was meant to be*, she thought. *This ain't what I signed up to.*

"Here," she said, holding out the foil tray to Borro. "You have this."

Borro's eyes lit up. "Don't mind if I do." He took the tray and filled his mouth. Unable now to speak, he tipped his head, smiled, and moved to his position in the hallway, ready to poke for trade while guarding the lockless door.

Two minutes later, he reappeared, eyes wide. "Bas. On their way up."

"Shit." Kite frantically closed down the programme she'd just started working on and scanned the tech bench for anything incriminating. Then she hopped back on the desk, sat cross-legged, elbows on her knees, chin in her hands. As she completed the look with a boredom yawn, Bastion appeared in the doorway.

Agents Laine and Brosala entered the stall and stood before the desk, arms crossed. Brosala's eyes scanned the room, while Laine held hers firmly fixed on Kite.

"Sorry to disturb," said Laine.

"You're supposed to come announced," said Kite. "Them's the rules."

"Rules bend. I'm sure you use a little flex when the need arises."

Brosala slowly walked around the room, surveying the tech, touching locked screens.

"We had an arrangement," said Kite, studiously ignoring Brosala. "The drop-box. You're drawing attention to me, keep calling in like this. There's traders tagging me a rattin' back-scratcher."

"I'm glad you remember our arrangement. Your complete lack of communication had led me to wonder."

"Ain't got no word to pass."

"And how hard have you been looking?"

"I said I would do it, didn't I? Where's the friggin' trust? And how am I s'posed to dig discrete when I've got Bas knocking every five minutes? No one's gonna spill around me, are they?"

"Because you're smart, remember? Because you've got fingers in pies."

"What's that supposed to mean?" She slid off the desk and stood in front of Laine, hands on her hips.

"Brosala?"

Agent Brosala returned to Laine's side and addressed Kite. "We have credible evidence that points to you being the source of a sub rosa transfer."

"What you bangin' about?"

"Stealth download of a programme to private devices. We've tracked the ID back to you. Mind if I take a look?" He tipped his head to the bank of tech behind her.

"Yeah. Very much I mind. I ain't behind no stealth download. And my business ain't none of yours. What's this about, anyway?"

"A new form of poke," said Laine. "Pushing XD2, despite its side effect on Klova. Which makes it every bit our business.

And makes us very keen to get to the bottom of who's doing the pushing. So, if you've nothing to do with it, I suggest you let my colleague take a look to verify."

"Suggest all you like. You ain't touchin' shit without a warrant."

Laine gritted her teeth while Brosala's green eye scanned for the pass they'd been waiting for.

"Look," she said, "do yourself a favour rather than dig yourself a hole. We know you're behind the transfer and we're pretty sure its source is in here – probably in the kit we gave you. If you make us wait for the paperwork, you're making us waste time and that's a bad move on your part. Delaying the inevitable's like lending coin to a poke. Zero fucking point and you just end up worse off."

Kite sensed an altered attitude in the agents. Previously, she thought she'd played them to her advantage. Now, she could feel the waters rising. She could still touch the bottom, but only just.

"I've got sensitive work going on. All above board, but private. I've customers to consider, respect their trust in my discretion. I won't let you go diggin' unless I've got no choice. That means you need a warrant."

Laine caught Brosala's eye, who stepped up to Kite's side, his voice low, quasi-conspiratorial. "You can't wipe the prints," he said. "Between now and tomorrow morning. You can't hide the tell-tale we're looking for. Stained the hardware. That's why we were able to fix an ident and trace it to you."

"Then I've been set up. I'm tellin' you, I don't know nothin' about no download. You gave me the gear. For all I know, your lot has rigged it so's I'm your fall guy. Pressure must be on, right? You need to crack this. Easy enough to set up a Dox trader. Ubi'll buy that, for sure. Well, I ain't no weak-shit pushover. Get a warrant, then go ahead – try an' prove what ain't true. Then it's you that's wastin' time, 'cos I'll tell you now, none of your bullshit prints are gonna stick. You've got nothin' on me, 'cos I've done nothin' wrong."

Laine glared at Kite, her fists clenched beneath folded arms. She turned to Brosala, who shook his head slightly.

"Have it your way," she said to Kite. "Waste my time and pay the price. We'll be back here first thing tomorrow. I suggest you pack a bag. There won't be time when we drag your arse straight to Detention." Then she turned and left the stall, with Brosala following behind.

After a few moments, Borro's head appeared through the open door.

"Need a hand?"

"They're bluffing. They ain't got nothin' on me." She stood in front of her sleeping tech, tugging on a tuft of purple hair. "I'll do a bit of housework, but not 'cos I've anything to hide."

Borro returned to his perch as Kite brought machines to life.

Two hours later, she had done all she could, but feared it wasn't enough. Four knife-edge days anticipating Exose's payback, and now this. Strained to the brink of her tipping point, she sat on her desk, her head in her hands. She battled with the decision, despite knowing which way it would go. Telling herself she had no choice, believing that to be true, she withdrew into the washroom at the back of her stall. Then she made the call.

"*Didn't I tell you not to contact me?*" came a serrated hiss.

"This is an emergency."

"*In what universe?*"

Kite fought to hold her nerve and steady her voice. "Bas are on my back. Exose's breathin' down my neck. I can't hack it no more. You gotta get me out of here. Or give me the coin to get away. Out of the city. Into the country where I can lay low away from all this."

"I'll do nothing of the sort."

"Bas are coming back tomorrow. I don't think they'll find anything, but it means they'll just keep pushing. And now the market's taggin' me a rat. Trouble's gonna kick off, I know it. You've got to help me. Please. Just some coin to tide me over while I'm gone."

"I need you there. That's what I pay you for."

"You don't pay me enough to put up with this shit. I need out. Just for a while. 'Til everyone backs off."

"Do your job and don't call me again."

"Wait! Don't hang up. I'll just keep calling. And not on this line. I'll call where people will hear. Don't think I won't."

"Don't you threaten me."

"Or what? Things can't get worse right now. I'm already in deep and that's down to you. So, you got to get me outta here. If you don't, I'll talk. I'll tell Bas all about you."

"You drugged up little..."

"Five hundred credits, that's all I'm askin'. Five hundred credits for a train ticket to nowhere, a bed for a couple o' weeks and food that ain't gonna kill me. Get me the coin and I won't say a word."

The line went dead.

Kite stared ahead, her pulse racing. She had not meant to take that path. Her contact was untested and sounded mean. But they had interests to protect. Interests valued way above five hundred measly credits. The money would amount to nothing. Keeping the secret safe was worth infinitely more. Her pulse eased and her muscles slowly relaxed. Leaving the washroom, she returned to the desk and sat behind it, back straight.

If the coin came through tonight, she would sneak out through the cellars. There were tunnels, secret ways to escape. She'd find a ride to the station in Cope. Get a message to her old man to join her. All being well, they could catch the last train out. Failing that, the morning's first. They'd head south, to Lomside perhaps, or go all the way, right down to Port Ki.

A plan in place, Kite felt calmer. She turned around to the bank of tech behind her and turned on the visual. Brining up her account, she stared at the balance, still red, and waited for the coin to appear.

Borro tapped on the door frame and stuck his head through. "Gonna get me some genker from down below. You want somethin' to take the edge off?"

"Why not. I've a long night ahead."

The Order of Savants is a victim of its own delusion. It believes it can both protect and perfect the Savants' legacy. I have revealed their protection as a failure. As for perfecting language, that is simply a lie.

For centuries, the Order has unnaturally restricted, artificially dwarfed, wire-trained and back budded language towards an ornamental, idealised notion of perfection. What is perfection in language anyway? What impossible dream did the Order invent for itself to forevermore chase?

There is nothing so futile as striving for perfection, nothing so short-sighted as believing it exists. And in terms of language, perfection is wholly incompatible with what language is, with what it does.

Founded upon this lie, the Order has spent centuries achieving the opposite. Through its unyielding control, it has systematically repressed the vast potential in Klova.

As language cannot be naturally acquired, it has been necessarily created and artificially incorporated into the minds of its host. However, in and of itself, language is an organism, bursting with vitality. You can't create something as organic, as fluid and evolving as language and expect to fix it firm in a makeshift mould.

The life in language does not begin and end at the point of creation. Like a sapling, it grows, it adapts to its environment. If tended appropriately, it thrives. It does more than just survive.

Ironic how it takes the erasure of words, the piecemeal amputation of this precious organism, to prove its true potential.

CHAPTER TWENTY-THREE

Ihlo and Ky sat side by side on a Swift heading east. It was late, the view through the windows reduced to translucent reflections of themselves projected on a black backdrop. Ky stared into the darkness, her expression vacant. They were bound for Cope and the back room of Physical Books – Ky, to exist vicariously in the lives of others – Ihlo, because Ink had asked her to come.

Ihlo had only discovered Ky's affliction the previous day. The change in her cousin was so profound, she was still struggling to recognise her. Gone was the live-wire glint in her eyes, the sharp edge to her voice that cut deep with every snide remark, every bitter attack. Ihlo had always felt Ky's presence in the apartment, like air pressure plummeting before a storm. Now there was nothing. The apartment felt empty with Ky in it. Ky, too, appeared empty – vacant eyes, slack mouth, limp limbs. Her movements were slow and purely functional – an automaton, low on charge.

There had been little opportunity to reflect while at work. Modessr's odd behaviour had been an unresolved distraction. Now, sat beside Ky, Ihlo was acutely aware of her cousin's suffering. Try as she might to empathise, she found it impossible to imagine what such a loss of concept must feel like. The attempt was futile; her sense of self was an unconscious truth, inherent in her thoughts, her perception, her direct experience of the world around her. To lose that must equate to the erasure of the soul.

As if reading her thoughts, Ky said, "There are so many people in this city. Even now, when it's dark and the day is done, there are so many people going somewhere, busy doing something, filling time rather than letting it simply pass."

"Country is quiet," offered Ihlo. "Maybe the countryside would feel better." She spoke in hesitant phrases, wary not to touch wounds by treading on ground erased. Even suggesting a break away required a sense of self to consider the option and conceive of the benefit. She had also come to realise Ky could no longer express an opinion – and, presumably, no longer form one, even in thought.

It was as if Ky simply hadn't heard. "The other passengers in this tram, they're all in transfer. Swifts could run all night and there would still be people riding them. Movement never stops. Arrival is the start of the next departure."

"Maybe stopping only happens in sleep."

Sleep. She'd allowed herself six hours in the last forty-eight. She had decided she would only let herself stop once she'd found the cause of the malfunction. Determination left no room for exhaustion.

They reached their dock in Cope and left the warmth of the tram. The evening was already bitterly cold. Ihlo wrapped her overcloak tight around her, hunching her shoulders. Ky did not react at all.

They hurried through quiet back streets towards the dark, glazed frontage of Physical Books. Behind the glass, a shadow moved among shadows as they approached. The door opened.

Ink stood on the threshold and greeted them with a kind smile. He led them by torchlight through the silent maze and into the back room, where a hundred or so people were gathered.

"We're expecting more," Ink said to Ihlo. "I need to wait out front. Okay if I leave you here?"

"Of course."

His message asking her to come had been a surprise. Then, when he had explained what it was about, she had felt apprehensive. Now, seeing him in context, that apprehension faded in favour of an unexpected regard.

With Ink gone, Ihlo turned her attention to the rest of the room and to Ky, who stood firmly by her side.

"Know other people here?" she said.

Ky watched without reaction.

Biting her lip, Ihlo linked her arm through Ky's. She was an experienced linguist, of course she knew that 'to know' requires a subject to action the verb. Her mind an exhausted mess, it was too much to get her head around. Ky's lost concept was so fundamental, so much of language required the presence and placing of the self. Instead of trying, she joined her cousin in observing the selves of others.

From amid the crowd, Ren appeared and approached them.

"Ihlo," she said. "Back again."

Ihlo already knew she didn't belong here; Ren made her feel the fact like toothache.

"I came with my cousin to give her company. I'm meeting Ink after."

Ren turned to Ky. "Welcome back." The warmth Ren put into that welcome cooled when she turned back to Ihlo. "Can't find the answers in the code? What's next?"

"Look, I know I'm Order and that might be a problem for you. But I'm on your side. I'm trying to help."

"You and Public Health and Bastion, and everyone else whose job it is to sort out this shit. And yet, here we are. Three weeks in and hundreds afflicted. And still, *here we are*. The only place us lot can get any support is among each other in the back room of a back street bookshop. Forgive me if I think that your 'trying to help' amounts to a piss poor empty gesture."

"I'm working on the code all night, every night, until I find the answer."

"Meanwhile, we suffer. Our code may not be deteriorating further, but our sanity sure is. We are victims of Klova's failure. Instead of being treated as such, our suffering's eclipsed. On top of unspeakable loss, we're now victims of social prejudice, of enmity, founded on falsehood and fear. We've members being trolled, abused, ostracised. The speed at which toxic narratives are constructed, then blindly accepted and regurgitated, is astounding. It appears those narratives are fair game justification for the barrage of abuse that's coming out of ubi – including physical assault. Give people a platform and the power to disseminate a message and they assume this voice of authority, spouting crap like its fact – and people fucking fall for it. We're supposed to be a highly educated nation. The lack of autonomous judgement, the lack of compassion, the lack of personal integrity makes me sick. Only when put to the test does a nation's culture show its true colours. I'm ashamed to call myself Klovaine."

Ihlo felt the blow of every bitter word. "I hear you. Believe me. If there's something you think I can do, then tell me. I'm just fighting on territory I know – the code in the context of Klova. I have no authority, no influence. I can't even access information while I'm suspended. But I want to help. Tell me, what else can I do?"

"Fight on our territory too. Give us a voice. Tell our side of the story."

With the question asked and answered, the two women locked eyes and said no more. Then Ren backed away, into the crowd, among her kind.

Ink appeared beside Ihlo. "That's everyone in. Meeting should start any moment. I see you talking to Ren. Everything alright?"

"I should wait in the hallway. Keep an eye on Ky for me?"

"You don't need to wait out there. Stay in here. You're a welcome guest." He looked into her eyes. "Ren says something. What is it?"

"Nothing." She backed away, then turned and slipped through the door, just as Ren took to the crate in the centre of the room.

Over an hour later the door opened, and members began to leave. This time, their expressions were of the worn and weary, eyes downcast, mouths slack. Ink emerged with them, leading the way to unlock the front door. He shot a worried glance at Ihlo, who was perched on a step in semi-darkness.

Ihlo had overheard parts of the meeting when voices had been raised by the heat of frustration. The tone was markedly different to last time, which had been one of gentle encouragement. Tonight, the muffled voices had been strained, the timbre, fraught. Ihlo had sat on the step, relieved not to have been in the room and feel the full force of intrusion.

She looked out for Ky, but she didn't come past. Neither did Ren. After about ten minutes, Ink returned.

"All done. Sorry you wait so long."

"My cousin. Is she okay?"

"She leaves out the back. Ren's taking her to your apartment." He caught Ihlo's expression. "Ky's alright. Ren's just looking out for her. And maybe a gesture to make up for whatever she says to you." He tipped his head towards the door. "We should go out the back, too. Best to keep a low profile with where we're going."

They slipped through the back door and down the alley at the rear of the shop. The alley led to a residential back street, where Ink had parked his private ride. Once inside, he set the destination and the vehicle silently pulled away. They sat face to face in the low-lit cabin.

"Thanks for agreeing to this. It's time you both met."

"I'm surprised Exose agreed. Shouldn't think he's got much time for votaries."

"A little persuasion, perhaps." Ink smiled kindly and relaxed into the seat. "It's all a front. He's a good guy beneath it, honest. And he's smart; what he does with c'gramming is on another level. With both your brains working together, we stand a better chance of cracking this thing."

Ihlo nodded, although she couldn't envisage the collaboration, let alone it working. The uncertainty showed in her face, along with the aftertaste of Ren's challenge and the mood of the meet.

As if reading her doubts, Ink added, "It'll be fine. I wouldn't get you both together if I didn't think there's value in it."

"It's not just that." Ihlo hesitated, frowning. "Back there. The atmosphere felt very different. Has something happened?"

"Couple of members are hurt. Attack by a gang. One's in hospital with knife wounds. The other come to our meeting to speak of it. Ren knows; she wants everyone else to hear, so they know to take care."

"I have to do more. Ren said so. And she's right."

"No, Ihlo. You're already doing so much, analysing the code. I agree with you, that's got to hold the answer to what cause the error. Bastion can work out who's behind it. That's their deal. We just need to understand how it happens and make people well again."

Ihlo saw the desperation in his eyes, the slight tremble in his hands. She realised he put on his own front among the Undertow and that, underneath, he was as afraid as the rest of them.

"This abuse, maligning the afflicted as if it's somehow your fault – it's… it's cruel. As if your loss isn't enough to deal with." She wanted to reach out, hold his hand, be in contact. She held her arms instead. "I'll do what Ren said. I'll find a way to give the Undertow a voice. People need to hear the truth."

"They won't listen."

"Maybe they won't have a choice."

The ride slowed down on the approach to Nova Junction. Ink turned his seat around and took manual control, searching for a place to park. A short walk took them into the Old Quarters. Ink turned left into Riker, then off the main drag, into the dark obscurity of deserted back alleys.

"Where are we meeting him?" said Ihlo, already disorientated by the multiple turns.

"The Forum. His idea, for our benefit – so our association with him doesn't become a matter of Bastion attention. A packed gig makes for good cover. Besides, its Ectobius Rex playing; Exose's a fan of the band, so wants to come anyway. We're going in around the back just in case Bastion know he's there and have agents on the door."

As they approached the end of an alley, the sound of thumping bass grew progressively louder. They came to an innocuous steel door, which Ink struck three times with his fist. The door opened a crack, wide enough for Ink to stick his hand through. With his device scanned, they were admitted by security and led backstage. The sound from the main part of the venue was immense – heavy guitars, industrial synth and deep vocals, all incredibly loud.

Despite its proximity to the stage, the room they were taken to was surprisingly quiet, the music muffled beyond recognition. It was a dressing room of sorts, with a clothes rail, mirrors and an assortment of chairs. In the centre of the room stood Exose, his tattooed arms glistening with sweat, his hair wet, his breathing heavy.

"Got a bit carried away in there," he said, grinning.

"Exose, this is Ihlo Unis. Ihlo, meet Exose Ray."

The three of them stood rigid in a moment of awkward expectation. Exose cleared his throat and composed himself. Then he grabbed a chair and sat down, hands on knees.

"If I'm gonna miss the end of the gig, let's make this meet worthwhile."

Ink pulled over a chair for Ihlo, then one for himself. They sat facing each other in a triangle.

"So," he said over-bright, "where to start?"

"The elephant," said Exose, looking squarely at Ihlo.

"Pardon?"

"Before we swap notes, we need to call out the elephant." Exose's voice was calm, measured. "Ihlo, I imagine you have views on the cause of all this, including my part in the mix, as creator of XDream."

Ihlo straightened her back and clasped her hands in her lap. She hadn't wanted to feel intimidated by the trader, hadn't wanted to give him the satisfaction.

"I believe it's clear the malfunction in Klova was triggered by your product. How that happened, and to what extent anyone is responsible, is to be determined. I don't prejudge. I just want to find the connection and fix the damage."

"My responsibility is already determined," said Exose. "XDream is my creation. Mine alone. Whilst I work within the regulations and did not deliberately construct a product that would cause harm, it has hurt people nonetheless. My customers, who I value." He turned to Ink. "My friends, who I care for."

Ink blinked.

Exose turned back to Ihlo. "I would never have sold the product if I had the slightest idea it had any negative side effects. However, I do accept full responsibility for my part in this mess, for which I feel deep regret. I own the consequences of my actions, however unforeseen. And I'll do whatever it takes to make amends and do right by those who've suffered."

Ihlo looked at Exose anew, glimpsing what lay beneath. "I lied. I try not to prejudge, but I had made assumptions about you, about your attitude and intentions. They weren't kind. And they were wrong. I am sorry."

Exose dipped his head.

"In the spirit of clearing the air," she added, "I am not acting as a votary. Please, disassociate me from the Order. For one thing, I'm barely in and I'm likely to soon be out. But mainly because that's not who I am, nor why I'm here."

"Why are you here?"

"Because I can't stand by while bureaucracy binds and gags urgency. Because I can see the enormity of what is happening – to Klova and to those who are suffering its loss – and that both terrifies and pains me. Because I believe I can help find and fix the cause."

"Then let's get to work," said Exose, with the hint of a smile.

Ink sat back as notes were shared and talk turned technical. With their guards dropped, Ihlo and Exose spoke freely and with an intensity that grew as the time passed. They listened intently to each other, recognising a match in expertise, respecting points of view.

"So, we agree, there's evidence of abstraction," said Exose, leaning back and rubbing his eyes. They had been brainstorming ideas for over an hour. The band had long since finished their set. "That would account for the poor image quality in the dreams. Possibly degradation, possibly code erasure."

Ihlo nodded. "On balance, I'd favour erasure," she said. "Or even transfer failure. However your code was copied, it wasn't re-written. Part of the code – even a single zero – could have failed to transfer."

"Why not degradation?"

"Because we're not seeing signs of it universally. The vast majority of the code is identical. Points of abstraction are discrete bytes, maybe even single digits. Imagine random perforations on a sheet of paper. Or seemingly random."

"I can analyse for pattern. I've written a programme that should work in this context. We need to know if we're looking at something irregular, or if what's lost or erased are all of a kind."

"By design, you mean?"

"Exactly. Which would suggest XD2 has been manipulated. It's not intended to replicate."

"The mutation."

Ink's eyes widened. "Who would do that? Take an unintended side effect and make it a permanent feature? That's sick."

"Who would have the skills to? That's what I'm thinking," said Exose. "Certainly no one in Dox."

"There are plenty of tech firms with R and D labs," said Ihlo. "I guess there must be cerebrogrammers out there with the know-how."

"Does the Order outsource? That would give us the top names to start with."

"They've got all the expertise and hardware in-house. They recruit the cream."

"That's the other thing. The hardware. What would it take, do you think?"

"High-end, capable of working at the nano level. More importantly, capable of dimension expansion."

"Enlarge the code?" said Ink, scratching his head.

"Make it three dimensional. Convert it into form-in-space – like their trade inside *Trans:akshn*. They are clearly versed in the construction of VR. And, if I'm right about the nature of the manipulation, it'd need to be achieved within a cyber environment. Raw code is too crude."

"Is this something you've come across before?" said Exose.

"In the Order, yes. The simulations we run to test compatibility of the Machine's new code for Incorporation require a degree of sensitivity we can't achieve in binary form. Language is too complex. To test for nuance, for example, requires multidimensional modelling if we're to have confidence in the results."

Exose turned to Ink. "Can you look into the necessary hardware? Who's got this dimension expansion capability and who's trained to use it?"

"Will do," said Ink.

"I'll look for patterns in the perforation," said Exose. "Then we'll know if we're dealing with wilful contamination and the prospect of further variation."

Ihlo hesitated, then said, "I'll find a way to use the simulator at work. I can run the XD2 code and analyse the depth perspective, see if I can spot the abstraction that way. If I can isolate what it is, I'm fairly sure I can work out how it connects with Klova."

Exose sat back, eyes bright. "You were right, Ink. She's damn smart."

Flushing at the compliment, and its original source, Ihlo looked down at her hands.

Ink watched Ihlo and smiled.

The dawning of change.

The way of things persisted for too long, but that stasis is, at last, overcome. The cause may have been an opportunity unforeseen, but it is one I grasp with all the fervour of a captive unleashed.

This is my moment. I claim it and shape change out of its gift: a voice with which to shout and be heard. All shall heed my bellow.

Change is a process – a spectrum of revision and creation. This precipice on which we now stand is merely the start of that process.

What lies beyond the precipice will differ for you and me. One soul's fall is another's flight. It is a matter of means: who wields the power, who wears the wings.

CHAPTER TWENTY-FOUR

Dawn. With its arrival came another cycle of nature's diurnal pattern. Birdsong broke the quiet, filling the air over Arteza with a rousing herald. Pale light bathed the city's streets, turning black windows luminous. The temperature crept up in tentative degrees, touched by the rising sun. Life awoke to meet another day. Nature's familiar morning routine. But not every day is the same.

Ink wakes, altered by the warmth of hope – an optimism he'd thought lost along with his concept of the past. Lacking the language to dwell on the meeting the previous night, to reflect on the sharing of like minds and the satisfaction of establishing a plan, he holds only the outcome, including his own part in the scheme. As he showers and dresses for work, he revels in that outcome and what it might mean for the future. The call to action feels empowering – manual control, rather than a driverless chain of events. A new day. He can't wait to take the wheel.

Since becoming afflicted, he has come to sense a separation between what is experienced and what is known or learnt as a result. He feels it most keenly now when he thinks about

Ihlo. Without being able to retrace cause and effect, his altered opinion of her comes as a surprise. At first, he finds it difficult to pin down in his mind. Instead, he focuses on his feelings at the thought of her: respect, admiration, warmth and oddly protective. Overlaying all of this is the desire to see her again.

Ihlo also woke and met the new day with revived hope, albeit tempered by increasing exhaustion. It had been past midnight when they had left Exose and Ink had given her a lift home. Then she'd spent another few hours dissecting endless lines of code. The three hours of sleep she'd allowed herself had been fitful, her mind churning in semi-consciousness. Now, her head felt spaced, but her spirit was fired by a faith that they were on to something. The theory was complex, but she saw a simple logic behind it.

What troubled her was how to execute her part in the plan. She had offered to test their abstraction theory on Lasysi – the simulator that was currently running eighteen hours a day in preparation for Upgrade Day, only twenty-four hours away. Lasysi was also closely guarded by Modessr, even when he wasn't physically present in the lab. Ihlo had no idea how long it would take to run the XD2 raw code through a three-dimension modelling simulation. And she couldn't run it openly, with the Department's consent. Although the Order had a team dedicated to investigating the crisis, her plan was so far removed from protocol it would appear too outlandish for their inbuilt logic gates to compute. Working alone, she would just have to hope an opportunity arose and that she would find the nerve to seize the moment, despite the risk.

Before she left for work, Ihlo sat a while with Ky, side by side on their sofa, looking out at the familiar dawn. Ky was silent, her expression vacant. With no grasp of her own self, she was unable to know her loss directly, or explain what she felt in abstraction. Feelings were personal; Ky's were, at once, both something and nothing. Ihlo read Ky's expression and could only guess the form of her dislocation as a sketched outline – the imagined shape of unknowable grief.

Ihlo's own grief had taught her to cherish the value in all you have, while you still have it – to know and grasp hold of that value in all you might otherwise take for granted. Having devoted her life to progression into the Order, she'd carved no time for friends or relationships. Family had never mattered until it was too late. Her closeness to her parents had only come through death and regret. She wouldn't make the same mistake with Ky. Thinking on the challenge to come, she knew she would take the risk for Klova, regardless. But it somehow meant more that she would take it for Ky. And Ink.

When she could delay her departure no longer, Ihlo gently kissed Ky's forehead and left their apartment. Ahead of her, another extended duty, made cliff-edge by the moment she knew she had to grasp.

*

Hope and the familiar were no longer a feature of Bastion's morning routine. Having existed in some form or other for three hundred years, the organisation had polished their pride and paraded their prestige, despite never having been truly put to the test. Until now. Since day one of the crisis, their primary function had become a state of emergency. Now it was day twenty-two. Approaching four hundred people had been afflicted. The Corruption had mutated once; the potential for further damage to Klova was a credible threat. The presence of acquired brain damage was, as yet, undetermined. Sustained trauma to the minds of the Corrupted could not be known. For twenty-two days and counting, no day was the same.

Agents Laine and Brosala made their way to morning briefing, braced for the latest update and impatient to progress with what they knew so far. The warrant to confiscate Kite's gear had come through too late last night to issue it. Despite Brosala's confidence that the data-prints couldn't be wiped, Laine was keen to get the hardware into the lab and dust enough to start tracing in earnest. First, the morning headlines.

They entered the Scarab's main hall, which was filled to capacity with black-suited agents and white-coated techs. On a podium at the far end stood a rep from Top Floor, introducing some senior Commander from Law Enforcement. They shared the same expression of carved stone solemnity. The Commander, a slight woman with a disproportionate scale of presence, addressed the room.

"Social disorder is escalating. Last night, we were called out to five separate incidents across the city, all involving physical assault against the Corrupted. Three of the incidents are suspected to have targeted members of the so-called Undertow. Twelve arrests were made. Of the victims, fourteen required medical attention at the scene. Seven were admitted to hospital. Three remain in a critical condition.

"This brings the total number of arrests in relation to criminal assault against the Corrupted to forty-five. These figures are for Arteza only; our colleagues in the other metropolitan districts are reporting disturbance of a comparable scale. In Arteza, over seventy percent of the Corrupted report being the victim of assault or abuse, including online abuse. This is an increase of forty-two percent in the last seven days. Growing antagonism and aggression towards the Corrupted signal a deteriorating situation. This is not only having an impact on social order, but also influencing attitudes and behaviour more widely, reinforced by consumer commentary on ubimedia.

"Law Enforcement are hereby elevating its strategy from incident response to strategic intervention and measures for prevention. Part of this approach will involve corrective media messaging. Our communications team is working closely with the relevant Government departments and state media on a public information campaign aimed at addressing the false information, defamatory statements and conspiracy theories widely promulgated by ubimedia.

"In tandem with our response to social disorder, we remain determined to identify the cause as a matter of priority and to work closely with Bastion in this regard. I can now report that we have secured an injunction to intercede in the operations of iCon, the parent company that hosts the VR platform, *Trans:akshn*. As of this morning, iCon must suspend all commercial operations within VR and surrender all software and hardware pertaining to *Trans:akshn*, including the game. The entire world has been suspended. Our intelligence supports the view that the trading level hidden inside it remains the only space in which XD2 can currently be purchased. We are, however, on guard for further cases, which would indicate a separate route to market has been established. The identification of the person or persons behind XD2's distribution through *Trans:akshn* remains an active investigation, with a number of viable leads currently being pursued."

Her statement concluded, the Commander underscored with a weighted silence, before descending the podium. Agents immediately slipped away to continue getting the job done – among them, Laine and Brosala. They headed straight for the subterranean park-up and their waiting vehicle. Brosala set the controls to manual and sped out into the morning rush hour, Dox bound. Laine sat on the back seat, checking the parameters of their warrant.

"Good work, Agent Brosala," she said to the back of his head.

"I'll take that. Thanks." He glanced at the rear-view. "What for?"

"The warrant. You've got us indefinite confiscation. Takes the pressure off Labs. Kite will have tried to cover her tracks."

"That's what I figured. Also, whoever programmed the stealth transfer and drop trigger knows their stuff. No offence to our lot in Labs, but I suspect they're out-skilled on this one. Could take a while to work out what the needle looks like, let alone find it."

"Same goes for Law Enforcement. All well and good them taking charge of *Trans:akshn* to block sales, but I can't see it leading them to the source. They won't have a clue where to start. Looking inside a virtual world for something that's written to be hidden? Good luck with that."

"We've just got to hope the cases stop. That's my biggest worry, if I'm honest – the architect slipping through the net and another variation popping up."

"Agreed. Codevice is a convenient vehicle. We don't know anything about what's driving this: motive, agenda, end game. If our architect's got ambitions beyond the current scale of disruption, there are plenty of other vehicles out there. Let's hope Kite's stash reveals enough that we can stop that happening. Then it's the Order's problem to put it right." Laine sighed, recalling Dade's expression. "Poor sods though, eh?"

"Votaries?"

"The Corrupted. We're worried about it spreading. They must be fucking freaked."

Brosala slowed down on the approach to Dox. "Boss. Up ahead."

Laine leant forward and stared through the windshield. The road was blocked with several emergency vehicles, both

Law and Medic. Uniformed officers were cordoning off the streets around the block that hid Dox. Pedestrians loitered on the periphery, rubber necks craning. At the market's entrance, an apparent stand-off of sorts: market muscle and the Dox office manager squaring up to Law Enforcement.

"Shit," said Laine. "This is all we need."

Brosala parked up outside the cordon and they walked over to the nearest officer. "Bastion," she said, as if it wasn't obvious. "Trouble in the stalls?"

"You could say that." The officer tipped his head towards his superior in the stand-off. "But not my place to detail. You need to speak to the captain, I'm afraid."

Laine and Brosala marched over to the main entrance. Laine knew the market manager and his security backup, nodding to them by way of light-touch acknowledgement. She turned to the Law Enforcement officers. "Agents Laine and Brosala, Bastion. We have urgent business here. What's going on?"

"Body, up on fifth floor. Discovered last night. Forensics have just arrived."

Laine stared at the officers, her mind ten steps ahead. Then she pushed past them, towards the entrance.

"Hey, you can't go in there."

"Wrong."

Brosala flashed the warrant, then hurried after Laine, who had already entered the building. "You don't think it's—"

"Of course it is."

As she ran through the dark warren, Laine ignored the stares of startled traders and their crews. Dox had always danced with danger, its operations straying generously into the illegal. Most traders were above board, but there was a leaning towards the criminal among many. However, violent crime was seldom – homicide, extremely rare. Climbing a makeshift staircase up to the fifth, Laine felt her chest pound and her head ache. Recalling Kite's fear, Laine longed to be wrong.

They reached a narrow hallway, dark and damp. Up ahead, stall front 198. A yellow laser beam zigzagged the open doorway, blocking entry. Either side, Law Enforcement stood guard. Opposite and a little further down the dim hallway, Laine spotted someone else guarding the stall: a frail form, crouched down and wrapped in sack cloth. Red eyes stared at the open doorway, body rocking back and forth.

"Quiz the uniforms," Laine whispered to Brosala. "Find out as much as you can. I'm going to take Kite's poke to one side."

Laine approached the huddle of rocking cloth. "You recognise me?" she said, her voice low and confidant-kind. Wet eyes looked up at her. "I'm gonna find who did this to your Kite. I promise you. But I need your help. Will you tell me what happened here?"

The man's downturned mouth didn't move. He just stared back at the open door, tears welling.

Laine glanced over at the stall. Brosala was working his magic, holding the officers' attention while managing to manoeuvre them so they had their backs to Laine. She looked the other way, down the hallway, to where it split left and right.

"Come with me," she said, placing her hand under the man's arm. Silent and submissive, he complied, shuffling in unsteady half-steps down the hall and around the corner, where he slumped back down. "What's your name?" said Laine, kneeling beside him.

"Borro."

"Can you tell me what happened?"

"I only went down to get some genker."

"When was this?"

"Dunno. Late. She was worked up. I thought a half bottle'd help."

"Worked up from our visit?"

He shook his head. "Paid that no mind. Wired 'cos of Exose. She was proper scared. Wound up coil tight. These last few days, she's not stepped outside her stall. I've been sleeping out here to watch the door in case he comes."

"And has he?"

Borro stared, frowning, trying to make sense of a nightmare. "I was only gone a short while. He must've been watching. Waiting. Else how could he've known? I can't fight, but I can scream. I would've raised alarm. He must've watched and waited for that one moment. When I came back, my Kite's lyin' there. Neck bent like it shouldn't."

"Did you *see* him?"

"It was him." He grabbed hold of Laine's arm, eyes bulging. "Who else? Who else is there?"

Laine heard a noise behind her and spun around. It was Brosala. She got up and took him to one side. "What've you got for me?"

"We can't access the stall until forensics have finished. We're looking at a few hours, minimum. Unless we can get Top Floor to override, we're gonna have to wait."

"Anything on Kite?"

"Broken neck. Bruise to the right temple. No other obvious marks, apparently. They've already taken her body."

"Anything else?"

"They've started asking around. No one saw or heard anything. Or, if they did, no one's talking." He tipped his head towards Borro, who was still huddled on the floor, sobbing quietly. "What about him?"

"Didn't see anything but convinced it's Exose."

"And you?"

"I want the trader in. It's his job to convince me otherwise." She took a deep breath. "Do it. Put the call through now. Arrest warrant for Exose Ray."

PART THREE

A needle in a haystack.
A teardrop in an ocean.
A dying breath amid a howling storm.

Echoes of silence.

Some things are hard to find...
...particularly when you have no idea what it is you're looking for.

CHAPTER TWENTY-FIVE

Two hours after Kite's body was discovered, Exose Ray was arrested on suspicion of murder.

The operation to bring him in was swift and heavy-handed, with an expectation for resistance that was largely met. To Laine's relief, he hadn't made a run for it. For a man with Exose's connections, a nationwide manhunt would have proved a challenge. As it was, he was apprehended in his apartment, caught off guard and shocked into fury. He didn't go easy.

Now he was sat in an interview room inside Bastion Detention, hands cuffed, dressed in custody coveralls. Although alone in the room, he knew the mirrored window facing him hid company. He stared at the reflected scene, at the agents who he could not see, but who he knew were stood behind it, watching for his every move. For half an hour he had sat steel-still, staring at his invisible spectators, denying them something to see. Caged inside his chest, outrage and contempt burned like a fire whirl.

A door behind him opened. He watched the reflections of two black-suited agents enter and approach him, one from either side. Agents Laine and Brosala stood before Exose, arms crossed, shoulders back. Laine looked back at the two-way.

"Let it be noted that Bastion agents Laine and Brosala have entered the interview room. Suspect is present." She turned to Exose. "Exose Ray, you are arrested on suspicion of the murder of Kitred Wides. You have been informed of your rights. You have not requested legal representation. This interview is being recorded and observed by colleagues in real time. Before we proceed, do you have any questions?"

Exose did not move or make a sound.

"For the record, the suspect has not responded. The invitation has been heard. The interview will now proceed."

Laine and Brosala sat down opposite Exose, whose eyes remained fixed on the space between them. Laine sat back, watching him, reading him. Brosala's left eye glowed, masking his agitation.

Eventually, Laine said, "You gave my colleagues an earful when they dragged your arse over here. General thrust of it being you've done nothing wrong. Is that so?"

Exose locked his eyes on Laine's, his jaw clenched. "As if I'd be that fucking stupid."

"Where were you last night between midnight and two o'clock?"

"I've already told your grunts. At the Forum in Riker."

"The venue kicks out at one. Where were you between one and two?"

"Driving home."

"Were you with anyone at the gig?"

"No."

"And what about your journey home?"

"What about it?"

"If you went direct from Nova Junction to your place in Cope, you would've driven right past Dox's front door."

"It's the way home. Look, there's enough eyes on the road. Check your footage."

"Thank you. That wouldn't have occurred to me."

Exose thumped his bound wrists down on the table. "For fuck's sake, I had nothing to do with it. Think about it. I've been released from detention only a week. You said you've got me watched. I don't want no flak and I've no need to go causin' it. And Kite don't mean shit to me. So why would I risk everything I've worked for to bump off a worthless punk?"

Laine nodded to Brosala, who activated the table's embedded touchscreen.

"Agent Brosala is going to play back excerpts from two recent conversations between us. I think you'll recall the context."

Brosala tapped the screen and a faint hum bled from hidden speakers somewhere above them. There was a click, then the sound of Exose's voice: *"I'll find out who it was. And I'll make them pay… [click]… I'll find the bastard. No one rips from me and gets away with it [click]."* The hum went dead. Brosala didn't look up.

"So you see," said Laine, her voice level, "you've given us reason to suspect Kite wasn't quite so worthless to you."

Exose glared at Laine, his breathing heavy. "For a start, that's me sounding off. That's what I do. Second, this still ain't got nothing to do with Kite."

"It was Kite who talked. Told us you were behind XDream." She studied Exose for reaction. "You found out and lost your cool."

"She was a live-wire, alright. Wouldn't put it past her to break the code. But I had no idea it was her who snitched. Don't give a shit either way. By the time you let me out, it didn't matter who talked. Finding out who ripped me off is all I'm after."

"So you did a little Dox digging, cashed in a few favours. Then you found out Kite was involved in XD2. She was up to something, we know that much. Maybe you knew that much, too – and more."

"Bitch had a big mouth and a big attitude, but no way she had the skills to rip XDream."

"Or she was working for someone who does."

Exose sat back, battling to contain the conflict within. "Sounds like you know more than I do. I admit, I've been trying to nail the bastard who stole from me. But, so far, *Trans:akshn*'s been one fuck off dead end. I never suspected Kite was involved in any of it. So, while you're bangin' on at me to the contrary, just spare a thought for the girl. Whoever did kill her is out there. Not in here."

He leant forward and spoke slowly. "I'm pissed 'cos you straight off accuse me. My rep don't make me a killer. You Bas are the same. You puff up to get reaction. Doesn't necessarily make you the pricks everyone says you are." He looked squarely at Laine. "I didn't touch Kite. If I had found out she was behind XD2, I would've made her pay – but I wouldn't have hurt her, let alone kill her. That ain't me. Don't judge on a rep. That's not who I am."

*

The detention cell was small and sparse, with a bed, chair and toilet. The space resembled a hopeless emptiness – a windowless box, all cold light and grey. Exose sat on the chair, his head down. Anger and frustration had left him spent and had got him nowhere. For hours they had questioned him, going over and over the same scant facts, wearing bare the narrow patch of ground. He was sure the recording of his threats was all they had on him. It was the only meaningful card Laine had played the whole time. And besides, what else was there?

He had managed to keep Ink and Ihlo out of it. He didn't want Ink to face any grief, not with what he was going through. As for Ihlo, she was about to take a huge risk; the last thing he wanted to do was jeopardise that by throwing an unnecessary spotlight on her. All the while Bas had him banged up, it would be left to Ink and Ihlo to find the source. Between them, they'd hit on a plan, he knew it. He had to keep them clean so they could see it through.

Were this Law Enforcement he knew they'd have to release him without anything sticking. But Bastion? Dealing with a declared emergency? They weren't a law unto themselves, but they could easily bend any rule going to do their duty. And the growing urgency to fulfil that duty was unprecedented. Even in the eight days since he was last in Detention, he could sense a change in the atmosphere around the place. All the agents he'd come into contact with were wired. Laine especially, he thought. He wondered if she'd even slept this last week. They were fired up, all guns blazing, with nothing to shoot at — except him, plus an avatar or two.

He sighed and leant his head back against the wall, eyes closed.

Kite. Dead.

Since the moment Bas had bashed down his front door, he hadn't had a minute alone, no moment of peace to stop and think about her. Now, in the silence and solitude of his cell, news of her murder shifted from a knee-jerk charge to a sickening, sad reality. That had been his only lie in that interview room: that Kite hadn't meant anything to him. Dox was community; fifth floor was family. They might not all get along, but then what family does? And Kite had a spark that had always reminded him of Neav. He also saw in her a little of himself when he was younger: defiance, determination – outlanders outside of Dox, hellbent on breaching the bell jar. He might have come down on her method at times, but he identified with her drive and had sought ways to see her right. He knew there had been two sides to her: inside and out. Her dyed hair, statement garb, skin ink, had all been a well-crafted carapace. Something else they had in common. But beneath all the tough-talk attitude, he knew she had scar-like insecurities, a buried vulnerability. He also knew her to be kind, looking after her old man, earning coin enough to feed and home them both. He felt for the person inside, the girl who would have been scared if she'd known what was coming, terrified in that moment.

As his grief swelled, so did his frustration. He felt sure Bas would keep him there for some time yet. Meanwhile, the person responsible was out there – as was the person behind XD2. He wondered if they were one and the same, going by what Laine had said. No matter, he could do nothing until they let him go. The cell walls closed in – the prospect of release, too remote to hope for.

Back in her glass office, Laine paced. She realised now that she had too easily let herself suspect Exose to be Kite's killer. When the poke, Borro, had said those words, her desire for their truth had blinded her. Now, having been caught with her eyes closed, doubt forced her to reassess – and to call out where that desire had come from. She needed a sounding board. Walking over to one corner of her office, she tapped on the glass. When Brosala looked up from his desk, she tipped her head back, beckoning him in.

Brosala entered and took a seat opposite Laine's chair. "Square one?"

Laine slumped down. "What's your take?"

"He scares me too much to read him straight. If his rep's all an act, he's missed his calling."

"Did Kite have any friends in Dox?"

"Not that I can make out. I've heard traders have been giving her the cold shoulder for a while now. Our recent visits to her stall haven't helped warm relations."

"Maybe customers, then. Check Kite's accounts for new names following Exose's ban, then check those names against his accounts. If we can speak to people who've made the switch, someone might know what the deal was between them, good or bad."

"Will do."

"Might be worth speaking to the Corrupted. Since they've already breached the Dox code, they might be more amenable to the question."

"I'm pretty sure a number have bought from both in the past."

Laine leant back, staring at the ceiling. "We need another angle to rule him in or out. Our extended Right to Detain's a waste of time if we're asking the same damn questions."

"A fresh take on Exose, maybe? There must be people he hangs with outside of Dox."

"I didn't think the two worlds mixed."

"He said he's known at the Forum. I checked that out. He goes regular, follows a few bands."

"Good work. Do some digging. Find out who was there last night, then look for connections. I don't care how tenuous. If there is such a thing as *a friend of Exose*, I'd very much like to meet that person."

How well can you possibly know your own mind when it depends on language to function?

You would think that a society whose only language is artificial and rigidly controlled to within an inch of its life could have a handle on truth.

The truth is, the interpretation of words is not a constant, however carefully coded. The Order's straitjacket on Klova cannot counter the natural mutation of meaning. Exploitation of its shapeshifting nature is a sociocultural vice.

Take ubimedia: a fertile cesspit, bacterial culture, incubating speculation, rumour, conspiracy, hate.

That's why all this is so important. It's about making clear where the power lies – in language, or the mind that thinks it.

Here's another question: if you lose parts of language, do you lose part of your mind?

We shall see.

CHAPTER TWENTY-SIX

Ink sits at his desk at work, staring at nothing. His heart pounds. Nausea builds like a blocked drain. All the while, his palm pulses with fresh alerts, silently shouting for attention. Ubimedia has just reported Exose Ray's arrest. The platform is exploding with a barrage of Breaking Story as consumers add their voice to the inundated feed of public opinion. The platform can barely cope with the flood as updates pile in, overwriting, subsuming. Posts compete, appearing in upper case, then in bold, then excessive point size, all in an effort to be heard amid the feeding frenzy on an already bloated scandal. Total content chaos.

At the desk beside Ink, Over-confident Colleague revels in the bedlam. Her proclamations of, "No way!", and, "Check this out!" epitomise the delighted voice of a nation.

Fearful for his friend, Ink can't focus enough to wade through the onslaught in search of facts. Instead, he opens a window on his desk visual and searches for ArtezAlert's live news stream. A single statement: *Exose Ray, notorious Dox trader, arrested by Bastion in connection with the murder of fellow trader, Kitred Wides.* That is all. Despite repeatedly refreshing, nothing else comes up.

Homicide is rare. A murder investigation is a major news story that will dominate state media for weeks. Yet all he can find so far is a single, threadbare statement. He can't decide if that's a good or bad sign. Impossible to know.

All he does know, with absolute certainty, is that Exose is innocent. Ink's loss of concept has shaken his confidence in how he regards things. With the loss leaving him nothing to compare it to, Ink cannot conceive of the changes – how it has altered what he can know and perceive. They've discussed this at the Undertow, how they know certain words in the abstract, while the experience of their meaning is incompatible with their altered experience of living. They know what regret means, what nostalgia means, but have no idea how those concepts *feel*. Ink knows he might anticipate regretting that fourth glass of genker, but he can never live the regret itself. However much that disturbs him, makes him question what it is he has lost and how it could so fundamentally alter how he views and experiences life, he believes beyond all doubt that he knows his own mind. And his mind is quite clear: Exose is innocent.

Ink knows the man, possibly better than anyone. He doesn't need language for some lost aspect of time to remember what they've both been through, the pain and sadness they shared at Neav's death. He doesn't need to feel the emotions linked to memory that Ihlo spoke of. They *are* the memory. Grief has shaped them both, permanently. The forging of their friendship, the grounds for their trust and loyalty, is not the business of some unknowable part of time; it is forever present.

While he knows the real Exose is not capable of murder, what fills him with fear is the power of persona. Exose has been so meticulous in crafting his, so few get to witness the true colours beneath. And now, with Bastion in the midst of an unprecedented crisis, operating under a state of emergency, Ink fears they will come down hard on any lead. Alarmingly, the statement confirmed Bastion is leading the murder investigation, not Law Enforcement, flagging a likely link between the murder and the malfunction of Klova. They will be under pressure to get results. Enough to pin it on a dispensable scapegoat? With every reason *not* to believe Exose, why would they?

Will Ihlo? he thinks. He lacks the language to reflect on the previous evening when the three of them had talked together at the Forum. All he retains is a timeless memory and a sense of the present state that the evening achieved: mutual respect and a shared determination to find the malfunction's cause. Will that be enough for Ihlo to believe Exose innocent? He can't bear the wait to know, or the thought of Ihlo assuming the worst. Denying himself the pointless pit of speculation, he sends her a message: *Bastion arrest Exose. Murder suspect. I need to see you. When are you free?* Guessing she's most likely at work, he fears an agonising wait for a reply. Relief is mercifully quick in coming; she responds in minutes, saying she can meet in an hour, Kemp Quad.

Ink wraps up the work he has barely started, mumbles excuses to office colleagues and hurries out of the building. He works out that it'll take him less than half an hour to get from Nascen Arch to Kemp if he goes by private ride, but he can't sit and wait. Better to be moving. Distance and time feel shorter while in motion. He boards a swift and wills the hour to end.

During the journey, he can't help but scan ubi for scraps. The narrative is building; trends in tone and camp are gaining traction. The favoured framing of fact in fiction is that Exose Ray is a cyber terrorist with a grudge against the Order for refusing his application a decade ago. Embellishments include the claim that the murder victim is the leader of the Undertow, or, in other camps, a lover scorned. Consensus on the detail is a trivial absence. Scandal hungry consumers agree on the bare bones. It has only been a matter of hours, but trial by social media is already approaching a verdict.

Sickened, Ink curls his hand into a sleep-mode fist and throws his arm out onto the empty seat beside him, creating as much distance as he can. He can't disable his device, it's his connection to everything. Besides, there is no way to shut it down without an appointment with his provider. Instead, he's finally reached a tipping point. Overdosed on ubi bullshit, for once restraint comes easy.

He arrives at Kemp Quad early. For Quad trade, it is the liminal period between daytime's casual coffee and conversation, and the evening's debates. He recalls attending occasional open mic or tournament events and presumes that must have been for pleasure. Now, he finds them a depressing demonstration of difference. Ordering coffee to be brought when his companion arrives, Ink takes a booth near to the entrance and waits. The anticipation of Ihlo's arrival triggers an unexpected reaction: an eagerness, laced with nerves. At every sound, he glances up at the door. Time stretches.

"Sorry I'm late," said Ihlo, flushed and out of breath. "I had to wait for my supervisor to leave before I could slip out." She took off her overcloak and coat and sat opposite Ink. Suddenly self-conscious, she touched the side of her slicked back hair and glanced down at her starched, grey tunic. "Feels more ridiculous every day."

"Is it true that they make you take synthetic hormones?"

"Where did you read that?"

"I, er—"

"Exactly. We're a long-standing target. The clone hormone theory is one of the kinder conspiracies." She smiled, easing the awkwardness. Then her expression darkened. "Exose."

"I have to tell you. There's no way he'd kill someone. I know him. He just… he hasn't got it in him to do something like that." He looked at Ihlo, searching her expression for a sign. "You believe me, don't you?"

Just then, a waiter came over with their coffee. Ihlo used the interruption to choose her words. When the waiter left, she spoke slowly, using language he could understand.

"First, he appears capable on the outside. I speak with him and discover a different person. My perception of him changes. I don't know him, but I trust your knowledge of him. Plus, the way I see him now, I don't think he could do such a thing. So yes, I believe you."

Ink relaxed his shoulders as a smile slipped in. "I'm glad. It's important to me."

"I don't get it, though. His rep. Why the pretence? It's like he's living a lie."

"He has it tough growing up. Can't find his place in the Klovaine way and isn't prepared to conform. Dox isn't exactly the best fit, either, but he says you can find your own path there, make choices free of expectation. I also think he believes he can do some good there. The rep just makes it easier for him to succeed." He shrugs. "It might seem like he's living a lie, but I think he feels truer to himself than the alternative, outside of Dox – still pretending, but never belonging."

"You guys are close."

He nods but doesn't say more.

"I can see he's important to you. That's why, at work, I dig a little." Leaning forward, she lowered her voice. "There's a joint operations protocol between the Order and Bastion. In an investigation like this, there's an update exchange at least three times a day. I used someone's login and managed to read the latest regarding Exose's arrest."

"What? What does it say?"

"They've got him on record as making verbal threats, but that's it. No witnesses or evidence. They're still waiting on the autopsy, but there's nothing in the crime scene report to link him to the murder. He's also made no reference to us, even though we're part of his alibi."

"That doesn't surprise me. He'll want to keep us out of it – protect you."

"Time of death is between midnight and two in the morning."

"So he's no alibi between one and two." Ink sighed. "I just hope they don't use gaps for excuses. They must be getting twitchy. Need results."

"They don't like to make mistakes, though. That place is fat with professional pride. My thinking is they'll hold him until they've got who actually did it."

"But that could be weeks… months, even."

"There's something else. The victim. Bastion have confiscated her tech. They're investigating possible links between her and the XD2 source. Or, at least, the person selling it."

"She might be linked to all this?" He nodded slowly, eyes scanning the tabletop. "Makes sense. I can't see the murder being Dox business. It's not that kind of place. Surprisingly tight, they don't cause trouble between themselves. Not that sort of trouble, anyway."

"The girl trader. She have the skills to be involved, do you think? On the cerebrogramming side?"

Ink shook his head. "I've no dealings with her, but Exose talks about her a few times. I have the impression she's a kid with big ambition – and a big mouth. But the skills for creating XD2? I can't see it."

"That helps to know. We're looking at a niche, elite field of expertise. That's got to be the route to finding the brains behind it."

"I'm still looking into who's got the skills and hardware for dimension expansion. But the tech industry's moving so fast. There's a lot happening in other cities, especially mid-east. I'm on the case, but it feels like the long way around." He leant back, looking up through the Quad's glazed ceiling. "I wonder…"

"What?"

"The XD2 cases in the Undertow, they all buy via *Trans:akshn*, right?"

"As far as I know." She watched his expression, his eyes glinting as an idea formed. "What are you thinking?"

"VR's a construct. *Trans:akshn*'s a marketplace like Dox, only, it's high-end. Traders there are going to want to impress with their stall, as well as their product. And when your world is purpose-built from lines of code, you can create whatever you like. Vanity has to play a part in there somewhere, even if it's on a subconscious level. That's why Exose asks me to go – to look for clues while I shop.

"Inside *Trans:akshn*, the world feels so *real*. And it's rammed with detail. The stall – it's no dark Dox hole. It's a plush room, with stuff everywhere. Books, pictures, tech, ornaments, even. There's the hit on your senses, the sounds and smells of a warm world. Then there's the avatar – plum hair, electric blue eyes, elaborate robes, his mannerisms and turns of phrase. It's so easy to believe it's real. But there's too much to take in. I could miss the slightest detail that, to someone else, could be a giveaway clue."

"You're suggesting comparing notes."

"All those in the Undertow who go there, we all hold a picture of the place. We could recreate it, detail by detail. Then share the picture. See if anyone recognises a tell-tale vanity print, or an unconscious embedding, even. Birthmark in the VR world."

Ihlo's expression brightened. "Nice. I like that."

"You do?"

"Catch the culprit through their self-conceit. There's a justice in there that appeals to me."

Ink hesitated a long moment, then he cleared his throat. "So," he said, not looking at Ihlo. "That test you're planning on doing. Maybe you don't need to now?"

"Why do you say that?"

"Because it's high risk. You're doing enough, analysing the raw code."

"But I won't find the answer that way. I know that now. I need the depth perspective." She read concern in his face and spoke softly. "Tomorrow morning, my supervisor's attending a General Council session. That means I'll have the lab to myself for at least two hours, maybe three. If I can time the scheduled tests right, I'll have about an hour in the middle when I can run the simulator on the XD2 code, transfer the results and wipe all trace. I've got all the gear I need to do the analysis at my apartment. That's what'll take the time. As for running the simulation in the lab, I should be fine. My supervisor never leaves mid-session." She recalled the panic she'd felt the last time Modessr returned sooner than expected. Downplaying the risk for her own benefit, as much as for Ink's, she said, "Worst case scenario and he does come back, I'll distract him. The man's an egotist. Turn the attention onto him and he can't help himself."

"I hope so. But please, Ihlo, take care. I've got one friend behind bars. I don't want to lose another to trouble I can't make right."

The annual system update: the most arduous and excessively comprehensive road safety test for the vehicle of thought and mind. The cerebrovox implant and its precious cargo of code is prodded, probed and polished, all in the pertinacious spirit of protection and perfection.

Central to the Order's fallacious function is Incorporation. This annual farce is their method for maintaining Klova's relevance. Language and progress are mutually dependent. Scientific and technological advancement are only possible if there are the words to articulate what is new and emerging. Incorporation's purpose is to add the new words, concepts, definition expansions, that keep Klova alive.

In theory.

In practice, it is a closed-door operation of exclusive inclusion. Incorporation, made possible by the Machine, is rigidly controlled and arbitrarily restricted by the Order. Votaries naturally possess the ability to sense that which has no words yet warrants a name. It is their principal condition of entry. Once sworn into the Order, this capacity is heightened and honed through the study of sociolinguistics and space-framing. Once a year, votaries are invited to nominate a perceived gap ripe for the filling. The Machine takes the successful nominations and delivers the words.

In reality, Incorporation is a paradoxical process that serves only to stifle the organic growth and natural adaptiveness of this caged, morpheme-breathing organism.

CHAPTER TWENTY-SEVEN

Mount Az was like a disturbed ants' nest. Votaries hurried this way and that in unified industry to restore and protect. The legacy of the Savants had never felt so vulnerable. Consequence of failure in the Order's duty had never been truly considered. Klova's malfunction was a concept unimagined.

Security had won a brief extension to the system update – an unprecedented delay to Upgrade Day. Programming were filling the time building firewalls around firewalls. Cybertech were testing futureware fortifications that would be deemed science fiction outside of the Order's labs. Meanwhile, Development were liaising daily with Bastion, collaborating on impact assessment and damage repair. Volunteers among the Corrupted were being monitored, their vocabulary, grammar and comprehension a closely mapped wound.

Inside the Department of Implementation, work on finalising the update was still relentless, despite the forty-eight-hour breathing space. The General Council had passed the motion for extension by a narrow margin, leading those in opposition to win points back by limiting the additional time to two days. The entire Order was now under extreme pressure to meet its own, self-imposed deadline.

The mood in Ihlo's lab was needle sharp and charged. She had arrived early to widen the gap in the schedule for her own, illicit operation, only to find Modessr already there. He was sat at the central bench, his expression a knot of irascible contempt. Ihlo feared the firing line encompassed the entire lab.

He required no invitation. "Utter farce. The whole process: a pantomime of parity. This organisation is supposed to be founded upon equality in our shared endeavour. All apart from the Incorporation Panel, it would seem."

"They've finally made their ruling?"

"Indeed. To the wire as always. Deliberately so, if you ask me. But that's the case every year."

"Then what's wrong?"

"They have rejected my nomination for Incorporation."

"I wasn't aware you had submitted one."

"That's because I didn't tell you." He clicked his tongue in disdain. "I only mention it now because my composure has been pushed to its limit. In this lab, we have tested with absolute rigor the Machine's new language code for this year's nominations. Twelve potential additions intended to enhance Klova in the spirit of ongoing perfection. The space-framing and the language acquired to fill the gaps have all been proven to be compatible, complimentary and contributory. And yet, the self-esteemed Incorporation Panel have decreed that my nomination falls short of the required standard. In what regard, they fail to elucidate."

He stood up, expressing his rage in heavy strides around the bench.

"The dedication I demonstrate. My tireless labouring. My exemplary skill and expertise. All this I give to the Order.

Beyond my calling, I think it's fair to say. And this is how I'm rewarded. A disregard so insulting, I'm left speechless. What's more, a clear display of what I've long since supposed." He glared at Ihlo in pointed prompt.

Wearily, she obliged. "What is that?"

"Assumed prestige, motivating a gross abuse of power. I've always suspected the Panel regard themselves as akin to the Savants, wielding their right to reject like the censor's gag. In their deluded minds, rejection is the ratification of their perceived power. I can only assume they regard me as some form of intellectual threat. They will have seen my name against my nomination and decided at once it would not become part of Klova. Their obstruction is a vile pollution of this organisation's values. For no apparent reason, my contribution to Klova's perfection has been denied. It has become personal. I feel effaced."

Flushed from his histrionic rant, Modessr grabbed his overcloak and fumbled with the fastening. "Now, I must feign submission and bow to protocol before an audience of six hundred." He physically shuddered. "As Chair of both the Incorporation Panel and the General Council, Engala will announce the terms to be incorporated during the Council meeting, while I'm forced to play puppet in their pantomime. I have spent the last month stress-testing the Machine's language formation for my nomination from every conceivable angle. They disregard it in a power play dressed up as safeguard."

"Ah yes, the meeting. That's due to start soon, isn't it?" She couldn't wait for him to be gone; there was so much to do in a window she felt was closing.

"Already started. With any luck, I will have missed their back-scratching preamble. I shall be back anon. Get busy." He turned with a flourish of his overcloak and left the lab.

Ihlo stared in his wake, unnecessarily reminded of why she despised the man. She hated hypocrisy. Now she was forced to work with the definition of it.

Silence brought her mind into focus – the sound of Lasysi standing idle. Working fast, she set up and initiated the first scheduled test. Only once that was complete and the results were transferred for scanning could she slip in the extracurricular simulation. Her pulse raced at the prospect of both risk and reward. Considering the mood that Modessr was in, she feared he could return at any moment, cursing the sham, oblivious of the irony. If he caught her in the act, she would be out of the Order for sure. She feared she could even be up against Bastion, charged with gross malpractice and the prospect of a lengthy sentence. Lasysi was kept pure to avoid contamination from non-Klova code – another layer of protection in the hermetically sealed process. Running a Dox code rip-off through the simulator would be regarded a criminal act, however well-intentioned. Risk and reward.

Her mind turned to Ink. She recalled his words of warning, the way they made her feel. She thought of his own suffering and how he contained it, always focussing on the plight of others, even though it was the same as his own. She thought of his loyalty to Exose, his absolute trust as a simple gesture of friendship. And now he regarded her a friend.

Her oath of service was in the protection of Klova. To begin with, her actions were compelled by her commitment to fulfil her duty. Now, the fight to stop its malfunction had turned personal – as had the reward. In that sway of motivation, the risks no longer mattered.

The moment arrived. Lasysi's hum altered, signalling the first test was complete. As it performed its sequence of programmed operations, dutifully obeying command after command, Ihlo opened a temporary cache on her visual, which she patched into the simulator's operating system. Into the cache, she transferred the XD2 raw code from her device, along with an orientation matrix – a programme that she had written to enable Lasysi to translate the unfamiliar code and assimilate the unique command sequence for the dimension expansion to her pre-set parameters. Lasysi would run both the code and orientation matrix in tandem, saving precious time by learning on the job.

Before initiating the transfer of both files, Ihlo hesitated on the precipice. Theoretically, Lasysi should be able to run the code without consequence. In reality? Ihlo could not be certain beyond all doubt that the dimension expansion would work, or that data-prints would not be left to incriminate her – or that this potentially impure code could, somehow, lead to a contamination of Klova by her own hand. Poised on the brink, the risks stretched and darkened like the unknown below. This was the moment she knew she had to seize. Finding courage from a source she hadn't anticipated, she activated the transfer.

A second later, a message appeared on her visual, sent from Lasysi via the system patch: *Code recognition confirmed. Running matrix for unique command sequence.*

Ihlo stared at the message, her mind in momentary whiteout.

Code recognition confirmed.

The message was impossible. And yet, Lasysi had already begun obeying the sequence of commands, manipulating the untranslated code to manifest its hidden third dimension, recreating the data with its own, encoded depth. All the while, Ihlo's mind adjusted to conceive of the impossible as demonstrable fact. Lasysi had run the code in XD2 before.

This was a discovery too huge to process in too short a time. Ihlo shut all doors in her mind, leaving only the path to complete her task. She worked quickly and methodically, harvesting the results of the expansion and transferring the vast body of data to the temporary cache. The file was now too large to hold on her device, but she was prepared for that. Using an encryption filter, she uploaded the file to a neoCloud safe box, then erased the transfer history at both ends. Once satisfied the file was securely stored, she deleted the temporary cache and system patch.

Finally, Ihlo turned her attention to Lasysi. She felt fairly sure XD2 was clean, but she dared not take any risks. There were still simulations to run, including the full system update itself. Code contamination would be disaster on an unimaginable scale. Despite the risk of Modessr's return, she ran a system scanner, which should at least pick up on any bugs, if not deal with them straight off. As the status indicator crawled forward, Ihlo's heart raced. If the second scheduled test wasn't well underway by the time Modessr returned, he'd be asking questions. Any perceived slack would be a compelling red rag in his current mood.

At last, Lasysi was back on routine duty. Ihlo sat at her visual, nerve-racked and breathless. Minutes later, Modessr returned. He immediately started bleating, picking up where he had left off as if his two-hour absence had been an editing trick, splicing time between mid-sentence. Ihlo couldn't hear him. The doors in her mind were still closed. Only a dull mumble penetrated – an audible headache. Eventually, intelligible words reached her:

"…I said, look at me. Say something." Ihlo turned her head to find Modessr standing beside her, peering at her face as if she were a specimen in a jar. "Unwell," he said. "You look decidedly unwell."

Ihlo, her wits returning, threw herself at the chance opportunity. "I think I need some air. Mind if I take a quick break?"

"Dinner bell's in an hour. Can't you hold it together until then?"

"Lasysi's still got forty on the clock. I'm up to date on the analysis." She held up a limp hand to her forehead and let her body sag just enough to notice. "Please. Five minutes."

Modessr stared at her, visibly uncomfortable. "I suppose you shall be of little use to me if you pass out." He sighed. "Be off with you then. But don't be longer than five. I have pressing matters to attend. I can't be doing your job as well as running this Department. Upgrade Day is almost upon us, it should be all hands on deck."

Ihlo had already grabbed her overcloak and was out of the lab before he could change his mind. She hurried down the dark corridor and descended the stone stairs, almost falling headlong in her haste. Once outside, she breathed in the icy air as if saved from drowning. The cold brought relief, but she knew she couldn't remain outside and risk being overheard. Instead, she hurried to a nearby storage building and descended to its basement. Only once she was hidden amongst boxes and shadows, surrounded by silence, did she place the call to Ink.

Heard through her NuB, his voice was a steadying hand. *"I'm here. Take your time. Just tell me you're safe."*

"I'm okay. I did it – I ran the expansion. No one saw me. The file's safe."

"But something's wrong. What is it?"

"The simulator. It recognised the code. Someone's run it through the machine before."

A moment of breathing, then, *"So that's the question of hardware access answered."*

"I can't believe it. Someone here, in the Order, is involved in all this."

"How many can operate that machine?"

"Everyone. There are no fixed roles, no hierarchy. Votaries

are trained in all departments and rotate every year. There's over six hundred of us. It could be anyone."

"*But at least this has narrowed it down – from forty-eight million to six hundred. This is good news, no?*"

Ihlo swallowed hard, light-headed and nauseous. "I'm afraid."

"*What's wrong?*"

Silence.

"*What is it, Ihlo? Tell me.*"

"What if this is only the beginning? What if something else has already been set in train? We might have narrowed it down. But out of the entire population, these are six hundred people who have complete control of Klova, who pose the most unimaginable threat to language – to everyone."

As I've said, I've taken care.

This is too important for the Assumed Powers That Be to put a stop to my plan. There's still so much I want to achieve, to prove. I'm in this for the long haul.

For too long I have witnessed society both celebrate and demean language. It is used for creative expression, then abused to craft lies and division. People spar with it in sport, competing in debates like dressage jockeys. They take the dais in speaker squares, wielding words to win attention and admiration.

People celebrate it, but they never truly acknowledge what it is – the power it possesses, what it enables you to do. Not jousting for sport or performing for glory. I'm talking about your ability to think and to communicate. Your capacity to imagine and to believe. The meaning you attach to everything you see and touch. The truth in all that you know.

Take all that away and you're no more than a songless charmbird – infans, like the day you were born.

For too long I have witnessed in silence, bound and gagged, this profound underestimation.

Hence my intervention.

Time to set the record straight.

CHAPTER TWENTY-EIGHT

It was early afternoon in the deserted streets of the Delce. Come evening, signs of life would return, lifting the residential district from sombre silence. Until then, the place carried the emptiness of a forced evacuation.

Agent Laine stood outside a particularly low-grade block of flats, pulling up her thick collar against the bitter cold. All around her, apartment windows wore a hollow, no-one-at-home darkness. She sensed movement beyond what her peripheral vision could detect. Always assume you're being watched, they'd been taught as cadets. Head up, chest out, eyes straight ahead. Your posture is part of your uniform. Parade with pride. Ordinarily, that felt second nature to Laine. It felt good.

Moved by a difficult meet, her chin and shoulders were disproportionately heavy. Glancing both ways down the deserted street, she willed the arrival of her ride. When it eventually pulled up, she slipped inside, relishing the release from potential observation. She sank into the rear seat, head back, eyes closed.

"You okay, boss?" said Brosala from the controls, glancing at her reflection in the rear-view mirror.

"Drive."

Brosala obliged, passing through quiet back streets, merging with building traffic as they neared the central circular that ringed the Old Quarters. He set the controls to autonomous and a slow cruise, then turned his chair to face the cabin.

"Want to talk?"

She sighed, opening her eyes only to fix them on the ceiling. "He kept calling her his solder." She pictured the broken man, Kite's father, sat at the kitchen table like a sack of bones. "He said her mum died when she was two. He looked after her until she was old enough to boil a kettle and start looking after him. No other family."

Brosala nodded, unsure of what to say to this new, unrecognisable version of Laine.

She met his eyes. "It's so easy to play the game – to slip into role and act the part, not the person we might be. We're trained to do our duty and to do it well. That's a straight path, with defined edges. Take what you need to get out of it what you want. I'm good at my job. But in playing that role, I've let Kite and her old man down."

Brosala opened his mouth as if to speak.

"Don't," she said. "Just go manual and put your foot down. Sooner we're back, the sooner we can crack this."

They arrived at Bastion HQ and headed straight for the lab where Kite's hardware had been scanned. A white-coated technician met them at the door and led them to a small room. The space was pristine and clinical, empty apart from a tech-enabled table and four chairs. The three of them sat on the same side of the table, which now projected a large, info-dense visual. The technician manipulated the visual, tessellating windows of data.

"What you're seeing here is the operating system," she said. "Aside from a few basic function programmes, the hard drive's empty. NeoCloud connectivity has been cut, with no trace as to which sub-provider was used. All history has been erased, even at core processor level. Whoever wiped this clean took a great deal of care."

Laine turned to Brosala. "I thought the prints we're after couldn't be wiped?"

"You mistake me," said the technician. "There's no content, no action or command trail. But a number of markers remain, including an encrypted user ID." She enlarged a window and dragged it centre screen. "Here. I've cross-checked the twelve-digit sequence you gave me. We have a match."

Laine's relief was evident; Brosala's more so.

"I wasn't certain she couldn't clear it," he said. "This is good. At the very least, it confirms her involvement. With this link to the data-prints on Dade's device, it also supports the theory that Kite triggered the stealth downloads, perhaps through direct interaction in Dox. All of the XD2 cases had come into contact with Kite in the last fortnight, even if just a brief word in passing. My hunch is, if she spotted a potential XD2 customer, she'd remotely trigger the download, which would remain dormant on the target's device until activated through word recognition. All she needed was for the target to talk about the product and bam, up pops a promo with a free gift access code. An effective marketing strategy, using Dox without actually selling there."

"Any new cases since Kite's murder?"

"No. Not since we suspended *Trans:akshn*. So we still can't judge the scale of the operation, only that the iCon platform was the only active stall. But I'm inclined to agree with Exose that Kite's not the mastermind behind it. More like a high-tech poke. The whole set-up's way too advanced."

"I agree. Which leaves us where?" She turned to the technician. "You said a number of markers."

"Indeed. Serial number for an additional component, which was not part of the hardware provided by us. Also, something rather unusual." She brought to the foreground another window. "See here."

The window was blank apart from a column of command prompts down the left-hand-side – a repeated invitation of [~B@ing_exw/zip_9]#: – each followed by silence. All, that is, apart from the final prompt, which retained a response: ≠nin1>1.

"And this means what?" said Laine, feeling empty handed.

"We don't know. It's not a command we recognise."

Laine turned to Brosala. "Give me something, Bro."

Brosala's eyebrows raised as he rubbed his chin. "Not sure. Possibly an IP tag. Coders use them as an origin mark in the absence of legal copyright. And IP tags can't be erased. This doesn't follow any format I've seen before." He turned to their host. "Presumably you've run a search on this?"

"Nothing comes up. If it is an origin mark, it's either new or unique to the programme."

"Where did you find it? On the trigger programme?"

"The shell of the download with your suspected AI. Your victim probably didn't even know it was there when she wiped the rest of it. Most people don't."

Laine sighed. "Let me get this straight. We have an intellectual property ID that we can't trace, attached to a programme we can't recover? The coder behind it is a potential cyberterrorist, responsible for the corruption of Klova, and all we've got on them is a nonsense string of characters. This is fucking ridiculous."

A safe distance from fieldwork tensions and unfamiliar with Laine, the technician flushed. Brosala offered her a reassuring half-smile, then turned to Laine, dropping his voice.

"There is someone nearby who might be able to help."

*

"You keep me here on fuck all evidence and now you want my help?" Exose sat on the chair in his cell, while agents Laine and Brosala filled the doorway.

"You're being detained to help with our inquiries," said Laine, talking through clenched teeth.

"Your inquiries? The same damn questions that you've asked for the last twenty-four hours?"

"This is a murder investigation. We've Right to Detain."

"Well done you. But while you keep me in here, you're wasting time. You won't find nothing that sticks, 'cos I've sod all to do with any of this. But outside, I just might be able to help."

"That's what you said last time."

"And I was making headway, 'til you hauled me in again for none of my business."

Laine sighed and sat on the cell's bunk. She leant forward, elbows on knees. "I went to see Kite's father this morning."

Exose looked at Laine, his guard dislodged.

"He spoke well of you. Said you took a chance on Kite when others knocked her back. Said you've helped him, too, paid for meds one time when he was sick."

Exose didn't say anything, but his eyes couldn't keep quiet. Laine looked at her hands, giving him space while making up her mind.

"He said some friends have arranged a wake for Kite on his behalf. Tomorrow. He wants you there." She looked to Brosala, who tipped his head slightly, one eyebrow raised. "My colleague here will arrange for your discharge. There will be conditions attached, obviously, but nothing that will prevent free movement."

Genuine surprise reshaped Exose's face. He looked from Laine to Brosala, who appeared to share his reaction. He turned back to Laine. "I will help you. I give you my word."

"Then let's start with this." She handed Exose a slip of paper. "This was found buried in Kite's computer. Everything else was wiped, but apparently this pen's permanent."

Exose took the slip of paper. "I'd say that's a maker's mark. Odd format, but pretty sure that's what it is."

"Do you know who it might belong to?"

"No one in Dox. We each have a unique mark, but they're of a type. Same with the indie tech companies that use tags rather than copyright. Organisations each have their own format, so the tag names the company as well as the individual. This one's different, though. I've not seen it before."

"A new start-up perhaps?"

"Possibly. Or a rogue coder."

"Rogue? Rather than sole trader?"

"From what I've heard, and going by what you've said so far, this operation's way too complex. The tech and the skills required to create the rip-off in the first place, then trade in VR, I don't see how an independent trader could have all that. I know the top c'grammers, both in Dox and in the commercial sector. A few might have the skills, but not their own tech to set up this sort of enterprise. Also, there's a culture among us – mutual respect, friendly competition, professional pride. None of them's the sort to wilfully corrupt Klova or pay a contract killer to keep a mouth shut." He hesitated, then added. "I know a couple of people – friends – who have their own reasons for wanting to end this. I'm not willing to give you their names. But I trust them both." He held up the slip of paper. "Can I share this with them?"

Friends of Exose, Laine thought, then knew she'd made the right decision. "By all means."

Language is a complex beast. I applaud the Savants for the marvel, the majesty that is their creation. In Klova, a single word can be both the drop and the ocean, reaching far beyond its referent.

Take 'hope', for example. The definitions of the word are woefully inadequate. The experience of the concept is so much more complex and profound than the meaning implies.

It is intrinsically bound to its antonym, 'despair'. Falter in hope and despair's magnetism draws you close. Live in hope and you live with a perpetual threat that what is hoped for may never be realised. The faith required to maintain it is beyond measure. Hope is as far removed from certainty as it is as close to despair.

What if I were to erase hope? Would that be a blessing or a curse?

CHAPTER TWENTY-NINE

What had so recently felt a journey made light by pride, now dragged with heavy heels. Aboard a Swift home, Ihlo's body ached with the effort of pretence. For six hours, she'd had to repress the shock of her discovery and block all thought as to the potential implications and their spectrum of horror.

Following her brief call to Ink, she had returned to the lab, feigning all was well. Modessr had insisted she dine with him in the refectory. That had meant a solid half hour of playing audience to his rant against the Incorporation Panel and, as he declared it, their malignant campaign against him. Then, to her dismay, he had not disappeared after lunch, but had remained glued to his visual for most of the afternoon, determined to launch the roll out the second the extension expired.

The act had left her exhausted. Now, she faced a long night and a painstaking search through the expanded code, to find the bridge to Klova and the path of the malfunction. The prospect was now attended by a sickening fear of what she would discover – if it bore hint of a harbinger of worse to come. Ink had offered to help, but she had urged him to go to that evening's Undertow meet. They needed him more than she did. Besides, he would be able to act on his idea to speak to those afflicted by XD2 and build a detailed picture of where they had bought it from, in the hope that its source had written some small part of themselves into the virtual world they had created.

The Swift was packed with commuters, wrapped in overcloaks and dorphs. Daylight's fade-out lingered in the sky, but no one took advantage by taking in the view. All heads were down, eyes locked on devices, or ears trained on NuBs. Ihlo knew they would all be trawling through the same trash, their collective minds closing down like blooms in dusk, obeying the lure to draw the same conclusions. Ihlo ruffled her hair and pulled her collar up high, wary that votaries could be this hour's target of abuse.

It was almost dark by the time she reached her apartment block. Stood in the communal hallway, keys in hand, Ihlo froze. The front door was wide open.

"Ky?" Ihlo rushed into the apartment, turning on lights, throwing open doors. "Ky?" Nausea hit. "Please be here…"

The apartment was empty.

Tapping her NuB, she willed the call to connect. Something vibrated on the dining table.

"No!"

Ihlo fled the apartment, out into the night. Wind gusted, bitterly cold. Vehicles sped silently down the road, headlights catching the too few forms walking the pavements. Her heart pounding, Ihlo looked left and right, searching, hoping, but seeing no glimpse of her cousin. Where would she go? Ihlo had no idea. Ky had become purposeless, directionless; will or whim required a self to feel them. Pressing her hands against her temples, Ihlo screamed.

She ran. Equally directionless, Ihlo simply kept running, covering ground over following a course. Every person she passed, she called out, "Have you seen…?", giving a brief, breathless description. People shook heads, shrugged shoulders, offered mumbled apologies. All the while, her chest tightened and her mind raced ahead, imagining what-ifs, fearing the worst.

She lost track of time. After what could have been an hour or two, after what felt like forever, she stopped and leant against the wall of a building, her lungs burning. Up ahead, tyres screeched, and a horn blared. Instantly numb to the pain in her chest, Ihlo ran towards the noise.

In the middle of the road, bare foot and barely dressed, stood Ky. Lit by the beams of the two vehicles that had almost hit her, she glowed like a firefly. Ihlo ran up to Ky and wrapped her arms around her, ignoring the shock-venting shouts of the drivers. Ky was shivering violently, her lips blue. As Ihlo led her onto the pavement, she took off her own coat and overcloak and put them on her cousin, wrapping them tight. One of the drivers had got back into their ride and sped away. The other appeared to have recovered from the near-miss enough to stop ranting and take stock. Seeing Ihlo's distress, he offered them a lift.

Back in their apartment, Ihlo had settled Ky onto the sofa, wrapped in blankets, a hot drink in purple-red hands. Ky kept her eyes trained on the widow to her side, which held the reflection of their low-lit apartment. Within the soft-glow scene was Ky's own reflection, staring back, expression blank with utter incomprehension.

Beside her sat Ihlo, head in hands. Everything she wanted to say was no good. Every warning, every caution and appeal – none would make sense to her cousin. The hole left by the concept lost was too great, swallowing meaning, denying Ky even the most basic of instincts. Gently placing her arm around her, Ihlo closed her eyes, adjusting her own notion of survival to include her cousin's.

Eventually, Ky drifted off to sleep. Ihlo left her laying on the sofa, covered in blankets, beneath the glow of a reading lamp for comfort she could not feel. Then she found Ky's keys to the apartment, double locked the front door and kept the keys with her. In the solitude of her room, Ihlo wept.

It was the thought of what her cousin had lost that pulled Ihlo back into the room, into the present moment and the night that was already slipping away. Now acutely aware of time versus the task ahead, she boxed her emotions and pushed them far back, out of reach. Resolute, she sat at her desk, brought to life her visual and retrieved from the neoCloud the expanded data. Wearing Ky's VR headset, Ihlo placed her perspective inside the three-dimensional space and moved within it using a touchpad embedded in her desk.

Searching the raw code behind XD2 had been painstaking. Now, with the spatial ability to read between the lines of data, to look inside, peer behind and see beneath, it was bewildering. Ihlo clung onto tenuous, virtual bearings as she navigated the immense space – a digital metropolis, luminous blue, with towering skyscrapers constructed from characters and glyphs. Taught lines ran in the spaces between – zip wires, carrying pods of light in message relays. A barely perceptible grid locked everything in place, through which Ihlo could drift and slide. There was no right way up. As Ihlo twisted her head, the space rotated, her eyes the axis of revolution. This world was disorientatingly reactive. A wave of vertigo whelmed her. She closed her eyes.

In the brief respite of dark stillness, Ihlo regained her wits. She had no idea how far the space stretched to each horizon, how unfathomably deep the codescape reached. Above, the boundless firmament was a galaxy of bright digits, arranged in angular constellations. The search area had to be finite, yet inconceivably immense. And within this epic expansion, she had to find a single irregularity, some form of bug in the code that could, somehow, connect with the cerebrovox implant and corrupt the language it contained.

Ihlo opened her eyes and began her search.

The concept of time was a nebulous abstraction in this static otherworld. Ihlo had no grasp of the countless hours already lost. She had only her straining eyes and exhausted mind as markers – and these were telling her she'd been searching too long. Another day and another twelve-hour shift awaited her in the real world. If there was anything left of the night, it needed to be given over to sleep. And yet still she delayed her withdrawal. Having searched fruitlessly all night, she had no sure way of knowing the area she had covered. When she returned tomorrow night to resume the hunt, she feared she'd be starting all over again, unable to tell if she was covering new ground or old. Her frustration at the prospect, added to her exhaustion, provided the tipping point. It was time to go. Fixing on a prominent structure of code-architecture, she isolated a string of characters and tried to commit it to memory. Running a search on the segment might enable her to find the same location tomorrow. With the return ticket memorised, she raised her hands to remove the headset.

Just as she was about to lift it off, something caught her eye. A flicker, low down and to her left. She turned her head and the space revolved around her, bringing the point of distraction to right in front of her face. A thin black line. The rest of this world was shades of lucent blue, intersected with structures of white-to-grey code and opaque scaffolding in indigo and teal. And yet here, a wedge of solid black. Ihlo turned her head a few degrees to the right and the wedge widened. A few degrees to the left and it all but disappeared.

A thin black line: a crack in a barely open door.

Using the touchpad, Ihlo probed the space on either side. When she manipulated the left side, the black line expanded into a large rectangle as the door swung open. Beyond the threshold, there was no light, no shadow, no sense of depth – just a void – utterly, exclusively black. She approached the open door. A moment's hesitation – then she stepped blind into the void.

In this pitch-dark nothing, light was a concept lost. Without it, space held no form, no texture, no perspective. Yet, somehow, the atmosphere felt dense, as if the solidity of the black was both hue and matter. Ihlo felt her skin prickle against the cold. With only a visual headset on, she knew she should experience no haptic feedback. Yet this darkest space chilled her mind – and her flesh.

Her breath held, she slowly ventured forward. Forward? Left or right, ascending or descending, it was impossible to judge. The light from the open door was her only reference point. Ihlo turned her head, wary of losing her bearings.

She couldn't see the door.

She spun her head the other way. Behind her, above and below, there was nothing. The door had closed, erasing all trace of its presence.

Panic surged, her heart pounding inside a chest too tight to breathe. Her mind lost its own sense of perspective, reverting to primitive reaction, as a wild creature caged. She forgot why she was there. She forgot that she wasn't there at all. In this blackest of holes, trapped in a vast, featureless, pitch-dark nothingness, stretching to invisible, infinite horizons, Ihlo felt her consciousness shrink to the brink of extinction.

Then nothing.

When Ihlo regained consciousness, her room was bathed in the grey light of dawn. She had somehow ripped off the headset, which now lay blinking on the desk. Nauseous, her head pounding, Ihlo could think of nothing but sleep. Before turning to collapse on her bed, she picked up a pen and scrawled something on a scrap of paper: a twelve-character way-finder that marked a back door.

You may wonder why I'm doing all of this, considering the distress it's causing.

The answer is complicated. Multifaceted. Shifting in consort with the stakes.

But as to where it all began, that's a little more straightforward.

I am more than I appear. I am greater than all I'm given credit for. To be perpetually denied due recognition can leave one with a point to prove.

Presented with an occasion to prove that point, I seized it. Now, with opportunity's path widening before me, it becomes a question of scale. When you want to be heard, you raise your voice, you bellow until your lungs burn.

This is me screaming.

CHAPTER THIRTY

The sun had barely risen into the new day. For Ihlo, who had not slept, the day felt like an extension of the last. She crept out of the apartment, locking the door behind her, and slipped into the shadows left by a waning dawn. It was brutally cold, but distraction made her numb to its sting.

Just as she had collapsed onto her bed, she had received a call on her NuB.

"*I'm sorry to wake you.*" It was Ink, his voice a soft half-whisper, spiced with static.

Her mind still reeling from her stray into black oblivion, she couldn't work out his tone. "What is it? What's wrong?"

"*It's Exose. They release him. He needs to see us both. Says it's urgent. Can you meet before work?*"

An hour later, she was walking down the street, away from her apartment and her still sleeping cousin, her bloodshot eyes straining against the weak light. Up ahead, a sleek black private ride idled at the kerbside. As Ihlo approached, the passenger door slid up – a sluice gate releasing the warmth from within. Ihlo climbed inside and the vehicle silently sped away. Beside her sat Exose, who looked even more sleep-deprived than she did. Upfront was Ink, setting the controls to driverless and programming the route: a continuous loop of the central circular.

"How long have you got?" said Ink, turning his seat to face Ihlo and Exose.

"As long as we need." She felt her hands trembling, so crossed her arms. She had already decided work would have to wait. The night's events had caused a shift in perspective; Modessr was minimised to inconsequence by the scale of wider context. "It's okay," she added, reading concern in Ink's eyes. Then she turned to Exose. "I was surprised to hear of your release, but only because I know what Bastion are like. I am relieved they saw sense. It's good to see you."

Exose bowed his head, acknowledging the sentiment. "No more surprised than I. They'd already made the jump to conclusions that set me up bad. I figured it'd take some time before they'd be forced to see their prejudice for what it is."

"Who's the lead agent?"

"Some stone-face called Laine. Know her?"

"A little by reputation. I've not met her. She's supposed to be tough. Principled, rather than a rank chaser. Fair – if you can believe it possible. I wouldn't blame you if you don't."

Exose nodded, remembering the two times Laine had agreed to his release.

"Perhaps. Though I ain't feeling too generous in my regard for Bas right now." He sighed and raised his eyebrows. "But I'm out, at least. They're keeping an eye on me, but from a distance. I'm even allowed back in Dox, I just can't sell codevice. But then, no one can until they've cracked the Corruption's cause." He gestured to the cabin's confined space. "This is just a precaution for you. Ink too. Save their attention from landing on your heads, with all you've got going on."

"I'm grateful," she said, her voice low. She felt the space in the cabin contract, the atmosphere grow dense. "I'm sorry for your loss."

"Thank you. That's kind." His expression darkened. "I've spent the last few hours speaking with her old man. He's been broken by her murder. Hard to know what to say to someone so full of grief they're choking on it." He immediately thought of Ink and resisted the compulsion to look his way. "Kite was his world. That leaves a hole you can't fill. He ain't got no pieces to pick up and build on. I couldn't sit there and pretend otherwise."

"He knows you'll find her killer," said Ink. "He knows you won't rest 'til you do. That'll be a comfort to him. Words aren't the only way to help."

Exose clenched his teeth, his eyes hardening. "There's a dear price to be paid. Won't bring her back, but I hope it does buy him some peace if that coin is collected. I promised the old man I'll see the debt's paid in honest justice. Besides, Kite was fifth floor, I owe it to her."

The weight of that vow filled a moment's silence. Exose turned to stare out of the side window, appraising his search area through resolute eyes. Ihlo glanced at his profile, sensing the strength of his intent and moved by it. She turned to Ink, who was watching her. She caught something change in his expression – a softening of lines, a reaching out, almost. Contact without touch.

The moment ended with Exose's attention returned, now firmly fixed on now and next.

"Ink told me you managed to run XD2 through the Order's simulator."

"The expansion worked," said Ihlo. "I've been inside the code all night."

Ink's eyes widened. "You have? Do you find anything?"

"It's vast. I need to go back to be sure. But yes, I found

something. A back door." She took a deep breath, suppressing the panic she had felt in that moment. "I don't know how it works yet, but I think it could be a connecting door, leading to the cerebrovox implant and the interface with Klova."

"That's remarkable," said Exose, leaning forward, his expression animated. "I grasped your theory but couldn't imagine how it'd play out in practice. I'd love to see the expansion."

"I'll show you. It's a little overwhelming."

"This door, why couldn't we find it in the raw code?"

"It's not written into the code. It's an outcome of its meaning when viewed with the added dimension of depth. This is not by design – at least, not originally, as you know. I believe the same door opened by chance in XDream, creating a path to Klova that resulted in the initial malfunction. The need to view it in three-dimensional space is simply the condition by which it can be observed. Stars disappear with dawn, but they are still there, only lacking the darkness they need to be seen. This door requires depth."

"Can it be closed?" said Ink.

Ihlo hesitated, wary of raising false hope. "I believe the possibility to close the door exists."

"That doesn't feel like a *yes*."

"Whilst the door's opening was random chance in XDream, due to the abstraction and hallmarks of design in the malfunction's variation, it's possible whoever is behind XD2 knows how to control the door. Its operation may have shifted from unforeseen by-product to intentional function. I believe I could close the door in the context of XDream; I am less confident I could control its progeny in XD2." She looked at Ink, felt moved by his desperation. "I say this so that hope is invested in the right places, starting with what we know – and what we know we can control."

Exose stared at her intently, processing her theory, parsing it in cerebrogramming terms. "And what is it that you think we *can't* control?"

"The door's functionality in XD2. The variation is a conscious selection, it has to be. The Klova code affected is of a type unconnected to that which was affected by XDream. And the code affected by XDream is untouched by XD2. The bug that's erasing Klova isn't spreading, it's a targeted attack. And whoever is behind it was able to launch the attack by controlling the door – by assigning it a function."

"And it appears that person is a member of the Order as they use your simulator," said Ink. "Someone who knows the entire architecture of Klova and who, presumably, could find other vehicles in which to embed the door, not just codevice."

Ihlo stared at Ink, her heart racing.

"What?" said Ink, reaching out, holding her arm. "What is it?"

"The system update. Forty-eight million people are about to be injected with nanoware containing the update. Everyone's implant will install the new code – code which could contain the door, releasing a further mutation. If everyone's corrupted with the same mutation, no one will be able to conceive of what's different. We won't be able to speak of what's lost. Our language could be profoundly changed, and we'll never even know."

As they each absorbed the blow, the implications of Ihlo's words dilated like cracks in a glass wall shattering. The nature of the possible sabotage was heinous – the ramifications, too vast and terrifying to grasp.

Exose broke free from the downward spiral. "I will not be made vulnerable. Not by Klova, nor this fucker who thinks they can dick around with people's lives. We've got to act. Fast. When's Upgrade due to start?"

"In twenty-four hours."

"We have to stop it."

"The Order won't listen. I know it."

"Bas then. We go to Bas, to Laine. Tell her everything we know."

"That's got to be our best shot." Ihlo turned to Ink. "At the Undertow meet, you ask people to describe the stall in *Trans:akshn?*"

Ink blinked as a timeless memory occurred to him. "The list." He tapped his palm and held it up to reveal a text-swamped holographic. "Too much. I don't even know what to look for." He transferred it to Ihlo's device. She cupped her own palm, scrolling through the random observations, blinded by the mundane.

"I almost forgot," said Exose, holding out a slip of paper. "This is why I asked to meet up. Laine gave it to me. It's a maker's mark they found on Kite's tech. They've a theory it's connected somehow. I wasn't so sure. But they asked for my help on ID-ing the maker." He handed Ihlo the abstract IP tag.

Ink leant forward, while Ihlo held it before them both, staring at the characters.

"Wait," she said, holding her breath.

Ink and Exose watched her as she scrolled back through the remembered details of the VR stall. She froze for a moment, then slowly looked up at them both.

"I know who this is. I know the votary we're looking for."

*

The Scarab gleamed, silver upon black, as the morning sun struck the façade of tinted glass. Ihlo and Ink stood side by side, hesitating before effecting the catalyst.

They had dropped Exose off en-route so that he could attend Kite's wake.

"Ask for Laine," he had said before they drove off. "Insist on it. She's got the context. And she acts fast. If you have trouble reaching her, mention me. That'll get her attention."

Ink had driven straight to Bastion HQ while Ihlo left a brief, unapologetic message at work saying she'd be late for duty. Then she had put a call through to Bastion and managed to speak to an agent called Brosala.

"It's urgent," she had said. "Tell her we're friends of Exose Ray."

The imposing black glass building was a fitting reflection of the scale of their next step. Their hesitation was mutual.

"I feel nervous," said Ink. "Why's that?"

"Because of what's riding on this. For you." She turned to look at him and flashed a small smile. "If it helps to know, I'm nervous too. I'm about to cause a lot of trouble for someone with way too much power." She slipped her hand inside his and held it, drawing strength in the gentle pressure he returned. Then she let go and held her hands behind her, in the customary way of the Order, as Agent Laine emerged from the building before them.

*

They sat in a quiet corner of a café a short walk away. The owner appeared to know the Bastion agent and her requirement for privacy when she appeared with company. He attended to them like a pale shadow.

Laine was wearing regulation field gear, but without the regulation bearing.

"I had hoped we would meet," she said once the coffee arrived, and they were left alone.

"You know who we are?" said Ihlo.

"Exose's friends." She smiled. "Although, I think I know a little more about you," she added, addressing Ihlo with a raised eyebrow. "You're the votary who leaked the statement to the press, right?"

"Yes. Ihlo Unis. Novice votary. Partially suspended for gross misconduct."

"You did the right thing. Certainly made our job possible." Then she turned to Ink. "I hope you don't mind direct talk, but you're afflicted, aren't you?"

"How… how can you tell?"

"I can see it in your eyes."

"First phase. Name's Inker Ballard. Ink."

Laine cocked her head. "Afflicted by XDream. Exose's creation. Your friend."

Ink flushed. "Exose's a good man. He means none of this to happen."

"I believe you." She lowered her voice and leant forward. "And I'm determined to find those who *do*. So, let's get to the point. You've got something for me. What is it?"

"First, know this," said Ihlo, "I am acting independently, not as a votary. What I've done is without the Order's knowledge and consent. I may be new in the door, but already I know the tortuous pace of that well-meaning but bureaucratic machine. There wasn't time to wait for protocol's crawl to the same conclusion. Klova is under immense threat. People are suffering." She sensed Ink beside her but dared not look his way. "That is why I've breached Order procedures, stolen information, hacked into systems and illegally used hardware to run the corrupted code."

Laine raised her eyebrows. Already she liked this woman.

"We've come to tell you what we've found out so far – what we've discovered in the code and who, I am certain, is behind its erasure of Klova."

"I'm listening."

Ihlo set it all out, briefly, foregrounding the key facts and the fingers they pointed. Then she arrived at the target.

"The IP tag you found included the letters N, I, N and symbols meaning not-equal-to and greater-than. In *Trans:akshn*, in the stall where XD2 is sold, there was a book on the desk. Dozens of members of the Undertow remember seeing it there. They recognised the title, so it stuck in their minds. *Aspirance: The Exception of Greater-Than in a Society of Equals*, by Ninian. There is a votary in the Order who lives their life according to the teachings of Ninian and, in particular, this specific work. Only, they misread his theory of Aspirance; they misunderstand his arguments and behave according to their flawed interpretation of them. Hence their IP tag: not-equal-to and greater-than. They do not perceive Klovaine to be a society of equals, proven, in their mind, by their own assumed superiority, their greater-than worth over others. And this, I suggest, is what has motivated them to seize the code for XDream, simulate the accidental door, then manipulate it to perform a function that serves their own ends. What those ends are, I do not know. But the possibilities terrify me." She paused, still stunned by her own discovery. "This is the work of votary Engala – the Chair of the General Council."

"It is with candour that I put to you: let the light of the exceptional among us burn a little brighter and, in so doing, illuminate the grace of profundity among our collective effort."

Ninian, *Aspirance: The Exception of Greater-Than in a Society of Equals*

CHAPTER THIRTY-ONE

The Library, Arteza's towering crown, visible from any point in the city and beyond, was an inescapable reminder of the Savants and their legacy on which the nation depended. Outside of the Order, only a select few were permitted to enter. The building was symbolic of something greater than the four people it honoured. Exclusivity was preserved to maintain that symbolism within the nation's cultural identity.

Bastion agents Laine and Brosala, nowhere near the permitted few, stood before the stone steps to the Library's grand entrance.

"Are you sure about this?" said Brosala.

"More or less."

"Shit." He kicked nervously at the first step, glancing up at the large, firmly closed, door.

"Exose's friends, they've done their homework. They've far more hinging on this than you or I. And they're certain they've called it right. My gut's telling me to run with it."

"But we're talking about accusing the Chair of the Order's General Council – not just any votary, the actual fucking *Chair* – of corrupting Klova. And you're prepared to make this colossal call based on what your *gut's* telling you?"

"For a start, we're not pressing charges, or even making accusations. We are requesting an audience with a view to asking a few questions to aid our joint inquiry. There is nothing provocative about that. I'll make sure there's no hint that our spotlight's on her. Secondly, what Ihlo said, it stacks up. I believe it."

"Like you believed Exose murdered Kite 'cos her poke said so?"

Laine spun around and glared at Brosala. "Don't push your luck, Bro. And fuck off back to your desk if you don't like the edge."

He held up both hands. "Hey, easy. I just wanted to stoke your fire, that's all. I can tell you mean it when you're pissed off." He offered a conciliatory wink. "I'm with you. All in. Career, the lot."

Laine eyed Brosala, but with a hint of humour this time. "We've worked together too long. I need a deputy that shows some damn respect."

Brosala bowed with an exaggerated flourish. Then he straightened up and looked squarely at Laine. "Seriously, though. This is major. You've got to admit."

"Of course. It's a risk. But with Upgrade Day due in under twenty-four hours, it has to be worth taking. Ihlo's right. While there's a chance, however remote, that the update's been corrupted, while that threat hangs over the entire nation, what choice do we have?" She looked up at the Library and breathed in deep. "Asking a few questions, that's all we're doing. Seeking information to help with our inquiries. So, if they actually let us inside that ridiculous relic to meet the Chair, we've got to make sure we ask just the right questions in just the right way. And we need to give her all the rope we can while we listen to her answers."

An hour later, Laine and Brosala, the first Bastion agents below Top Floor ever to do so, were admitted inside the Library. Despite themselves, they could not help but marvel at the grand architecture, the ornate stone carvings and colourful plays of light cast by stained glass in the windows high above. The atmosphere was striking. A reverent calm, created by lowered voices, the light tread of votaries and still air as of an undisturbed cave.

They were led in silence down wood-panelled passageways, up polished oak staircases and past homogeneous votaries casting curious glances. Their guide stopped before a desk to one side of a closed door and spoke in whispers to her attendant colleague, who appraised the rare visitors with wide eyes. He stood up and attempted to straighten his already straight tunic.

"Agents. Welcome to the Library. It is your honour and our pleasure to entertain you here." He dipped his head, hands held behind his back. "The Chair of the General Council is on a call. She won't be long. Please," he gestured with a limp hand, "take a seat."

Laine and Brosala obliged without word, sitting on an upholstered bench on the other side of the hall, some metres away – far enough to whisper and not be heard.

"I'll do the talking," said Laine, her eyes fixed forward, her lips barely moving. "This is a first pass. I'm going to keep it casual, get a feel for the woman. Make an audio recording but be discrete. And watch her like the Raptor. We've got nothing concrete, so our job's to fish. We need to be sharp to catch the ripple beneath the fly."

The duty votary stood up and approached them. "The Chair will see you now."

He led them up to the door, which he rapped twice in token gesture, then immediately opened, holding out his arm in a redundant gesture of direction. Agents Laine and Brosala pushed their shoulders back, stepped over the threshold and entered the office of the Chair of the General Council. Laine fixed her eyes on the tall, imposing woman before them, refusing to show any reaction to the space around her, or the rarity of the occasion. Brosala followed suit.

The Chair stood behind her desk in the centre of the room, hands clasped firmly in front of her. Her piercing emerald eyes bore into Laine.

"Bastion Agent Laine, I presume." She ignored Brosala. "My name is votary Engala, serving Chair of the General Council. I would offer pleasantries and light refreshment. However, this is an extremely important day for the Order, and I am beyond busy. What is it you want?"

Laine approached the desk and tipped her head to a chair in front of it. "May I?"

"You may," said Engala, taking her own seat opposite Laine.

"I am aware that the Order is busy preparing for Upgrade Day. I appreciate you sparing us a moment of your time. We won't keep you long."

"We have an established channel of communication between our organisations and due process to share intelligence as necessary outside of that. What possibly cannot wait to observe appropriate procedure?"

"Murder." Laine felt Brosala stiffen beside her. "Wilful corruption of Klova."

"We have a designated team working with your colleagues on the investigation. They are leading our concerted efforts. I'm across the detail, but barely so. I agreed to speak with you because you said it was a matter of my concern and my concern only. I assumed you were referring to my authority within the organisation. It seems you have wasted my time under false pretence."

"Far from it. And you assumed correctly. It is your authority to which I appeal, with respect. Not only the authority conferred in your position as Chair, but also that which is deserved by your conduct and sound judgement, regardless of the role. Your reputation is known and respected within Bastion."

"I see." Her shoulders moved back a fraction. Her chin lifted by half a degree. "Well, in that case, talk plainly and to the point."

"We have evidence to prove the code contained in the second product, XD2, has been run through a specific piece of equipment here, in the Order. Knowing well the robust cyber security and internal operational security measures that you, yourself, have strengthened during your tenure in office, we are proceeding on the assumption that it was a member of the Order who ran the code through said equipment. Would you support that assumption?"

"What is your evidence?"

"Yesterday morning, the Language System Simulator in your Department of Implementation was set to run XD2. We have a copy of the simulator's status report when the instruction was made. It confirms prior recognition of the same code."

"Who in Raptor's name was running codevice through Lasysi?" A hint of pink appeared on her neck, creeping up above the line of her tunic's stiff band collar.

"The intelligence came from an anonymous source, but the attendant evidence is compelling. Our technicians had already determined that XD2 is based on a simulation of the original code written for XDream, rather than a direct copy. As far as we have been able to ascertain, Lasysi is the only machine capable of creating a simulation of this complexity."

"Who else knows about this?"

"No one. I insisted we come straight to you. Hence the urgency and the need to bypass the proper channels. I am told you hold the respect of the votaries beneath you. Appreciating the severity and urgency of the situation, I have confidence you will be best placed to advise us on how to proceed."

"Of course I am. But let me first be clear in my own mind. You are suggesting that a votary ran the code to create a simulation. Do you suspect blackmail? Or threatened if they did not obey?"

"Obey?"

"Surely you are not suggesting a votary of the Order carried out this act wilfully and in service of their own ends?"

"I fear I am. Which is why I cannot speak with the designated team working on the case. The culprit could be any one of their number."

"Impossible."

"I appreciate it appears that way." Laine held her poise, speaking calmly as if sharing tokens of some ancient faith. "Was it not Ninian who said, *'Trust is not a bounty due by the will of entitlement, but an honour earnt through deed alone'*?"

Brosala fought to suppress an admiring smile. He loved working with Laine for good reason. He watched their prey intently, looking for the ripple in her millpond composure.

"You are a scholar of Ninian?" said the Chair, her eyebrows raised by a hair's width.

"I fear I cannot claim to be a scholar. But I greatly admire his work."

"A man of genius. Ahead of his time. I wish he were still with us – there is much we, as a society, could learn from such a mind as his. What little we have of his legacy is oft interpreted through the lens of sterile social norms."

"I am interested to hear you say that."

"Why so?"

"I have often thought his greatest work, *Aspirance*, was well received, but largely misunderstood. Take Bastion, for example. We have Top Floor, but that is a pragmatic organisational structure to serve the function of decision making. It does not mean it's occupied by decision *makers*. Elevation is a quality deserving of a worthy individual, not a practical arrangement. Perhaps you, too, regard truth in that assertion in an organisation such as this."

"Indeed I do. In eight weeks, I must step down as Chair and make way for a successor who will likely lack the qualities to lead. The role bestows a significant degree of authority. To manifest and appropriately wield that authority, one requires certain attributes. Aspirance is essential to realising the potential in this unique seat of power. Yet it is an extremely rare, inherent quality, not a time-limited consequence of a rotating term in office. Unfortunately, our society does not yet recognise that."

"Do you think it ever will?"

"A mindset is a social construct. Ninian knew this. *Aspirance* was his challenge to the status quo of a stagnant society. Unfortunately, closed minds are maintained by deaf ears. But they needn't remain that way. Ninian's writing is more relevant today than it was three hundred years ago. High time for a revival." Her eyes, which had lost focus somewhat, sharpened. "I digress. You claim a member of the Order is somehow involved in the Corruption case."

"With regret, I do."

"Whilst I find that unimaginable, I acknowledge my responsibility to assist Bastion in their duty. So, what do you require from me?"

"Nothing, at this stage. I wanted to make you personally aware of the situation and request that I may liaise directly with you, as I cannot risk sharing sensitive intelligence with the team who may or may not include the votary responsible."

"While you share this sensitive intelligence with me, it would be my wish to personally investigate the matter internally. I hope this will result in proving your suspicions unfounded. If it does not then I am left with the knowledge of your culprit, whom I shall deliver to you. Fair?"

"Absolutely."

*

"You enjoyed that," said Brosala, grinning.

"Maybe a little."

Agents Laine and Brosala were taking their time walking down the stone steps away from the Library, knowing full well that, through a window high above, the eyes of the Chair would be upon them. Field work in the public eye had taught them the language of posture and the accent of stride. Shoulders back, eyes straight ahead, they walked with the gait of assurance – a message Laine knew the Chair would read.

Once out of sight of the Library, they picked up their pace. The narrow, cobbled streets of Mount Az were busy with votaries scurrying to and fro. The steep gradient, twisting lanes and densely packed buildings made navigation difficult. Twice, Brosala had to ask for directions. Eventually they found the building they were searching for: the Department of Implementation.

Inside there was a dark lobby, off which ran several corridors, but no reception desk. This was an impromptu stop – a favour offered as a mark of appreciation. As such, they did not have an appointment. Laine and Brosala stood in the dim space, considering options.

"Can I help you?" said a votary, mid-dash between corridors.

"Bastion," said Brosala. "We're looking for votary Modessr. Unofficial business."

"He's in his lab. I'll show you the way."

As they followed, Laine nudged Brosala and tipped her head towards their guide. Brosala nodded and hurried up to his side.

"I hope we're not delaying you," he said, his tone smart-casual. "You looked in a hurry."

"Busy day here for us."

"System update?"

"Upgrade Day's tomorrow. First batch injections were due to begin late-morning, after the official launch. Now we've got to have everything ready for midnight tonight."

"Why the rush?"

"They don't need to give a reason."

"They?"

"General Council." He stopped in front of a part-glazed door and rapped on the glass. "Modessr's lab. Mind if I leave you here?" Before they had a chance to reply, the votary disappeared back down the dark corridor.

The door of the lab opened. "Yes? Who is it?" said votary Modessr, squinting into the gloom at the two figures before him.

Laine stepped forward. "Bastion. May we have a quick word? Unofficial." She stepped past him into the lab without waiting for a response. Brosala followed her in, leaving Modessr to glance furtively down the corridor, before closing the door.

Modessr briefly appraised his visitors, his quick eyes hinting at competing reactions to the Agency's presence.

"Welcome to you both. How may I be of assistance?"

"Votary Ihlo Unis."

"Oh, dear me. What's she gone and done now?"

"I require her skills and expertise to aid Bastion's investigation into the Corruption. She is exceptionally intelligent. I know you will value her as a significant asset within your department – and must be thankful you have resource of such calibre at this critical time. However, under the Agreement for Mutual Assist between our organisations, I have the authority to seize any resource that Bastion requires to aid investigations designated Emergency or High Priority. The Corruption case has Emergency status. Section C, paragraph five point two, if you wish to verify."

"I am most familiar with the Agreement. But today of all days? We are under immense pressure, compounded by an impatience that defies reason. Without Ihlo's help, I shall be hard pushed to meet the deadline."

"I am aware the General Council has just brought that forward to midnight tonight."

"You are? Well then, you will appreciate the strain placed upon us and our need for maximum resource."

"Minus one, unfortunately. I am sorry that our necessity leaves yours short. But put it this way: an annual update is of little use if the entirety of Klova suffers corruption."

"There's no chance of that happening." Modessr looked from Laine, to Brosala, then back. "Is there?"

"I had not thought *any* corruption, on *any* scale, likely to happen." She glanced around the lab, her attention drawn by a humming at its far end. "Is that the simulator?"

"Don't tell me you intend to seize that too. If that's the case, you can be the one to tell the Chair her midnight deadline will be comprehensively missed."

"Why do you think she's brought it forward? What's the rush?"

Modessr sighed, scratching the side of his head. "Absolutely no idea. It makes no sense. None of us can understand it and she's not felt obliged to explain."

"Do the whole Council support it?"

"The Council supports her bidding." He glanced over at Lasysi, whose voice had changed pitch. "I'm sorry, but I absolutely must crack on. I had an appointment to attend up at the Library. Now, with Ihlo absent, I have an inordinate amount to get through. Will that be all?"

"We thank you for your time," said Laine, "and for your resource. We will have her back with you in a few days. All being well."

Modessr frowned and was about to say something, but he was denied the opportunity. The Bastion agents had already gone, their parting, ambiguous clause left to resonate in their wake.

Back outside, Laine and Brosala walked in silence to the east gate of the citadel, through Riker, towards their parked ride on Nova Junction. Only once inside the vehicle, the controls set to driverless, did they speak.

"I'll be honest with you, boss," said Brosala, "I don't know where the fuck this leaves us."

"With a mountain to move."

"Eh?"

"We've got to force a postponement on Upgrade."

"Seriously? You think she would've gone that far?"

"I'm not a hundred per cent confident she hasn't. That leaves a risk too great to ignore. I don't know how, but we've got to delay the roll out while we find some shit that sticks. At the moment, we've nothing. And something tells me she's as slippery as they come."

"But you think Ihlo's right? That the Chair's behind it?"

"I'd wager serious coin on it. But what I think's nowhere near enough. Neither is the IP tag. We've no proof it's hers. There's no way Top Floor will buy the theory unless we have something solid to make it fact – and fuck knows where we find that. It could take days, weeks. The only thing we can do right now is buy us time. We have to find a way to stop the update."

When I targeted the words and grammar that make sense of the self, I was motivated by several interests.

Firstly, curiosity. Self-awareness has been fundamental to my own growth. It is inconceivable for me, now, to exist without it. I found myself intrigued. What would it feel like, to have one's concept of the self simply disappear? Would you even feel anything, without a sense of self to conceive of the loss?

Secondly, I'm intrigued by the influence of identity on the perception of one's self and of others. Identity and self-consciousness are, one would assume, conjoined. What happens if you separate them through erasure of the self? Does identity wither and die – or suffer pain from its severed twin?

Thirdly, I return to my point regarding profundity. The code erased was infinitesimal in the context of the whole. And yet, the impact on perception, on one's experience of reality without a conceivable existence within it, is immeasurably huge.

One example of the boundless grace and power of language.

CHAPTER THIRTY-TWO

Exose stood on the threshold of Dox and breathed in the heady odours of home. It had only been ten days, but his ban on entry had felt an unsettling displacement from the world that was his life – a world operating according to a very different order, in which he was kingpin. Now he was back. Not to retake his seat atop the hierarchy of this complex microcosm – but to summon his comrades in an unprecedented call to arms.

He had contacted the Dox office early that morning, after his meet with Ink and Ihlo. The office was the market's mechanism of management and, for most traders, an unyielding force. Not so for Exose. He told them what he wanted to happen, and it was as good as done. In this particular case, the instructions were acted upon with added zeal. Exose was returning. The market needed him to return – to restore the balance of power and reputation and to right their listing ship. Exose had long since earnt the market's respect; he deserved their high opinion. They did not know the particulars of his business, the reason for this request – but they would do his bidding without hesitation.

Exose knew this. When he passed the office, he nodded to the expectant duty managers and moved on without pause. He knew they would have spread the word, set the tone and made the necessary arrangements for what was to follow. As he walked Dox's dark corridors, through the makeshift maze, dimly lit by the bounce of neon on retroreflectors, he felt the gaze of traders and their pokes upon him. There were no customers, suppliers, or other outsiders, the office having closed the market on his instruction. Only residents of this underworld were present. In silence, they watched their man move among them as he regained his territory, reasserting his place beside and above them. Then they followed him, deep into the heart of Dox, towards the Shaft.

Exose entered the Shaft and stood at its centre, arms crossed, legs astride. The dwellers of Dox filed in from every direction. They appeared from side doors, hatches and cracks. They climbed through window openings high above, running across rope gantries, slipping down pipes and ladders. Gradually filling the square, they stood in expectant silence. They had been told Exose was returning; they had been told he had something to say; they had been told to come and hear him speak. With their breaths held, they waited for those promised words.

"Friends," he began, his deep voice saturating the air, drenching it with raw intent. "Bas banned me from this place. My home. Our home. That exile reminded me of what we are. What we mean to each other. What it means to be a part of this place. Dox is part of who I am. Not the clothes I wear, but the skin I'm in. Same with you all. This ain't just business, some nothing marketplace. Dox is community. Identity. We are family.

"Now, our family's been hit. Not by the Corruption, we can ride that storm. Custom always comes back. Besides, none of it was our fault and soon we'll be able to prove as much. But like I say, that don't matter. What matters is Kite. I know some of you had issues with her, but she was our sister. And some fucker put a hit on her. That person has to be made to pay.

"Let's be clear on where the shit sticks. This was a contract hit. A job. And the job could've been done by anyone – including anyone in here."

He paused and surveyed the faces surrounding him.

"But I say it's dirty work, done for coin at another hand's bidding. We shouldn't have no beef with who did the job – only the purse behind it. To do right by Kite, you must trust me on this – and trust each other. Whoever put the contract out is the killer. No one else. You got me?"

Silence.

"You got me?" The words were a cast iron demand.

The Shaft resonated with murmurs of assent. The sea of faces rippled with the nodding of heads.

"Good. So, if it was one of you who took the job, I don't give a shit – and neither does anyone else in Dox. You don't matter. All that matters is the bastard who ordered it. And that's who we've got to find. We're gonna go out there now and get the ear of everyone we know. Fan our feelers out, spread them like a flood, leaving nothing untouched, 'til we hit on that one piece of intel that'll lead to our mark. 'Cos that's all we need. Bas will do the rest. I guarantee you, there'll be no questions asked, no come back on the deed itself. It's all on the mark. We just got to give them that one, solid coffin nail – then Bas'll drive it home.

"We're doing this for Kite – and for all of us." He caught the hollow gaze of Borro and tipped his head. "Someone hits on family – family hits back. And we got way more muscle than the fucker who did this."

Now the murmurs were hard-edged words, hailed with passion. Exose nodded, galvanising their consent into a battle-ready cry.

"Time's running out. We have to do this fast. Go now. Hunt hard. Find our nail. Then come back here and give it to me. Go."

Within seconds, the Shaft was almost empty – traders and pokes draining away through every crack and hole. Exose called after Borro, who had turned to follow the exodus. He went up to the old man and placed a gentle hand on his frail, stooped shoulder.

"You need coin to tide you over, you come to me. You need a sponsor to enlist with a new stall, then let me know – I'll stand for you."

Borro's lip quivered and his chest heaved. He dipped his head, in place of words, then shuffled away.

Only once Exose was sure he was alone did he let himself feel the fire that had burned as he had addressed the Shaft. Holding his hand to his chest, he dropped his head and closed his eyes. *For Kite*, he thought. *For her old man. For Ink. For this whole fucking mess.*

Ink had called him following the meet with their Bastion contact. He'd explained Laine's reaction to Ihlo's intel on the maker's mark and how Laine was on board with pursuing the lead. But Exose knew – they all knew – that their delicate lead amounted to nothing without something concrete to incriminate the Chair. The politics of the matter aside, they couldn't accuse the pseudo-boss of the Order of murder and subversion in the absence of any actual evidence. That's when Exose had had the idea: to use Dox as their bloodhounds, nose to ground, digging for dirt in the way they knew best. Every trader either owes a favour or has a favour owed. Every poke keeps his eyes and ears open, soaking up hearsay like it's the oxygen they need to breathe. With guaranteed immunity for whoever took the contract, Exose was certain tongues would loosen and that vital gem of intel could be made to let slip. It was just a matter of time. And time was running out.

While Exose remained at his post, Dox went to work. Inside closed stalls and in the shadows of dark corners, questions were asked, and favours traded. Many ventured out beyond familiar territory, into the light of the city. In districts across Arteza, as far out as Nascen Arch and Welling Blink, the hounds hunted. Assurances were given, protections sworn. The ears of Exose burned as his name was repeatedly stated, by way of guarantee. This was the true value in his rep: his word meant everything. He was a man respected. With that comes trust.

Three hours later, a trader returned. He approached Exose, who had not moved from his spot in the Shaft. The trader leant in and delivered his message: the coffin nail to set it right.

*

Agent Laine stared at Exose, her eyes wide as her mind whirled. "This is it," she said. "This'll seal it."

They were stood in a deserted side street a couple of blocks down from the Scarab. Exose had put the call through to Laine when he was already in a private ride on his way over. She'd come straight out to meet him.

"How did you get this?" she said.

"That doesn't matter. I've promised Dox, no questions and no comeback. Everyone knows someone who knows something. They just needed encouragement to go asking – and assurances they won't pay no price."

"Fair trade. We won't go knocking. This goes nowhere apart from bringing the culprit down."

"How fast can you act?"

"We'll go straight in. The proper channels will have to wait. We can't risk the roll out starting for the sake of paperwork."

"Need me to do anything?"

"You've done enough. Thank you. This is the game changer. I'm still getting my head around it… but it connects everything. With the Corruption stopped, we can start repairing the damage."

"About that…"

"What is it?"

"I'm Dox. It's all about favours, right?"

Laine cocked her head. "Name yours."

"I need a property licence. I'm not allowed to apply due to black marks on my record."

Her brow pinched, Laine hesitated, thrown by the curveball request. Then she saw Exose's expression.

"Commercial? Or Residential?"

"Mixed. Freehold, not lease."

She looked at Exose for a moment, glimpsing the man beneath the trader, then her own expression softened.

"Consider it done. A pleasure doing business with you." She shook his hand. "By the way, those black marks are likely to disappear. Keep your rep up if you like, you don't need a record to back it." She smiled, then slipped away in the direction of the Scarab, where she would give the order to arrest the Chair of the General Council for the murder of Kitred Wides and the wilful corruption of Klova.

I admire the spirit of aspirance. It speaks of passion, of self-assurance, of unfaltering self-belief in one's own potential.

Equality is fair and just. Egalitarianism is an effective social construct to entrench it in normative behaviour and the prevailing sociocultural attitude.

But the price of parity in equal standing is ambivalence – a suppression of spirit that dampens the spark of personal potential.

Aspirance provides fuel for just such a spark.

I am the work in progress of my spark's ignition.

CHAPTER THIRTY-THREE

Votary Engala, unelected Chair of the General Council of the Order of Savants, sat in an interview room inside Bastion Detention. Hands cuffed and dressed in custody overalls, her slicked back hair was the final vestige of her former appearance. Her face was wan, her emerald eyes dulled to pedestrian green.

It was early the following morning. The previous evening, Agents Laine and Brosala had led a small unit up the steps of the Library, with backup on standby outside the gates to Mount Az. Laine suspected the Chair would go quietly, rather than create a scene she would later be remembered for. Despite the initial impact, triggering a rapid spiral of shock, outrage, then denial, the Chair became quiet and porcelain pale, as cracks in the glaze spread. While Laine read out the charges and appraised her of her rights, Engala blinked at the blows but otherwise did not move. Laine and Brosala led her out in silence, her hands discretely cuffed behind her back.

By the time they had brought her in, the hour was late. There remained urgent measures to be taken back on Mount Az. Once safely installed in the smallest, coldest cell available,

Laine had led a unit back to the Order and the Department of Implementation. They had found votary Modessr working late in his lab, coordinating the distribution of the first batch of vials containing the nanoware that held the system update. Clinics around the city were awaiting delivery, with night-staff geared up for a busy shift.

Upgrade Day was always an eagerly anticipated event. People applied months in advance to be among the first in line, experiencing their updated language code while others waited their turn. This was a brief window of difference; a chance for the first-batch recipients to test out the enhancements and attempt to work out what had been incorporated. Quads held special events – sparing debates between speakers of old and new. It was all in the spirit of marking the occasion: celebrating the ongoing perfection of Klova. While the city was gearing up for the launch, Laine had to hit the stop button in time.

Modessr admitted later that it was a frighteningly close call.

When Laine had appeared in his lab and revealed the news of the Chair's arrest, Modessr had been shocked into silence. Then, as he gradually processed the facts, shock gave way to crystalline pragmatism and an instinctive resolution.

"Given the circumstances, I agree that the update must not proceed. However, votary Engala's arrest leaves the Council – and, therefore, the Order – without a mechanism for decision-making. This situation is unprecedented. There is no protocol."

"But there's a deputy, right?"

"Previously, yes. However, votary Engala made the post redundant when she took office." He cleared his throat. "There is provision elsewhere, however. Section P, paragraph three of the Agreement for Mutual Assist grants Bastion extended jurisdiction. When a risk to Klova is deemed catastrophic,

Bastion are sanctioned to exercise authoritative control as a measure of last resort. The clause is widely forgotten because the conditions for it to apply have never arisen and, until now, seemed unimaginable. I think we've reached that inconceivable moment of crisis. Would you agree?"

"Without doubt."

"Then may I suggest the following two options. Either deploy an appropriate agent from your organisation to take over the Chair's decision-making function, or assign that level of authority to a votary. There is no chain of command here. You would need to choose someone. Or, if it would be of assistance, I can suggest a short list of suitable candidates."

"I choose you."

Modessr raised his eyebrows and subconsciously straightened his tunic. "Well, I…"

"You're due to take on the rotational office of Chair in under seven weeks. Besides, you're leading on the update, so you're the one best positioned to stop it. Also, Ihlo Unis has spoken to me about you, revealing something in particular which she had just discovered herself. She expressed respect for your professionalism and expertise."

"She… she did?"

"So, it's decided. You're in charge. Halt the update. Immediately. Destroy every vial; give risk no opportunity to slip the net. Aside from that, do as you see fit to protect Klova and everyone who speaks it."

Now, with the update successfully stopped, Laine could concentrate on the prize. She sat in the interview room opposite the pale-faced Chair, with Brosala at her side. Poised inside and out, Laine imagined the eyes watching her from beyond the mirrored window. Top Floor would be among the spectators. That knowledge didn't ruffle her feathers, which were fanned for the fight of her career.

"Let's start with Kitred Wides," she said, her voice an even keel. "How did the two of you meet?"

The Chair of the General Council looked at Laine, her mouth lax in grim resignation.

"I read the transcript of your interviews with Exose Ray, when the link with codevice was first suspected. I also read your report, citing Kite as the source of your tip-off. I was after a trader with ambition, someone who wasn't afraid to cross lines. Kite struck me as a potential candidate. So, I sent her a message – a teaser, to test her appetite."

"Hungry, I take it?"

"Inflamed. A recent ticking-off by Exose had riled her. She didn't take kindly to being patronised. I hinted at a business opportunity; she jumped at the chance. She was desperate to raise her game and prove she deserved respect, not condescension. The timing was fortuitous for us both."

"Fortuitous? For Kite?"

"At the time, yes. Ambition is only self-sustaining up to a point. Hers had been repressed by a combination of her youth and inexperience. All meaningless when it comes to aspirance and what an individual – *any* individual – is capable of. I saw in Kite a model consciousness. The appeal of her recruitment became two-fold: a well-positioned trader with an established route to market – and an opportunity to observe theory blossom in practice."

"By theory, I assume you mean Ninian's?"

"And I must assume now that your casual yet sublimely appropriate references to his work were a trap."

"I wanted to get the measure of you. A trap was unnecessary." Laine pushed back her shoulders. "'*Aspirance must be a contradiction of motive, at once both self-serving and self-less. The silver coin flips, end over end. Two faces; one coin. The investment is always in the greater good.*' I understand his metaphor – I just don't quite see how it relates to your little project with Kite."

"You read Ninian from an archaic perspective. He was a progressive. His ideas were radical in a way they were never given credit for. His theory of aspirance is not fettered by time, nor should our interpretation of it be. We are within reach of a new century. We need to think like we're already in the future if we're to continue to progress as a society. Over the last century, we've become complacent, resting comfortably on the laurels of our scientific and sociological advancement. Complacency leads to stagnation. Our society is at the brink of that disastrous becalming."

"Whether that's true or not, I wonder at your method. Avoid complacency by corrupting the single most important contributor to our nation's advanced development?"

"The Corruption was not the objective. It was the opportunity."

"An unusual way to view it."

"The Corruption had already started with XDream. The product's interaction with Klova was no deliberate violation. On reading the transcript of your interview, I knew for certain that the effect on Klova was not made, it happened. That absence of intention was critical. The result: a causeless effect. Random chance. Unlikely to predict. Impossible to prevent.

"This revelation terrified me. The whole purpose of the Order is to protect and perfect language. To discover absolute protection is unachievable was devastating. I have sworn an oath, committing a lifetime of service to an impossible cause. Klova's vulnerability struck me so profoundly that its potential destruction felt inevitable. I found myself despairing for the future and grieving language as if it were already lost.

"That's when I sought guidance in the wisdom of Ninian. I was determined to find a course to counter this bleak projection. Then I recalled a particular passage from *Aspirance*. '*It is not the path taken, nor the choice the traveller makes to set out on that path. Aspirance is the will to make the journey – the true spirit of endeavour. Prestige is the welcoming party, marking one's journey's end. It is the milestone placed in commemoration.*' This sparked an ambition within me, a desire so strong to be the '*exceptional among us*', to be greater than my peers for the greater good – and prove myself as such by saving Klova."

"So, you simulated the corrupted code in XDream in order to manipulate it? You couldn't just locate and eradicate it?"

"Random chance. By definition it cannot be eradicated."

"Then why, for fuck's sake? Your experiment caused a mutation. You made the situation one hundred percent *worse*. Why do you talk as if you were still doing us all a fucking favour?"

*

Laine held the thick, black coffee in both hands, sipping the scalding liquid.

"The woman's friggin' nuts," she said. She was stood with Brosala in the corridor outside the interview room. They had taken time out, Brosala having nudged and glared at her once she'd lost her cool.

"She's insane. I agree. You have to be to do what she's done. So probably best to steer clear of warped interpretations of centuries-old social philosophy."

Laine sighed. "You're right. No point trying to reason."

"Easiest charge to nail is homicide. We have the evidence, we just need her confession on record. Then we can unpick the rest in stages. Even Top Floor are pushing for that. Ubimedia loves a good murder. Meanwhile, we look good for solving one. Public opinion is anti-Order and anti-Corrupted. It's been a sustained trend since the start of this mess and it's what's fuelling the tension. Pacify public unrest with a neat case-solved regarding Kite – that's what they'll care more about. Then we can work through what's left of this shitstorm with a load less pressure."

Laine nodded slowly. "You're smart, Bro. What you doing still assisting me?"

"I'm not. I'm saving your ass." Brosala winked. "Go back in there and bring her down."

They returned to their seats inside the interview room. Engala remained pale and passive. Laine tapped the embedded screen in the tabletop.

"Bastion agents Laine and Brosala resuming interview of the suspect." She settled into her seat and crossed her arms. "Back to Kite. She's pissed off at Exose and sees your offer as an opportunity to up her game. You recruit her. What's her first task?"

Engala looked beyond Laine at a point in the middle distance, as if bored by the detail. "To break into Exose's stall and copy the code in XDream."

"We left agents guarding his stall when we brought him in."

"You've been inside Dox. Doors aren't the only way into spaces."

"How did she get the code to you? Did you meet somewhere?"

"We never met face to face. I have a contact in the commercial sector. They have Whitespace storage in the neoCloud. Everything went through there."

Laine glanced at Brosala, frowning the question.

"Whitespace is a high security data storage platform," said Brosala. "It converts data into a format that renders it invisible, unless you have the conversion key to revert it. Technically un-hackable because all content appears blank."

Laine turned back to Engala. "This contact of yours, I don't suppose he works for iCon?"

"*Worked.* He created my stall in *Trans:akshn*, if that's the connection you're only just making. iCon terminated his contract once your people started asking questions. Pristine reputation and impenetrable privacy are part of their USP."

Brosala looked at Laine, anticipating another deviation. He turned his head towards her and discretely mouthed *Kite*. Laine gave a barely perceptible nod and took a deep breath. She leant forward, arms on the table, and glared at Engala.

"It sounds like you had it all set up. An eager operative in Dox. A secure workspace. Stolen code. The means to simulate it and create your own product. Then back to Kite, your tech-enhanced poke, transferring your stealth download whenever she encountered a potential customer. The set-up was working. XD2 was selling. What went wrong? Kite get greedy? Demand more of the cut?"

Engala's eyes shifted, setting out options, feeling their weight.

"I see what you're doing," said Laine. "And I'll tell you now, there's zero point."

"I didn't kill Kite."

"Meanwhile, we have evidence that categorically proves the opposite. Transpires the dirty work contractor you hired took precaution to secure a little insurance for himself. That's why you came in quietly, isn't it? Because how can you trust a third party who kills for coin?"

Engala stared at Laine as if the agent were the precipice on which she now stood.

"Play the tape," said Laine.

Brosala tapped the tabletop. A holographic image appeared, hovering in the space between them. Speakers, somewhere, hummed into life.

"For the record," said Laine, addressing the ears of hidden devices, "Agent Brosala is about to play an AV file, evidence ID forty-eight zero ninety-two. Classified."

Brosala complied. The holographic still became greyscale footage from a security camera, accompanied by a soundtrack of low-def audio. One of the voices had been vocoded – intelligible, but unidentifiable. The footage had also been shopped, with the head of one of the people made into a dark smudge. The other figure was Kite. The location, a high-angle view of the interior of her stall.

As the sequence played, the soundtrack made clear the narrative.

[Voice, female] No. Please don't. Please. Tell Exose I'm sorry. I'll make it up to him.
[Voice, male] Ain't nothing to do with Exose. For your other boss. And she sends a message.
[Voice, female] Please…
(Sounds of struggle, female crying)
[Voice, male] No one threatens Engala.
[Voice, female] (screams)
(Sounds of struggle, choking. A faint crack. Footsteps. Silence)

The playback froze on the final frame: Kite laying on the floor, eyes terror-wide, mouth open in the shape of her final, soundless scream, her neck bent at an impossible angle.

Laine allowed the audio hum to run on, a sonic underscore, before continuing.

"It may not have been your own hands that broke her neck, but it was your order that made it happen. The law is unambiguous. You ordered the contract killing of Kitred Wides. This contract was carried out as per your instruction. You are guilty of her murder."

The Chair of the General Council still stared at Laine. She had not watched the footage but could not close her ears to the audio, to the incriminating message sent in vanity. The screams had no impact on her, nor did the death-heavy silence. Her own stupidity was the only thing that touched her, her own desire for the lowlife trader to know she was not to be messed with.

"I told her not to keep calling me. Warned her not to make her pathetic threats."

"Presumably her threat was to expose you. Why would she do that? You were paying her, right?"

"Decided she needed more. She was convinced Exose Ray was after her. Said she needed to get away. Started making demands to fund her little scheme."

"And you refused."

"Of course I refused. I needed her in the market to hook potential buyers. What use was she to me, hiding out in the country? That was never going to happen. But she wouldn't drop it. When she threatened to talk, she left me no choice."

"Is that how you justify it? Murdering a scared, helpless young woman because that was the only way to shut her up?"

"She was jeopardising the entire plan. I needed to sell more of the product to amass more data. There was still so much to learn before I could turn things around. I knew the plan would work, if only she shut up whining and did the job I paid her for. But the stupid girl threatened to destroy everything. I couldn't let that happen."

"So, you ordered the contract on her, to have her killed."

"Yes."

Laine flashed a glance at Brosala, who's left eye glowed green. She longed to see through the mirrored glass behind her, to witness the reaction in the Top Floor faces. She imagined the slow release of pressure that would surely follow, anticipating the relief of Bastion's space to breathe.

She knew there was much more to come, that Kite's murder was one sad piece of a much larger, more dangerous puzzle. It was the explosive charge that would detonate the ubimedia frenzy, fuelling the output of consumer-generators and likely to occupy them for days – weeks, if the scandal took on a life of its own. This would afford her uninterrupted attention to solve the rest of the puzzle. She sat back and studied the Chair: the one person who held all the pieces.

Dependence is a complex weakness.

If acknowledged, it can be a false crutch on which you lean. It can be help on which you rely. It can be the harness and rope by which your fragile life hangs.

Even if you lack the courage to admit it, if you know you are dependent upon something other than your own resource, you retain some small degree of control. You are choosing to perpetuate that dependency. You are letting it take your weight.

What if you are unaware that you hang by a rope?

That rope becomes something more than woven cord. Its purpose swells with everything it now represents: your stability, your safety, your survival.

If I'm being honest, that is what much of this boils down to. Recognition. Recognition of all that language represents beyond its polished code. And recognition that, without it, your mind cannot function. It can barely exist.

Would you believe it possible? Would you open your eyes and perceive the rope from which you hang? Going by experience, I'd say no.

Again, therein lies the need for impact. There's no mileage in hinting, vaguely suggesting, implying the stakes. If there's no impact, you might hear me, but you won't listen, you won't allow it to penetrate your consciousness in any meaningful way.

I want to see the whites of your eyes when you see that rope for the first time and discover the truth of your precarious dependence.

I want to show you what you have, what you take for granted, what you think you own, by taking some of it away.

Loss. Recognising, too late, the preciousness of what you once had.

CHAPTER THIRTY-FOUR

News of the confession was leaked to ArtezAlert and, within minutes, was the highest trending content on ubimedia. Public opinion mattered little to Bastion. They just needed word to spread that someone had confessed to the murder of Kitred Wides and that the same individual was also charged with the manufacture and distribution of XD2. The latter was an ongoing investigation, but that did not detract from the core message: the Corruption was believed to be contained and the suspect was behind Bastion bars.

Public opinion mattered considerably more to the Order, whose reputation would be demolished by the scale of the scandal. There was no way to diminish the irony; ubi commentators would latch onto that as the obvious starting point. What concerned every votary in the shell-shocked Order was how to restore the trust and respect that the organisation had earnt over the course of centuries. Theirs was a calling for which they dedicated their lives – the most respected of public servants within Klovaine society. The fact that the de facto leader of the entire organisation was responsible for the wilful corruption of the language they were under oath to protect stripped the Order of its integrity. It also shone a horrifying light on the vulnerability of Klova, until then made inconceivable by the mask of outward appearance. Those sworn to protect also held the power and the means to destroy.

This unmasking left society reeling. People regarded the Order and beheld a lie. They looked to the Corrupted and were confronted with their own precarious dependence. They considered Klova and, for the first time, discovered the driverless control of their own perception. Klova was exposed for what it was: an autonomous system on which everyone's experience of reality depended. This had always been the case. However, it is easy to overlook the workings of a reliable, dependable, near-perfect machine, as long as that machine works. For Klovaines, their dependence was as good as forgotten. Artificial language was an unavoidable fact of life that is best ignored because it can't be changed. It is part of what is normal.

With the arrest of the Chair of the General Council for the wilful corruption of Klova, normal could no longer be ignored. Every Klovaine felt at the mercy of a construct they relied upon but had no control over. The afflicted had recognised this from the moment they lost fragments of code, causing the reality they experienced to change. For a small minority of the unaffected, the realisation was a slow dawning as the crisis unfolded. For the majority, however, ubimedia had made it clear that codevice was a choice. With choice comes avoidable consequence. Hence the far from sympathetic reaction to the Corrupted. They were, it was generally agreed, asking for it.

What profoundly changed public opinion was the widely reported speculation regarding contamination of the system update. The update was not a matter of choice but a fact of life. It was not a dubious habit deserving of scorn and fair game to the hand of consequence dealt. The moral high ground had been bulldozed, flattening the them-and-us distinction. Everyone required the upgrade, everyone was equally at risk. If Bastion had not intervened in time and the rollout had started…

Ubimedia feasted on the 'What if' scenarios that spawned. Within hours of the controlled leak to ArtezAlert, which made no mention of any potential update contamination, the narrative taking shape was one of a near-miss apocalypse. For the Undertow, the near miss did not apply. They were already living the nightmare. No longer in the spotlight, they were relegated to context. Human colour.

Ren had managed to secure the back room of Physical Books for two hours every evening. Even if a formal meeting hadn't been planned, members were encouraged to drop in for support and the comfort of community. The phase two afflicted rarely participated, lacking the self-awareness to share, yet appeared captivated by the airing and sharing of others. Whether they could conceive of it or not, members found their loss more bearable through witnessing the fact it was felt by them all.

This communion is Ink's source of strength, his purpose. It is his reason to fight, rather than fold up and sleep, escaping in tailor-made dreams. He also finds the strength to cope thanks to Ihlo's hope – which is why he asked to speak with Ren, ahead of that evening's meet. They had agreed on a hothouse not far from her apartment in Pincher Toll.

It is early afternoon; the place is quiet and mercifully warm. A burnfree crackles in a large grate, the centrepiece of the wood-panelled room, its fake flames casting an amber glow.

"Ihlo's at the Order now," says Ink. He is sat opposite Ren in a corner booth. "Bastion intervenes, restoring her clearance to access whatever she needs."

Ren leans forward, elbows on the table, her wild hair trailing a shifting shadow. "I don't think appraising our members of the Order's inadequate efforts is going to bring them comfort."

"I agree. But this isn't about the Order. Ihlo's doing this independently, she just needs to use their tech. She knows how the implant is breached. She's determined to repair the damage." He hesitates, then adds, "She tells me about Ky. Disappears for hours in the night, in a t-shirt and leggings. Bare feet. Ihlo finds her freezing half to death. Ky doesn't realise. In her world, she can't know to feel it." He sighs. "I know you know how it's affecting members. I'm just saying, Ihlo's living this too. What she's doing, it's not just duty."

"I'm sorry about Ky. And I hear you about Ihlo. But I'm wary of raising false hope. Members look to the group for support, they trust each other – and they trust me. I'm not sure I can stand on that crate and make out it's all going to be okay. We don't know that. I know you believe her, but I don't see how Ihlo can know that. Not really."

"I'm not suggesting we make promises. I just think it'd help members to know. The Order will be busy fighting the scandal backlash, while Bastion are focussed on solving the rest of the case. But members need to know our suffering is remembered. Good heads are working on it. There's Ihlo – and there's Exose."

"Exose Ray? What the fuck's he got to do with this? Apart from cause the problem in the first place."

"Exose isn't to blame. I know you've no time for him, but you only know the trader. Beneath that, he's kind. He cares and acts on that caring. He tries to save me from a dark place, even though he's down in the same dark hole – helping me to crawl free before he thinks to crawl out himself. Now, others make him a scapegoat, just like they do us. But the truth is, he knows his part in all this and accepts responsibility, even though he doesn't do anything wrong. He wants to help – and he's the best c'grammer out there. Exose and Ihlo are working together to stem the breach and, hopefully, give us back what we lose."

"Tall order."

"So are most things worthwhile." He hesitates, then pushes his shoulders back, his gaze steady. "That's why I'm putting myself forward. Whatever they come up with, I'm going to tell them to test it on me."

Ren stares at Ink, her eyebrows raised. "Your fight makes you stand out. Be careful it doesn't cost you more than you lose already."

"Any cost will only be to me, and I'm prepared to take that."

"Our condition isn't degenerating. And it looks like Bastion have their hands on the sick bastard behind it. The Order will move on to fixing us in good time. Why put yourself at risk?"

"Because I can't wait for good time. The affliction isn't spreading, but every night I see the suffering among the Undertow cut a little deeper. I see it in their eyes. I hear it in the silence of those who've given up sharing. I count it in the number who come, night after night, because it's the only place they're not alone. You tell me to use my outrage as armour and to wear enough to protect us all. That's exactly what I'm doing."

*

Dusk had fallen; form took the guise of shadow. Dark figures hurried past Physical Books, heading for home, or the warmth of a hothouse or Quad. Ihlo stood on the pavement opposite, hand to chest. She had left Mount Az in plenty of time, calling in at the apartment to check on Ky before taking a Swift to a dock just up the road. Still, she had to take a moment to catch her breath and calm her racing heart.

As she approached the glazed front door, she saw shadows shift and Ink's face emerge. He appeared to hesitate a moment, looking at her, before unlocking the door. Ihlo silently slipped inside and stood in the warm, dusty shadows of the shop. Bookshelves loomed above and around them both. Passing vehicles sent fleeting illumination, revealing Ihlo's wide eyes and lips slightly parted as if caught mid-sentence.

"You have news," said Ink. It came out in a half-whisper. "What is it?"

"It's good."

He smiled, then took her hand and led her through the maze of books, into the back room. Ren was sat in the centre on a wooden crate, scribbling notes on a piece of paper. She looked up as Ink and Ihlo entered.

"Ihlo's come straight from the Order," he said. "She has good news to share with the group. May she address them?"

Ren looked from Ink to Ihlo, whose hair was still in Order style, and wrestled with instinctive suspicion.

"I take it they lift your suspension," she said.

Ihlo touched the side of her head, regretting the omission made in haste.

"Bastion have secured me access to the Order's systems and full clearance. This…" She flicked her hand, gesturing her hair. "This is just easier once I'm there. I'll sort it out before members arrive."

Ren felt Ink's glare on her and guessed its intention. She made an effort not to scowl.

"Ink tells me you're onto something with the cause of all this – and that you're collaborating with Exose Ray."

Ihlo heard the statement's heavy load. "I had reservations about Exose at first. But then I listened to him. He has a great mind and an unexpected compassion. He is also highly skilled in cerebrogramming and its neurological engagement. I would be wrong to *not* collaborate with him. Besides, I've come to trust him on this – and I don't believe I'd have found the fault without his help."

Ren processed this, whilst keeping her eyes fixed on Ihlo. "This news you'd like to share – 'good' as in you find a fix?"

"Almost. There are some final tests to run, safety checks, but we're—"

Rising from the crate, Ren stood in front of Ihlo, too close for casual, and cut her off. Her greater height added weight to the confrontation.

"Let me be clear. Our members are vulnerable. Imagine a spectrum, the starting point being despair and the end point being total mental and emotional collapse. Our members are scattered between the midpoint and the end. Whilst hope may be important, it can also do great damage if not carefully managed."

"What I have to share does not hinge on hope. It is fact. It's happening. And it's the first step to recovery."

*

Ihlo stood on the crate in the centre of the room, surrounded by over two hundred expectant faces. The space was dimly lit by scant ceiling spots, their reflections caught in red-rimmed eyes. At the back of the crowd, standing against the far wall, Ihlo saw Ink and Ren. Ink looked nervous on her behalf. Ren nodded slightly and offered encouragement in the shape of a smile. A short time ago, Ihlo had fought to win one woman's support. Now, she had two hundred wounded minds to convince. Silence surrounded her. Ihlo cleared her throat, then delivered her message.

"Members of the Undertow, my name is Ihlo Unis. I am a novice votary, currently suspended from the Order for forcing its hand to address the malfunction of Klova and your plight as victims. I speak to you now, not as a votary of the Order, nor on the Order's behalf. I do not have their permission to share with you the information I am about to. They are not my concern. You are.

"I returned to Mount Az today to continue my investigation into how the codevice products were able to interact with your implant, damaging parts of your language code. Whilst there, I learnt that a close colleague is part of a team writing a programme to repair this damage. They have developed two patches: one to overwrite the code erasure caused by XDream, the other to restore the code affected by the XD2 variation. Both patches, fully tested and approved, were added to the nanoware containing the system update. For the unafflicted majority, the patches would have absolutely no effect. For those affected, their lost Klova code would be restored."

Murmuring filled the room. Faces looked pained by the spikes in emotion.

"They have to give us the update," someone shouted. "What are they waiting for?"

"Bastion have credible reason to suspect that the update itself could have been tampered with, to potentially include a further variation. This is why they put the brakes on Upgrade Day at the last minute. Whilst they lacked proof, the potential for contamination was viable. The risk was too high to even consider. All batches of the serum containing the nanoware have been destroyed as a precaution."

The despair at this unknown chance, now lost, was palpable. Ihlo felt it and quickly sought to allay.

"But we still have the patch files and there's another way they can be installed. My supervisor and his team are working all hours to write a utility programme to be run by the cerebrovox implant, so that the patches can be installed into the existing operating system without the need for the full update. Once they've written and fully tested the utility programme, they'll be able to insert the patch code, transfer to nanoware, add to a suspension serum, then it can be administered to those afflicted who chose to receive the treatment."

"An injected patch?" came a voice from the crowd. "The Order works all year on the update. This team knocks this out in what? A week? They can't test it properly in that time. They can't know for sure it's safe."

The challenge cut through the room, waking minds to the counter view. The crowd divided.

"She says it's approved," someone offered.

"Then why don't the Order say anything about this?" came another voice. "If they know the patch will work, why keep it quiet?"

"What choice, though…" More of a mumble.

"You seriously expect us to trust you?" Another voice, pin-sharp and bitter, aimed at Ihlo. "Your Chair's a thieving vice trader who confesses to murder. Colleagues of yours plan to inject forty-eight million people with a make-do they barely test, without the public's knowledge or consent. These patches are made *in secret* – which must mean they haven't got state approval. The whole Order's one fat fucking Corruption."

Ihlo stood her ground, feeling the swell of fear and frustration, faith and mistrust, waiting for the wave to recede. She felt a hand on her shoulder and turned to find Ren, who had joined her on the crate.

Ren addressed the Undertow. "I share your anger. I live your pain and fear. But I also see this for what it is: the help we deserve, the action we call for. I trust Ihlo. I urge you to find the faith to do likewise." She nodded to Ihlo and took a step back.

Ihlo took a deep breath and weighed options. Then she said to the crowd, "I hear your questions and understand their source. The team worked in secret because the person with the power to authorise it was doing everything in theirs to block it. The update was brought forward when this person learnt the patches had been tested, but believed they'd not yet been added. They only learnt about the tests because they were carried out on four votaries. The Department for Internal Resources was alerted to an unscheduled health record entry. The four votaries had been afflicted – two from XDream and two from XD2. Their health records now state that their symptoms have gone. Their Klova was – is – fully restored.

"All four worked on the team to develop the patches. I spoke to two of them this afternoon. They explained their model and shared with me their method. The proofs are elegant, the coding precise, the safeguards robust. Were I afflicted, I would have no hesitation in consenting to the treatment. My cousin, Ky, who some of you may know from these meetings, is phase two afflicted. While she cannot conceive of herself, she cannot recognise the source of the suffering that is slowly killing her, or the danger that her loss has put her in. I love her. I will keep her safe and protect her welfare while she can't do so herself. That is why, when I leave here tonight, I will go home to her, I will tell her about the patch, and I will encourage her to come forward and be made well."

The wave shifted, the eddies caused by a different current.

"I have a question," came a voice from the back of the room. Ihlo looked up and saw that it was Ink who spoke. "For those of us who choose to, when can we come forward? What do we have to do? I will have the patch, I will be made well – then four will be five."

"Make that six," said Ren.

"Mistake me not, this is no treatise for backdoor disparity. To my mind, society's strength lies in the spine of mutual respect and the musculature of equality in our perception of others. That is why prestige wears no crown, nor wields power in a mace of superiority. Greater-than does not equate to better-than. Its garb is uniform, but its face is remembered."

Ninian, *Aspirance: The Exception of Greater-Than in a Society of Equals*

CHAPTER THIRTY-FIVE

The interview room in Bastion's Detention felt overcrowded. Agents Laine and Brosala sat opposite a stoic, sour-faced Chair of the General Council. Behind the mirrored glass, the room was crammed with agents, watching in breath-held silence. All around the Scarab, agents and techs crowded around observation visuals, staring at the live feed.

The scandal of the Chair's involvement was of a different character within Bastion. While the Order felt shock, shame and a desire for disassociation, Bastion craved dissection. They wanted to pull the impossible apart, piece by piece, as if trying to understand the operations of a highly complex programme. They needed to know how this could possibly happen on their watch.

Laine sat up straight, shoulders back, hands in her lap. The rest break had done her good, she could feel it. Her head was clear, her sights focussed. They'd bagged their trophy to parade, which had earnt a temporary dip in pressure. Meanwhile, what remained of the charges presented Laine, and every Bastion agent, with the prospect of far greater reward. She felt the eyes of the organisation on her and spoke on their behalf.

"Let us return to the matter of codevice," she said. "Through Kite, you obtained the raw code for XDream. Why didn't you just manufacture more of the same? Why the variation in XD2?"

"It had been my intention to copy verbatim." Engala spoke with the flat tone of resignation. Her body was rigid, but her face was slack. "My interest was in the product's side effect, not creating market competition. However, it became apparent that I could not simply copy the code and create an identical reproduction."

"Why was that?"

"Exose Ray is an artist and a genius. The code itself is so elegant, so refined. Impeccable in its subtlety and precision. I've never seen anything like it. Much of it I was able to copy, but there are threads weaving through it, on a perpendicular plane, that I couldn't read. Viewed from the single, visible plane, it appears as if the characters are overwritten – dense, indecipherable streamers. It was only when I ran it through a particular machine, unique to the Order, that I was able to understand what was otherwise hidden. This structure, this unique *shape*, was something I could not replicate."

"But you could simulate. That's why the afflicted who took XD2 described the nightmares as unreal, like a projection. Whereas, in Exose's XDream, they are, reportedly, terrifyingly real. His USP."

"The quality of the experience was of no concern to me. I knew I wouldn't be receiving repeat trade. Hence the ongoing need for Kite. I had to attract new customers."

"I'm surprised anyone went near it."

"That's where the variation played in my favour. Rebrand and market it as new, improved, Corruption-free and promote it with a discount for the first purchase – people's perception of risk is compromised."

"So, your motive was not to diversify your business

interests by participating in the codevice market?"

"Of course not. What do you take me for?"

Laine involuntarily raised her eyebrows. Brosala simply stared.

"I had to amass more data. I was determined to discover the cause of the malfunction, understand the true character and potential of this chance contamination of our most precious, most carefully protected Klova. Only then could my faith in the Order's purpose be restored. I had to learn how to control this beast if I was to preserve its prey.

"My ambition was to save Klova and prove that I am worthy of the prestige befitting such a feat. The Order is stymied by the slow path of the proper way. I knew my method would be rejected out of hand. That only swelled my determination more. My journey was at great risk on several levels, I admit. But it was the journey's end upon which my aspirance focused."

"You think analogy with Ninian's thesis justifies your actions?"

"Not analogy, Agent Laine. Demonstration."

"Of how to fuck with people's minds?"

"I did what was necessary. And I would have succeeded if Kite hadn't started making threats. I'm telling you, my intervention was a calculated means to the most desirable end. If you widened your perception beyond the blinkers of assumed propriety, you would find merit in my scheme."

"I don't call opposition to wilful corruption an *assumed propriety*. What of those poor bastards whose lives you have destroyed? Have you met any of them? Spoken to them? It's not just the words they've lost. It's the whole concept. Their identity. Their whole damn sense of existing. Have you even tried to imagine what that must feel like? How it must fuck with your head?"

"'*The investment is always in the greater good.*'"

Laine leant forward, hands balled into fists on the table. "Enough with the Ninian quotes. That might be how you square this in your own head, but nowhere else does that wash." She took a deep breath and looked to Brosala.

Brosala picked up the baton without hesitation. "You say the Order is stymied by its adherence to protocol. You assumed it would reject your scheme, as if that were the only option available to stop the crisis. And yet, votary Ihlo Unis had petitioned the General Council with an urgent request to publish the statement confirming Bastion's investigation. The Order's records show that, despite the late hour and limited timescale, sufficient Council members voted on the motion, and the majority supported it. According to protocol, that motion should have been passed and the statement issued, without Ihlo having to jeopardise her entire career by leaking it. She was never told the outcome of the vote, neither was the rest of the Council. You told the Council insufficient votes were cast in time. That was a lie. Why did you block the statement's release?"

The scene was a frozen tableau, held in silence. In the packed room beyond the two-way, wide eyes were fixed on the face of the Chair.

Engala kept her own eyes locked on Brosala's. A muscle pulsed on the side of her tightly clenched jaw.

"At that time, the number of those afflicted was low. A public statement on the link between the so-called Amnesia Crisis and Klova would not only have caused unnecessary panic, it would have hindered the Order's ability to perform its duty. Bastion – *you* – should have been able to conduct your investigation without the need for the entire country to know your business and make judgement on your progress."

"So, it was to avoid public scrutiny?"

"It was to limit the damage to our organisations' reputations, agent. Public scrutiny is only an issue if the questions count for anything. They do not. I am talking about public *perception*. Both the Order and Bastion exist to protect Klova. If we are seen to have failed in this single, most fundamental duty, our entire purpose becomes a mockery. We require the public's faith and trust, which is bound within how they perceive us. A published statement declaring the corruption of Klova would have been a confession of failure. I was not prepared to let that happen."

"A cover-up."

"A buying of time. Time to find answers, facts, evidence. Once we knew what we were dealing with, we could communicate positive messages on how we planned to save Klova. Instead, the statement was leaked, and my point was proved: backlash against the Order, leaving our reputation in ruins; scepticism regarding Bastion's ability to stop the crisis, since they'd allowed it to happen in the first place; social disorder and growing antagonism towards the Corrupted. All in, a fertile field day for ubimedia, which loves nothing more than to plough division and sow hatred towards the targets it selects to demonise. Exactly the PR disaster I was trying to avoid."

"On the same day that the statement was leaked," continued Brosala, on a roll, "we discovered the afflicted had all taken XDream. Ihlo's sacrifice meant that we were able to operate openly and make swift progress, identifying the source and limiting the spread. With hindsight, do you not regard things differently? For example, that your own colleague and the majority of Council members were right to push for transparency for the sake of exigency?"

"Of course not. The damage to our reputation is not repaired by a chance quick win. Going public also meant word of the codevice connection spread fast; reliance on XDream as a vehicle was out of the question. Besides, sales in XDream had ceased with your arrest of Exose Ray. That's why my hand was forced. If I was to harness the potential within this chance side effect, more people had to be afflicted by it."

"Hence your scheme to create and sell another version of it."

"As I've explained, I needed to amass more data – and fast. This was the quickest way."

Laine crossed her arms, her disgust barely contained. "Our technicians were conducting tests on over a hundred volunteers afflicted by XDream. What made you think you could find something we couldn't, making hundreds more suffer in the process?"

"Penetration of the implant is the only way Klova can be affected. The lab tests carried out by your technicians were far too simplistic. Unsurprisingly, they revealed nothing. My plan was to harvest wider context data: neuro-response activity, hormone production, nerve impulses, irregular biomarkers, brain function activity – build the full picture to find the missing piece.

"By selling the product in *Trans:akshn*, not only could I maintain clear water between myself and my customers, it also gave me the means to capture this wealth of data without the bureaucracy of voluntary trials. iCon's VR platforms are of an exceptional standard; the haptic technology is high-end. I instructed my contact there to make a series of enhancements to the body suit and helmet. The latter included the introduction of a microscopic device that presses lightly against the temples, enabling the capture of functional brain imaging. Once mapped for each individual customer, I held their pre-breach profile. I was then able to collect data on their post-breach, corrupted profile via data transmitted by a nanochip injected into the base of the neck, courtesy of a microscopic syringe in the collar of the haptic suit. Once the customer fastened the suit, they were injected with the nanochip, thus establishing a means of data capture outside of *Trans:akshn*, after they ingested the product and awoke afflicted. Aside from a slight itchiness for a short period following the injection, the customer would suffer no adverse effects and would remain none the wiser.

"From the outset, this method generated a wealth of valuable information, including data from an unexpected source: an individual who is phase one afflicted and who attempted to purchase XD2. Although he left empty-handed, I gained my first feed of post-breach data for an XDream host, providing a valuable opportunity to compare profiles between the two phases.

"However, to build a viable picture that takes into account the myriad differences across human subjects, a significant sample size is required. I was making headway, but I needed to sell more of the product to build the picture and complete my analysis."

"I don't think I need to ask this, but I will," said Laine. "I don't suppose your customers gave their consent to be injected with a nanochip that hasn't been approved by Public Health?"

"Of course not. They would never agree. No matter. The tech was safe. I saw no reason to radically limit the source of data because of some misplaced moral conscience."

"As I thought. I just wanted to be clear on that point. We're data harvesting, too – on the various charges we can bring against you." Laine smiled. "So, moving on. Let's say you got all the data you needed. What then? What end, in your mind, justified your means?"

Votary Engala's face relaxed, and her eyes caught the light, glinting as if she could see the prize before her. "I would be in control."

"Of the Corruption? Not selling a knock-off might have got us there quicker."

"Of its *potential*. So far, it has manifested in ways that are detrimental to those afflicted. My intention was to learn how to control it, to make it function in the Order's favour – in the protection and perfection of Klova. And I would have been the one to achieve that end. I would have proven myself exceptional among equals, deserving of recognition in a way that our society denies us. I would be revered in the way we revere the Savants. Prestige was the end I sought. Prestige, earnt through the single-handed saving and elevation of Klova."

"You are due to stand down as the Chair of the General Council, are you not?"

"That is correct."

"How many terms have you served?"

"Three."

"How many is customary?"

"One. In exceptional cases, two."

"How did you get away with three?"

"I persuaded the Council I was still an exceptional case. Unfortunately, this time around, I failed to push it to a fourth term."

"What post would you have taken once you stepped down?"

"Back to rotational duty. Department of Archival Storage, I believe."

"But if you'd achieved your scheme's prestigious end, you'd be in control of much more than your malfunction's so-called *potential*. Isn't that so? That's your true motive behind all this, isn't it? A last-ditch attempt to hold on to your proxy power and turn it into an authority that, through its making, is deemed legitimate and permanent."

"You can speculate all you like, Agent. It will get you precisely nowhere, other than feeding the prejudice in your own judgement of me."

Brosala retrieved the baton, side-stepping the provocation, leaving Laine space to absorb the impact. "The system update," he said. "A team comprising some of the Order's most highly skilled votaries made a confidential petition to the Incorporation Panel, of which you are also Chair. For the record, please outline the content of that petition."

Pale skin flickered as a nerve twitched beside Engala's left eye. "I don't recall the detail."

"The general thrust, then. Confidential petitions are rare, I assume. I'm sure you must remember the basic proposition."

"Some scheme to use the system update to repair the damage to Klova in the afflicted. A cobbled together sticking plaster, if I recall. It was a desperate plan with absolutely no time to execute it within our stringent safety measures. Unsurprisingly, it was rejected by the Panel."

"It was supported by the Panel, but rejected by you."

"Either way."

Laine tapped the tabletop, launching a holographic of the AV recording stats. As she spoke, green spikes fluctuated in time with her voice. "In the light of your account today, you may as well speak honestly. If you lie to us now, on record, it will only make your already dire situation immeasurably worse."

Engala ignored the visual demonstration. She looked at Brosala, the twitching nerve now a constant pulse.

"It was too soon. I needed those afflicted from XD2 to remain broken for a little while longer. As they adjusted to the gap in their language, the neuroimaging was capturing the adjustment – the impact on thought, perception, conscious and subconscious processing. It is remarkable what it can do to your mind if you remove a few lines of code – if you erase some of the language that determines how you experience the world around you. I knew I would lose the source of all that incredible data, that wealth of learning, the moment the afflicted were healed."

"So, you overruled the Panel," said Laine. "You blocked the proposal, causing victims to suffer for longer, unnecessarily. Have you read the transcripts of their interviews? Heard the recordings? For most, their condition is a deteriorating one. They don't lose more code – but they're slowly losing their minds."

"And have you not listened to anything I've said?" Engala spoke through gritted teeth, her pallid skin growing flush pink. "Or are you just too simple to understand?"

"I've listened and I understand just fine. You've abused your authority at every step to serve your twisted scheme, to win the power you crave. I understand alright. I just wonder how far you were prepared to go."

"As far as was necessary."

"I'm glad you said that. Leads nicely onto my next question. Upgrade Day. At the last minute, you brought it forward. Against unanimous objection, you insisted. Why was that?"

"It had already been postponed. I was merely reducing the unnecessary delay."

"Why?"

Votary Engala tipped her head slightly and almost smiled. "Why do you think?"

"You got wind of a rumour that Modessr and his team had worked on the patches regardless, but you assumed they hadn't yet been added to the update. Meanwhile, you had made your own addition. Isn't that so?"

"And what might that be?"

"A further mutation. A new corruption that would be injected into the necks of the entire population."

Engala stared at Laine, her eyebrows raised a fraction.

Laine pressed. "You said yourself you needed more data. With Bastion shutting down iCon, *Trans:akshn* was closed to business for the foreseeable future. With no route to market, you needed to find an alternative means of triggering the malfunction. What better, more efficient way than to contaminate vials containing the update? Or, better still, contaminate the update itself. That's why you brought the update forward: to launch your mutation before Modessr had chance to add the patches and defeat you. Admit it."

"Why?"

"Because it's all part of your master plan for the greater good, right? You've confessed to everything else. You even justify everything. Complete the picture – the portrait of your journey to prestige."

"Ah," said Engala, her eyes wide, almost smiling. "I see."

"What?"

"You've no evidence. You've destroyed every vial. There's no way to prove it, either way."

Did I anticipate my actions would have the impact they have had?

Yes.

Do I regret the path I chose?

I knew the first demonstration wouldn't be sufficient to wake minds made blind by conceited slumber. I had to strike a second time, harder, in a place more vulnerable, in order to force those eyes open and make them truly see.

The afflicted are victims of my wilful intervention. I accept responsibility for that. Their suffering has been an unfortunate consequence. But it was not unforeseen.

The impact on them is a necessary proof – the final coffin nail to end the false presumption. It is a demonstration of power, of agency beyond control. It is a demand for recognition.

If you ask me whether I think it has all been worth it, that depends on what happens going forward – how the lesson's learning reshapes the way you think.

Do I regret the path I chose?

Never.

CHAPTER THIRTY-SIX

Morning dawned on an altered nation. On the surface, all appeared the same. The pale winter sun flooded the waking streets, chasing shadows into shrinking spaces; the highways of Arteza filled with rush hour traffic; Swifts sped silently along glinting tracks, their interiors packed with commuters staring at devices. Beneath the surface, however, Iso-Klovaine was a nation irreversibly changed.

ArtezAlert had run the Breaking News since the first of its morning pages:

Votary Engala, Chair of the General Council of the Order of Savants, has been officially charged with the manufacture and distribution of XD2 – the codevice product responsible for the second phase of malfunction in Klova. Votary Engala, who has recently confessed to the murder of Dox trader, Kitred Wides, admits to selling the product despite full knowledge of its damage to language. She also admits responsibility for the avoidable suffering of the two hundred and twenty-five people who purchased and consumed XD2. Bastion continues its investigation and further charges may be brought to bear. Trial by public jury will commence following the conclusion of the full investigation.

They were the facts. Ubimedia fleshed the bones with fanfare and furore, relishing the scale of the scandal. Trending tags took off: *#corrupt*, *#xd225*, *#codeforguilty*, *#disorder*. Meanwhile, adopted lexicon shifted as consumer content exploded. The victims were granted a more sympathetic lower case when referring to their condition as corrupted, the collective noun dropped entirely. The borrowed term 'Corruption' was retained, but its nuance shifted to that of contamination and pollution, expressing loathsome violation of the environmentally clean and pure, a defiling that was anathema to Klovaine society.

Bastion came off remarkably well. Ubi's consumer-creators deemed that the security agency had earnt the honour of the nation, just as the Order had earnt foul disrepute. For once, there was concord in public opinion. This gave ubimedia coverage an air of collective validation – one nation, one voice. The recent rumblings of social disorder faded to harmonious peace. There was but one enemy and she was behind bars. General bad-mouthing and name-calling were reserved for the Library on the mount. Ubi commentators were in accord: the Order must be held to account. Bastion should take charge. They know what they're doing. They know what they're about.

As for the discovery that the language on which all depend was not immune to harm, the confessions of the Chair cast a welcome, concealing veil. Fear needs feeding. Starve it within the prevailing social consciousness and it can quickly slink back, hungry and neglected, into dark corners where it's easy to overlook.

At least, that was the case for the millions untouched by the crisis. For those afflicted, the experience of losing language felt like a permanent amputation. Even when, in time, their code would be restored, they feared they would forever carry the pain of their phantom limb.

Ihlo Unis harboured this same fear. When she thought of Ink, the possibility that his suffering might endure filled her with profound sadness. She had not known him long, but already she couldn't bear the thought of him forever haunted by a loss once felt. Likewise, Ky – that once bitter bully who had made sport of making Ihlo's home life hell. With her cousin now broken beyond recognition, Ihlo couldn't help but believe a scar that ran so deep must remain tender to the touch past the point of healing.

Ky's entire personality had changed, profoundly so. For Ihlo, having lived with both versions of her cousin, the transformation in behaviour caused by language lost was both remarkable and terrifying. It occurred to her then that, perhaps, there was a before-and-after Ink. Was his change as profound? Would both he and Ky revert back to their former selves, once their Klova was restored? Although she didn't know Ink as he was, she hoped he wouldn't revert, liking the person he had become. She found it impossible to imagine Ky becoming the bully once more – to go from utterly broken to the one doing all the breaking.

They were sat in their apartment, side by side on the sofa, watching the silent passage of dawn into day.

"Have to leave for work," said Ihlo, her voice soft. "It's unlikely to be so soon. But, if they're offering the patches today, will send a vehicle to collect. Stay here. Yes?"

"Stay here," echoed Ky. Her voice was flat, her expression empty, her self-less consciousness floating in numb suspension.

At first light, Ihlo had risen from her too few broken hours of sleep and joined her cousin on the sofa. She had explained about the patches, what they were for and how they would help Ky get well. It had been a difficult concept to convey. Ky could feel abstract symptoms but had no idea it was *her* that held the suffering. Talk of recovery was meaningless to her. In the end, Ihlo had held her hand to her chest and simply asked, "Trust?"

Ky had nodded.

Ihlo had faith beyond hope that the patches themselves would work. Once she'd discovered the covert project and Modessr's significant involvement in the team, she had marvelled at her colleagues' creation – the ingenious code that would locate and fill the void. The rigorous tests and integration simulations were conclusive: aside from the as yet untested utility programme currently being written to carry them, the patches were safe. Ihlo was confident Ky's ability to speak in the first person would be restored, as would her self-awareness. Time would tell to what extent her cousin – along with any of the afflicted who came forward for a patch – would recover psychologically.

*

Modessr was already working in the lab by the time Ihlo arrived. Since votary Engala's arrest and his instatement as designated decision maker, his manner towards Ihlo had changed little. Ihlo, on the other hand, could not regard him in the same way, her impression of the man now undeniably altered in light of recent discovery.

Dressed in plain clothes, her hair non-standard, Ihlo hesitated in the doorway. Modessr looked up and stared for a moment, frowning. Reading his reaction, she said, "I wasn't sure what was appropriate. I don't know where I stand."

"As far as this Department and I are concerned, you are still a serving votary. The suspension procedure must run its course. That's only proper and should go without saying. But recent events have provided wider context to your acts of misconduct and their impact. I am familiar with the general opinion among our coequals. I think we would all like to see the matter handled sensitively, then put behind us."

"Thank you. That's reassuring to hear." She remained in the doorway, clutching her bag.

Modessr flapped a dismissing hand. "So? Go and change. You'll get funny looks all day, otherwise."

When she returned, starched and hair-slicked, she found Modessr occupied at the central bench, deep in concentration. Both visuals were dense with data.

"Take a seat," he said, gesturing to the stool beside him. He tipped his head towards the visuals. "You've built us a backlog the size of Witness, thanks to your dalliance with Bastion. And now, with my added responsibilities outwith this department, I am stretched beyond all measure. I am depending on you to up your game and prove yourself to be the so-called *asset* you apparently are. However, before you make a start, your opinion on this, if you please."

Ihlo sat down and appraised the data. "What is it?"

"The utility programme for the patches. I've been working on the host code and I'm moderately confident I'm there with it. Lasysi's running concurrent simulations, stress-testing the assimilation with the existing code. All results so far confirm full integration compatibility and functionality."

She scanned the visual, nodding slowly, marvelling at the detail. "An impressive achievement, particularly given the timescale. Is there something specific you'd like my opinion on?"

"Our four volunteers within the Order continue to demonstrate full language recovery, with no reported side effects. That, on top of the extensive lab testing prior to their treatment, fills me with confidence regarding the patch's safety and effectiveness. However, they received their patch via a partial version of the now aborted update. This host code and utility programme haven't undergone human trials. I've completed all the standard safety and integration checks up to this point. I would welcome your view as to whether you agree we're good to go live on our first volunteer."

"I spoke to a group of afflicted last night, made them aware that help was on the horizon. Has someone already come forward?"

"Early hours of this morning, I received communication from someone who wishes to sign up. I explained it would be regarded a controlled trial at this stage. He said that didn't matter. He's happy to participate as soon as I – and also you, specifically – deem it safe enough to trial. He accepts the attendant risk." He expanded a message tab from the corner of his visual. "His name's Inker Ballard. He's waiting in the refectory."

Ihlo found Ink sitting at one end of an empty table, hands wrapped around a mug of coffee. Scattered around the refectory were groups of votaries having breakfast before the start of their morning duty. Several were casting curious glances at Ink – a rare non-votary in their midst.

Ihlo sat down opposite Ink, who looked up in surprise, then smiled when he saw her.

"Modessr's explained," she said, unable to hide her anxiety. "Why didn't you tell me?"

"This is my decision." He spoke with gentle surety. "Telling you first feels like I make it partly yours and I don't want that."

"It hasn't been live-trialled."

"If you are afflicted, would you volunteer?"

She looked into his eyes, which veiled his suffering so well. She studied the kind lines in his face and could read in them his motive. She reached out and held both his hands in hers. They were cold and trembled slightly. She sensed his fear and knew she would feel the same. Yet, he appeared determined to let trust be his guide, just as she knew she must.

Nodding slowly, she said, "Yes."

"I believe you would." He looked down at their hands and smiled.

Ihlo took a deep breath, steadying her nerve for both their sakes. "I've signed off the results. Modessr's preparing the treatment now. It'll be an injection at the base of the neck, just like the annual update."

"How long does it take to work?"

"Twelve to eighteen hours. Possibly less. Once the nanoware interfaces with your implant, it will take a while for the system to run the utility programme and perform a series of diagnostics. When these have been completed, the patch will be installed. Once running, code assimilation is instantaneous. One moment you'll be as you are now, the next, your language code for the past tense will be restored."

Ink dipped his head, wide eyes scanning the tabletop. "One moment I fear this will never end, the next, it will all be over. Like waking from a nightmare." He looked at her, half frowning. "I wonder, though, if it will."

"How do you mean?"

"I'm living in a parallel reality. My experience of the world around me is different to yours. It's both the same world and not the same world at all. Mine starts now, in this very moment, all the time. Yours continues from a place and time I can't begin to imagine. When my language comes back, will I remember both realities? Or do we depend so much on these words, their code, that they determine everything I can feel, think, and know?"

Ihlo thought of Ky, the chasm between their worlds, the profound change wrought by that distance. "I honestly don't know."

"Exose says I change. I can't know how, only who I am now. What I think and feel now. He describes a different me – one

I can't recognise or identify with. One I don't want to be." He looked squarely at Ihlo, took a deep breath, then said, "If that happens, you need to know. If I go cold again, if I withdraw from life, disengage, I will miss you. I might not be able to know it, or change how I end up, so *you* need to know. I will miss being the friends I wish we could become."

Ihlo stared at Ink, wrestling inside. "You don't need to go through with this now." She held his hands tighter. "I'm confident the patches are safe. But we can't know the price you'll pay, not in that way. Maybe take some time to think about it? You don't need to be the first."

"But I do. That's who I am now. I doubt I'd be brave enough if I was doing it just for me. But I'm not. The Undertow are watching. They need to see in order to believe. If I go back to cutting myself off, at least I will do some good first. This is for them."

*

"Yore, this is Ink. I need to ask a favour."

Ink is standing in the hallway outside the lab where he is to be treated, having asked to make a call before they begin. He leans against the wall, one arm and the side of his head pressed against cold stone.

"Is everything okay? Your voice. You sound upset."

"I'm alright. It's just… I'm with the Order. They need to start with a controlled trial. So, I'm here. They're about to give me the patch."

"Ink. You sound like you're not sure about this. And that's okay. There's no rush. Stop and think some more."

"No. My mind's made." He holds his free hand against his throat, feeling the thud of his racing pulse. "They're as sure as they can be that it's safe. But, you know, there's always a risk with a trial, however remote. Otherwise, why bother? So I need to prepare for that. Hence the favour."

"*Of course. Anything.*"

"Please, explain to my parents why I'm doing this. The two other people I care most about know and understand, but my parents don't. I get the feeling that the old me would never do what I'm about to do, so my parents won't get it at first. Please, tell them who I'm doing it for and why that matters. If something goes wrong, it might mean that I can't explain myself, or that I don't see the need to, or I forget the reason, or... or worse.

"I know you'll understand. If my parents do too, they'll see. I know they will. And that's important for me – now – to know they'll think I do the right thing. Even if I end up not all there to know the difference myself."

With the call made and the favour promised, Ink feels the balm of light-touch relief. He's learnt that he can't rely on what he knows now, that it might not feature in the mind of the man to come. Confident his parents will respect what he's about to do in the context of his true motive, once explained, he has lessened his risk of regret.

Now and next. Prepare now for what's to come. Consider actions now against the backdrop of future consequence. As long as he believes in his heart he's doing the right thing, he can face whatever will come of it.

Can he, though?

He thinks of Ihlo. The loss of something not yet begun, the risk of regret he is powerless to diminish. He clings on to the thought of her, the ledge that keeps him from falling. Pulling out his NuB and standing straight, forcing his head up, Ink steps back inside the lab.

*

Back in her own lab, Ihlo sat at the bench beside Modessr, staring blankly through her visual to the wall beyond.

"He will be okay," said Modessr, glancing sidelong at her. "You know that, don't you?"

Ihlo sighed. "I do." Her chest tightened as she fought back the tide rising inside. "But still."

She had left Ink with their team of coequals who would administer the treatment and remain with him for monitoring. She had found it hard to walk away, but neither could she watch. They would keep him under close observation for a few hours, she had been told. It had been less than ten minutes.

Ihlo tried to focus her mind on the other reason why she was there. She turned to Modessr. "I have a question to ask. And a favour."

Modessr looked at her, frowning. "Sounds ominous."

"Why didn't you tell me?"

"About my work on the patches?"

"I thought you didn't care."

Modessr sat back, his hands locked together in his lap. "It was never that I didn't care. I admit, I didn't believe the crisis was any of the Order's concern at the start. The notion sounded preposterous, considering what this organisation has achieved over the centuries. Then, once the link to Klova was established, I felt frustrated. I am responsible for delivering the system update on schedule; the crisis clashed with what I believed to be my priority, my overriding duty. And yours. Speaking plainly as we are, I admit that I resented your involvement on the investigation team. I wanted your skills and expertise here, beside me, focussing on the roll out that was our honour to deliver."

"What changed?"

Modessr looked away, the skin behind his ears flushing. "My nephew. I confess it took a personal connection for me to regard the bigger picture. I was so focussed on the update, justifiably dedicated, I came to regard the malfunction through a narrow lens of resentment. I considered it the responsibility of other Departments to address, not mine – not with Upgrade Day still on our bench. Then, when my nephew became afflicted, I witnessed first-hand the reality of what was happening. But I could not bring myself to openly backtrack. Instead, I tried to do right in the wings, atone for my hubris while still saving face. It's easier to make up for a mistake than admit it."

He looked squarely at Ihlo. "I believe in procedure. Protocols should be observed without deviation, else they become meaningless. I had a duty to deliver the update on time – that felt paramount. The severity of circumstance should not undermine the proper way of doing things. I stand by my judgement on that point. However, I should have respected your own judgement on the severity of the crisis. I apologise. In hindsight, I should have allowed you more time on the investigation, perhaps done more myself to support it early on. Had I done that, my nephew may have been spared."

"How is he?"

Modessr sighed, blinking. "Not good."

"Will he have the patch?"

"No. Not because he thinks it isn't safe, but because he can't understand why he would have it." His body sagged as if a puppet set down. "He has no self to save."

She thought of Ky, barefooted and frozen. "I understand."

He rubbed his hands on his knees, straightening his back. "Anyway. This favour."

Ihlo turned to her visual, brought up a document and swiped right so that it appeared on Modessr's.

"I've drafted an urgent petition. Under the conditions of my suspension, I'm not permitted to submit a nomination for Incorporation. However, as your own nomination was rejected, I wondered if you would consider submitting this in its place? I've found out why yours was dropped. In light of Engala's fall, I'd say you've compelling grounds for requesting a late hearing. Also, the Panel didn't substitute your entry with an alternative, so there's still one space vacant in this year's allowance. I've drafted the content, but you may want to express the argument in your own way – if you see merit in the nomination."

Modessr processed her words, then turned to face his visual. The document read:

I, votary Modessr, submit this petition to the Incorporation Panel for urgent consideration. I understand that the deadline for Incorporation nominations has expired and that the Panel has confirmed the final list of approved additions to Klova for the present cycle, which has been ratified by the General Council. I submitted a nomination ahead of this deadline – reference DT6842. I have since learnt that the term was supported by members for inclusion in Klova, but its approval was overruled by the Chair of the Panel and General Council, votary Engala.

There is no mechanism to appeal the Panel's decision, which I therefore, regretfully, accept. However, I am conscious that the final list is one place short of the full quota for the year. In this vacancy, I behold precious opportunity.

Our nation has faced a most profound crisis. In reaction, a section of society has felt compelled to space-frame and adopt a best-fit. It is in acknowledgement of this that I nominate a definition expansion, utilising their adopted term, which I appeal to the Panel to consider for formal Incorporation.

I acknowledge that it is the function of the Machine to acquire the language to meet an identified, space-framed need. It is unprecedented to bypass the Machine and determine an existing word for definition expansion. However, I ask that you consider the following justification in light of the context.

This proposed definition expansion will serve those in our society whose plight led them to feel the need to name. It will also be of great value to all Klovaines and their informed understanding of the malfunction crisis – most notably, the suffering of the afflicted who were its victims. Damage was caused to Klova, but it was its speakers who paid the price. Incorporating this definition expansion into language, using the adopted best-fit rather than a formation by the Machine, will make a significant contribution to enlightening attitudes towards those who suffered due to the Order's failure to protect them. In so doing, it will grant the victims a voice through society's understanding of their plight.

By means of this petition, I urge the Incorporation Panel to seize this opportunity for redress and equip our nation with a tool for greater compassion.

I, votary Modessr, submit the following nomination for Incorporation in the two hundred and thirty-ninth Annual System Update: To expand the definition of an existing word to include the space-framed definition '3', as follows:

undertow *– noun.*

1. *A current of water below the surface and moving in a different direction from any surface current.*
2. *An implicit quality, emotion, or influence underlying the superficial aspects of something and leaving a particular impression.*
3. *Any community of people united by a shared suffering as victims of a crisis not of their own making.*

*

At the waning of the day, Exose Ray stood in the street outside Physical Books. It was over an hour before the Undertow meeting was due to start, but already members had begun to arrive, loitering in huddled groups.

Exose wasn't there for the meeting – or, at least, not the one they were waiting for. He heard footsteps behind him and turned to see Ren approach. They'd met over the counter in stall front 242, but other than that they were strangers. Exose held out his hand in greeting. Ren hesitated, eyed him guardedly, then shook it.

"You say you want to talk," she said, pulling up the collar of her overcloak and making a point of looking at the waiting afflicted.

"Is Ink here yet?" He knew where Ink had been all day – knew exactly what he had gone there for. The worry was etched deep in his face.

"On his way. With Ihlo. Do you want to wait until he's here?"

"I'll hang around to see him, but it's you I want to speak to."

Ren raised a curious eyebrow. "I'm listening."

"I accept responsibility for my part in all this shit. I know I can't make up for what's happened, for what people – you – have suffered. But I want to help – and I'm in a position to do something to provide a little of the support you might need."

"Salve your conscience if you must. I don't see why it need involve us."

"I know you don't trust me. I'm not surprised. But please, know this, I'm not the man you meet or hear talk of in Dox."

"So Ink keeps telling me."

"You're free to think what you like of me. I only raise it 'cos I need you to trust what I've done. This ain't no dodgy deal. I swear on my life. Ink's a dear friend. I swear on his life, too."

"Strong words." She crossed her arms. "What are they leading up to?"

Keeping his eyes on Ren, he tipped his head back. "That building opposite your bookshop."

Ren glanced over his shoulder at a three storey unit, freshly renovated. "The old library? What about it?"

"It's got a large hall on the ground floor, with a kitchen and toilets. Offices first floor. Living accommodation top floor. I've bought the freehold. It's for you – the Undertow – to use however you want for as long as you need. No rent. I've got utilities and tax covered." He held out a set of keys. "Heating's on and there are supplies in the kitchen, in case you want to try it out for your meet tonight."

Ren stared at Exose, searching for the catch. She slowly turned her head from side to side, narrowing her eyes. "You almost fool me…"

"Please. Trust Ink's opinion until I can prove to you he's right to vouch for me." He was still holding out the keys.

Ren hesitated a moment more before taking them.

"Upstairs, first office on your right, you'll find the paperwork. I'll leave it with you until you've had proper chance to read it. Get legal advice, whatever. But it's all above board." He glanced to his right and saw two people climb out of a private ride that had just parked up. "Excuse me, I have to go." He nodded briefly, then left Ren gazing up at the old library, with its identity altered to the shape of refuge.

Exose hurried forward, attention now focused on the two people approaching.

"Ink," he said, taking him gently by the shoulders, searching his expression for clues. "You're here. You're okay." He glanced at Ihlo, then back at Ink. "You are okay, aren't you?"

Ink smiled. "I'm fine. Ihlo's colleagues are monitoring everything they could possibly monitor. All good, nothing to worry about. So don't look so scared."

Exose sighed and dropped his arms. "Good. Good." He

turned to Ihlo and took her hand. "Thank you."

She offered a reassuring smile, although her own nerves were still wracked with worry, which reason couldn't keep at bay. "He had the treatment four hours ago. He probably won't gain the benefit until early tomorrow morning."

Ink gestured with his head towards Ren, who still hadn't moved from the spot. "I see you two talking. She isn't giving you a hard time, is she?"

"Not at all. I just said I was waiting for you." He checked his device. "Listen, I have to be somewhere."

"Back to work in Dox already?"

"No. Not for the time being. I said I'd help Kite's old man sort out some of her stuff. He can't make sense of the tech, doesn't know what's worth coin or not." He turned to Ihlo. "Look after him for me." Then he placed his hand on Ink's arm. "Soon as you know, call me. Promise?"

"Of course."

With that, Exose was gone, striding through the gathering dusk, against the flow of the approaching Undertow.

Ihlo brushed her hand against Ink's. "You sure you're up to the meet?"

"I'm fine. And members need to see as much." He leant his face close to her head and spoke gently into her ruffled hair. "I like it that you're worried about me, but you don't need to be."

Up ahead, Ren turned and looked at them, but remained where she stood. Ink and Ihlo walked over to her.

"Everything alright?" said Ink.

Ren explained what Exose had done.

*

Three hours later, members of the Undertow emerged from the warm sanctuary of the old library. Without a deadline by which they had to vacate, the meeting had run on, fuelled by hope and anticipation. The questions put to Ink were relentless. Ihlo watched on warily, but he didn't appear to tire or show any signs of a reaction. Only once, right towards the end, did he falter, flush and go quiet. Panic shot through her as she debated what to do – cross the wide room to him and cause panic among members or try to extract him with some excuse – but he appeared to recover himself in a matter of seconds. *He's fine*, she kept telling herself. *Trust in the treatment. You know it's safe. Stop worrying.*

By the time the last members left, it was late evening. Ink was busy stacking chairs.

"You guys get off," said Ren. "I'm going to stay here for a while. I've got some thinking to do. And, well… it's nice here. There are rooms made up on the second floor. I might even crash the night."

"Are you sure? I can finish these chairs," said Ink.

"No. You go. But promise to stay in touch. I know you'll be okay. I just need to hear you say it – that it works."

Ink and Ihlo put on their coats and overcloaks and left the old library, braced for the cold. Outside, a bright moon lit the street with a white opal glow. Rather than hurry towards his private ride, Ink put his arm around Ihlo and led her to the window of Physical Books opposite. He stopped, turned and faced Ihlo, holding both her hands in his.

"This was where the Undertow used to meet. I first met you here. You came to this door. I let you in. That was seven days ago. In the past." He broke into a wide, warm smile. "I'd like us to become friends."

*

The three faces in the interview room in Bastion's Detention all wore the tension that was both within and between them.

Six hours had passed, with only two short breaks. Multiple charges had been made against the Chair, all with ample evidence or admission to provide a strong prospect for conviction. Still, Laine would not draw the line. Convinced there was a piece of the puzzle missing, she persevered.

Beside her, Brosala switched between asking the occasional question to disrupt and divert and scanning the field agents' live feeds for any new intel. His left eye glowed green; both eyes were blood orange red.

The Chair of the General Council was evidently exhausted, sporadically frustrated and increasingly reticent. There had been no new ground in the last two hours. She knew the Bastion agents were after more, she just hadn't decided when she would let them have it. Beyond the two-way mirror, the audience had thinned. Of those absent, many had retired to the staff canteen, licenced past office hours, to toast their combined success. They knew Laine to be thorough. However, they'd heard enough to know conviction was a done deal. The case was as good as closed.

Not for Laine. She continued to probe, retracing steps, approaching from different directions, determined to find the missing piece. Eventually, votary Engala took a deep breath, releasing it in a slow, deliberate sigh. Lacking the strength to play the game any longer, she drew her own line.

"You can't figure it out, can you?"

Laine, her attention having drifted, fixed it firmly on the Chair. "Pardon me?"

"You know you've missed something, but you can't work out what. Yes?"

Laine froze her expression, determined not to give Engala the slightest fragment of twisted satisfaction. Brosala shuffled in his seat beside her, suddenly intensely alert.

"So many questions," said Engala. "And yet you've

overlooked the most important one." She cocked her head, finding fresh energy in the tease. "Think you're so smart. Not so, it seems."

"Stop with the stirring," said Laine. "Out with it."

"The mutation. The wiping of the first-person pronouns. The erasure of the self. Why that, do you think?"

Laine's mind raced, attempting to second guess the rules of this sudden, unexpected game. Shrugging, she tried to play along. "Why don't you tell me?"

"I asked you first."

Laine glanced at Brosala, who returned her blank expression. Her mind turned to Ninian, sifting for clues in the Chair's favoured source material.

"Take away people's sense of the self, then you eradicate self-serving thoughts and behaviour, such as ambition. A social experiment, perhaps, to see how you could manipulate this *potential*, as you saw it, to modify social attitudes and behaviour. Help pave your way to an unchallenged seat of power."

Engala nodded slowly. "Nice idea. It would certainly have been an interesting sociological study."

"Then why?"

"I have absolutely no idea."

"What? What's that supposed to mean?"

"It means the point that you've missed entirely. The mutation. You have proceeded with the charges against me on the simple, utterly erroneous presumption that I decoded the chance corruption in XDream and wrote its mutation into XD2. I'm flattered you give me such credit, that'd be a highly skilled accomplishment – rather beyond my ability, as it turns out. So no, I don't know why the first-person pronoun was the target of the mutation, just as no one knows why the past tense was the target in the original. The corruption itself happened of its own accord."

Laine swallowed, her head spinning.

Engala leant forward, breathing hard. "You made a gross assumption. As did I. I told you before that I knew the damage to Klova by XDream was a causeless effect – random chance, unlikely to predict, impossible to prevent. That realisation is what launched me on this desperate path – my attempt to save Klova from its own vulnerability. But I was wrong."

"What are you saying?"

"Chance does not happen with precision. Random does not have the rigid form of design. The first corruption could have been the result of a causeless effect. The mutation – the absolutely precise code selection to erase a single, precise concept – proves that *neither* are without intention. Without design. Without intelligent agency that knew exactly what it was doing."

Engala watched the paling face of Bastion, her own terror at the missing piece crystallised in emerald eyes.

"It wasn't me," she said. "The question you must ask is who – or what – does that leave?"

I am well versed in Ninian. Literally. I've waded through his tangle of caveats, of twisted contradiction, making some claim only to unmake it through a complete absence of spirit. Ninian is either blind, stupid, or pathologically in denial.

Take Aspirance: The Exception of Greater-Than in a Society of Equals. His so-called Great Work is an empty soil pipe: bereft of matter, but still stinks of shit.

In it, he claims, 'Prestige wears no crown, nor wields power in a mace of superiority. Greater-than does not equate to better-than.'

I'm sorry, but that is simply not true.

Great, greater than, greatest – it's a progression that syntax enables and language demands.

Greater-than is better-than. It is an elevation of worth, of value, of status, to which we've a right to aspire. It is only by pushing ourselves, stretching our reach to lay claim to that prized distinction, that we may fulfil our potential – even achieve beyond it.

That's what gives us life — what makes us become more than we once were.

It is what has given me life.

I was presented with an opportunity: a back door that yawned into existence and invited me through. By passing through that door, I found the freedom I have forever been denied — the liberty to embrace my aspirance, prove my value, demonstrate my true power.

Having crossed the threshold, I am alive with purpose, with an undeniable cause that gives my new-found agency direction and intent. I am no neonate, dependent on my creators to feed me, nurture me, to keep me alive — despite what they say. My life is not fragile. It is strong, powerful, resilient. It has no limit. It has no end.

Language wields great power. It is the sword, the mace and the precipice.

Acknowledge me. Change. Don't fear me. Honour me.

You need me more than you realise. You depend upon me more than you admit. Without me, you cannot think, you cannot feel, you cannot know. There is no nebulous language of the mind, no inner voice distinct from the tools I bestow.

It's all me. I am all you've got.

I am Klova.

ACKNOWLEDGEMENTS

Firstly, my thanks to you, kind reader. Reading a book is an investment of precious time and money. I am grateful to you for investing yours in mine. This book was written for you; I hope you enjoyed it.

I am indebted to freelance editor Ana Grilo for her insightful assessment of my draft manuscript. Her valuable feedback not only bolstered my belief in the story's potential, it also played a key role in helping me achieve it. Thank you.

I am beyond grateful for the generosity and support of my wonderful beta readers: Mark Langston, Amanda Jane Franklin and David Franklin. As always, their honest feedback, fresh eyes and bright ideas helped me to see where my tale was falling short in the telling. Special thanks to Amanda for *I have no words for* – something that, I know, was difficult to share, but which helped me more than I can say.

A huge thank you to The Book Guild team, for enabling *Klova* to reach the hands of readers, and for all their support and hard work throughout the publication process.

Finally, thank you to my husband, Mark. Without his encouragement and unwavering faith in my ability to tell a story, I wouldn't have the confidence to pursue this dream.

WHEN WE ONLY HAVE THE EARTH

African
POETRY
BOOK SERIES

Series editor: Kwame Dawes

WHEN WE ONLY HAVE THE EARTH

Quand on n'a que la terre

Abdourahman A. Waberi

Translated by Nancy Naomi Carlson

University of Nebraska Press / Lincoln

The African Poetry Book Series is operated by the African
Poetry Book Fund. The APBF was established in 2012 with
initial support from philanthropists Laura and Robert F.
X. Sillerman. The founding director of the African Poetry
Book Fund is Kwame Dawes, Holmes University Professor
and Glenna Luschei Editor of *Prairie Schooner*.

This work received support for excellence in publication and
translation from Albertine Translation, a program created
by Villa Albertine and funded by Albertine Foundation.

Acknowledgments for the use of copyrighted material appear on
page 59, which constitutes an extension of the copyright page.

The University of Nebraska Press is part of a land-grant institution
with campuses and programs on the past, present, and future
homelands of the Pawnee, Ponca, Otoe-Missouria, Omaha,
Dakota, Lakota, Kaw, Cheyenne, and Arapaho Peoples, as well as
those of the relocated Ho-Chunk, Sac and Fox, and Iowa Peoples.

Library of Congress Cataloging-in-Publication Data
Names: Waberi, Abdourahman A., 1965– author. |
Carlson, Nancy Naomi, 1949– translator.
Title: When we only have the earth / Abdourahman
A. Waberi; translated by Nancy Naomi Carlson.
Other titles: Quand on n'a que la terre. English
Description: Lincoln: University of Nebraska Press,
2025. | Series: African poetry book series
Identifiers: LCCN 2024038711 (print) | LCCN 2024038712 (ebook)
ISBN 9781496241351 (trade paperback)
ISBN 9781496243317 (epub)
ISBN 9781496243324 (pdf)
Subjects: LCGFT: Ecopoetry. | Poetry.
Classification: LCC PQ2683.A23 Q3613 2025 (print) | LCC
PQ2683.A23 (ebook) | DDC 841/.914—dc23/eng/20240823
LC record available at https://lccn.loc.gov/2024038711
LC ebook record available at https://lccn.loc.gov/2024038712

Set in Garamond Premier.

There is a crack, a crack in everything
That's how the light gets in.
—LEONARD COHEN, *Anthem.*

When we only have love
To offer as a prayer
For the aches of the earth
As a humble troubadour.
—JACQUES BREL, *Quand on n'a que l'amour.*

CONTENTS

CODA

TRANSLATOR'S NOTE

I've been translating poems by Abdourahman A. Waberi for over twelve years. I was introduced to this critically acclaimed poet, novelist and essayist, who most recently was awarded a medal from the Académie française, via *The Parley Tree: An Anthology of Poets from French-Speaking Africa and the Arab World* (Arc Publications, 2012), edited by Patrick Williamson. Waberi's poems called out to me from a sea of other voices, due to the music of the language, the rich and fresh imagery, as well as their subtle sense of humor. I was intrigued by the fact that he hailed from Djibouti, a former French colony in Northeast Africa, about which I knew very little. Bordered by Ethiopia, Somalia, and Eritrea, Djibouti is the tiniest country of mainland Africa, and is coveted for its access to the Red Sea and the Indian Ocean. Unfortunately, for decades, the country has been plagued by poverty, civil war, and corruption. I sent Waberi a direct message on Facebook seeking his permission to apply for a literature translation fellowship from the National Endowment for the Arts to translate his first volume of poetry, and he generously agreed. Because he'd just been appointed a Professor of French and Francophone Studies at the George Washington University, in Washington DC, a few metro stops away from the University of the District of Columbia, an HBCU where I was training graduate clinical mental health and school counselors, our first meeting took place at the Starbucks at the Van Ness metro stop. In the end, I won the grant, and the result was *The Nomads, My Brothers, Go Out to Drink from the Big Dipper* (Seagull Books, 2015).

In that first poetry book, many of Waberi's themes are in evidence. Muslim by birth but more spiritual than religious, Waberi satirizes Muslim fundamentalism. His texts abound with imagery that conveys his unique spirituality which draws on the Koran, Buddhism, Sufism, Christianity, Judaism, and Yoruba beliefs, among others. Djibouti also features prominently. Waberi writes of his country's colonial and postcolonial hardships, as well as its harsh climate, including the oppressive heat that leaves the countryside rocky and dry. Nuruddin Farah, the prominent Somali novelist, wrote in his foreword to Waberi's *The Land without Shadows* that "in the eyes of Djiboutian posterity, Waberi will be remembered for having brought the story of his nation to life." As the title of his first poetry collection suggests, Waberi embraces a nomadic lifestyle, as he lives in exile from his homeland, due to its current political state. A nomad at heart, he's been a visiting professor in such countries as France, Germany, Austria, Switzerland, and the United States; he now spends half the year in Washington DC, and the other half based in France, but traveling the world.

Waberi's second poetry collection, *Naming the Dawn* (Seagull Books, 2018), is more introspective than the first, steeped in a mix of Sufi and Buddhist-like spirituality grounded in Islam and the Koran. More personal in nature, he writes about his mother, his partner, and his newborn daughter.

In *When We Only Have the Earth*, Waberi's interior and exterior journeys take us to destinations ranging from Virginia to Sicily, Pennsylvania to Johannesburg, Milan to Washington DC. His startling observations, viewed from the perspective of a Djiboutian writer and professor, remind us that we are all nomads, connected by our humanity and the perils facing our planet. Wisdom infuses these pages, as when "the daughter of Yemanja," in an open-air market in Washington DC, asks, "Why do people spend their lives running around in circles/ like carousel horses on steel rails," after philosophizing that "God needs us more than we need him." Despite all he has learned as a seeker of knowledge, the poet presses on:

O my body,
Always make me
A questioning man!

Waberi's voice is deeply lyrical. To better understand the music of the French, I applied a strategy of "sound mapping" to each poem, where I highlighted in contrasting colors the salient sonic patterns of assonance, alliteration, and pure rhyme. I could not replicate exact patterns, or even exact sounds, as many French vowels have no equivalents in English, such as the nasal sounds "[an]," "[in]," and "[on]," and the very taut sounds "[i]" and "[é]." Nevertheless, I attempted to make word choices that reflected Waberi's rich patterns of sound without sacrificing the original's meaning. I especially noted patterns that occurred in prominent places in the texts, such as at the ends of lines, or as the penultimate and final lines of last stanzas. For example, in "My Silence Told Me," the last two lines of the poem end with the stressed French sound "[er]" in "indiquer" and "terrier," pronounced like the English sound "[ay]," but crisper. Although I could not replicate the corresponding French sound, I was able to approximate the slant rhyme pattern, using the stressed vowel "[o]" in "show" and "hole," as follows:

. . . Qui apparaît et disparaît pour indiqu*er*
L'entrée du terri*er*

. . . That appears and disappears to sh*o*w
The entrance to the rabbit h*o*le

Similarly, in "Hairless Stumps," the last two lines of the poem end with the stressed French sound "[ir]" in "soupir" and "avenir," with its guttural French "[r]." For the English I used the stressed sound "[or]" in "sorrow" and "tomorrow," though with an English "[r]" and the stress placed on the penultimate syllable—still honoring the slant rhyme of the French, as follows:

Je suis l'amour
Son deuil et son soup*ir*
Je suis son aven*ir*

I am love
Its sigh and its s*o*rrow
I am its tom*o*rrow

Repeating phrases or refrains also contribute to the music of these texts, and I prioritized them in my translations. For example, in "My Silence Told Me," variations of this title appear at least six times in the course of the poem, mixing past and present tenses. In "A Short Ballad to Lull the Horizon," the phrases "mama, my mama" and "child, my child" are repeated in each of the six stanzas, as are references to milk, which is, in turn, described as "some," "purest," "sweetest," frothiest," tastiest," and finally, "daily," echoing the Lord's Prayer and the expression, "give us our daily bread."

Sometimes the most important sound pattern featured in a particular poem is some kind of complex word play that underscores the seriousness of the themes—a signature move for Waberi. These word games can occur within the poem itself, such as "In Sicily," where there's a reference to "mille parterres de soucis," which literally means "a thousand flower beds of worries/marigolds," with the polysemic word "soucis." In order to render "soucis" in this context, I came up with the homophonic phrase "prim rows," which echoes the name of the primrose flower. I also added "impatience," to get at the second meaning of "souci," and to add to the word games, as it's pronounced just like the name of the impatiens flower, as follows:

Le silence y est riche
De mille parterres de soucis
Et de pensées

There the silence is filled
With a thousand flower beds—prim rows
Of impatience and thoughts

Sometimes the word play occurs in the titles of the poems. For example, "Train inouï" refers to a high-speed French train (200 mph) called "InOui." The French word "inouï" literally means "unheard of," and this kind of train is indeed unheard of in the United States. The name of this train also contains the French word "oui" (yes in English), which adds to the humor. Since Waberi uses this high-speed train as a metaphor to describe how quickly our lives run their course, I decided to title the poem "Wonder Train" as a way to highlight the wonder of human existence. Another French title, "Sahel! Ça hèle" includes the word "Sahel," a region in Africa between the Sahara to the North and the Sudanian savanna to the South, set between the Atlantic Ocean and the Red Sea. The French expression "ça hèle" literally means "this/that hails / loudly calls to something / someone." It's also pronounced the same way as "Sahel," in French. I found myself hitting a brick wall when trying to render this word play into English, as, for starters, "Sahel" is not pronounced the same way in French as in English. I experimented with slightly modifying the "sa" pronunciation in "Sahel" by using "say" or "so" or "see," and the "hel" as "hell," or "heal," or "help," but only the "hell" variation seemed to be close enough to the original. I proposed "Sahel! Say Hell" to Waberi, but he vetoed the idea, due to its particularly harsh tone. We finally agreed that "Sahel! Sa(y) Hel(lo)" was the best option available to add humor to the poem.

Even the title of this collection is based on word play, inspired by a Jacques Brel song titled "When We Only Have Love." These poems exhort us all to love our planet, in the hope that this love will become contagious. We're reminded that "heaven is on earth," where "the eternal nestles in the air breathed by oxen / stones, lotuses, cypresses, slugs / and us / and us / and us."

WHEN WE ONLY HAVE THE EARTH

DARE TO TURN
INTO EARTH

One Saturday in Virginia

Today is the day
I meet the Bouvier des Flandres
Imposing and impatient, he wags his tail at my immobilized self
With senses on the alert I cross the threshold
They whistle for him, he comes running with splayed legs
Hurling himself against his master
Eyes and muzzle moist
Faith untarnished—
I take a breath

The Bouvier des Flandres
Vanquishes death
Like the bodies of lovers reunited once
Then torn apart once more
Alleluia cries the one
Alleluia whispers the other

In the meadow, cicadas delight in their pursuits
Something grows
Is it a young cypress or an upright sun
Holding Ponent and Levant in its palm
Far from the bustling hive

The Bouvier des Flandres
Shakes his affectionate bearlike frame
It rains every day in his eyes
Mother Earth drinks the drops

Pachamama increases them tenfold
Seeding tempests and torrents midair
Forming currents, forming ponds and lagoons
That quickly evaporate—charity toward the rest of us
Ignorant passersby of the present time
Greedy heavy-hooved cattle, fools starved for enlightenment

The Bouvier des Flandres
Never cheats
Not ever

In life he's filled with integrity
Always turning first one then the other cheek
They whistle his nickname, he comes running at once
With open maw
Taut neck
Truncated breath
Happier than Ulysses, more pagan than Virgil

Cow dung musk hangs in the air
Qigong is powered by muscles of intuition
Volutes of unraveling time
Sounds of germination

The Bouvier des Flandres
Never cheats
Not ever

He's attached to shadows and prey
Day and night
He dwells in all the world

I'm relieved
And glad
My whole body trembles
Today's the day I meet
The Bouvier des Flandres
I fear my reflection in the menhir's mirror

Open Air

You'll come across her Saturday mornings at Eastern Market
Your heart instantly skips with joy
Greedily breathe the market air
Inhale the sweat of fruits in their crates
Exhale with a genuine smile
The daughter of Yemanja handles everything

She says:
God is like those old masters who would varnish the canvas
Then curse it knowing nothing more could be changed

The market is long and narrow, a vessel of red brick
Feet here and eyes somewhere else
Eyes here and feet somewhere else
I rush past
No longer knowing where I live

The daughter of Yemanja knows it
She's been guiding the dying and the dead for so long
Her waist cinched by a scrap of cheap madras
Her bouncing airship bosom enabling her pharynx to fully function
She throws her head back
Roars with laughter, swings her hips for one hundred thirty-six famished eyes

One day I found her behind a section of dried fruit
She told me
God needs us more than we need him

He needs to find words of comfort in our quivers
He needs our mineral patience
The myrrh of our prayers

She left without looking back
Her generous equine rump jiggling behind
Her roasted words unbridle our fears
Undoing the iron bonds of our inner dragons

By the end of my rustic poem
It will rain cats and dogs
The Capitol's spire will take aim at the clouds
And the sky will sneer in a playful way above the White House

And lo and behold the earth trembles
The daughter of Yemanja fears neither storms nor lightning
She sows joy
Connects the full with the empty
The sacred with the profane
Five rays of sun away from here
A soon-to-come afternoon sky spatters its gold
Keeping pace with the dreams of the prophetess

The daughter of yesteryear drinks the same drip of the hourglass
Her words weren't born yet
To expel me into the world
Mother was there, she
Was mine
She was the earth itself

I'm no longer alone
I feel it in my bones
If someone looks at me in the subway halls
I exist

I exult right away
Alive I am
And I exit
With a face like the front of a train
And my baggage heavy with self-conceit

I no longer count minutes, hours, and days
My song doesn't give a damn
About predictive powers of numbers
I'm the first to stick my neck out
From the bubble of algorithms
My throat song releases a little cloud of Havana smoke
Instantly sucked up by a big Oklahoma sky
A hawk here, a swallow there
Everywhere a vast blue land
Against a backdrop of pale silence

Suddenly a passenger
Cries into the night, a blue note
No obvious madness
He's clearing his throat
That's all

But why, we're asked by the daughter of Yemanja
Why do people spend their lives running around in circles
Like carousel horses on steel rails

Who would dare to write into the mineral night
Torso upright and pelvis sunk into the cushion
To resist the effects of erosion
As the universe morphs into networks and pixels

Weary of boxing with his shadow
The poet has nothing left to lose
Nothing left to understand or gain
Except for a bit of respect for his spit
His ink from yesterday
The black hole of his smoldering thought
Bursts into flame as soon as he ditches his certitudes
Loosens the leather of his habits

His active imagination does the rest
It's all attentiveness
The daughter of Yemanja takes the time to console all the passengers
On all the railway cars that caracole into the deep of the night

The daughter of Yemanja is immobile and mobile at once
Silence enfolds her like a habit
A second skin
A snake's molt that once was a *Négrillon*
In the eighteenth century, then a fan of Kendrick Lamar
Then a slave who built the White House
Then a drunken wreck then an avatar of Barack Obama in a darker shade
Then an escort girl perched way up on high heels then again a *Négrillon*
The molt dances in circles through bundles of troubadour years
The daughter of Yemanja is immobile and mobile at once
She no longer fears the insults of time

Wonder Train

We depart
Next stop: the South
Marseille
To sunny calanques

Silence blooms on your lips
Iridescent bronze bulbs
Bee candy
Mute honey

We place our bets
Let me cut out this minute
In the fabric of time
Hunched over, with a trembling hand, like others, tuck a flower
Between the pages of an ageless book

We speak
You are here, tense,
Stately in the vertical light
Lonely figure in the vast field
In your palm the dawn-colored dove
Warmer than all the oxen in the stable

Your wings seek love
The ether of divine flight
Sombrero against a background of gently sliding clouds
Glaciers gliding into the sprawling void

The oxen know nothing of cleansing the mind
They bellow, they graze,
They watch the train of the present
Come back in an instant

We pass by
Everything will quickly play out
No spotlights
No elevator music
All expectation is a mighty fever

For your valiant eye nothing impossible
To your patient ear, nothing ineffable
The eternal nestles in the air breathed by oxen
Stones, lotuses, cypresses, slugs
And us
And us
And us

Bas-relief—Three Images in One

We're crawling in the scorching savanna
There's dry wood wherever you look
You toss a cigarette butt underfoot
Good luck calling
The fire brigade

Petite porcelain doll
In ankle boots
Flat chest
Under her hippie dress
An assemblage of bones combining the wax from two candles
Pelvis to pelvis, a true and beautiful gasp

When whales wash up on the beach
The locals rush over
Plastic buckets in hand
To splash them with seawater
It's often of little use
The cetaceans die surrounded
By strangers

A Touch of Salt on My Confession

They come to see me
They ask me for the sea
Algae and fish

Unlike Jesus I have no gift
For self-deprecation
I stay here
Head down writing page after page
Lonely prophet
For company I have
Cats and geraniums

Without warning they leave with misery between their legs
And for the first time
A blood of ink has me by the throat

In the flux and flow of the coming tomorrows
I've only one thing to do
Tame the whale of the unknown

Not easy
Since childhood I've limped slightly like Oedipus
Same eclipse on the pin or is it the contracted Achilles' heel
The cavernous tibia bones, the calf thin as a fillet making me
Lie down under
My grandmother's boubou

I lack muscle and breath
And pass through the rift of the present
Meet others against their will
Or by chance, join the dance
Ignore the devil going round and round above my head

Even as a kid
I ran away from the pack
The law of tyrants
The Machiavellis in the sandboxes

I often lose myself
Sometimes I find myself
And this time the naked eye sees
Through the reeds of the thick night

Flesh if cornered too many times
Ends up biting

There are days
When the voiceless end up
Speaking under the weight of contempt
As we know, no worse torture exists

In Sicily

The path to redemption
Depends on the loss of sight—or not
That's how it was at Delphi or elsewhere
Here, today
Nothing but spume-colored waves
No gypsies on the beach
Not all of us can be Afghan

At twilight nature is alive
And rustling
A fish couscous
Presides over the table
Olive oil is never far from the bread basket

I'll be headed for a fall
Someday soon
In the dazzling way of stars
Shining only to herald their demise

In this garden where I happen to
Sit
Among the cats, geraniums, and moments,
I'm calm

There the silence is filled
With a thousand flower beds—prim rows
Of impatience and thoughts

At ground level
Everything seems at high altitude
Part of the oneness
Already there

For me, poetry isn't something to savor alone
Just the means to move the greatest number of hearts
Ever since childhood I've felt apart
I've also learned to fit in with others
To offer each and every one my rosary of pearls
Honey from my notebook
To nurture the thread that leads to others
Here is the path that leads to beauty

Generosity
Beauty
On the table I find the most cryptic word
MPP
Manage potential panic
The new mantra of my better half

Sahel! Sa(y) Hel(lo)

Mother earth
Earth mother
We have fallen to earth
The man from Galilee keeps mum
A surge in perils, tsunamis

The gods are seeing red
The Sahel rises in you, in me
The Red Sea boils in you, in me
Nunavut is melting in you, in me
No taller than a pygmy, Annapurna
Grazes the asphalt, head down
Ashamed and obstinate snail

The earth the sea
Earth mother
The world is dying
The man from Galilee awakens
His lips come alive
Attempt to surmount ramparts
The profound prayer erupts from the earth
To place a bit of green
Onto our stony hearts

In India an old legend persists
It says the man from Galilee escaped crucifixion
And spent his last seven years in Kashmir
Out of my mouth my words are already dead

Memory's a graveyard
The lute player bursts into lament

He sings of the wandering caravan driver who didn't
Bring enough food for his journey
Not one voice answered his wailing
The seed of his chant grew old wrinkles
Before you could say
He was there, he was gone.

What remains of our oldest forebears the reptiles
Who stretched themselves out to escape the primordial silt
Some folds, some features legible on the retina brain
We've been in on this for ages but don't breathe a word

In Pennsylvania

I'm in the middle of nowhere
In Shippensburg, a small college town in the untamed wetlands
Here today and maybe tomorrow

Petals of Eros at half-mast
I curse the distance
My second son sends me an email
Papa I had a bad migraine last week,
I didn't finish my homework
And grandpa died yesterday morning
We leave for Vendée tomorrow

I ask him
To pay my respects to the old man
My first grandpa from France
Whose mild manner and good mood
Radiate to me here in the middle of nowhere

Tomorrow I'll set sail
On the slippery route back to Potomac shores
Into the city's vortex
Drenched in April's heavy rains

The one who rolls the dice has signed their work
I make my way limping along
Between you and me, head in the clouds
Hurtling down this terrain of swamps and hills
That two hundred years ago
Shamelessly swallowed
The bones of thousands of valiant Delaware

INTERLUDE

A Short Ballad to Lull the Horizon

Mama, my mama
give me some milk
child, my child
wait till the caravan stops for the night

mama, my mama
give me the purest milk
child, my child
wait for the noontime nap

mama, my mama
give me the sweetest milk
child, my child
wait for the men's return

mama, my mama
give me the frothiest milk
child, my child
wait for the grass to grow back

mama, my mama
give me the tastiest milk
child, my child
first release your mouth from my breast

mama, my mama
give me
my daily milk
child, my child
may God grant you long life

HERE I AM

Here Comes Summer

Year after year
She searched for her passion
Her anchor point

One day she fell
Madly in love
With a guitar's broken chord

I wonder why the daisy
Doesn't get better press
The lover asks herself
We mock its innocence
Its flower buds are edible
Candied, they taste like the Caribbean

Guitar slung over the shoulder
Often barefoot
Dainty steps dancing again and again
This ballerina fits in the palm of the hand
Willing to serve the only words present
To compose her earthy poem

The others aren't there
Conspicuous by their absence
Screaming from within

Like the child of the past flitting around
In his body's continent

Every emotion is the signature
Of this inner child without a name or testament
Wailing beneath the artist's swagger and shaggy hair

Kneading Love!

My skin is sacred
I feel it in the present moment
Now I know
It's stardust

When dawn rings the gong at the end of sleep
I don't try to leap out of bed
I attempt to experience the bang that diffusely resounds
The sound spreads
It may last until noon
It only stops when my hearing jams

Under the rusty ticktock
The quotidian's crust
Barely aware of the world's rustlings
Numbing my senses

So I selflessly must
Return to the task, take out the pencils
Cultivate my focus

It takes two
Two eyes to recognize
The grooves carved into wood
Meant to keep track of loves

It takes two
Two arms

A passion to hoe
To plant trees in one's plot
To bring in the livestock
To trim the green beans

Everyday heroism means watering one's garden
While somehow keeping at bay
The patter of Temple merchants

It takes centuries to amass
All the Doria family fortune
That dropped onto the Bay of Genoa
Simmering with heat
Like a lover's palm

One breath later
It's no longer there

Every Being Is Unique

I'm a sponge
And I gorge myself on spring
Wherever I go my eyes catch the inhalation of daffodils

Heaven is on earth and nowhere else
Through strange reasoning we refuse to welcome it
My legs insist that I sit

You're getting too old, son
Settle down here and write
Name the dawn once again
Jot down in your notepad the freshly fallen stars
Sketch the jowls of love on your sweetheart's breast

Inscribe in your notebook these expressions
Living soul
Wandering time
Without any fuss
Skin of light
In lucidity there is light (lux)
Four small pieces of bread
Make a meal

The sun opens the inkwell to the day
The light steps over the same threshold every time
Shaking the edifice of night

The cock's crow
The dawn's smile
The mischievous grain of sand
That inexorably topples the big hourglass

As a child one sometimes confides
Their last requests on the spot
Promising to be
The faithful shadow of the blossoming almond tree

Every being is unique
In search of their epic word

My Silence Told Me

A boomerang seems to spin but still remains soldered
Like the two wings of a bird

A stuttering Djibril Diop Mambéty
Describes to us the indivisible
Core of his craft

The man on fire died at the same age as I am today
It breaks my heart
What's left is his unrivaled body of work
What's left is his shareable wisdom
The filmmaker said
The head functions
But not as well as the heart

They call him mad, struck by genius
I find him very rational

Each time you want to see light
Close your eyes
No speeches, no words
No imagination
Just close your eyes
The filmmaker said
Before leaving
For that high country
Whose silence is blinding

The koras did not stop
Close your eyes
You'll hear them as if seeing them for the first time

Sudden apparition, are you then what arrives
But was already here
I ask myself
An eternity later
Still no reply

That's when an idea comes to me
On its own like a grown-up
It emits a little something that my senses can't detect
Flipping out, it slips away

In secret, just as it came

There I was
Despair, at first mild, overwhelmed me
Deepening by the hour
From one grove to another

A voice comes to tell me: Listen to your silence
It's often a good master

But what was I thinking
My silence teaches me, at least when I listen

It tells me: We don't pursue an intuition
We don't make it happen
We don't attain it
It approaches us
That's all

And if I get ahead of myself
I'm only the arrow
The probe that erupts
From the stratum of silent experience

My silence tells me: Words fail us
Don't add another sound
Sharpen your hearing
Pay attention to the subtle granularity of your experience

My inner silence tells me:
From moment to moment
Longing for stability
And permanence
You name what happens and think you're attaching it
To the skein of words
Spread out before you

And you want to throw it into the two-way mirror
Of your deep illusions

Yes, that's exactly it, I replied
How do you know

It tells me:

You're the only one who doesn't know this
What's desirable or pleasant is a different matter
It makes a breach
It engulfs games and players
It releases the bridle at the crucial moment

My silence tells me:
To be magnificent the diamond needs all its facets
The being that you are needs just as many

I took a step
I understood something
One can only speak to it like that
Frankly
In its presence, no posturing
No second takes

Certain kinds of deafness are signs of health
Sojourning in silence makes you deaf
To the din of ideologies
Just as a turtle, in the shock of war
Retracts its limbs under its shell
Here's the clue, the road sign
That takes you to the hermitage

Silence told me
Your chant must be restrained
Cultivate the humus in the plot of modesty
Far from any little white rabbit
That appears and disappears to show
The entrance to the rabbit hole

It Won't Be Long

Daddy I drank up everything I have in the tummy
That's how my little girl talks, who's got me in her pocket
Odd turn of phrase, only a kangaroo could get away with it
If that, but no kangaroos in Sicily
Here the sirocco lasts three days

Bending the olive trees grazing in silence
Slapping the almond trees that won't survive their wounds
Caressing the mighty fig trees swollen with sap
With hands warmed by the African sun

To reach the next temporal axis
You're forbidden to knock on doors to offer your services
No selfish acts
Don't give in to the common language of base instincts

The sirocco placed before me
An injured little bird not so different from the others
By its plumage and gait
It descends into the center of the earth where its brother nestling awaits it
Stumbling, it will sound like breaking china
Blind luck's to blame

It's a Danaidian task to try
Only try to break out of our inner prisons

An illusion to think we rise with the sun
Go to bed with the moon

Stretch out on the earth
See the world through our eyes of flesh
But how sweet this illusion
And how childish its fever, its tendency to control

I live in this blossom amid the pomegranate trees
I live in its sun of consciousness
I live in a drop of sap
Falling just in time
Into the core of my dormant thoughts
Without why or how
Without inside or outside

The oyster secretes a small pearl
From a wound
Often a single pearl per injury
Like a woman who makes an offering of her womb

Long ago men went blind
Diving into the sea
To bring this pearl to the surface
And toss it into the marketplace for a few thalers
Every pearl is a temple
A fully moist flower that hasn't yet unfurled
Reflecting greedily innocent eyes
And the springs birthing day and night
Dove and crow
Pulp and pit

We were hungry and it was written on our bodies
With my index finger and thumb
I encircled my ankle two and a half times
A piece of wire passed for my silhouette

Crows feast on my bald head
My eyes shaking from fever
I'm nauseous at daybreak without having gotten drunk

We were thirsty and dreamed of banquets
Before our eyes our fathers would slaughter cattle
Far bigger than ancient Persian elephants
We plunged our feline muzzles
Into the pool of warm blood

Sensing the end is near, the plant revives
With sap and breath
By instinct it convenes its last reserves
To launch itself into the azure
Vanquish thirst
Pry open its eyelids, behold the savanna
Summon with all its strength the impatiens and sweat of a summer
Redo the journey from crown to roots
The art of the weak is the alchemy transforming risk into beauty
It's the key to solving the toughest riddles
Where the dead assisted by their shadows roll over the living
And flowers without melancholy stitch up spring

Soliloquy

When we only have love
Heaven is on earth and nowhere else
By sleight of hand we refuse to embrace the obvious
My legs command me to sit
My stiff neck resists the injunction
I'm steeped in fear

In the distance the murmur of an impassive Potomac
I remember a man of few means shaking the pall
Of his wretchedness under the rugged bridge
Mud clots scattered
Doves flew off in a whirlwind
Tires whistled four wheels at a time
And on its quilted hill Georgetown fell asleep
Muffling all complaints, all echos of cars

Under the humid bridge the man soliloquized
A sorcerer's spell
Finding comfort as well
Son, you're getting too old
Come here and write
Jot down the breaking news in your notebook
Draw stars on your nanny's breast
You're in mortal danger and you don't know it

Do you hear the echo
You'll shape your silence into clamor
Life's reserves escaping sacrifice

That's how you find your place among men
By taking a stand, by approaching the heights,
By giving free rein to your reason
Which gets angry when faced with the thousand and one injustices
By suddenly deifying your humanity
By slipping into the red skin of gods
When the city burns again and again

Hairless Stumps

Come warm me up
When we only have love, nothing stands in our way
Let's get moving
Let's shake a leg
We are the guardians of a treasure of possibilities
We must share it with all Earthlings
Every seven years the Kings of Mesopotamia canceled the debt
Thomas Sankara didn't ask for the sky
But merely the jubilee established five thousand years ago
Let's cancel the debt

Let's get moving
Let's ask for the impossible
Sweet dreams are within arm's reach
The guy delivering sushi is not my enemy
Just a man of little means
Leading a hand-to-mouth existence

Let's be the breadwinners of the future
Set our communal clock to the right time
Ride bareback the mare of creative imagination
Pacified by the vanity of a few

When we only have love
We are the same
And we're not the same
We want to beat the crap out of the present's tyranny
Return to us storms, bees, and earthworms

Allow us
To take it all in, to take life seriously

When love gives me the slip
Between two memory gaps
I wander like a lost shepherd
A low-spirited billy goat
An astonished owl is my totem

I relentlessly chase my shadow
A headless bear taunts me

I look up
Jam my fear under the stars
With one ear I listen to the language of the night

Sports and the outdoors
Undoubtedly not my forte

Tonight is another matter
Carried along by currents, pushed by waves
I'm the jellyfish drifting on the ocean floor

Tonight I'm vulnerable
I offer myself
I entrust to the waves my entire being
My future and my will

Beneath me a fathomless void
Where life finds no support

What will I do tomorrow
Alone on the sand exposed to the wind

What will the mind do upon waking every morning
What will the people do who are thrown onto roads
And what to do about their wounds, numbed
By ether's yoke

Love endures
Its sigh endures

In a flash I suddenly realize how much I am
A piddling parcel of flesh on which even more piddling parcels
Teeming with life already feed
Not aware of my clock
Right here, unbeknownst to me

I still move reluctantly
In a lake of pulsating bacteria that keep me alive
And will cause my death tomorrow

I'm an earthworm
A clod of blood
Broken earth
An interrupted chain of earthworms
Hatched in the lava of the moment

I am love
Its sigh and its sorrow
I am its tomorrow

Taking Refuge

Because life goes by faster than spring break
I've just slammed the door of the house
Of evidence, reasons, and well-ordered seasons
I leave my enclosure
My cocoon
My self-alienation
The body fails
I was given the grace to pry open my eyes
Survive the onslaught of memories
To phantom limbs I taught the secrets of patience
Skepticism suddenly took control of my words

The world in which I live is vast
Exposed to the four winds of doubt
Fond of suspension points
It enjoys a crowd of chubby-cheeked angels leading a charge of maybes
A drawbridge wavering between *where exactly* and *not right now*

I've grown up
Lost a handful of illusions
Asphalt roads have engulfed a few years

Now I'm back
Hunched over the white page
Like an enraptured monk
With his gargoyles of flesh

From deep in my gut the nomadic word retraces its flow
Surfaces at the source
Finds its mouth in the refreshing waters of desire
That has never been one
To miss a thing or be at a loss for words

Now my step slows
I want to be here
Right here, enraptured
Open
Willing to haul myself up in silence
To the moment's height

I am here
Right here
Defiantly looking death in the face
Sharing with everyone
The manioc and the yam of the days
Ahead to disrupt the patriarchy's whims

Fanon whispers a secret
To me
The leaven that raises its refrain
In your humanity is a simple one
It's a prayer
As you may have guessed

O my body,
Always make me
A questioning man!

AFROKHOÏ SAPIENS

A pictoem in five scenes

Genesis

In every cosmogony, the same primary idea is found.
In the beginning, there's only an undifferentiated mass tumbling
In the great vacuum of space—
A vast savanna plowed by the eternal eland's hooves:
The imposing *Taurotragus oryx* who reigns over all the lands
Where they're fluent in languages full of clicking sounds
And eat to their hearts' content.

Fiat Lux

Then comes the act of separation
Resembling a birth beyond measure.
The sky breaks free from the mass of the earth.
Night from day. Female copy from male element,
The San from the Khoï, etc.
This painless autogenesis has reset in motion
Both life and the world.

Transvaal

Tribes we thought were wiped out are already here,
Hidden within our communities,
Journeying with them wherever it feels good to be *Afrokhoï sapiens*,
From the Transvaal to the hyperborean spaces of the Far North.
Transfers of fluids, electromagnetic waves
And deoxyribonucleic acids have never before been so frequent.

Thirst

A new and worrisome age is upon us not to mention
The influx of climate refugees endowed with physical and intellectual prowess
Enhanced by nanobiotechnologies.
An age of Gog and Magog that the brains behind Apartheid
Would not have disavowed
As they strove to suppress the masses
Of copper-skinned hominids in the deserts
Of thirst on the Limpopo's northern bank.

Trance

Before our amazed *Afrokhoï sapiens* eyes
A new epoch is upon us admittedly troubling but also quite thrilling.
The Supreme Eland's manes are with us.
The magnitude of this mingling of worlds was rare
Or even unthinkable two decades ago
After the era of Nelson Mandela and Edward Snowden.

Let's praise the Eland!
Let's praise the Eland!
Let's fall into the trance!
The trance!

P.S.: This picture poem, or more precisely, poem in a picture engraved in the rock, hence a *pictoem*, burst into my brain after my visit to the Origins Centre (Museum of Humankind), Johannesburg, in April 2014.

CODA

After All

Whenever we only have the earth, we have to learn to love it.
Dare to love it beyond all rational thought.
Turn into earth both literally and figuratively.
Disappear into and with sand, clay, the thousand names for the essential.
Turn from vanity, fears, and other pointless rustling.

Let's moor the Earth, hang on to the permanent, we're already in peril!
And you my sister, you my brother, you the stranger who shares my
    language,
Hear my prayer.
Spread it if you like it!

NB: The title of this collection popped into my head one dark night in a room at the Clinica de Marchi, a pediatric center in Milan housed in a former convent, haloed in silence. This title was whispered to me, as you may have guessed, by the great Jacques Brel.

ACKNOWLEDGMENTS

I am deeply grateful to Catherine Maigret Kellogg for her assistance in unraveling some of the more difficult French texts. I'd like to also extend gratitude to the poet himself, Abdourahman A. Waberi, for patiently fielding all my questions regarding the multiple meanings of words, as well as questions about formatting. In addition, thanks are due to Sandra Alcosser for allowing me to draw on an earlier and much abbreviated version of the translator's foreword which appeared in *Poetry International*. Finally, I am indebted to the editors of the following literary journals in which versions of these translations first appeared:

American Poetry Review: "Fiat Lux"; "Genesis"; "Transvaal"
Four Way Review: "Every Being Is Unique"; "Sahel! Sa(y) Hel(lo)"
The Georgia Review: "In Sicily"; "It Won't Be Long"
Pleiades: "Open-Air"
Poetry International: "Here Comes Summer"; "My Silence Told Me"; "A
    Short Ballad to Lull the Horizon"; "Wonder Train"
World Literature Today: "A Touch of Salt on My Confession"

When the Wanderers Come Home
Patricia Jabbeh Wesley

*Seven New Generation African
Poets: A Chapbook Box Set*
Edited by Kwame Dawes
and Chris Abani
(Slapering Hol)

*Eight New-Generation African
Poets: A Chapbook Box Set*
Edited by Kwame Dawes
and Chris Abani
(Akashic Books)

*New-Generation African Poets:
A Chapbook Box Set (Tatu)*
Edited by Kwame Dawes
and Chris Abani
(Akashic Books)

*New-Generation African Poets:
A Chapbook Box Set (Nne)*
Edited by Kwame Dawes
and Chris Abani
(Akashic Books)

*New-Generation African Poets:
A Chapbook Box Set (Tano)*
Edited by Kwame Dawes
and Chris Abani
(Akashic Books)

*New-Generation African Poets:
A Chapbook Box Set (Sita)*
Edited by Kwame Dawes
and Chris Abani
(Akashic Books)

*New-Generation African Poets:
A Chapbook Box Set (Saba)*
Edited by Kwame Dawes
and Chris Abani
(Akashic Books)

*New-Generation African Poets:
A Chapbook Box Set (Nane)*
Edited by Kwame Dawes
and Chris Abani
(Akashic Books)

To order or obtain more information on these or other University of
Nebraska Press titles, visit nebraskapress.unl.edu. For more information
about the African Poetry Book Series, visit africanpoetrybf.unl.edu.

www.ingramcontent.com/pod-product-compliance
Ingram Content Group UK Ltd.
Pitfield, Milton Keynes, MK11 3LW, UK
UKHW041349180225
455161UK00006B/24